The Revenge of the RADIOACTIVE LADY

Center Point
Large Print

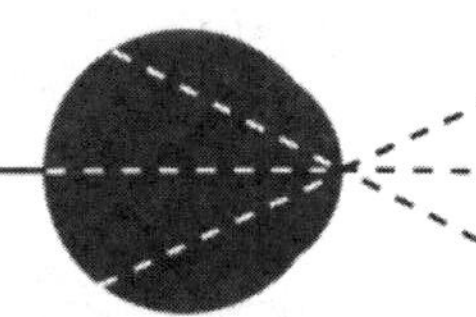

This Large Print Book carries the
Seal of Approval of N.A.V.H.

The Revenge of the RADIOACTIVE LADY

ELIZABETH STUCKEY-FRENCH

CENTER POINT PUBLISHING
THORNDIKE, MAINE

This Center Point Large Print edition is published
in the year 2011 by arrangement with Doubleday,
an imprint of The Knopf Doubleday Publishing Group,
a division of Random House, Inc.

This book is a work of fiction. Names, characters, businesses, organizations, places, events, and incidents either are the product of the author's imagination or are used fictitiously. Any resemblance to actual persons, living or dead, events, or locales is entirely coincidental.

The text of this Large Print edition is unabridged.
In other aspects, this book may vary
from the original edition.
Printed in the United States of America
on permanent paper.
Set in 16-point Times New Roman type.

ISBN: 978-1-61173-134-7

Library of Congress Cataloging-in-Publication Data

Stuckey-French, Elizabeth.
The revenge of the radioactive lady / Elizabeth Stuckey-French.
p. cm.
ISBN 978-1-61173-134-7 (library binding : alk. paper)
1. Older people—Fiction. 2. Florida—Fiction. 3. Domestic fiction.
4. Large type books. I. Title.
PS3569.T832R48 2011
813′.54—dc22

2011008587

For Ned, Flannery, and especially Phoebe

Part One APRIL 2006

Marylou

By the time Marylou Ahearn finally moved into the little ranch house in Tallahassee, she'd spent countless hours trying to come up with the best way to kill Wilson Spriggs. The only firm decision she'd made, however, was that proximity was crucial. You couldn't kill someone if you lived in a different state. So she flew down from Memphis to Tallahassee and bought a house on the edge of Wilson's neighborhood. Doing so had been no problem, because she had a chunk of money left from the government settlement as well as her retirement and social security. She furnished her new place quickly with generic "big warehouse sale" furniture. Back in Memphis she rounded up a graduate student couple she'd met at church—a husband and wife who both needed to give their spectacles a good cleaning—to house-sit, and then she transferred her base of operations to Tallahassee, informing friends only that she'd be taking an extended vacation.

Completing her task in Florida, unfortunately, was taking a while. Every morning when Marylou and her Welsh corgi, Buster, left their house at 22 Reeve's Court and set out on their walk toward Wilson Spriggs's house at 2208

Friar's Way, Marylou chanted to herself: *Today's the day. Today's the day. Today's the day he'll suffer and die.* Every morning she fully believed that by the time she'd walked the three blocks to Wilson's house she'd have figured out how to do him in, despite the fact that she'd been setting out on this very walk a few times a day for the past two weeks and it was nearly May and the best method and right time had yet to present themselves.

She tried to spur herself on with angry thoughts. Would she feel better after she'd killed him? Darn tootin'. She didn't expect to go around giddy, not after all that had happened, but she expected to feel relieved, to have a sense of accomplishment, like when, fifteen years ago, she'd stepped out the doors of Humes High School, never to have to spoon-feed Chaucer to tenth graders again. It must be a good sign that she was now living in a neighborhood where the streets were named after Chaucer's characters. *The Canterbury Tales* had returned to mark this next big passage in her life.

It didn't help that the walk to Wilson's house was so pleasant. Canterbury Hills was once a suburb of Tallahassee; but the city, moving northward, had swallowed it up, and it was now spoken of by Realtors as Midtown. The homes in Canterbury Hills, mostly ranch houses from the fifties and sixties, weren't as stately as the houses in her Memphis neighborhood, but they all sat on spacious lots full of flowering shrubs and well-tended flower gardens, shaded by live oak trees; and Marylou enjoyed looking around so much that she was always rattled when she found herself standing, again, in front of the evil yellow house where Wilson Spriggs lived with his daughter and her family, so rattled, in fact, that it took her a minute to reenter the murdering frame of mind.

She would stall in front, while Buster sniffed around in the grass, and stand beneath the magnolia tree that bloomed with fantastically white blossoms, hoping that Wilson himself would pop up in front of her and ask to be killed, please, and hurry up about it. When this failed to happen, she hoped to at least be struck either with the courage to storm the house or with a clever idea about how to sneak in undetected.

But she was struck by neither courage nor inspiration, and by the time she got back home she was so hot and weak and discouraged she had to lie down and rest.

In the evenings, after she'd eaten some dinner, usually a fried egg and slice of toast, a kind of Chaucerian meager repast, she'd hook Buster's leash to his collar and they'd walk over to Friar's Way again. Sometimes she saw a gray Volvo turn into the driveway of the yellow house or a navy blue minivan pull out of it, but she was never close enough to make out who was actually in the car. One time she saw a middle-aged man in a grungy black T-shirt—must've been the son-in-law—mowing the grass in the front yard, but he refused to look up at her; and one time she saw a girl and a little white dog running down the driveway. It was like they, the Spriggs family, were purposely keeping their distance from her—but how could they, when they had no idea she was nearby and looking to get even?

The whole being-in-limbo thing, the looking-to-get-even thing, was getting old. She was growing weary of wanting to kill Wilson, of imagining herself killing him; she was itchy to actually do it.

At first all the planning to kill Wilson had been, well, she had to admit it, fun. The idea started forming in her mind six months earlier, right after she'd stumbled across the article about Wilson Spriggs on the Internet. She'd been googling "Dr. Wilson Spriggs," as she did every so often, without ever finding anything recent about him, and one day there was a link to a little piece in the *Tallahassee Democrat* about Dr. Wilson Spriggs helping his teenage grandson Otis Witherspoon win a science fair prize. As she read the article, which had an accompanying picture of Otis holding the blue ribbon he'd won at the Leon County Science Fair for his poster about the upside of nuclear power, she knew she had to *do something,* that Grandpappy Spriggs could not be allowed to go on living the way he had been, untouched by his cruel deeds.

Marylou and her former husband Teddy had recently stopped corresponding, so there wasn't anyone she could talk to about how she felt when she found the article. She began to scheme all by herself. She didn't tell another soul what she'd decided to do, and she wrote nothing down, but she made the plot she was hatching into a story in her mind, a horror story, like that wonderfully dreadful old movie *Attack of the 50 Foot Woman.*

In the summer of 1958, when Helen was five, she and Teddy had gotten a babysitter and gone to see that movie at the Orpheum Theatre in downtown Memphis. Teddy had howled with derision all the way through it, as did most of the audience, some of whom began throwing their popcorn at the screen, but Marylou thoroughly enjoyed it, trashy and badly made as it was, especially the scenes of the giant (much taller than fifty feet) vaguely annoyed-looking heroine, Nancy Archer, stuffed into an unexplained bikini top and miniskirt like Jane of the California desert, scooping up a police car and throwing it, tearing apart electrical towers, ripping the roofs off buildings, slapping her weaselly husband and his tarted-up girlfriend and their drinking buddies across the bar like so many pesky insects.

After she'd found the article about Wilson Spriggs and gotten swollen up with rage all over again, she remembered the fifty-foot woman. She and Nancy Archer were sisters in some strange way, sisters who were involved in parallel stories. They had both been poisoned by radiation; they both desired to get even with a man who'd done them wrong. Unlike Nancy Archer, Marylou hadn't been touched by a giant hairy alien hand, but she'd swallowed a deadly radioactive cocktail and she was walking around, very much alive. Marylou wasn't fifty feet tall, but the radiation she'd swallowed had surely given her supernatural powers. If she only knew how to use them! She could be the Radioactive Woman! She really didn't like the word *woman,* though, because of the way her grandmother used to say it: "*whoa*-men." So she thought of herself as the Radioactive Lady. Close cousin to Nancy Archer and the Wife of Bath—lusty, powerful, ready to get hers.

Of course, the radiation she'd swallowed had made her sick. Weak. Anemic. Dizzy. Prone to headaches. Bleeding gums. And because she'd swallowed it, she'd killed Helen. After Helen's death she'd had to focus her anger somewhere, and since the government of the United States as a thing to hate was too unwieldy, and all the idiots who got caught up in cold war paranoia—the morons who devised and funded and carried out the radiation experiments—were too numerous and anonymous to collectively despise, she focused her hatred on Wilson Spriggs.

She used to hate herself as well, hence the need for electroshock therapy, but these days, whenever her thoughts drifted again toward blaming herself, she steered them in another direction—toward the fact that she did not know what she was doing when she swallowed the poison. She was young, she was pregnant and vulnerable, she was ignorant, she was naive, she was a hundred million other things; but the fact remained that *she did not know,* because she was tricked. Wilson Spriggs had instructed his minion to trick her into drinking poison, and now, finally, when she and Wilson were both old and he was least suspecting it, she was going to play a deadly trick on him.

But exactly what sort of trick should she play?

For a time she daydreamed about a much younger, fifties-looking version of herself, looking like pre–alien encounter Nancy Archer in a black-and-white film, clutching a fluffy white pillow to her ample bosom, tiptoeing in a slinky dress and high heels toward an old man in his bed—Wilson had aged while she, miraculously, hadn't—but when she tried to imagine the ensuing struggle, she turned back into a frailish old lady and it seemed too risky.

She entertained another fantasy that was just as delicious as the Nancy-with-a-pillow fantasy. She would sneak up behind him with piano wire (whatever that was) and garrote him. However, the thought of his old head rolling on the ground, blood gushing, eyes staring, was so hypnotically alluring that whenever it popped into her head she forced it away by singing a hymn, as she was afraid that even allowing herself to imagine such things meant she was teetering on the line between avenger and sicko. Same with stabbing him. She didn't want to enjoy herself *too* much.

She considered poisons. Poisoning him, in some ways, would be the ideal revenge, because it was so tit-for-tat. You could find anything on the Internet these days. She'd googled "how to poison someone" and got more than enough information. She was thrilled, and horrified, to discover that you could order chunks of radioactive uranium ore "for educational and scientific use" from amazon.com. There would be a nice symmetry in poisoning him with the same stuff he'd given her, but she had no idea how to go about forcing him to ingest a chunk of rock, so she crossed radiation poisoning off her list.

One of the most appealing methods of poisoning was described in a book she'd read to Helen years ago, when Helen was sick, a Nancy Drew book, the one set in Hawaii, *The Secret of the Golden Pavilion*. In that book, Nancy receives a lei from one of her enemies, a lei made with purplish black funereal orchids, and hidden among the flowers are tiny tacks "soaked in poison." She couldn't get this image out of her head, the image of a wizened old man with a garish lei around his withered neck, being poisoned while simultaneously looking frivolous and stupid. Of course, it would be impossible to make such a lei and force someone to wear it. What did it mean to "soak tacks in poison"?

As far as poisons went, given her in-and-out time frame and lack of round-the-clock access—in other words, she wasn't his long-suffering wife—it seemed like putting antifreeze in something sweet would be the best option. But after more research, she had to admit that, on the whole, poisons weren't such a hot idea, because they were all readily detectable these days, not like the good old days when someone at the coroner's office would write "heart failure" on the death certificate and be done with it.

And now, here she was in Tallahassee, so close to her quarry, but she couldn't decide. She and Buster walked up and down Canterbury Hills and her thoughts went round and round. What about "accidentally" running over him? Knocking him down stairs? An "accident" like that might not kill him, though, and injuring him just wouldn't be the same. She could push him off a cliff! Were there any cliffs in Tallahassee?

Canterbury Hills was certainly hilly, and the hills were much bigger than any hills in Florida had a right to be, but there was nothing resembling a cliff, not even any large rocks. She did see a Merchant's Lane, and a Nun's Drive, and Cook's Circle, Prioress Path, Knight's Way, but no Wife of Bath anywhere. Where the hell was the Wife of Bath? Did somebody have a problem with the Wife of Bath? Bath. On TV, people were always killing people by drowning them in a bath. But how would she happen to be there when he took a bath? What about a swimming pool? She enjoyed swimming, but she was no Esther Williams, and even a man in his eighties could probably fight her off.

And so it went, until, one evening, when she and Buster arrived at the yellow house on Friar's Way, she spotted an elderly man watering a flower bed in the side yard and felt a jolt in her brain like electroshock therapy, but instead of knocking her out, it woke her up and set her tingling. Was the old man Dr. Wilson Spriggs? The devil himself? This old man, who might be him, who surely *was* him, didn't glance Marylou's way. Arrogant prick. He was standing sideways, near the bottom of the sloping driveway. She could see only his profile, but it was him, all right; she recognized his insolent slouch. "The very one," she muttered to Buster, who was too busy nosing at some dried poop to care. She'd seen this man twice before, once on the happiest day of her life and again on the worst day, and he'd been a jerk both times. Memories of those two times wouldn't leave her. Even electroshock therapy hadn't dulled them.

The first time she met Wilson she was three months pregnant with Helen, in 1953, when she was visiting the University Hospital OB clinic for her first checkup, and she'd just been told, by the older doctor with a crew cut who'd just examined her, that everything with the pregnancy looked fine and that she was past the danger stage when miscarriage was common. She was only twenty-three, but she'd had two previous miscarriages, and those first few months she was pregnant with Helen she could barely breathe she was so worried. (Years later she'd wondered if they'd chosen her as a subject for their experiment because of those miscarriages, because they thought that she'd probably lose this baby, too, so it wouldn't matter what the radiation did to it. But after the hearings in Washington she read that they'd just chosen the eight hundred women at random—all poor and powerless, though; they'd made sure of that by conducting their study at a clinic with a sliding fee scale.)

But on that joyous morning, after her examination by Dr. Crew Cut, she had no idea she'd been randomly chosen for anything besides the privilege of becoming a mother. She'd gotten the all clear! She was going to have, at last, a baby! She sat up on the examining table, bare legs dangling from the mint green gown with the baby rattles pattern on it, breathing so deeply she felt light-headed, and then a nurse waltzed in and gave her a cold metal cup of pink fizzy liquid that smelled like strawberries and iron and told her to drink up quickly, that it was a vitamin cocktail to keep her baby healthy!

In her mind, many times Marylou has said, "No thank you," or asked, "What, exactly, is in this so-called cocktail?" Or thrown the drink in the nurse's face, screaming obscenities, or leaped on the nurse and forced *her* to drink it, or just jumped up and ran, bare assed and barefoot, out of the examining room and down the hall and out of the hospital and into the late September sunshine. Safe!

But no. No, no, and no again. What she actually did was drink the poison while the nurse, who wore a name tag reading Betty Bordner, watched her with big blue eyes and what became, in Marylou's memory, a greedy and sinister smile. The drink tasted so bitter that Marylou's eyes were watering when she handed the cup back to the nurse, and just as she did a young doctor passing in the hall paused in the doorway of her examining room. He had longish hair and wore round tortoiseshell glasses and a bow tie. Foppish. Pretentious. A dandy.

"Oh, Dr. Spriggs!" gushed the nurse. "This is Mrs. Ahearn, one of our pregnant women!" At the time Marylou thought this was an odd thing to say, but so what? Medical people said all kinds of odd things, in her experience: *Have we had a movement lately? Have we had any nervous imaginings?*

"We appreciate your cooperation, honey," the doctor said to Marylou, nodding at the empty metal cup.

What the hell did that mean? Who knew?

"Back atcha, Doc," Marylou said, acting like a smart aleck because she was twenty-three and happy. Also, although it made her sick later to admit it to herself, she was flirting with him. She knew she looked cute, sitting there bare legged in her gown, and, she supposed, she must've been attracted to him, God knows why.

Betty Bordner turned to Marylou, clutching the metal cup between her pointed bosoms, nearly cross-eyed with reproach. "Dr. Spriggs is in charge of the entire clinic. He's head of our study! He hardly ever comes down here!"

"What study?" Marylou had the presence of mind to ask.

The nurse flushed and went silent, her gooey orange lips working nervously, and she fixed her eyes pleadingly on the great Spriggs.

"I'm in charge of all kinds of studies," he said, and clearly, as his manner indicated, this was rightfully so.

The nurse set the metal cup down on the counter with a clunk. "How *are* you today, Doctor?" she said, and Marylou thought, Calm down, Nurse Bosom, you're twenty years too old for the baby genius.

Dr. Spriggs spoke no more—their time in his presence was up. He smiled, gave a silly wave, and disappeared; and that little scene with nurse and doctor was the only thing Marylou remembered distinctly about that day, although she knew that she and Teddy had later gone for a stroll beside the Mississippi River and then to Checkers Barbeque to celebrate.

And now, in 2006, there he was again, standing at the bottom of his pollen-covered driveway waving the garden hose, like a drooping old penis, over his azalea bushes. Still tall and lean, but no longer foppish! No visible ass. A sailor hat and thick glasses and ugly orthopedic shoes.

Marylou's ankle ached and sweat slunk sheepishly down between her drooping breasts.

If she had a gun, she could just walk up to him and say: "This is for what you did to me and Helen and those seven hundred and ninety-nine other women and their children, you son of a bitch," and shoot him. Would it really matter if she was tried and put in prison for the rest of her life? Or even put to death?

Well, yes, it would matter. People said that living well was the best revenge, but wasn't it enough, really, in her case, at age seventy-seven, to say simply that *living* was the best revenge? He dies, she lives. So she'd not only have to do it but get away with it.

It hadn't rained here in a coon's age. Motes of dust and pollen swarmed up into her face. She and Buster stood at the top of the driveway watching the old scum overwater his bushes, hating every fiber of his being with every fiber of hers. But what to do? If only she were fifty feet tall! Fifty feet tall, twenty-three years old, dressed in superhero attire—Amazonish costume barely covering her giant bosoms—raging and focused as fifty hurricanes, she'd fly at him and fling his parts all over the flat-assed state of Florida.

Just then he cocked his head, as if he'd picked up the stirrings of a storm. He threw down his garden hose and, without looking in her direction, turned and shambled off behind the yellow house, out of sight. Walking away from her once again.

"Mur-der-er!" she bellowed, and Buster flattened his yellow ears and rolled his eyes up at her. But she wasn't finished. She yelled again, even louder, "Where's your fucking bow tie now!" which was not at all what she meant to say. What she meant to say was "Eat leaden death, motherfucker!"

She waited, heart skipping merrily in her chest, but the murderer did not reappear, so eventually she and Buster started back home, unfulfilled, a familiar condition for both of them. Why couldn't she think straight? Of all the things she could've yelled. His bow tie! How inadequate was that? She'd had the beast in her sights!

When she got home, she lay down on her cold pleather couch and closed her eyes and heard Teddy's voice. "You act just like you drive, Lou. Go, stop. Go, stop. Gas, brake. Gas, brake. I'm getting motion sick." When he'd said that to her, years ago, he'd been joking, sort of, but he was also speaking the truth. She was still that way—wishy-washy, indecisive—and she hated that about herself.

For a time after that evening, the evening of the bow tie insult, Marylou shifted into low gear, continuing to roam the streets of Canterbury Hills with Buster—Miller's Ride, Nun's Priest Place—waiting for either courage or inspiration to strike, enjoying in spite of herself the low humidity as well as the slight breeze that would be gone in a few weeks, not to return, unless there was a storm, until October, according to the Channel 9 weatherman. The late April air had begun to smell like October—smoky, because of nearby forest fires—prescribed burns, according to the *Tallahassee Democrat*. Hurricane season, according to countless billboards around Tallahassee, was only a month away. "According to," "according to"—these were her friends now, these public postings.

While walking she met some of her neighbors, including a nice minister's wife, a chipper blond gal named Paula Coffey who always wore a white sun visor, and they talked about the pollen, which Marylou had never seen the likes of. When she'd come down to Tallahassee in March to look for a house she'd been amazed by the steady stream of brown oak leaves raining from the sky—evidently they shed their leaves in the spring and not the fall—leaves that looked like palmetto bugs swarming all over the ground. But in April the pine trees cast off little brown tubes of pollen that blew everywhere. Everything on her screened porch was coated with green slime. Trails of pollen, like ooze from giant snails, lined streets and driveways. Even though Marylou parked her rented Taurus under the carport she had to hose off the front windshield every time she wanted to drive somewhere.

Paula listened to Marylou complain, and her response was, "Get ready! After the pollen comes the mosquitoes and no-see-ums! It's always something!"

Paula called on Marylou a few times, once

bringing her lasagna and another time a key lime pie. When Paula brought the pie, her daughter Rusty came with her, a thin teenager dressed in black, skulking behind her big healthy mother like a dark cloud. When Marylou opened her front door and turned on the porch light, Paula introduced Rusty, who was holding the pie, but Rusty didn't say a word to Marylou, just stared at her sullenly. The black rings around her eyes looked like she'd drawn them on with Magic Marker.

"Rusty made the pie," Paula said, thrusting Rusty forward.

Rusty gave Marylou a squinty look. A little leather medicine bag hung on a cord around her neck. "Didn't make it for *you,*" she mumbled.

"Rusty!" her mother said. "That's not nice!"

"*I'm* not nice," said Rusty, but she held out the pie, wrapped in foil and smelling delicious.

"I'm not nice either," Marylou said. "Join the club." She knew she should invite them in and offer them some, but she couldn't do it. She took the pie, planning to eat the whole thing as soon as she could get to a fork and a table. "Thanks so much, sweetheart!"

At this, Rusty gave her an even colder look. I should hire this kid to kill Wilson, Marylou thought. She could picture Rusty delivering a pie laced with antifreeze. But, no, she wanted the satisfaction of doing it herself.

As Paula and Rusty turned to leave, not being able to tell, apparently, that she was speaking to the Radioactive Lady, Paula invited her to go to church with her family.

"My husband Buff's the youth minister at Genesis Church," Paula said. "We'd love for you to be our guest! It's a big church with a small church feel!"

"Oh God, here we go," Rusty groaned. She hurled herself off the porch steps, black shirt flapping like bat wings, and darted across the street toward their house.

Paula stood there in her yoga suit, grinning at Marylou, and for a few seconds Marylou seriously considered saying yes right then but finally told Paula she'd think about it. Going to church with Paula's family might make her feel less lonely, but she hadn't moved to Tallahassee to make new friends. She had priorities. She had a vermin to exterminate.

So she and Buster walked and rested and walked again. And then one day, with no plan in mind, bereft of courage and inspiration, Marylou got the opportunity she'd been waiting for.

Part Two MAY 2006

CHAPTER 1 *Suzi*

Q: How many times had Suzi been warned?

A: Every time she turned around.

Every time she turned on the TV or opened up a newspaper there were stories about perverts who scooped up children, locked them in closets, tortured them, raped them, strangled them, and buried their bodies in crawl spaces. What *was* a crawl space? And those were just the stories she found on her own, trolling the Internet. She was also warned directly by her parents, by the plastico chick on the evening news, by an Officer Friendly visiting their school who wore a protective puffy suit so he looked like the Michelin man and encouraged the kids to attack him with fury. "If someone tries to grab you, yell *fire* and run! Kick and punch and poke. Even adults you know might have bad intentions. Teachers, scout leaders, ministers, even Father himself. If an adult makes you uncomfortable, get the hell out of there. Tell another adult, hopefully not another child molester. Don't be fooled by the ploys: 'Your mother sent me. Help me find my lost puppy! Want some magic dust? Come to my house and drink beer and watch a dirty movie! Want to sleep in my tent?' Don't walk to school, or wait for the bus alone. Don't ride your bike alone. Never be alone."

But who would've suspected that an old woman living in her own neighborhood, a woman who walked her corgi morning and night, who would've thought that this white-haired, slightly humpbacked old woman was the *very person* Suzi should've been on guard against?

Suzi had drawn the task of walking their mini poodle, Parson Brown, each morning before school and each evening after dinner, and her mother made her wear a whistle around her neck so she could blow it if someone tried to mess with her. Like a whistle would stop a maniac! Oh well, it showed that her mom cared about her at least a little. Suzi hadn't blown the whistle in earnest yet, although she'd huffed on it a few times just for fun.

Her mother had also told her to cross the street when she walked past one particular house in their neighborhood, a house where a registered sexual offender in his thirties lived with his parents because he'd just gotten out of jail. But then she told Suzi that she'd done an Internet search and discovered that all the guy had actually done was drug a woman—probably at a bar—and then, you know, taken advantage of her, so he wasn't a *child* predator, which was the kind they really had to worry about, but even so, be careful! Like drugging and raping anybody wasn't that bad! The way adults could talk themselves into and out of feeling okay about something always amazed her.

As she walked Parson through Canterbury Hills, Suzi played out scenarios in her head—Ted Bundy Jr. creeping up behind her with a fake cast on his arm—she'd kick him in the nuts and run to the nearest house. A bus full of gangstas offering her a milk shake with date rape drugs in it—she'd throw it in their faces and run to the nearest house. A pimpled geek on a bike exposing himself—she'd blow her whistle right in his ugly face. But never once had she imagined an encounter like the one she was about to have, nor could she have imagined the consequences of it.

It was too bad, really, that everyone tried to scare the crap out of kids about hanging out in their own neighborhoods, because if she didn't always have to be "on guard," these walks with Parson would've been her favorite part of the day.

On the morning she met the old lady she turned right at the top of her driveway so she could walk past her favorite house—the neighborhood's original plantation, a two-story white clapboard house built in the 1800s. In their side yard there was a bronze tortoise, which the homeowner had ordered online, as big as a VW Bug. As Suzi and Parson walked past, she surveyed the plantation house and the tortoise and the front porch lined with rocking chairs as if it were her own house, just waiting for her to move in.

Their next-door neighbor John Kane, setting out in his Ford Ranger for his insurance business downtown, gave her a wave and a smile. Suzi waved back, deciding not to attribute his friendliness to a sick and twisted plan. From somewhere in the trees above her came a pileated woodpecker's nutty laugh. She tried to imitate it and strike up a conversation, but the bird must not have been fooled, because it flew away, a shadow fluttering off through the live oak limbs. Its mother had probably warned it about people posing as woodpeckers.

She turned the corner, and she and Parson went down a small hill, passing a group of middle-aged women who walked together every morning, blabbing and hogging the whole road, then she started down Nun's Drive, staying under the shaded canopy. She stopped beneath the line of confederate jasmine bushes to inhale their sweet smell, and this was when the old lady and her dog cornered her.

She'd seen this particular woman, in various spots around the neighborhood, a number of times on her walks (Suzi didn't walk the same way every time, per instruction), and she didn't pay much attention to her (old ladies are interchangeable), but her dog was cute. Parson thought so, too, and always whined and lunged toward the corgi, desperate for contact. Suzi always managed to pull Parson away and keep walking, but that morning in May, when the two dogs were lunging at each other, the old lady spoke up and said something more than the usual "Isn't it a lovely day?"

"How about we let them get acquainted?" she said in a twangy Southern accent, an accent Suzi's friends referred to as "country." "Buster here's been awful bored with just me for company."

Suzi—who'd been daydreaming about a certain boy in middle school to whom she was sending carefully plotted mixed signals, Dylan B. (there were four Dylans in middle school) with his shaggy red hair and deliciously round freckled face, calculating how much time she had to spare to placate this old woman before she was late getting home and would be late to school and unable to walk by Dylan's locker and pointedly pretend not to notice him—decided it would be easier to go along than to be rude, which was, unfortunately, a decision Suzi often made.

The two dogs did their doggy sniffing thing, Parson Brown gradually becoming less interested, turning her head, then her body away, and the corgi, Buster, became more and more frantic trying to get her attention. Note to self, thought

Suzi. Here was proof, straight from the animal kingdom. She was always trying to instruct Ava, her clueless older sister, not to seem so *interested* in a boy she liked, but would Ava listen?

"What's her name?" the lady asked. She wore a straw hat; khaki pants; white long-sleeved shirt; and hideous, puffy white walking shoes. Typical old person. Even though it was May, and in the eighties, we have to keep every inch of our flesh covered! It looked like the old lady had no breasts at all under her shirt.

Suzi wore a denim skirt, flip-flops, and a tank shirt, and she felt suddenly like the sleazy little tramp her mother often suggested she looked like without ever actually coming out and saying it. "Are you going to wear *that* to school?"

The old lady's blue eyes, in her pale face, were wide and intense. "Your dog's name?" she said.

Suzi explained the origin of Parson's name. Christmas, five years ago, they brought the poodle home and they were listening to that song all the time, and it was her favorite, "Winter Wonderland," the Johnny Mathis version, and she noticed that their new little poodle, sitting on her hind legs, looked just like the snowman they built in the meadow, hence, Parson Brown, even though the poodle was a girl. She tried to tell this in an animated way, even though she was sick to death of the story. They ought to just rename the damn dog.

"Well, isn't that cute!" said the old lady, and then, with hardly a pause, "Where do you live?"

Suzi told her, thinking that this woman surely knew already, because she'd seen the woman watching from afar when she and Parson ran down their driveway, but maybe the old woman was just being polite.

"I live on Reeve's Court," the old lady volunteered, "down at the dead end, white house with blue shutters."

Suzi made a polite sound, thinking of her soccer uniform and how she hadn't assembled the parts yet and how angry it made her mother when she didn't do it the night before, which she never did because she liked to live dangerously, and, okay, it was entertaining, she had to admit, watching her mother getting angrier and angrier while trying not to, so predictable, but she had to make sure her mother didn't get too angry, or it would quickly stop being funny and start being scary. Whew. It was hard work being thirteen.

"You have a brother, am I right?" said the old lady.

The two dogs were sniffing each other's faces now, so Suzi decided to give Parson another few seconds. Buster was so cute, with that long sausage body and little flap ears. If she ever was allowed to get another dog, she wanted a corgi.

"How old is he?" the woman asked her, leaning forward slightly. "Your brother?"

Suzi thought it was a rather peculiar question, but what else to do but answer? She told her about Otis, sixteen, and Ava, who was eighteen, and added that she was thirteen.

"I live alone now," the old lady volunteered. "I moved here a few months ago when my son got a job teaching at the FSU medical school, but then he lost his job—long story—and they moved to Houston and here I still am! I reckon I ought to follow them, but I just bought the house and I like Tallahassee." She stretched her lips out in a sort-of smile.

The old kook must be as lonely as her dog, telling her whole life story to some random kid. And Suzi could've sworn she'd seen the woman for years in their neighborhood, but maybe not. "Oh," said Suzi.

"Mrs. Archer's my name," said the woman. "Nancy Archer. My friends call me Nance."

Nance? What kind of nickname was that for an old lady? Suzi—full name Suzannah—when she turned eleven, had toyed with the idea of making people call her Zan just to piss them off, but decided it wasn't worth it.

"Who else lives in your house with you and your brother and sister and doggie?" Nance asked her. Buster was busily sniffing a mailbox and Parson was watching him, looking a little forlorn. This was another abnormal question, but Suzi answered it. Mom, Dad, Granddad. And now she really had to go, she said, or she'd be late for school. Nice meeting you!

"Oh, yes. I've seen your granddad. Working in the yard."

Wait. So Nance already knew where she lived and that she had a granddad. But old people did get confused. Maybe she was just asking to make sure.

Nance suddenly reached out and grasped her wrist. "What's his name?"

"Granddad's?"

Nance nodded briskly. Her eyes, shaded by the hat, stared up at Suzi unblinkingly. Why was Nance holding her wrist this way? Should she blow her whistle?

But Suzi was way taller and stronger than Nance. She backed up, and Nance let go. For a second she couldn't remember his name. He was Granddad. "Umm. Wilson. Wilson Spriggs."

"That's what I thought." Nance let out a hissing little breath.

Wait another minute. What was all this about? Did she have a crush on Granddad? Was that it? Suzi couldn't wait to tell her friend Mykaila. A crazy old woman had a crush on Gramps! She was stalking Granddad! All adults were insane!

"And your grandmother?"

Suzi didn't get why Nance kept asking about her family, but she couldn't think of a good reason not to answer, so she did. "My stepgrandmother. She died two years ago." Suzi didn't like thinking about that—the hot day of the funeral, sitting under that blue tent in folding chairs and watching her mother crying and hugging people. Suzi's mother had never known her real mother, but she always told people that she'd loved Verna Tommy like a mother. Suzi'd held somebody's baby, called Dee Dee, four months old, and gazed into Dee Dee's face whenever she felt like crying, 'cause who could feel sad when they looked at a baby's face? Would Dee Dee even remember that day and how Suzi held her?

Nance was staring off down the street, like she was spacing out, not like she was actually looking at something, and she didn't say sorry about your grandmother, like people usually did, but oh well.

Suzi said again that she had to go, nice meeting you, blah, blah, blah, and Nance suddenly turned to her. "Every time I see you, I think, there goes a smart, beautiful girl with a great future ahead of her. You've just got that air about you."

"Wow. Thanks!" Suzi was used to old people remarking that she was smart and beautiful—and she never minded hearing it again—but she especially liked the bright future part. She planned on becoming a famous soccer goalie, and thought about telling Nance that she was going to statewide Olympic Development

Program soccer camp in July, but, for God's sake, she really had to go.

She said good-bye and ran all the way home, as fast as she could run in flip-flops, and by the time she got home, where her mother was out in the yard, hands on hips, waiting for her, she'd mostly forgotten about Nance, but she was in a good mood the rest of the day.

Suzi's life went by in a blur of soccer practice; soccer games; school; homework; texting Mykaila and Sienna and Sierra and ignoring texts from Davis; pretending to ignore Dylan B.; fighting with her sister, Ava; and the dog-walking thing, of course, took up just a tiny fraction of her day, and it was the most boring part, something she protested about having to do, but mostly on principle. It was a relief being alone, watching Parson sniff the same bushes with the same intensity, not taking her cell phone with her even though her mother wanted her to, not having anyone expecting great things from her, or even little things. And she found she looked forward to meeting Nance, the dog lady, whom she ran into now nearly every time she walked Parson, and who always asked her questions and seemed so pleased with the most mundane information.

Nance wanted to know all about her family, so Suzi told Nance that her father worked at Florida

Testing and Assessment, and her mother, right now anyway, was a stay-at-home mom; and Nance nodded approvingly. For some reason Suzi kept talking, revealing things she'd never tell most people, had told only Mykaila before, that both Ava and Otis had what is called Asperger's syndrome, which was bad enough in itself, but what made it worse was that Ava took up *all* her mother's time. Got more pity than anyone ever had in the history of time. Their mother was always taking Ava to counseling and different therapies, trying to turn her into a normal person who was going to go off to college and get a job and get married, which was never going to happen in a million years but her mother refused to admit it.

"I see," said Nance, and nodded as if she did see. She didn't ask what Asperger's syndrome was, thank God, because it was nearly impossible to describe. "What about your brother?"

And Suzi told her how Otis was a science geek who did experiments in his shed out in the backyard and nobody ever paid any attention to him except Granddad, who gave him advice and things to read about science.

Granddad seemed to be the one Nance was really interested in.

Nance asked how long Granddad had been living with them—two years—and where he'd lived before that—Iowa, until his wife, Suzi's stepgrandma, died.

Oh, Nance seemed puzzled, knocked off balance. Where did he live before Iowa?

Memphis, Suzi said, wondering why she cared.

"Oh," Nance said, now in a totally different way. "Memphis!" She seemed thrilled, and then revealed why. "I lived in Memphis for a long time myself." She looked at Suzi expectantly. "I'd love to meet your granddad and talk about Memphis sometime."

"You should stop by. He's always home." Suzi wanted to howl with laughter. The poor woman had a crush on Granddad! It was the most ridiculous thing she'd ever heard. Should she tell Nance that Granddad was in the early stages of Alzheimer's? Three people in her house had some kind of official label, given to them by doctors, but Suzi could label the others, too. Her mother was a helicopter parent, hovering around Ava. Her father had turned into a workaholic; and when he was home, all he did was watch for hurricanes on the Internet. He was also a soccerholic. He went to all Suzi's games and gave her advice on how to be a good goalie, and most embarrassing of all he coached her from the sidelines. Like he knew anything about soccer. Sometimes it seemed like he cared more about Suzi being a soccer star than she cared herself. Everyone expected her to be the perfect one, the one with no problems, the athletic one, since Otis and Ava were so uncoordinated they couldn't tie their own shoes.

Suddenly Suzi realized—oh my God—they were standing on the corner of Squire's Drive and Cook's Circle right in front of the *sexual predator's* house—a boxlike brick ranch house with a boring flat yard. His white van wasn't there, but Parson was sitting in the *perv's* yard, next to the *perv's* fire ants. She gave Parson's leash a little jerk and pulled her into the street, where she sat down next to a tuft of Spanish moss, which was probably full of chiggers and ticks, but oh, well. Suzi'd never actually seen the pervert, but she'd seen his picture on the Florida Department of Law Enforcement Web site, and he was just a normal-looking dark-haired dude—didn't have squinty eyes or tattoos or a cauliflower ear like the bad guys in the old Nancy Drew books that Suzi read and reread. But it gave Suzi a thrill to stare at his house, where the shades were always drawn, and give it the stink eye.

Just then, on the road behind them, a black SUV—whew, not the white van—came roaring down the hill on Squire's Drive and then slammed on the brakes like the stop sign had jumped out in front of it, and then peeled out like the driver was pissed off about having to stop for two seconds. What was the big fricking hurry?

"That's my neighbor. Reverend Coffey. They call him Buff," Nance said, waving at the person in the SUV, who was already long gone. "He's a minister, but he drives like the devil!"

Suzi smiled politely. She pulled Parson across the street from the stop sign and the perv's house, and stood back underneath the McPhersons's live oak tree, out of the late afternoon sun. Nance and Buster followed. It was almost dinnertime. She could hear the McPherson kids in their backyard pool, yelling, splashing. It smelled like they were having a cookout. Suzi's family hadn't had a cookout in ages.

Suzi hadn't changed out of her soccer shorts and stinky shirt but was wearing her favorite flip-flops, and her feet felt wonderfully unencumbered. The dogs had already sniffed hello. Parson had plopped down on her stomach in some weeds, and she was gazing up at Suzi like, Can't we get going already? No, Suzi silently told her, we're going to take our time. Buster leaned forward on his squat little front legs, soft white belly pouching out, and watched some squirrels racing about in the tree like they were on speed.

"When?" Nance asked her. "When should I stop by to meet your family?"

Didn't the woman know that Suzi was just being polite? She was about ready to say anytime, but remembering her menopausal mother, she thought better of it. On her mother's recent birthday she'd stayed in bed all day and could barely get up the energy to blow out her birthday candles—a group of four and a group of eight carefully arranged by Suzi, who'd had to carry the cake—one she'd made herself—to her mother's bedside. Suzi'd had to pitch in and help her mother blow out the candles, which caused Ava—Miss Letter of the Law—to cry because they weren't following proper birthday-candle blowing-out procedure. Otis leaped forward as soon as the flames went out and yanked the candles out of the cake so that he could be the one to lick the bottoms. Then he and Ava begin to fight over the candles, dropping a few of them on the bedspread, while her father yelled at them to stop. Happy birthday, dear Mommy! All Suzi's efforts to please her mother were wasted.

"I'll check and see when you can come by," Suzi told Nance. Suddenly she felt deflated, but she didn't really know why.

"What else interests you, besides soccer?" Nance asked her.

"I used to be in drama," Suzi said. "I love being in plays, but I don't have time now. I really want to travel, go to Europe. Italy." I just want to rest, is what she really felt, but didn't know how to say it. I don't want to have to work so hard at being perfect. But nobody would admit that out loud because it would sound like bragging. And there were perks that went with being thought of as perfect. She had to fend off the girls who wanted to be her best friend and boys, too, except Dylan B., who looked right through her.

"Italy," Nance said, nodding. "I've always wanted to go there, too. Rent a villa in Tuscany. Sleep late every morning. Walk into a village for bread and fresh vegetables and gorgeous leather shoes. Tour the little churches. How does that sound?"

It sounded great, even the church part. "I go to Faith Presbyterian. My dad's an atheist and my mom hates having to be nice to people."

Nance didn't respond to this revelation. "You and I should go to Tuscany together," Nance said. "Have a true vacation. No soccer allowed."

As if, Suzi thought, but she smiled. "Read all day," she said. "That's what I'd really like to do." It was curious that she and Nance barely knew each other and were already talking about going on an overseas vacation together. Okay, *curious* didn't even begin to describe it. But, she realized, she liked the idea of going to Italy, even with an old lady she barely knew. Especially with an old lady she barely knew. Her age and her lack of connection to Suzi might make her the ideal traveling companion. She could suddenly see it, the two of them, herself and Nance, reclining on lounge chairs in a lovely courtyard with flowers and a fountain, Nance wearing her usual white shirt and khakis and her funny hat, reading a book, and herself reading one big fat Scottish romance after another. No cell phones or soccer dads or people with Asperger's talking about Elvis or nuclear bombs. Maybe a couple of good-looking guys standing by the fountain. Young good-looking guys, trying to get up the nerve to speak to her.

"Here's my phone number," Nance said, suddenly reaching into her pants pocket and pulling out a little white card. She'd already had the card prepared—she'd written the number in ink. Suzi took the card.

"Ask your mother if it would be all right," she said.

"If we go to Italy?" Suzi felt a little confused, dazed from the Italian sunlight in the courtyard.

"Let's start with me coming by for a visit!" Nance said. "First things first. I'd love to talk about Memphis with your granddad."

Granddad again. Suzi put the card into the pocket of her soccer shorts. She'd throw it away when she got home.

"I had a daughter," Nance said in a low voice, looking off somewhere down the street, as if she could see her daughter standing in somebody's front yard.

"What's her name?" Suzi said, because she didn't know what else to say, pretending that the daughter was alive, when she could tell by how Nance had said it that she wasn't.

"Helen," Nance said. "She died when she was eight years old. You remind me of her. She was a beautiful girl."

"I'm sorry," Suzi said. She wanted to ask what had happened—how would an eight-year-old girl up and die—but it wasn't polite, and did she really want to know, so that she could obsess about it night and day? Maybe a sexual predator got her.

"Her hair wasn't curly like yours," Nance said. "Hers was blond. Straight and blond." Nance reached out her wrinkled hand as if she were going to touch Suzi's hair, but then she dropped it down by her side again.

"At least you have your son," Suzi said, proud that she'd remembered Nance's doctor son, but as soon as she said it, she knew it was a stupid thing to say.

Nance smiled at her, even though it was a mournful little smile. "I do have my son," Nance said. "That's right. But I miss my daughter every day."

Suzi thought about how she could embellish the story when she told Mykaila. She sees her dead daughter, Helen, walking the streets of Canterbury Hills! She thinks I'm Helen reincarnated!

But really, Suzi felt bad for Nance who seemed

to be a nice but melancholy woman who wanted to take Suzi to Tuscany. Suzi didn't throw the card away after all, but she didn't take it out of her soccer shorts pocket, and these were the lucky shorts she never washed. She left the card there in the pocket like a talisman to remind her that a strange old woman found her interesting enough to invite to Tuscany.

Fast-forward a few days.

During dinner one night, Suzi gave in to her dark impulses and started tormenting Ava, just a little light torment, even though she knew she shouldn't, and even though she knew she was doing it because she was tired and pissed at herself for letting Elana, the girl who bragged about her thong underwear, get one past her at soccer practice and her middle finger on her right hand felt sprained, and her knee hurt but she couldn't complain because her father would overreact, and she'd gotten an isolated lunch at school for answering some twerp's questions during study time, and, okay, she just needed a little fun.

Suzi made her eyes big and wide, leaned forward, and said, mimicking Ava's deep voice, "I love Elvis even though he wore thong underwear."

Ava did not *overreact,* the word her parents use for Ava's wild, physical outbursts. She turned red but kept eating her well-salted chicken Alfredo. She reminded Suzi of a long-necked goose.

Otis lay down his fork and grinned in anticipation of a rollicking good sister fight. He came to the table with greasy hair and dirty fingernails, but Mom and Dad had stopped caring.

"Would you look at that tree," said Granddad, who still had half his dinner left. He sat next to Suzi, looking out the window and eating so slowly he made her feel like a greedy pig. He was talking about the live oak right beside the deck, a tree with long curving branches as thick as most tree's trunks. Every time he sat down to eat, it was like he'd never seen that tree before. "Isn't that the most beautiful tree you've ever seen?"

"Yes, Dad, it's the most beautiful tree in the whole wide world," Suzi's mom said.

Ava smiled at Granddad, ignoring Suzi, so Suzi kept talking, saying whatever came into her head, because it didn't matter: whatever she said would do the trick. "Elvis loved black people. Even loved geese. I declare, he's a saint."

Suzi's parents, at opposite ends of the long trestle table, glanced up at each other, their faces sagging with tiredness, and Suzi knew she should keep her mouth shut, and probably would have, but her mother said, "You can't let us have one dinner in peace."

"What?" Suzi said. "She always talks about Elvis. Why can't I?"

Ava couldn't stand it any longer. "You don't like Elvis because he's part Native American! And part Jewish. You're prejudiced."

"No," said Suzi, "I don't like him because he sings like he has a stick up his butt."

"I like him," their father said, a little too heartily.

"I don't *dislike* him," Suzi said. "I just think he has a stick up his butt."

"Eat. Your. Supper." Mom's hair was frizzed out around her face from the humidity in the kitchen, and she slumped over the table like she was 110 years old.

"Don't you just love trees?" Granddad said, and took a sip of his water. "I think that tree has to be the most beautiful one ever."

"Yes, it is, Granddad," Ava said. Miss Suck Up.

"I wonder," Suzi asked, "did Elvis have a syndrome, too? Like Asperger's? Ass stickers?"

Otis barked out, "Shut up. Freakazoid foundling." He meant that Suzi must have been adopted because she didn't have Asperger's and had kinky, curly hair.

"Don't say 'shut up,' " Mom told Otis, then threatened Suzi with lack of phone privileges.

For a moment there was only chewing and

swallowing. Parson Brown wound between their legs under the table, snuffling for crumbs. Outside, the evening sky was turning a pale yellowish color.

"This is very good," Dad told Mom, indicating the chicken Alfredo, which was one of the four dishes she cooked because everyone would eat them. Mom didn't even look up.

"Yes, it is, honey," said Granddad, and took an actual bite.

Mom said thanks like she didn't mean it.

"Tropical storm Alfredo's headed right for the Panhandle," Dad went on and said, "St. Marks, maybe."

"Who cares. It's not a hurricane," Otis said. Elbows on the table, he went back to his chicken, bent low and shoveling it into his mouth. He chewed with his mouth gaping open. Both he and Ava had terrible table manners, and Suzi was sick and tired of having to watch them eat, but she decided to practice self-control and refrain from imitating them or saying anything about how gross they were.

"It might turn into a hurricane," Dad said.

"It's *Alberto*, not Alfredo," Ava corrected Dad, who smiled. He'd been testing them.

Suzi felt stupid that she hadn't caught Dad's error, so she tried out another angle on Ava, saying something that could, if she had the right attorney, be construed as an innocent remark in a court of law. "Will you tell your roommate at college that you have a syndrome?" she asked Ava.

Ava couldn't help rising to the bait. "I don't have it anymore. I've outgrown it."

"Isn't that just the most beautiful tree ever?"

"Yes, Dad. The most. Beautiful. Ever."

When Granddad first came to live with them, all three kids had cut back on their fighting, at least in front of Granddad, but after Suzi noticed that Mom and Dad seemed to be fighting more than ever, she went back to her wicked old ways, and so did the other two. "You don't *outgrow* Asperger's," Suzi announced primly. "You and Otis will have it your entire lives." Facts were facts, after all.

Ava's face scrunched up. The moment had come. What would Ava do? Would she throw herself across the table and try to strangle Suzi? Would she pick up her glass of milk and toss it onto Suzi's head? Would she scream about how much she hated Suzi's guts?

Suzi tensed up, waiting for Ava to emit the high-pitched yell she usually gave before she attacked, but this time the yell never came.

Ava thrust her chair back and left the table. Had Ava finally developed self-control? At first Suzi was disappointed, but on her way past Suzi, Ava reached out and gave Suzi's hair a good hard yank.

"Ava!" Dad said. "No bodily contact."

Granddad was studying his tree with a pensive expression on his whiskery face, probably wishing he lived in a nursing home.

"I didn't do anything!" Ava yelled from the hallway. "I just accidentally bumped into her."

"Liar!" Suzi, relieved to be the one wronged, howled, held her scalp, and burst into tears.

Mom told Suzi that she had provoked Ava and so she was grounded until further notice. "We all see what you're doing," Mom told Suzi, "and we all know why you're doing it." She looked at Suzi like she hated her.

"How do you know? You can't read my mind." Suzi bawled harder and ran from the room and down the hall. She slammed her door shut and threw herself on her bed. Her wailing, now muffled, continued. She'd started the whole thing, it was true, and she'd been mean and even disgusting, picking on poor defenseless Ava, but she felt like she'd exposed some deep truth that they all needed to face, and there was some relief in that.

This was the truth: her own mother didn't like her.

From Ava's room, Elvis sang with bold abandon: "Ta-reet me like a fool, / Ta-reet me mean and cruel, / But love me."

I'm not a bad person, she wanted to tell her mother, and she didn't think she was, really, only why did she feel compelled to pick on Ava? Sometimes she really didn't blame her mother for hating her. She promised herself she'd never pick on Ava again. But couldn't Ava listen to something else once in a while? Even someone else old and embarrassing, like Frank Sinatra?

And her mother had actually encouraged Ava's obsession with Elvis by taking her to Memphis to see Graceland over Christmas break. Only Ava was allowed to go, and since then, Ava'd been even more fixated on the King, and her mother had come back talking about her own mother, who had left her when she was a little baby, not even a year old. Her mother had started asking Granddad lots of questions about her mother, but Granddad didn't have answers and her mother cried awhile about that, saying that when she was in Memphis she kept thinking about her mother and feeling down.

Well, hello! Suzi wanted to yell at her mother. How do you think I feel! You've never loved me like you do Ava. But she felt bad for her mother, too, because she knew what it felt like to miss your mother's love.

After a while she started fishing around in her shorts pocket for some Kleenex, but instead she found the card with Nance's phone number. She held it and looked at it a minute, and then, without even thinking about it, got up and walked back into the kitchen, where her parents were sitting, glaring at each other and then at Suzi. Granddad and Otis had disappeared.

She handed the card to her mother and explained how she'd met this nice old lady out walking her dog and that she was from Memphis and really cool and she really liked Suzi and thought Suzi was special. "She invited me to go to Italy with her," Suzi explained. "We're going to stay in a villa in Tuscany. At the end of the summer. Can I go?"

"And miss soccer camp?" said her father, acting like the trip was a joke.

But she wouldn't let him. It wasn't a joke, not to her. "I said at the *end* of summer. August."

Her mother was looking at the card, and she glanced up at Suzi. "Why would she want to take you?"

"That's real nice," Suzi said, hurt, of course, but grimly gratified to have more evidence.

"I didn't mean it like that," said her mother. "What I meant was, she doesn't even know you. It's kind of strange, don't you think?"

"No," Suzi said, even though *strange* was exactly the word for it.

"She can tell you're fun to hang out with, I guess!" her mother said, smiling like it hurt her face.

"I *guess*."

Her mother sighed, *can't do anything right,* and

studied the card again. "Nancy Archer. Wonderful name."

"It sounds made up," Dad said, but nobody ever listened to him.

Vic CHAPTER 2

He never would've hooked up with Gigi if his kids had been out front of the roller rink, SkateWorld, like they were supposed to be.

Inside, Otis and Suzi were whizzing around the rink under the disco lights, and although he was annoyed by the crowds and the blaring music and the flashing lights in the dimness and the smell of grease and sweat and by having to come inside to get his kids—again!—it also did his heart good, as they say, to see his children enjoying themselves, even though they did it in very different ways.

Suzi swung around the rink hand in hand with Davis, a dark-haired kid who was a couple of inches shorter than she was. Davis was something of an Eddie Haskell type, somebody who could charm any adult he saw fit to charm, but Vic liked him. He came to most of Suzi's local soccer games. He left messages on their voice mail, pretending to be Bob, a Sears appliance guy, because he knew Vic thought it was funny.

Suzi skated carefully and had Davis to hold on

to, and Vic was glad. He had to keep himself from forbidding her to do any activity that might cause an injury and ruin her chance to go to the Olympic Development soccer camp in July. She hadn't made the cut last year, but it was just *so cool* that she'd have the chance to participate this year and hopefully get chosen to go on to regionals in New Orleans in January. And then . . . but, no, he wouldn't let himself get his hopes up too high.

Free spirit Otis, on the other hand, swooped around the rink alone—around and around and around he went, skillfully avoiding other people, just as he did in real life. Otis never seemed to need, or want, any attention or affection, so most people eventually let him be, even, to a degree, his own parents; but it was either let Otis be or struggle with him constantly. Skating was the only physical activity Otis had ever enjoyed, and he was damn good at it. Even so, Vic had to force him to go skating on occasional Saturday afternoons, and he had to drive him there because Otis wouldn't waste his own gas. The only place Otis ever really wanted to be was working on his science project in that hideous shed. This place, at least, was an improvement over the shed. Without noticing his father, Otis swung past again, wearing a glow-stick necklace, which meant he'd once again won the boys speed skate for his age group.

Vic was standing there, admiring his progeny, when he felt a hand on his shoulder. "Victor? Victor Mature?" Only one person ever called him after the B-movie actor from the forties and fifties—the chump who played opposite Rita Hayworth in the forgettable *My Gal Sal*. Vic smelled her perfume before he turned around. Prada—the same scent Caroline used to wear before she pitched her bottle along with all her fancy face lotions.

There stood Gigi Carter with the tousled blond hair, a smart Southern belle who was going to seed, in a sexy way. Gigi was a friend of Vic's from graduate school at FSU. Gigi had finished her Ph.D. in English—focusing on Southern women's literature—but she had a trust fund income and didn't have to look for a full-time teaching job. He saw her occasionally in the halls of Florida Testing and Assessment, where she temped from time to time. She preferred temping, she'd said, because it gave her more time to ride horses and write.

Vic gave her an awkward hug.

Gigi was wearing a sundress, so obviously she wasn't skating. She didn't seem like the skating type. In fact, Gigi wasn't athletic looking—she was pale and knobby—but in her case, appearances were misleading. She trained and boarded horses and taught riding lessons and was a skilled rider herself. She'd given riding lessons to Ava and they'd gotten along famously—until Ava had fallen off one of Gigi's horses and hadn't wanted to go back.

Gigi asked Vic where his family was, and he happily pointed Suzi and Otis out to Gigi, who hadn't seen them in a while and made the appropriate fuss about how grown-up and good-looking they were.

"Is Travis here?" Vic asked her over the refrain of "YMCA" by the Village People. Travis, her son, was Ava's age.

"Travis wouldn't be caught dead in here," Gigi said. "My niece's birthday," she said, indicating a picnic table in the snack bar crowded with small kids eating giant saggy slices of pizza. "Buff's daughter. Angel. She's four. Let's sit." She pulled Vic gently back onto a big carpeted block of wood that served as an observation bench beside the rink. Her brother, Buff, she reminded him, lived in Canterbury Hills. "They have two daughters, Angel and Rusty. You know them? The Coffeys?"

Caroline, Vic's wife, knew Paula Coffey from school committees and disliked her because she was too peppy. Vic had never met Buff, but according to neighborhood gossip, Buff would preach the socks off anyone he could corner. He was a minister at some wacky fundamentalist church. "I know *of* them," he told Gigi.

"Rusty's headed for trouble," Gigi said. "She

used to be such a great kid. And she's so smart."

Vic said he was sorry to hear that, and decided not to mention all the neighborhood gossip he'd heard about Rusty. According to the stories, Rusty was more than *headed* for trouble. She'd already been suspended for having pot in her locker and had been caught shoplifting at Hot Topic. She skipped school and periodically ran away from home. Supposedly, she was one of the vandals who occasionally swept through Canterbury Hills at night. So far, they hadn't done any major damage, and their pranks were kind of funny if it wasn't your mailbox sprouting a spray-painted penis and, of course, if it wasn't your teenager doing it. He didn't think his teenagers were doing it, but he'd probably be the last to know.

"Hey," Gigi said. "See that old lady sitting over there with them?" She pointed.

Vic barely looked. "Uh-huh."

"Just moved in across the street from Buff and them. But it's y'all she really wants to meet. Seems to know a lot about your father-in-law. Come on over and I'll introduce you. Her name's Nancy Archer."

It was the old lady who was supposedly going to take Suzi to Italy. "Does Suzi know she's here?"

"They were talking up a blue streak earlier. They're real buds."

"Don't make me go over there," Vic said. "I don't want to meet any new people. I know too many people already."

"Fine, Puddleglum." Gigi was scanning the skaters. "They should serve martinis to the adults who're brave enough to come in here, don't you think?"

"I do think," Vic said, but, actually, he found the skating rink, once he got acclimated, to be mesmerizing. He got a kick out of watching not only his kids but people of all ages and races and types, from the little dreadlocked five-year-old boy to the older white woman in Ice Capades attire, forming the letters *Y, M, C, A* with their arms as they skated past.

Vic never was much of a roller skater, but back in Iowa, he and Caroline, before they had kids, used to go ice-skating on Lake Macbride. He could still picture that silly fur hat and old yellow ski coat Caroline used to wear. Those exhilarating Sunday afternoons, holding hands and moving together over the dazzling white lake, looking forward to a warm fire and split pea soup and an evening reading and talking, were some of the happiest days of his life.

"Hey, Mr. Mature," Gigi said, squeezing Vic's elbow. "Good news. I've been assigned to your portfolio project."

The Great Portfolio Project! Vic and his team had spent months designing it, convincing the higher-ups that it would be a better way than the usual standardized tests and timed writing essays to assess high school students' writing. Eleventh graders in participating high schools would assemble portfolios of the best writing they'd done that year in math, language arts, science, and social studies, and trained FTA scorers would evaluate them. Following the national trend in education, FTA would be encouraging writing not only in language arts, but—and here came the buzzwords—*across the curriculum*. The plan was that after they'd tested the project and gotten it up and running, they'd sell it to various school corporations across the state, who, hopefully, would be delighted to jump on board.

FTA had lined up ten high schools from around the state to participate on a trial basis at no cost to them, with the understanding that, depending on how happy they were with the results, they could later buy into the project at a discount. Vic was more excited about going to work than he had been in years, but he was more stressed-out as well. There were big bucks involved and a strict timetable, and his ass was on the line. Human Resources had hired Gigi and fifty other temps for the trial scoring.

"You'll be my boss. Can you handle it?" She swung her crossed leg, silver high-heeled sandal dangling from her narrow foot.

It would make everything more fun to have

someone he actually knew and liked working with him. “You can help me train the language arts scorers.” He made this statement without thinking about it first. As soon as he said it, he knew he shouldn’t have. But for the first time in forever, he felt a bit reckless. He was aware that he was willing to risk pissing off his boss because he wanted Gigi’s company, but what was wrong with that? Why was he arguing with himself?

Suzi and Davis, gliding past, waved at Vic. Then Suzi clapped her hand over her mouth, meaning, Uh-oh, I forgot what time it was!

Otis continued round and round with smooth scissor strokes, looking neither left nor right, his shaggy hair flying out behind him. A couple of tweenage girls struggled valiantly to keep up with him. He would never notice them.

“Don’t you have to be, like, a permanent employee to train scorers?” Gigi asked him. “I mean, it’s not that I don’t want to. . . .”

She was right. Temps weren’t supposed to train people. “I can assign you any job I want to,” Vic said. “That’s why I make the big bucks!” Gigi kept staring at him quizzically, so he kept on, digging himself deeper into the hole. “I know you’d be good at it. You won a teaching award, right? So, congratulations! You’re a trainer! If they sold booze in here, I’d buy you a martini to celebrate.”

“Rain check!” Gigi said, moving aside as Suzi

came hurtling toward Vic, falling on top of him and nearly knocking him down.

"My friend's here!" Suzi said to her father, clambering shakily to her feet. "My friend Mrs. Archer. The one who wants to take me to Italy. Come meet her."

"Don't have time right now, kiddo," he said, waving and smiling at the old lady, who sat by herself at a small table on the edge of the party. She waved back, and for a moment he was afraid she'd get up and come to them, but, thank God, she didn't.

Suzi went over to Mrs. Archer before they left, her Rollerblades slung over her shoulder, and gave her friend a hug good-bye. Now, as Vic often did, he felt proud to have a daughter like Suzi. She always put herself out for people. Everyone except her own sister.

Vic thought that the best way to handle the whole Italy thing was just to ignore it, but Caroline thought differently. She wanted to meet Mrs. Archer and size her up, and she wanted Vic to be there with her.

"You're not thinking of actually letting her go off to Italy with a total stranger," Vic said.

"What I *think,*" Caroline said, "is that Suzi probably read too much into a casual invitation. Let's find out for sure instead of *thinking.*"

"Why do you hate me?" Vic asked her.

She sighed, looking even more exasperated. "What kind of nincompoop question is that?"

"We should rent a villa in Tuscany," he suggested, "Just you and me." Neither he nor Caroline had ever been to Italy.

"Like I have time," she said. "Have you seen the pile of laundry in there?"

Nowadays everything Vic said got on Caroline's nerves, so he tried to stay out of her way. In the evenings he'd been escaping to his little study (closet) in the basement to check out the National Hurricane Center Web site. After supper and before Nancy Archer was due to arrive, he snuck down and sat in his dark study bathed in the blue glow of his Mac laptop.

Praise be! A new hot spot! He clicked on the little orange circle on the map.

> A TROPICAL WAVE IS LOCATED OVER THE FAR EASTERN ATLANTIC OCEAN ABOUT 350 MILES SOUTH-SOUTHWEST OF THE CAPE VERDE ISLANDS. THE ASSOCIATED SHOWER ACTIVITY CONTINUES TO SHOW SIGNS OF ORGANIZATION . . . AND SLOW DEVELOPMENT OF THIS SYSTEM IS POSSIBLE OVER THE NEXT COUPLE OF DAYS AS IT MOVES WESTWARD AT 10 TO 15 MPH. THERE IS A MEDIUM CHANCE . . . 30 TO 50 PERCENT . . . OF THIS SYSTEM BECOMING A TROPICAL CYCLONE DURING THE NEXT 48 HOURS.

Oh, the possibilities! Thanks to the Internet, you could now watch a storm during its inception and incubation through all stages of development, which in turn allowed you more time to obsess, if you were so inclined. Conditions had to be just right for a hurricane to develop. First of all, he'd discovered, for a trouble spot to form, ocean waters had to be warm, warmer than usual, and along with that you needed a cool upper atmosphere. There also had to be a disturbance near the surface of the water, an inverted trough of low air pressure moving through, such as a West African Disturbance Line—a line of convection that formed over Africa and moved into the Atlantic Ocean. Many factors could dilute storm activity—the infamous El Niño causing vertical wind sheer, a dry dusty Saharan Air Layer cooking the upper atmosphere, an area of high pressure hulking like a big bully, deflecting all storms. The 2005 hurricane season notwithstanding, the more Vic knew about hurricanes, the more it seemed a sort of miracle that one ever formed at all.

Vic would never have admitted it to anyone, but part of him was hoping for a hurricane to hit Tallahassee. Growing up in the Midwest, he'd always run outside, instead of into the basement, when the tornado sirens started wailing, but he never actually got to see a funnel cloud. Now he wanted more than just to see a storm coming. He wanted to be *in* a storm. Period.

Almost every summer, tropical storms flooded Tallahassee, but a tropical storm, nasty as it might be, wouldn't do. It had to be a big mother. Cat. 3 or better. Chances this year were good. According to the weather experts, the 2006 hurricane season was supposed to be as bad or *worse* than the previous season, which was the most active hurricane season in recorded history, the season of Dennis, Emily, Rita, Wilma, and Katrina. He'd watched news coverage of those hurricanes and found himself, in a sick sort of way, envious of the survivors he heard telling their stories. They'd lived through a natural disaster of legendary proportions, they told awe-inspiring stories, and their lives would never be the same. Of course there were tragic losses, and he felt bad about the losses, when he thought about them, which he didn't spend much time doing. Instead, he kept imagining what it would be like to be right in the middle of all that fury, and hoped he'd get the chance.

Tallahassee was twenty-five miles inland, but that didn't make it safe from hurricanes. People still talked about Hurricane Kate, which wreaked havoc in 1985—ten years before Vic and his family moved from Iowa to Tallahassee. People said there were trees down everywhere, especially the big pines, power and water out for six weeks. There hadn't been any direct hurricane hits since then, but Vic was hoping for the worst, which, he supposed, made him a selfish and callous person, but as long as he never actually voiced this desire, who would know? It's not like he could *cause* a hurricane to come there. Get bigger, he told the little orange circle that wasn't quite a storm. It didn't budge.

Mrs. Archer showed up right at seven thirty p.m., and Vic was annoyed to be summoned out of his hidey-hole, but he tried to cover up his annoyance by offering the old lady some chocolate cake, and of course Caroline and Suzi wanted some, too, so he divvied up the remains and gave himself the smallest piece. Carrying their slices of cake on Caroline's precious Jadeite dessert plates, they paraded into the living room—Vic, Suzi, and Caroline and Nance, as she insisted on being called. The rest of the family was nowhere to be seen. Otis was out in his shed, Ava was in her bedroom, supposedly doing homework, and Wilson was downstairs "resting." None of them wanted to be subjected to an awkward evening with Nance, the fool who was dangling a trip to Italy in front of Suzi.

Vic's living room felt more cramped and shabby each time he entered it. One side had big windows looking out at the front yard, and the other walls were covered with bookcases and flea market oil paintings and old family photos—of *Caroline's* family—in antique frames. Every flat surface was littered with fifties knickknacks—souvenir ashtrays, chalk bookends with animals heads on them.

Once upon a time Vic had welcomed all the stuff Caroline brought home from her excursions, but that was back when the kids were little and it felt like they had room to spare. Now they were living with three hulking teenagers and a dog and Caroline's ever-present father—who'd always been kind to Vic, even though he'd been an English major, and had paid for private elementary school for all three of his grandkids, so how could Vic complain about his being there? It was just that this house was starting to feel just as chaotic and unwelcoming as the house he grew up in. If a hurricane did come through Tallahassee and their house was flooded, all Caroline's crap would be ruined and they'd get to start over again.

As soon as Nance spotted the old photographs, grouped together on one wall and lined up on top of a short bookcase, she shuffled over to see them, oohing and aahing. Suzi told her who was who. Nance seemed most interested in photos of Wilson and his wives. Suzi pointed out Wilson's later wives, Lila and then Verna Tommy, both of them plump and blond and sweet faced, unlike Caroline's own mother, his first wife, Mary, who was dark and serious looking. Nance picked up and closely examined the oval sepia-toned portrait of Wilson and Mary on their wedding day, both of them gazing down at her bouquet of daylilies like it was the most compelling thing in the world. "What a lovely couple!" Nance said. "Oh, I just love old photographs." She turned to Caroline, who was slouched at the other end of the couch from Vic, waiting to be able to politely eat her cake, as he was. "Your mother made a beautiful bride," Nance said to Caroline.

"She left when I wasn't even a year old," Caroline answered. "Never heard from her again."

"Oh, dear. I'm so sorry." Nance set the photograph back down in front of the others, positioning it carefully. "She must've been out of her mind. Simply out of her mind to do that."

"Okay, time to eat." Suzi knew when to head her mother off. She herded her new friend, both of them clutching their cake plates, forks, and napkins, over to the old red armchair in the corner, where Nance settled down.

Suzi, her wild curly hair pulled back in a ponytail, plopped down between Caroline and Vic, emitting waves of lemony smelling perfume.

Nance sat on the edge of her seat and began to eat daintily, careful not to drop a crumb. She was the kind of person who was easy to overlook.

She had a short white cap of hair and pale skin. She had a dark place on one cheek, like an age spot, and legs speckled with bruises, which Vic assumed were from bumping into things. She wore a flowered skirt and tucked-in blouse, and the whole affair rode up too high on her waist. This was the only fashion faux pas Vic ever noticed in anybody, because he'd once been accused of high-waistedness himself.

In between bites of cake, Suzi reached over and adjusted the strap of Caroline's tank top so that it was covering the tattoos on her left shoulder.

Caroline, his former sprite of a wife turned menopausal mess, yanked her strap back down.

"You're just as cute as your daughter," Nance said to Caroline.

Caroline shook her head, ungracious about the compliment.

She used to be cute, Vic thought, until she gave up on herself and everyone except Ava. When Vic met Caroline she'd been a fashion merchandizing major at the University of Iowa, working part-time at a clothing store, called Barbara's, in downtown Iowa City. After she graduated and married Vic she was promoted to store manager. Women from all over Johnson County—and surrounding counties—flocked into Barbara's to get Caroline's sartorial advice. She used to wear slightly unusual but pleasing combinations of clothes, like plaid Bermuda shorts and a ruffly top, or a slinky dress and cowboy boots, and she'd always gotten stylish haircuts. Back then she'd had a calm sense of purpose about her, but these days she was either comatose or bristling with manic, angry energy.

Now she was wearing a pair of baggy, ripped-up shorts and a tank top with Gumby on it, her face puffy from an earlier crying jag. She'd scrunched her hair up in a bunch of tiny ponytails to keep it off her face and neck, which made her look like a crazy person. She'd tendered this invitation to Nance as a concerned parent, but she did not project either competence or hospitality. What Nance didn't know was that she'd actually dressed up for her. She'd put on a bra!

Vic knew how he looked to Nance—a run-of-the-mill middle-aged white guy, curly hair in need of a trim, an eager-to-please smile meant to cover up his desire to get the hell out of there.

Nance was glancing around the room like she was looking for something or someone. She turned to Caroline. "Your yard is so beautiful. Who does it?"

"We do," Vic said.

Caroline gave him a cold smile, because, it was true, she'd been doing the yard work of late, but it was because he was either at work or at soccer with Suzi.

Nance smiled eagerly. "I believe I've seen your

father out there from time to time. I'd love to talk to him about Memphis. I lived there for years."

"Oh," Caroline said.

"Is he here?"

"He's napping," Caroline said.

"Maybe another time?"

"Sure."

Vic sighed. Why were they talking about Wilson and Memphis instead of Italy and Suzi?

"This is just the best cake, Caroline!" Nance said, dabbing at her lips with a napkin.

Vic waited for Caroline to correct Nance and give Suzi credit, but she didn't.

"I made it," Suzi said. "For Mom's birthday."

"All by herself," Vic added.

"Well, it is scrumptious!" Nance said, then went on nervously. "It's so nice to meet more neighbors. I feel so blessed. I just happened to buy a house across from the youth minister at the Genesis Church. What church do ya'll go to?"

"We don't," Caroline said.

"Not very often," Vic added, trying to smooth over his wife's bluntness.

"I go with my friend Mykaila," Suzi said. "Mykaila's African American, but they go to a white church."

"I swan," said Nance.

Everybody went back to eating.

A churchgoing Southern lady who used old-timey expressions like *I swan* and took vacations in Italy. She was too good to be true, like some innocuous creature in a mystery novel who actually turned out to be a ruthless criminal.

"That Reverend Coffey's daughter's kind of strange," Nance continued. "I came home from Publix yesterday and found her in my carport, just sitting there!"

"Did you ask her what she was doing?" Suzi asked.

"She wanted to know could she wash my car for eight dollars. I found that peculiar. Why eight dollars?"

"I know her," Suzi said. "Rusty. She must need the money for drugs."

"Well, that's just great," Nance said, waving her hand dismissively. "I live next door to a dope fiend."

"Let's talk about Italy!" Suzi announced, setting down her cake plate on the coffee table.

"Yes, let's do," Vic said, setting his plate down, too.

"Italy?" Nance said.

"*You* know," Suzi said, speaking to Nance like she was a child. "Our trip to Tuscany. How about early August? After soccer camp and before school starts."

"Sounds good," said Nance, nodding vigorously. If she was surprised by Suzi's insistence, she didn't show it. "That would be the *perfect* time."

"You really want to take Suzi?" Caroline asked. "May I ask why?"

Did she have to be so openly suspicious of the woman? "We wanted to make sure," Vic said, "you know, that Suzi didn't misread your invitation."

"No, she did not!" Nance smiled at Suzi, who glanced down at the carpet, pleased. "One of my childhood friends has a villa just outside Lucca," Nance said. "Her better half recently died and she's been after me to come visit and I've been itching to go, but I need this young thing to come along and help me."

A villa outside Lucca. Sounded heavenly. He and Caroline were the ones who ought to be going there.

"I've *always* wanted to go to Italy," Suzi said. "Ever since I saw *Under the Tuscan Sun* with Diane Lane. You didn't tell me about your best friend's villa, Nance."

"We can't afford that kind of trip right now," Caroline put in.

"Maybe Suzi could earn the money," Vic suggested, realizing that he was mostly championing the trip because Caroline was against it.

"I'd pay for everything," Nance said. "Should've mentioned that right off. Money isn't a problem for me, thank the Lord."

"But why Suzi?" Caroline persisted. "You just met."

Nance explained that she didn't have any children and that she herself had been an only child and didn't have any other living relatives. "I lost my daughter a long time ago," she said. "Suzi reminds me of her. I've never stopped missing her."

Vic said he was sorry, but Caroline said nothing.

Suzi said, "What about your son? The doctor?"

Nance looked briefly confused, then she smiled. "That's my stepson," she said.

Suddenly Caroline turned to Nance, and asked, in an accusatory voice, "How long did you live in Memphis?"

"Since the early fifties."

"Have you lived anywhere else?"

"Little Rock, when I was a child. After the war I moved up to Memphis with my first husband."

"So you've been married more than once," Caroline said.

"Twice. Just had the one daughter. But I didn't get to see her grow up." Nance set her empty cake plate and fork down on the mosaicked end table and dabbed at her little bowlike mouth.

Caroline handed Vic her empty cake plate, like he was supposed to do something with it. He set it down, too hard, on top of his.

"That spot on your face," Caroline said. "Has it been there a long time?"

What was with all these random personal questions?

Nance touched her cheek. "It's a birthmark."

Now Caroline seemed agitated. She shifted around on the couch, tucking her legs underneath her. Vic could tell that she wanted to get back to her bedroom and shut the door on all of them. Their bedroom had somehow become *her* bedroom. In the last few years of their marriage, Vic had been eased into the category of people who got in Caroline's way.

Now it was Nance's turn to ask Caroline a question. "When did your father live in Memphis?"

"He grew up there. Got his first job there, after medical school."

"How interesting! And where did you say his job was?"

"I didn't."

Why was Caroline being so grudging toward Nance? She was the one who'd insisted on inviting Nance over. It was obvious Nance was lonely and Memphis was something they had in common. Would it hurt to just humor her a little?

"Wilson was a researcher at the medical school," Vic said.

"I wonder if I ever ran into him," Nance said. "I went to the free clinic at the medical school. Lived in Lauderdale Courts at the time. Didn't have much money then."

There was a loud startled cry and then, with a great flapping, Ava swooped down the hall into the living room. She perched on the ottoman, knee up like a large bird. She wore white cotton socks with her shorts because her feet were always cold. "Where did you say you lived in Memphis?" Ava asked Nance.

"This is my daughter Ava," Vic said.

"Hello, Ava. Nice to meet you. We were living in Lauderdale Courts. Public housing."

"Wow," said Ava. "I can't believe it."

"Oh no," Suzi groaned. "Here we go."

"Did you ever meet Elvis?" Ava asked Nance. "He lived there in the early fifties."

"I knew who he was. Didn't really know him. He used to play his guitar in the courtyard."

"Oh my God!" Ava jumped and began to pace back and forth, back and forth, the width of the living room, head tilted, twiddling the fingers of one hand, the way she did when she got excited. Vic watched Nance watch Ava curiously, wondering, no doubt, what was up, why a young woman would act this way. The pacing was an Asperger's thing, and Vic found it charming, because she did it when she was excited and happy. Caroline, however, found it embarrassing.

Sure enough, Caroline told Ava to sit down.

Ava didn't seem to hear her mother. "Did you talk to Elvis?" she asked Nance, pacing.

"Not really," said Nance. "Just to say hello. To me he was just a white boy singing colored songs. How wrong I was!"

"Oh, I wish you'd talked to him when you had the chance!" Ava said. "You're so lucky! Mom and I went to Memphis over Christmas break. We got to see Graceland and Lauderdale Courts and Sun Studio and Humes High School. All the old Elvis places."

"Please stop talking about Elvis," Suzi said. "We're trying to plan our trip to Italy."

"Please be nice to your sister," Caroline told Suzi.

"Please sit down, Ava," Suzi, the assistant parent, put in.

"Please shut up," Ava told her.

"You shut up."

"Stop it, you two," Caroline said, in that same flat voice she'd been using too often lately.

"Nance's going to think you fight all the time!" Vic said.

"We do fight all the time," said Ava.

"It was a joke, Ava," Vic said.

"A lame joke," Caroline said, without looking at Vic. "Go finish your homework, Ava."

"I can't. I'm going to fail!"

"No, you're not."

It was obvious by then that Vic's family couldn't hold it together for five minutes, not even in front of a guest. It's time to go home, lady, Vic silently told Nancy Archer. Just leave us to feast on one another's carcasses. "Goodbye, Ava," he said. "Do what your mother asked you to do."

"I taught at Humes High School," Nance put in, "for fifteen years."

To his relief, Ava didn't respond to this. She slunk back to her room.

"So that's what you were doing," Caroline said, half under her breath.

Nance turned to Vic and asked him about his work.

Vic picked up his favorite pillow, a suede pillow with a fuzzy dog embroidered into one side, clutched it to his chest, and told Nancy all about the portfolio project. As he talked, he thought of something he could do for Nancy, a way he could arrange for her to meet more people, nice people, unlike his wife. "We'll start scoring about the middle of June," he told Nance. "You probably don't need the extra income, but if you want to get out of the house, it might be fun. We hire lots of retired people. All you need is a bachelor's degree. The scoring will last about a month. You can set your own hours!" Vic was aware that he sounded like a game show host, but his enthusiasm wasn't put on and he knew that some of it had to do with Gigi.

Nance clapped her hands together. "I swan. I just might. Thank you, Vic!"

"Will it be over by the time we go to Italy?" Suzi asked.

"It'll be over in about six weeks," Vic said, "God willing."

“Dad went to graduate school in English,” Suzi told Nance.

“He had to drop out so he could support us,” Ava yelled from her bedroom.

Ava was right . . . well, half right . . . but Vic hated to hear such excuses. He’d applied to graduate school because he loved Fitzgerald and Hemingway, but not long after he’d enrolled he was informed that his literary heroes were beyond passé, a couple of sexist old drunks, and he felt trapped in classes where politically correct theory heads pontificated. But he’d dragged his family down to FSU from Iowa so he’d hung on for a while, too long maybe. Finally he grabbed his M.A. as a kind of consolation prize and got on with things, taking a full-time job at FTA. He was fine with his decision. He actually liked his job at FTA and was good at it.

“Is Dr. Spriggs going to score papers for you, too?” Nance asked him.

Caroline answered for him. “Dad’s memory’s not so good.”

“How bad is it?” Nance frowned intently.

“Bad,” said Caroline.

“It’s not that bad,” Vic said.

Caroline made a scoffing sound. “I’m the one who looks after him all day. I should know.”

Suzi clambered to her feet. “I’ve got some social studies to finish. The Incas and Mayans.”

She smiled politely at Nance and thanked her for coming. Then she stopped, just before rounding the corner, and stood there dramatically. "So can I go to Italy with Nance? Can I?"

"No, you can't," Caroline said.

Suzi said, "What? Why not? She needs me."

"We'll talk about it later," Vic said, when Caroline didn't reply.

Suzi waved at her friend and disappeared.

Nance scooted forward in her chair and gazed at Caroline. Vic expected her to make a case for Italy, but she surprised him. "My new house doesn't have any yard to speak of. I miss it so much. Maybe I could come work in yours sometime."

"There's not much to do," Caroline said.

Nance began blinking her eyes rapidly, obviously disappointed.

"Come by anytime," Vic told Nance.

"Mary," Caroline said, apropos of nothing.

Nance jerked her head quickly toward Caroline, frowned, then looked quickly away.

"What?" Vic said. "Why'd you say that?"

"Mary?" Caroline said again. "Isn't that your name?"

"It's Nance." Nance giggled, even though she was having to apologize for not being Mary.

"Oh, right."

Had Caroline really forgotten the poor woman's name that quickly? Vic was living in a house full of lunatics. He wouldn't blame Nance if she never darkened their door again.

Nance was the kind of woman he'd always wished his own mother could have been—helpful, interested in other people, someone who wasn't afraid to be ordinary, domestic, happy. She had no idea about the nest of yellow jackets she'd just stumbled into.

CHAPTER 3 *Caroline*

Everything that used to work didn't.

Even with the air-conditioning cranked up, she was hot. She kicked the covers off during the night and lay there fuming, and during the day she wore tank shirts and boxer shorts around the house. She couldn't stand her hair touching her face and neck. She was always "sweating like a hog." One time Ava made the mistake of reminding her that hogs don't sweat. "Come over here and feel my chest, then," Caroline snapped, which caused Ava, and everyone else, to flee the room.

She was awful to her husband. She once informed him that she never wanted to have sex again . . . with anyone, she assured him. She couldn't stand anyone "at her, wanting something." Then, another time, she blurted out that she felt like having sex with every man she saw. Well, almost every man, she added, as if that made her statement more palatable.

"Me, too?" Vic had asked, just to humor her, she could tell, because, well, she was a sweaty hog with scary ponytails.

Even though she didn't have high expectations, when they did have sex she had to conceal the feeling afterward that it hadn't been worth the bother. Maybe she was done with the whole nonsense. How depressing was that?

She was awful to her children. To her own dear children! She was used to having her hands full, but this summer, because of the older kids' developmental lags, the adolescent desire for distance from one's parents seemed to come over all three of her children at the same time. Caroline couldn't engage any of them in conversation. She got only monosyllabic answers to her questions, eye rolling, deep sighing. Of course, she was in demand as a driver, as there were doctor's appointments; counseling appointments; Suzi's soccer practice; Ava's piano lessons and classes at the community college, where she was finishing up her first year; carting Otis to his part-time job at McDonald's and to Sunny Side High School, when he didn't have gas money for his Pontiac; and of course there was always shopping, laundry, meal preparation, fight referee—but she could do all these things on autopilot. On many occasions her presence was required, and her cooperation was always expected, but she was supposed to perform her duties and stay in the background.

She often felt helplessly reduced to her children's level. Below their level. One time she slapped Ava in the face for getting an F on her take-home algebra exam—she'd spent hours working on it and then forgotten to turn it in. Another time she scattered Suzi's basket of clean laundry in the front yard because Suzi wouldn't fold it. She held her nose around Otis because he stank like McDonald's and refused to take a shower. After these occurrences her family had to endure her self-flagellation and profuse, weepy apologies. There were more incidents like this than she cared to count.

She was awful to her poor father, who enraged her by sitting at the kitchen table, patiently drinking coffee, waiting for her to read the newspaper to him because he couldn't see well anymore, or waiting for her to take him to a doctor's appointment or out to Target or CVS or Lake Ella to look at ducks. She'd taken to hiding from him in her bedroom, wondering how it could be that she had another person to take care of, cursing her gadabout younger brother who couldn't take care of an ingrown toenail, hoping that the old man would finally give up and shuffle back downstairs to his little bedroom.

Her father's presence in her home was a constant reminder that she'd never had a mother—a fact that she'd been more successful at suppressing when he was living back in Iowa. The old question kept resurfacing—what had her father done to run her mother off? The answer to this question had never been obvious. Caroline had never seen him drink more than the occasional glass of wine, and there was no evidence that he'd spent money wildly—but he hadn't clutched at it in a miserly way either. He'd lavished love and attention on the two wives—one nice, one mean—that he'd had after Mary Conner. He'd never shown signs of being a philanderer. But her mother wouldn't have left behind a nine-month-old baby girl unless Wilson had done *something* to force her away. He'd never been willing to talk much about it, not while Caroline was growing up and not now. He didn't talk much about anything anymore. On her worst days it seemed like he was simply there in her house to remind her of her mother, to give her more work to do, and then to die where she'd be the one to find him.

She was tired of being awful to the people she loved, but since she couldn't stop being awful, the only alternative was to get away from all of them. Leave them far behind so as not to expose them to her anger. Maybe this was how her own mother had felt—that her family would be better off without her. But her mother had left a tiny baby! And never came back! Caroline would only be taking a sabbatical from grown and half-grown people who either resented her or took her for granted, or both—not leaving for good, just until she stopped wanting to slap them all silly. Suzi dismissed her. Otis patronized her. Being around Vic the way he was now—middle-aged—frightened her, because when she really noticed him, she was reminded of who they used to be and never would be again. Two people who'd backpacked in New Mexico on their honeymoon. Who'd howled with wolves from a canoe in northern Minnesota. Who, when they couldn't afford cable TV, watched Lawrence Welk on Saturday nights so they could dance to Myron Floren's accordion. Then the kids came along, and everything was different but always a new adventure. Now she felt like they were waiting for it all to be over. She couldn't wait anymore. She wouldn't. Next! But what was next? Leaving was next. It was the only option she could come up with, because she was losing her mind.

The truth was, Caroline had been losing it for a while. But she didn't want to go down without a fight.

Three years ago, when she turned forty-five, after having spent most of her life laughing at the suckers who'd buy such things, she started hemorrhaging money on expensive face creams with pseudoscientific names that promised miracles. She would apply each cream hopefully and study herself in the mirror, asking her husband periodically if she looked any different, and every time he said, "Yeah, sure," until she stopped believing him. Around this time she started wearing T-shirts with skeletons and rhinestones on them and, with her already-tattooed friend Billie, she went downtown and got the names of her three kids tattooed on her left shoulder. Her family was horrified, which pleased her.

But after a while all this age-fending-off behavior started feeling like wasted energy, a finger in the dike. The sure prospect of old age and death hits different people at different ages. For Caroline, forty-eight was the magic year. She turned forty-eight on May 2, 2006.

The day after her forty-eighth birthday, that dreadful birthday when she couldn't get out of bed, Caroline dumped all her expensive face creams in the trash and gave all her rock T-shirts to Ava, since Suzi tended more toward stripes and Nike swooshes. That's when she started in with the boxer shorts and tank shirts and the little ponytails and the simmering anger and longing to run away, the same shameful longing that her mother must've felt, and then Mrs. So-called Nancy Archer appeared in her living room, the first time when Suzi invited her, the second time when she dropped by with a book about Elvis—one of those huge coffee table books of photographs that end up in the remainder pile at Barnes & Noble.

The poor woman had lugged that big useless book three blocks in the heat. She was so thin and pale and dry, and not a smear of sweat anywhere on her—it was like she was trying to mock Caroline, who was red-faced and sweaty and not yet back—mentally, that is—from her morning run. She and Vic used to run together, but now, because he went in to work so early, he got up to run at five a.m. Caroline ran slower when she ran by herself, but she tried to stay in decent shape, which meant something different at age forty-eight than it did at age twenty-eight.

She didn't know what to make of this insistent old lady. Caroline didn't trust her, but what could she do but invite her in?

"Well, for a few minutes," Nance said in her breathy voice, stepping quickly into the house.

Oh, but this was an opportunity, Caroline realized. Vic was at work, Ava supposedly studying in her room, Otis at Sunny Side High School, and Suzi at Miccosukee Middle School. Her father was in the den, and she would get to witness the meeting between Nance and her father. It would be a big moment. Either it would be a reunion between her parents, or else a first meeting of two strangers. She'd surely be able to tell which one it was when she saw it happening.

She suggested that Nance set the Elvis book on the dining room table so Ava could look at it later. Then she explained that she'd just finished reading the *New York Times* to Wilson, who liked to be kept abreast of the news, and that the two of them were now working on the crossword puzzle—they did it on Mondays and Tuesdays but after that, forget it, it was too hard.

"I'd love to help, but I'm not too good at crosswords," Nance said in the dim hallway.

"Neither are we," Caroline said, wondering if poor crossword solving skill was genetic.

The previous evening, after Nance had left their house, Caroline called her best friend, Billie, and told her what she suspected. It was when Nance mentioned having lived in Memphis when her father had and having been a patient at the clinic where he worked that Caroline began to feel that there was something else going on with Nance, a hidden agenda. Then when Nance talked about the daughter she hadn't gotten to see grow up, the suspicion began to form in Caroline's mind. She knew that her mother had met her father at that clinic—that her mother, Mary, had been a patient there. And the daughter she hadn't known? Might that be Caroline? And then there were the identical birthmarks—the same place on Mary in the wedding photo and on so-called Nancy Archer.

She knew better than to tell Vic what she suspected—he'd tell her she was imagining things and accuse her of letting Billie egg her on. It was true—Billie did egg her on, but that's what any good friend would do.

"My God!" Billie said to Caroline on the phone that night. "She *could be* your mother. But why has she come now? What does she want? Why the secrecy?"

"Exactly," Caroline said, feeling slightly sick and dizzy. She was sitting in her own living room, usually her favorite place in the world. Who had picked out that pink floor lamp? Who were the innocent-faced children in those watercolor portraits?

"Maybe she's afraid you hate her," Billie suggested. "If it is her, she's got a reason to be afraid. Abandoning you like that."

"I don't hate her," Caroline said but knew she'd spoken too quickly. Her feelings about her mother changed periodically—had gone through various permutations over the years, and could even bounce all over the map—anger, sadness, longing, acceptance, hatred—in one hour. "Maybe she just went out of her mind and had to leave," Caroline had said to Billie, and Billie snorted.

"She's still out of her mind, if she's showing up and pretending to be someone else."

And now she'd shown up again! It was an

opportunity for a do-over. During Nance's earlier visit, Caroline had gotten more and more addlebrained when she began to suspect Nance of being her mother. She had acted rashly, pretending to have forgotten Nance's name and called her Mary. Nance had seemed startled, but really, who wouldn't have been if they'd been called Mary out of the blue? Right now Caroline had no proof of anything, there were only some odd coincidences and her own intuition. Today she would remain calm. She would strive for detached curiosity. Not an easy state for her to achieve these days, but she'd try.

She led Nance back into the little sitting room where her father hung out. Each time she entered that oppressive room she was struck again by the old man smell. Sometimes she felt like everyone in her house was trying to take it over, take up all the air and space and sound waves until there was nothing left for her. The big old farmhouse she and Vic had rented in Iowa haunted her. The quiet. The space. And they'd been so eager to fill it up with kids! What the hell were they thinking?

Her father, the old man who smelled, sat in his favorite chair near the TV, the nubby chair with the permanent imprint of his butt in the cushion. They'd have to throw it away when he died. Not that she ever thought about that.

"You must be Dr. Spriggs!" Nance gushed. "So

good to finally meet you." She glanced around the room and then arranged herself on the love seat across from him, settling in among the pages of the newspaper.

Her father stared at Nance in bewilderment.

If this woman was his long-lost wife, wouldn't he recognize her? True, it would have been forty-eight years ago that she left him, and his mind was going. But maybe he was only *pretending* not to recognize her.

Nance kept staring at him, looking him slowly up and down.

Wilson Spriggs was a commanding presence, even in his old age. If you saw him working in the yard, you might think, if you were a certain age yourself: why it's Cary Grant's look-alike! The old Cary Grant, when he wore those cool black glasses. And if you were to stop and talk to him, you'd think that he must be a paid advertisement for Geritol. Clear-eyed and friendly but not overfamiliar. If you talked to him only briefly, you would never suspect that his mind was slipping. Wilson still radiated that doctor vibe: *I'm important! Pay heed!* The man had been married three times, the last two times to adoring nurses. But now he was unshaven, wearing his hideous brown bathrobe. If Caroline had known that Nance was coming over, she might've insisted that her father get dressed and shave. She felt like a matchmaker.

Nance didn't appear to be smitten. She now gazed at him with a stony expression that contradicted her earlier gushiness. "Finally," Nance muttered. "Wilson Spriggs, in the flesh. As I live and breathe." And then, in a louder voice, "Yep, still living and breathing here, Wilson Spriggs!"

"Me, too," Wilson said in a jovial way.

"So I see. *Dr.* Spriggs." Nancy Archer, or Mary Conner, seemed to be harboring resentment toward Wilson. How could she resent him if she didn't know him? Interesting.

"Nancy Archer is our new neighbor." Caroline had to speak loudly, because her father wouldn't wear his hearing aid. She was speaking too loudly, but she didn't care. "She brought Ava an Elvis book."

"Good morning," he said to Nance, and smiled like his old charming self.

Nance refused coffee, and glanced at Caroline expectantly. Entertain me, is what her expression said. Christ, another person who wanted to be taken care of. If this woman was her mother, had she come expecting Caroline to nurse her in her twilight years? Was she looking for a handout? Nance had claimed to have plenty of money, but was that true? There were many questions that must be answered, and answered to Caroline's satisfaction.

Back in Iowa City, when Caroline was in junior

high school, Wilson had told her what he knew about her mother, which was disappointingly little. The two of them had known each other only two months before they got married, Wilson explained, and they got married only because Mary was expecting a baby. Mary was eighteen at the time, a country girl from Arkansas who'd come up to the city to seek her fortune. Wilson claimed he knew nothing about her family or exactly where she'd grown up. How could you not know those things? Caroline had always wondered.

Later on, when Caroline was in high school and Wilson was married to wife number three, he revealed to Caroline what had happened the day Mary disappeared back in 1959. He'd dropped Mary and baby Caroline at his mother's house in suburban Memphis and had gone off to do some errands downtown. When he returned a couple of hours later, Mary was gone. What did he mean, gone? She wasn't there. She'd left. Didn't he ask his mother what had happened? Sure, but his mother swore to her dying day that she didn't see Mary leave and didn't know why or where she'd gone. Didn't he try to find her? Sure he did. He checked with all their friends, visited all their old hangouts, like the Arcade and the Tick Tock. He even put an ad in the paper. No, she never asked for any of her things. Oddly enough, Wilson said, his mother's precious grand piano also disappeared a few days after Mary did, and his mother claimed that she'd just felt like selling it. Wilson immediately suspected that his mother, who'd never liked Mary, had offered to give her the piano if she'd disappear, but he didn't voice his suspicions to his mother, who would've denied it. So had Mary been a music lover? Had she ever taken piano lessons or expressed an interest in playing piano? No, Mary had never shown much interest in any kind of music. But what kind of person would swap an object they didn't care about for their own baby? Mary, apparently. What kind of person would deprive a child of her mother? The child's grandmother, evidently. Why would you suspect your own mother of secretly bribing your wife to leave and then lying about it? He did, and he couldn't explain why. The whole thing was too vexing to think about.

Caroline had long since given up expecting her mother to show up on her birthdays or to call, even send a card. Maybe that's why she'd always hated her birthday. So what had prompted her might-be mother to return now?

Keep quiet until you're sure, Caroline told herself. She sat down at the other end of the love seat, picked up the paper, shook it, and read, too loudly, "Six-letter word for animus."

"Romulus and Remus," said Nance in a singsong voice.

Okay. Caroline took a sip of her cooling coffee. "Dad? Animus."

He shook his head slowly. "Do we know any letters?"

"No! I told you that."

"Hate," he said.

"Six! Letters!"

"Betty Bordney fairy sway," Nance said, and snorted with laughter.

Her father laughed, too, a startling sound. Caroline hadn't heard her father laugh in ages. The crossword puzzle segment of their morning was usually done in a businesslike manner, because it was one of the things the doctor had said they needed to do to help keep Wilson's memory intact. Caroline had suspected that her father didn't enjoy it much either.

"Who is Betty Bordney?" Wilson asked Nance.

"A lady I knew. In Memphis. A nurse. Betty Bordney fairy sway. That's what we used to call her. Or was it Betty fairy *Bordner* sway?"

"Did you hate her?" Wilson asked. "Was there animus between you?"

"Oh, no. The opposite. She and I had a lesbian affair."

Wilson blanched, uncomfortable about such things being said boldly aloud.

Was her mother a lesbian? Was that why she left? Caroline felt hysterical laughter bubbling up and tried to swallow it.

"Just playing with ya," Nance said. "I'm not a lesbian."

"Betty Bordney sounds like a cow," Wilson said.

"And fairy sway sounds like a dairy dessert."

"Moo," Wilson said.

What the hell? Was this an inside joke from when they were married? Caroline broke out into snickers, clamped her lips together, then exploded with laughter. She laughed and tried to stop and stopped and started up again, the way she and Vic used to laugh, the way she and her high school buddies used to laugh, the way she never laughed anymore; and she kept it up until she was crying. No. Not that. She finally got control and wiped her eyes with a handy napkin.

Both Nance and her father were staring at her, her father with a worried smile and Nance with a big pumpkin grin. This Nance was a different person than the one who'd sat in their living room a couple of days earlier—the old Nance had been earnest and eager to please, even if she hadn't been convincing talking up her and Suzi's trip to Italy.

"I'm sorry, kids," Caroline said in a jolly voice. She dabbed her eyes and blew her nose. "Let's get back to the crossword puzzle. Okay. Thirty-two down. An eight-letter word for nocturnal creature."

"Huh," Wilson said. He glanced over at Nance.

Nance pursed her thin little lips and shook her head. "Armadillo?"

"That's nine letters," Caroline said. "Good guess though."

"I saw an armadillo in your yard just now," Nance said. "He squeezed out from under that shed in the back."

"That's my pet armadillo," Wilson said. "Animus."

"Tee-hee," Nance said.

Caroline set down the newspaper. She picked up her coffee cup, wanting to hurl it across the room. "Anyone else want coffee?"

They both refused, eager, Caroline felt, to get rid of her.

When she returned, blowing on her third cup of the morning, Nance was reading an article from the paper aloud to Wilson, her voice changing when there were quotes. Caroline always read the paper in a bored monotone. Nance must've been able to tell, just by being around Wilson for a short time, that he was in dire need of levity and a fresh face.

Caroline stood in the doorway to listen. She studied the old woman's sharp features. She could see no resemblance at all between Nance and herself.

"Frank Comas," Nance read in a newscaster's voice, "a physician, appeared before the president's advisory committee to defend the work done by the Oak Ridge doctors." Here Nance's voice changed to a basso profundo. "'It is with some sadness and also some annoyance, I must confess, that I am obliged to try to exonerate ourselves for something perceived by some as devilish acts where science was God and damn all other considerations.'"

Wilson sat in his chair, head down, his fingers twined together in his lap. Caroline hoped he wasn't falling asleep. It was odd. She'd just read most of that section of the paper to Wilson, and she didn't recall the article that Nance was now reading.

Nance went on reading, something about a committee and a hearing, blah, blah, blah. Caroline stood and listened for another minute—well, not really listening but watching her father to make sure he seemed content—and then, with a slightly lighter heart, she drifted away.

She knew she should stay away from Ava, but somehow she found herself in the hallway outside Ava's door, where she often ended up, back at the scene of her many failures to communicate with her daughter, wondering whether or not she should go in to make sure she was studying for her algebra test. Ava, when she was involved in some activity, could react angrily to being interrupted. Caroline knew this from years of experience, but of its own accord her hand was on the doorknob, turning it, and she was looking into the room where Ava sat cross-legged on the bed, studying a book, the big book of Elvis photographs Nance had just brought over. How had she gotten hold of it so fast?

The sound of Elvis's melodramatic, self-mocking voice came from Ava's room from morning until late at night. "Polk salad Annie, / the gators got your granny."

"Ava," Caroline said now. "Please turn the music down."

Ava ignored her.

"Shouldn't you be studying algebra?"

Ava kept studying the photographs, hunched over, her dark hair hiding her face, the fingers of one hand busily rattling the corner of the page she was looking at. She sat surrounded by all her Elvis memorabilia—her Elvis posters, *Jailhouse Rock* Elvis clock, Teddy Bear Elvis pillows, Aloha Elvis lamp. She wore a new Elvis T-shirt, a fitted pink one which showcased the fifties Elvis. When had she gotten that one? How had she paid for it? "Ava!"

Finally Ava glanced up at her, disoriented, like she'd just woken up. "This has some pictures in it I've never seen before," she said. "From when he lived in Germany. Where'd this come from?"

Caroline explained that Nance had brought it, which made Ava sit up straighter and smile. If only Ava weren't so beautiful, Caroline thought for the millionth time, and then scolded herself for thinking such a dumb thing, for wishing ugliness on a girl who already had the cards stacked against her.

"After you finish studying, there's some forms you need to sign," she told Ava. "For Rhodes College."

Ava kept looking at the book.

Elvis sang that he was just a roustabout. Going from town to town.

Caroline marched over and pulled the plug on the iPod dock. "We need to get those forms in the mail as soon as possible."

Ava, surrounded by pictures of Elvis, kept looking at the book with a little smile on her face that indicated total absorption. Mother did not exist. Nothing else existed but Elvis.

Caroline considered her options. She could go get the forms from her desk and thrust them in front of Ava's face. She could rip the Elvis book from Ava's hands. She could thrust the math book in front of Ava and yell at her about passing math and how she wouldn't get into Rhodes College if she didn't pass math this time. Ava would scream back at her that she didn't care, didn't care about math or college or anything and just wanted to be left alone, and she might even start in yelling about how dumb she was, how ugly, how fat, and even start hitting herself, until Caroline ran from the room holding in tears.

This scene had happened many times, even

though Caroline knew better than to start it, knew better because of all the years of therapy they'd had and books she'd read about how to deal with Asperger's syndrome; but it was hard to act like a calm, disinterested therapist with your own child.

Caroline, like all the other mothers she knew who had autistic kids, had become the designated therapy parent in the family. Vic's only contribution to their therapy was to get the kids hooked on watching reruns of *Seinfeld.* He pointed out that the show was all about social gaffes and miscommunication, and, who knows, it could be that watching *Seinfeld* and afterward discussing the many ways that Kramer, Jerry, Elaine, and George screw up might help Ava and Otis more than anything. Could be, Caroline agreed, but we can't just stop there. Sometimes she admired and envied his ability to stay aloof, but other times it maddened her. She needed help and he wouldn't help her. She knew it was good for the kids to have one calm person in the family, but why did it have to be him?

When Caroline got Ava diagnosed at age nine, she flung herself into trying to fix her. She quit teaching preschool in order to devote herself full-time to the cause. There were the no-wheat no-dairy diets that the family endured for only a month before Caroline called it quits, then the vitamin and mineral supplements, physical therapy, occupational therapy, Relationship Development Intervention, HANDLE neurological therapy, chelation—removal of toxic heavy metals that might be making things worse—tutoring, counseling, support groups, psychiatrists, etc., etc., etc. The trouble was that all these so-called therapies were very expensive, and they never had any measurable results. Caroline could never tell what worked and what didn't work, because they did many things at once. They had to. They couldn't afford to waste any time.

And Ava did seem to get better, leaving some of her bigger, more obvious problems behind her—such as public temper tantrums and huge social gaffes—but that could have been due to growing up as much as to any treatment.

Otis, when he was about five, was also diagnosed, but in a pro forma way. Caroline and Vic saw the signs early on—the stiffness, clumsiness, intolerance of change, lack of desire for physical contact, precocious verbal development. But by this time Caroline was so exhausted by her efforts with Ava, and she was so depressed about Otis having the same problems, that she couldn't bring herself to try every new treatment that came down the pike on Otis—and there were new theories and treatments popping up on the Asperger's Web sites every week. As a result, Otis had no special therapies whatsoever, nothing but what he got in school, and it was hard to see that he was any worse off, or better off, than Ava. The awful truth: she had the energy to try and fix only one of them.

Suzi turned out to be their comfort child. Caroline and Vic watched baby Suzi fixedly, and when they saw no signs of autism they were so relieved they couldn't even speak of their joy, and the guilt they felt about their joy. Caroline would carry Suzi around, reveling in her affection and attentiveness, and then some kind of internal alarm would go off and she'd shove Suzi aside and go running back to Ava, whom, she thought, really needed her.

Caroline, because of all this intense activity, had come to depend on Ava's disability to give her life focus. For years she'd been quietly anxious at the thought of Ava moving out on her own, but that ended once she got the idea of sending Ava to Rhodes College. Now it made her panicky when she considered the possibility of Ava flunking algebra for the second time, of her not having the grades to transfer from Tallahassee Community College to Rhodes College in Memphis, where she'd decided that Ava had to go, because—although she hadn't told anyone except her best friend, Billie—she planned on moving to Memphis with Ava and living in an apartment in midtown while Ava lived in a dorm and went to college.

Ava would need her to be close by, she'd tell Vic. And you and Suzi and Otis are doing fine here. What would she do about her father? Vic shouldn't, couldn't take care of Wilson. She could hire someone. Maybe Nance! Or maybe the two of them would realize that they still loved each other and get married again. Everything would all work out. It *had* to work out. Of course, Ava could stay here and go to FSU, but it was such a *huge* school, so big that she wouldn't make friends and her professors wouldn't know her and she'd flounder, whereas Rhodes was small, had small classes, and the professors wouldn't let her slip through the cracks. The kids would be nicer, more motivated, more accepting. And the thing was—if Ava stayed here, then Caroline wouldn't have an excuse to leave herself.

Caroline had no idea, until she visited Memphis last December, how tired she was of the whole kit and caboodle at home. Trying to keep everything running smoothly. Anticipating everyone's needs. Nodding and pretending to be interested while her husband droned on and on about portfolio scoring. Driving the same routes over and over again, passing the same Tire Kingdom and BP station and the Melting Pot fondue restaurant where a customer's hair and face had once caught on fire—every time she drove by she felt compelled to imagine it—and the Christian School with the electronic billboard informing you that All Roads Lead to Jesus! where the parents picking up their saintly children pulled out right in front of her or rode her bumper. Forcing herself to smile at the same competitive soccer moms who forced themselves to smile back. Measuring everything she said in the Asperger's support group so as not to seem to be one-upping or condescending to the mothers whose kids were either more or less affected than Otis and Ava. Fixing the same unappreciated lunches; sorting the same mounds of vile sour clothes; nagging people to do their chores.

How wonderful to be in someplace totally different from Tallahassee, someplace gritty and urban and mysterious and where she wouldn't run into *anyone* she knew! Her father had been the youngest of four children, but his older siblings had already passed away. None of her cousins still lived in Memphis. She had no obligations to visit anyone there. And how cool to discover that, when she and Ava visited, she actually *liked* the city of Memphis, found it fascinating, when she'd never appreciated it before. The wonderful old buildings downtown. The civil rights history. The place where the blues and rock and roll took off. The place where her parents had lived together for a year, and where her mother had come, as a young girl, to seek her fortune. A whole new old world lay before Caroline, waiting to be explored. She loved being a stranger in her own hometown. Because Memphis *was* her hometown, even though she'd lived there only until she was two.

She simply had to live in Memphis for a while. Had to.

Caroline was standing there, in Ava's doorway, on the verge of screaming at her daughter once again, when she heard a voice behind her.

"Does she like the book?" Nance asked.

Caroline hadn't heard the woman approach, wondered what she was doing at this end of the house.

"I was looking for the little girls' room," Nance said, laying a hand on her elbow. "Your daddy fell asleep."

Ava, hearing a voice other than her mother's bothersome one, glanced up and smiled her brilliant smile.

Caroline felt something inside her settle a little. All she wanted was for Ava to be happy. And to have her own place in the world. Well, that wasn't all she wanted. She herself wanted to wander free in Memphis, tethered, only lightly, to Ava.

"Thanks for the book," Ava said to Nance.

"It was very nice of you," Caroline said to Nance. Then she turned to Ava. "But right now you need to put it down and study for your algebra test."

"Just let me finish this," Ava said.

It was one thing to be ignored when she was alone, and another to be ignored in front of an audience. She wanted her could-be mother to see that she'd become a good parent in spite of being abandoned as a baby. "You need to do it now," Caroline told Ava in her stern voice.

"Okay!" Ava hurled the book across the room. It slammed into her bookcase and landed, open and pages folded, on the floor.

"I'm sorry," Caroline said to Nance. She walked over to the book, picked it up, smoothed the pages, wanting to howl and gnash her teeth and laugh at the same time. "Ava doesn't like math. Her tutor is on vacation."

"It doesn't make any sense!" Ava said. "Who cares what *X* equals?"

Caroline agreed but knew better than to say so.

"I used to teach algebra," Nance said from the doorway. "Many moons ago. How about if I help you study?"

Ava didn't say anything, but her relaxed face told Caroline what she needed to know.

Caroline sat down on the carpet, clutching the Elvis book, which was shaped like a phonograph album. It was a bit strange that Nance would volunteer to tutor Ava—unless Ava actually was her long-lost grandchild. Either way, if it made things easier on Ava—and Caroline—and if it helped Ava pass algebra so she could get into

Rhodes, then why would she say no? She'd see that they studied here, so how much trouble could they get in? "We'd pay you what we pay Laura," Caroline said.

"Oh, no," Nance said. "Just leave us alone for an hour and I double-dog guarantee she'll do fine on that exam."

"It's only a couple of days away," Ava said, sliding to the edge of her bed.

"Let's not get our hopes up too high," Caroline said, but for the second time that morning Nance—Mrs. Archer, Mary, Mom, whoever she was—had caused her to feel lighter, less burdened; and as she sat there cross-legged on the floor, she could almost feel herself levitating, like those transcendental meditation people in Fairfield, Iowa, who claimed they could fly.

On the following Saturday, Caroline and her father and Nance worked in the yard. Caroline and Vic's property had been landscaped and well tended by the previous owner, so all Caroline's family had to do was maintain it. The backyard didn't take much work, being mostly ferns and monkey grass and English ivy shaded by live oak trees, so they usually focused on the front yard.

Nance, dressed in bleach-spattered Bermuda shorts and a big straw hat, waded into the English ivy and commenced weeding the Nandina, a nasty exotic bamboo that tried to take over, and Caroline's dad, covered from head to toe to prevent skin cancer and bug bites, got to work near Nance, planting some bulbs near the prickly holly bushes in front of the house. The bulbs, which Nance had brought with her, were daffodil bulbs and wouldn't survive in Florida, she informed Caroline, unless Caroline dug them up every winter and stored them in the freezer until spring, which she wasn't about to do, though she didn't say so.

Caroline supposed that what Nance might've wanted when she'd invited herself over today was to spend time with Wilson, try to get him to remember her. It was odd, but Nance didn't seem particularly interested in getting acquainted with Caroline, her long-lost child. Surely she must care about Caroline, the way she'd talked wistfully about missing her only daughter. But maybe Nance could focus on only one person at a time, and she'd decided to start with Wilson. Caroline told herself she was fine with that. She could wait until Nance was ready to be honest with her. That is, if the woman even was her mother and she wasn't just having paranoid delusions.

Right now she wanted to lose herself in yard work, which gave her immediate gratification. She forgot about Wilson and Nance while she mowed the front lawn. The cycle of summer soakings had recently started up again, and the lawn, newly fertilized, had turned a lush dark green—no brown spots or orange fungus yet. After the lawn she edged and blew the brick walk and driveway off with the leaf blower—tasks she'd recently taken over from Vic because he was always off at Suzi's soccer games on the weekends. And just like with running, she could get some of her frustration out this way.

When she was up on a ladder with Vic's electric trimmer, attacking the front hedge—Florida anise—inhaling the rich licorice scent, someone snuck up behind her and grabbed her calf. "Boo!"

The ladder swayed and Caroline's stomach lurched. She turned the trimmer off. "My God," she said, shaking free of Nance's gloved talon. "Be careful. This thing could slice us up."

Nance tipped her straw hat back on her head. Her face was coated with a sunscreen containing zinc oxide which turned her complexion chalky white. She looked like she'd escaped from *The Mikado*. She gazed up at Caroline. "I believe I'm done weeding for now," she said. "You have a hand trimmer in that little shed back there?"

Caroline explained that the shed had once been used to store tools, but they'd bequeathed it to Otis after they got tired of his blowing things up in the house. He was working on something in there now that had to do with smoke detectors. "I think he tells his granddad what he's doing but not me. He doesn't want any of us to go in that shed until he's ready." The hedge trimmer was getting heavy, and she was itching to turn it on again. She was itching, period. Biting things were nibbling on her legs. She swiped her forehead with her T-shirt sleeve. "Well, back to work," she said.

But Nance leaned on the ladder. "Aren't you proud of that Suzi?" she asked. "She's such a dynamo."

"I am," Caroline said.

"And Ava could be a model. Truly. You know that show, *America's Next Top Model*? She could win that."

"Never seen it."

"The winner gets scads of money!" Nance said. "And, believe me, she's got what it takes."

"Don't tell her that," Caroline protested. She had a horror of her daughters being caught up in the cultural obsession with looks and youthfulness, perhaps because she was fighting her own battle with it. "But you're very nice to say so."

"I'm not nice!" Nance protested. "That child is gorgeous! Just like her mother."

Caroline smiled. She and Ava looked like entirely different animals. "Where's my dad?"

"Weeding over in the side yard. I'm going on home now, hon. I'm just pooped." Nance waved good-bye and set out for home, walking quickly for somebody who claimed to be pooped.

Caroline finished clipping the hedge, which took another fifteen minutes, and then turned the trimmer off. She glanced around the front yard, a rectangle enclosed by white picket fencing on the short sides, their one-story yellow brick house on one long side and, on the other long side, next to the street, a wire fence hidden in the hedge Caroline had just trimmed. The metal swing, where Wilson liked to sit, dangled empty from the limb of the live oak tree in the center of the yard. Parson roasted in a spot of sunlight on the front porch.

She climbed down the ladder, wondering if maybe he'd gone inside. She didn't think her father would've wandered off anywhere, but with his memory getting worse, who knew?

She set down her clippers, and started calling "Dad!" like he was a missing dog. He wasn't visible in the side yard. She strode back through the front yard and into the house, tromping down the hall in her dirty sneakers, shedding flakes of dirt and grass on the hardwood floors that she'd have to clean up later, calling for her father as she went, her actual dog, Parson Brown, on her heels. But the house—upstairs and down—was silent, and Wilson wasn't there.

She stepped out onto the deck which overlooked the backyard, sloping gently downward, totally enclosed by trees and bamboo and viburnum. Otis's shed, in the far corner of the yard, was always locked. She couldn't see Wilson anywhere. She called his name a few times. "Dad! Wilson! Dad!" Nothing.

Her heart was beating fast now, painful adrenaline pumping through her like it did when one of her children had wandered off. She walked back through the house again, yelling Wilson's name, through the front yard and then up and down their block of Friar's Way, calling for him. There was nobody about, nobody that she could question. Should she start knocking on doors? He could be anywhere by now. Should she get in the car and start looking that way? She needed help. Vic wouldn't answer his phone. Ava was at Asperger's support group. Otis would be home from work soon, but she couldn't wait for him.

She trotted back home and, in the kitchen, Parson panting beside her, called the police. She'd just finished up giving her report, fighting back panic, when Wilson and Otis, in his McDonald's uniform, stepped in through the back door.

Wilson, red-faced under his brown safari hat, strands of his white hair pasted to his forehead, looked on the verge of heatstroke.

"Never mind," she told the woman on the phone and hung up. "Where have you been?" Caroline removed his hat, got him situated in a chair, and made him drink a glass of water.

"Hot as hell in there," he said.

"In where?"

"In my shed." Otis slapped his grandfather on the shoulder as if he were a naughty little rascal. "I heard him rattling the door, trying to get out."

"He must've locked himself in," Caroline suggested. "Did you give him a key?" Wilson had been advising Otis on his current project, whatever it was. They'd been science pals for years.

"It was unlocked," Wilson said.

Otis shook his head. "No, sir. I always keep it locked. There's a key hidden out there, but he doesn't know where it is. *Nobody's* allowed in there but me."

Caroline sank into a kitchen chair.

"I didn't *want* to go in there," Wilson said. "She made me."

"Who made you?" Caroline asked, but she knew the answer.

"The padlock was locked from the *outside,*" Otis said. "He couldn't have done it."

"That woman," Wilson said. "That strange woman. She pushed me in there and locked the door."

Caroline found herself wanting, horribly, to giggle, the way she had when they were attempting the crossword puzzle. "Why would she do that, Dad?"

"I damn near suffocated in there. Couldn't get the windows open."

"He shouldn't be in there," Otis said to his mother in a scolding tone. "There's dangerous chemicals in there."

"What chemicals?"

He took a few steps away from her. "Just my stuff. I know what I'm doing. But if you're in there, you need protection."

"Protection," Caroline repeated, and thought of birth control, which brought the giggles back up to the surface. She forced them down again.

"She hates me, for some reason," Wilson said.

"She doesn't hate you," Caroline said. "Why would she hate you? I'm sure it was an accident. You need to go lie down for a while."

So I can call Billie and give her an update, she finished silently.

CHAPTER 4 *Ava*

She hated the Asswiper Support Group, but her mother dropped her off at the Methodist Church downtown at one o'clock every Saturday afternoon. The Asswipers met in a dank basement that had one of those floors covered with tan linoleum squares that had been there since the dawn of time, or since the 1950s, and there were black scuff marks all over the floor that Ava stared at while the other people were talking—the guys were talking, because it was only her and a bunch of losers.

She didn't like looking at the guys, noticing all their facial irregularities—it was better to stare at the scuff marks on the floor and try to see pictures in them. Each week she made sure to sit in the same chair so that she could revisit the scuff mark pictures she'd already conjured up. There was the clipper ship she'd christened the *Ordinary*, and there was the tree of life she'd noticed for the first time last week, and over there the state of California, and right in front of her a profile of Elvis, the 1968 comeback Elvis, with sideburns and thin face.

Ava had seen the face of Elvis in the marbled swirls of a shower stall in a Super 8 Motel, in the clouds, in a half-used bar of olive soap from the Italian deli. Hang in there, Ava baby, he was always telling her, things *will* get better. He understood, because he had Asperger's, too, only he'd grown up in the good old days before people even knew what Asperger's was, so it was more of a live-and-let-live kind of a thing, instead of a live-and-try-to-fix-the-other-guy kind of a thing. Back then, you were just labeled a freak and left alone, which really wasn't ideal either, she had to admit, unless you also happened to be a gorgeous musical genius. Hello there, Elvis. She tapped his chin with the toe of her flip-flop. Hey, Elvis. Hey, guitar man.

One time she'd mentioned to the freaks in her group that, in her opinion, Elvis had Asperger's, and the only response she'd gotten was the most gung ho Christian guy going, "Rock and Roll music is sinful. The beat is meant to make you think of the sexual act. The phrase *rock and roll* is actually a euphemism for the sexual act. Even Christian rock isn't wholesome. Doesn't matter that the lyrics are about God." What could you say to this kind of nonsense? For somebody who was so against sex, he sure liked to talk about it a lot. Sexual act. Why add the *act* part?

And over there, by the group leader's Teva sandal, plain as day, was the Eiffel Tower with Madeline and Miss Clavel and the row of girls in two straight lines. In two straight lines they ate their bread, brushed their teeth, and went to bed. An ideal life for someone with Asperger's. Ava had always wanted to be Madeline, an orphan who lived in a cool old house with a solid unvarying routine, some built-in friends, and a nice old lady who was not your mother, like Nance.

Ava would've given anything to see a row of girls about then, because the guys in the support group were the most peculiar bunch of guys ever assembled in one room. They were mostly old and scary, not one potential boyfriend in the bunch. This week, though, there was a new guy there, baby faced, about her age, who said his name was Travis and that he didn't have Asperger's but that his mom had wanted him to come check out the group. Interesting! A non-Aspie, not bad looking, who wanted to check them out! She wanted him to say more, but the other guys wouldn't let him get another word in. Their voices droned on.

"Those Aspies are so repulsive," she'd complained to her mother once, who told her that it wasn't very nice to say things like that, and that she should give them a chance, and that every man wasn't going to look like Elvis, so she'd better face reality. She'd insisted that Ava join this group to improve her social skills—what a laugh. This group was the blind leading the blind.

So here she was, facing reality, and right now reality was the tall, hawk-faced Christian dude talking about his CD collection. His glasses hung unevenly on his face, one side lower than the other. She'd pointed this fact out to him once, and he'd told her that one of his ears was higher than the other. "There's a real disparity in terms of how many recorded minutes there are on different kinds of albums," he told the group. "There are twenty-two minutes on average for secular sound tracks and only fifteen for Christian music." He made this statement in the same flat voice he made every statement.

The rest of the guys in the group—there were six of them—didn't really listen to one another, but waited for a pause in the speeches to give their own. They were supposed to be learning conversational skills, but what they were doing wasn't having conversations. They were taking turns holding forth.

The man with the beard complained that Christian bookstores didn't carry any Christian computer games.

Then the group leader, the Teva sandals guy with the kooky name—Sumpter—started in about how Northern milk is better than Southern milk because Northern cows have different digestive systems.

What Ava wanted, more than anything, was to find true love.

So far she hadn't had any luck on this front. Sometimes she went out on a date or two or even three with some "typical" guy, and she'd get all panicked and excited and ask her mother, and even Suzi, for advice about what to wear. But after a few dates the boy would start backing away, and her mother told her that it was probably because of her Asperger's. According to her mother, who grilled her after every date, Ava did everything wrong. She smiled too much. Either stared too intensely or wouldn't make eye contact. Began pacing and twiddling her fingers. Stiffened up when she should've been cuddly or made awkward, sloppy physical overtures out of nowhere. Talked about mundane, unrelated subjects in an overpersistent way—the albums of Elvis Presley or the health benefits of eating walnuts, for example—and failed to ask questions of her dates or interrupted them when they were talking.

Her mother had it all figured out; and she always emphasized that it wasn't Ava's fault. The typical young men just didn't understand, her mother explained to her, that Ava didn't have the inner resources to think much about other people when she was nervous, not because she didn't care, but because she was focusing very hard about how she was supposed to behave, which caused her to come across as either strange and wooden or as strange and random. Like her mother's explanation would make her feel better. Her mother always seemed relieved that things hadn't gone well. She didn't really want a boy to fall in love with Ava. Ava's mother had married young, when she and Ava's father were still in college, but she didn't want that for Ava. She wanted Ava to live at home for the rest of her life.

It looked like her mother might get her wish, because any normal boy who showed interest in Ava would soon drift away, never giving her any satisfactory explanation as to why, but leaving her feeling that she'd failed yet again, that she would always fail because she was defective.

Even though she was pretty! Everyone said so.

"I'm going to be on *America's Next Top Model*," Ava announced, interrupting the guy who was mumbling about movie popcorn and how bad it was for you. There was silence. The coffeepot in the corner hissed and sputtered and stank. All the men, with their hairy nostrils and asymmetrical eyes, were looking at her, not into her eyes but at parts of her—her breasts, her bare toes, her hair—and not saying anything. The new guy, Travis, the tall guy with fat cheeks, was staring at her mostly bare legs. Probably none of them cared about what she was saying, but they were making a space for her, which, for them, was something.

"I made a new friend," she explained. She didn't need to tell them that her new friend was seventy-seven. "She's going to get me on that show. I'm going to win the contest and get a contract to be, like, a cover girl."

"There aren't enough healthy food options at movie theaters," said hawk beak.

"You're pretty enough to be a model," Travis said to her right knee. His side bangs hid one of his big brown eyes. "You could win that contest."

"Those reality shows are all scripted," said Sumpter, their self-appointed group leader, gazing sternly above her head. "It's not a real contest."

Ava felt she was being assaulted. Put on the spot. Their words felt like needles prickling her skin. She hoped they would shut up before she had to tell them to shut up.

"Do you want to go to the movies sometime?" Travis asked her now, in front of everyone.

"I don't know." Ava pulled her sweatshirt hood up over her head. It was always freezing cold in the basement, and the folding chair seats felt like blocks of ice.

"That's not appropriate, Travis," said Sumpter, as if he knew the meaning of the word *appropriate*. He thought he was more well-adjusted than the rest of them because he had a real job—even though it was a crummy job, doing something with computers, the kind of job Ava would never want in a million years. Sumpter was afraid of anyone in authority. Any parent, teacher, and especially God himself, had to be consulted and obeyed. These guys were all big on God. "Does your mother know that you're applying to be on *America's Next Top Model*?" Sumpter asked Ava.

"I told you, I have a friend who's helping me," Ava said. "Nance. She's like my grandmother. It's just between me and her."

"Ava is old enough to do what she wants," Travis said, and gave Ava a sweet little smile.

"How do you get to be on that show?" the guy with watery eyes asked her.

"You have to apply, send in pictures, all that. I don't have pictures. Nance's going to help me get them."

"Pictures like that are really expensive," Sumpter said. "My mother used to be on TV commercials. She was on one for Lemon Pledge. You have to get like a whole book of pictures in different poses."

"Nance is going to pay for them," Ava said. She felt elated. They were actually having a conversation for once, a conversation that included her. True, they were asking her challenging questions, putting her on the spot, which she usually hated, but at least they were paying attention to her.

Hawk face said, "You have to be careful of people offering to do things for you. I learned that the hard way. There was this history teacher at my high school who offered to tutor me, and one day he asks me if I want to see his penis."

"Did you see it?" said the man with the chapped lips who always wore a Sonny's Bar-B-Q T-shirt, the guy who usually never said anything.

Hawk face twisted up his mouth in that painful way he had. "I did want to see it, just out of curiosity, but even I knew that he wanted more than me to just look at it. So I said no."

"You missed your chance," said Sonny's Bar-B-Q. "I would have said yes."

"Gross!" Ava said—yelled, probably. Her voice always came out louder than she meant it to. "Keep it down!" people were always telling her. She flopped over double. That's it, she told herself. I can't sit here anymore. And I'm not coming back here, not for anything.

She just didn't like her own kind. She could understand why typical people avoided people with Asperger's. They were obnoxious know-it-alls. Just like her brother, Otis. Mean, but true. Maybe girls wouldn't be so bad, but she'd never been around any Asperger girls. It was depressing to realize that she didn't fit in here, and she sure didn't fit in with the so-called typical people. So what was left? Living with her mother for the rest of her life? She'd rather kill herself.

Her mother thought she was going to get into some fancy private college full of snobs and that somehow, miraculously, she was going to fit in and get straight A's and become a famous scientist. Her mother just couldn't face facts. She was never going to understand math in a million years. She'd passed her final algebra exam with a C, but no thanks to Nance, who hadn't actually tutored her at all. No, Nance had advised her to just forget about college and be a full-time model. Models didn't need a college degree, especially top models.

She was staring down at the floor so hard she

saw it, saw a new scuff picture she'd never noticed before, right there between her feet. Maybe she'd even made the picture herself, with her very own flip-flops. It was a picture of her—Ava Eleanor Witherspoon—one arm cocked up behind her head, the other one on her hip. The scuff girl even had long hair like hers. She was posing, the scuff girl, and that was a sign.

The next Saturday Nance had volunteered to take Ava to the support group, but once they got in the car she said she had a surprise for Ava—they were going to get Ava's pictures taken instead! Nance had arranged it all.

She agreed with Ava that the support group was a waste of time. "You've got more important fish to fry," Nance told her. "Your mama doesn't need to know about the pictures, not yet." Nance drove like a maniac, weaving in and out of lanes, speeding up quickly and then stepping on the brakes. Even Ava, who'd been too afraid to take driver's ed, knew that you weren't supposed to drive this way. "When you get famous, she'll be glad you did what you did!"

"Well," Ava said, thinking that her mother wouldn't really be pleased at all if Ava got famous, especially for something as shallow and superficial as modeling, but she wasn't doing this for her mother, she was doing it for herself. Ava rolled down the passenger side window of

Nance's Ford Taurus and stared at her face in the sideview mirror, at her long dark hair whipping around, her pale skin, her big blue eyes, her full pink lips. Ava felt a sickish kind of excitement bubble up inside her, the kind of excitement she felt when a new obsession was taking her over. Not that she'd totally leave the old ones behind—never Elvis—but a new one always took her over like coming down with a virus and pushed the other ones aside. The virus didn't hurt, but it created an ache, a need, that might be soothed but never satisfied. It always seemed to start with a picture—a picture she'd seen of an earnest-looking girl on a horse jumping a fence, a noble rescue dog in a field guide, a young Elvis on a train in 1956. This time it was an image of herself.

Ever since she'd decided to try and be America's next top model, she couldn't stop staring at herself in any mirror she found herself next to. She spent her time in her room, posing in front of her full-length mirror the way they did, hand on her hip, tilting her head this way and that. Sometimes she thought she looked better than any woman they had on that show, and sometimes all she could see were her flaws—her fat nose, her long neck, her big ears, her flat boobs. Then she'd run out and find her mother somewhere in the house and cry to her mother that she was ugly, hideous, fat; and sometimes she'd hit herself to drive the point home. Her mother did her best to ignore this behavior, but, Ava could tell, it took everything her mother had not to argue with her or try to soothe her or to keep from telling her to shut up and go away, because if she did any of these things Ava just latched onto her mother's words and incorporated them into her rant. It was all about trying to draw her mother into her circle of hell. She'd rather there were two miserable people dealing with all her faults than just one person, herself, because she felt so overwhelmed by these feelings she had to push them off onto someone else.

Now though, because Nance thought she was pretty enough to be doing this and had offered to pay for fancy photographs, when she looked at herself she saw a gorgeous model. "I won't have to take my clothes off, will I?" Ava said to Nance but looking at herself in the mirror. "For the pictures?" On the application form for *America's Next Top Model* there was a bulleted item that said you had to agree to pose naked. There was no way Ava was going to do that, no matter what they said.

"Oh, good Lord, no, honey," Nance said. They were downtown now, with real traffic, or what passed for traffic in Tallahassee, and Nance was watching for a certain street. "This is a reputable photographer we're going to. I asked around at church and got recommendations." She saw the street she wanted, slammed on her brakes and then, without turning on her blinkers, surged around the corner. Riding with Nance was like being at Wild Adventures. The Crazy Woman Driver ride.

"What does your grandfather like to eat?" Nance asked Ava out of the blue.

Ava couldn't think, for a while, how to answer this question. "He eats everything we eat," she finally said.

"I mean, is there anything special he likes? For a treat?"

"Pineapple upside-down cake," Ava said, because it was her favorite kind of cake.

The photographer was a man named Danny Boyle, or Danny Boy, something like that. He mostly looked at her through the lens of his camera. He had a nice, freckle-faced assistant girl, Marcy. For the first pose Marcy put lots of makeup on Ava, and Ava had to change into a black shirt with an elastic neckline; when they came out of the dressing room, Mr. Boy pulled the neck of the shirt and her bra straps down off her shoulders. Marcy turned a fan on her so that her hair whipped around and Mr. Boy took a hundred million pictures. Popular music blared from speakers, the same songs that played over and over again on Star 98. Big hot lights shone down on her, but it was okay, because the rest of the room was dark.

"Nice. Nice," Danny Boy kept saying.

When he said, little to the left, or little to the right, Ava froze up because she always had trouble remembering left from right, but Mr. Boy caught on and just told her to tilt her head toward Nance, who was sitting on one side of the room, or tilt her head toward the exit sign. "You're a natural," said Mr. Boy.

Marcy took her back into the dressing room, where there was a lighted mirror like in the dressing rooms you see on TV, and helped Ava change her black shirt for a striped button-down shirt and smoothed her hair into a bun and put fake glasses and pink lipstick on her and took her back out under the lights and sat her at a desk.

Mr. Boy unbuttoned a few of her shirt buttons before he started taking pictures. "The sexy secretary," he crowed.

Nance clapped when they finished doing the secretary.

Then Marcy made her into a tennis player wearing a visor and swingy skirt, then helped her get into a sundress, curled her hair with a curling thing, and gave her a basket of daisies to swing. Then she gelled Ava's hair and teased it up and put tons of eye liner on and a ripped T-shirt with chains hanging on it and tight leathery pants. For that pose she got to make angry, fierce faces.

The whole process seemed like it was taking hours. Much longer than support group was supposed to last, but Nance, no doubt, would give her mother some believable lie, and her mother would buy it. Why would Nance be willing to lie about such a thing?

A good question, one she didn't have an answer to, one that made her uneasy. But she found that she enjoyed posing, pretending she was in front of her mirror in her room, and also enjoyed just sitting there passively in the dressing room while somebody else made her up and fixed her hair and dressed her. It was sort of being like a kid again, all burden of responsibility for how you look removed from your shoulders. Ava kept smiling at herself in the dressing room mirror, and Marcy joked with her about it. Marcy had crooked teeth, but Ava's were white and straight.

The last pose was supposed to be in a bathing suit, one of hers from home. Marcy took off nearly all of Ava's makeup and wet down her hair with a spray bottle. But when Ava came out in her one-piece suit and the high-heeled sandals they'd given her, the beach towel draped around her shoulders, Mr. Boy, for the first time that day, took his camera away from his face and frowned.

"Is that the only suit you brought?"

"It's the only one I have," Ava said, which wasn't true, but it was the only suit she'd allow herself to be photographed in.

Mr. Boy bit his fleshy, wormlike lip and studied her with judging eyes. He motioned for Marcy to turn down the music, thank God, that annoying song about the black horse and the cherry tree. Mr. Boy studied her some more, and she felt, for the first time that afternoon, horribly self-conscious.

"You'll have to take it off. Take the suit off."

"Right now?" was the only thing Ava could say.

He shook his head, a swath of blondish red hair swinging. "No, dear, go into the back, take off your suit, wrap a towel around you and come back out. We'll do some nude shots. That suit doesn't work."

Her heart started thumping like something just woken up. No. She didn't want to do this. Did she have to? Of course, she didn't have to. Her mother had always told her that she didn't have to do anything involving sex that made her uncomfortable. Taking off her clothes for Mr. Boy had to do with sex, but it was also just playacting at sex, and it had to do with fame and fortune. She didn't want to do it, not because she had anything against sex and fame and fortune, but because she was ashamed of her naked body, that she was sure wouldn't measure up.

Ava glanced at Nance for help. "Can I talk to you?"

Nance came over and walked uncertainly out

under the big lights, blinking and squinting like a mole rat, her face a hypnotizing surface of crosshatched fine lines. It was all Ava could do not to touch them.

"Should I take off my clothes?" Ava asked her, her face flushing. She towered over Nance in the high heels.

"Absolutely not," said Nance in a low voice. She pulled on Ava's arm, trying to get Ava to lean close, but Ava couldn't help shrinking away. "Just put your clothes back on and let's get out of here."

"Okay." Ava let out a huge breath she didn't know she was holding.

"You didn't really want to get on that show anyway," Nance muttered.

Behind them, Marcy and Mr. Boy were laughing about something. Probably about her.

"What? I do too want to go on it."

"Well, you have to be willing to pose naked." Nance shrugged. "And you're not."

"Would you do it?"

Nance laughed that barkish laugh. "If I looked like you, I'd do it in a heartbeat."

"Who would see them? The pictures?"

"Just the judges. That's all."

"Nobody else?"

Nance grasped her arm again. "Not unless you want them to." She winked at Ava. Did she really wink?

There was something wrong with Nance. Ava might have a syndrome, but she could tell that there was something off about Nance. The way she'd used reverse psychology on Ava was creepy. Ava had learned about reverse psychology in school. "I don't trust you," Ava blurted out.

"Why not?" Nance backed up, with an inscrutable little smile, and Ava knew then that Nance was no Miss Clavel from the Madeline books. Nance, unlike Miss Clavel, didn't care about something being not right.

"Are we ready?" called Mr. Boy. "Chop-chop."

Lounging naked in a beach chair and letting Mr. Boy take pictures of her turned out to be the easiest thing she'd done that day. It was easy as soon as she decided to act the same way she'd acted when she'd had sex with that boy from her writing class. He'd taken her to a motel room on Monroe Street, the Prince Murat, and asked her to pose for him on the bed, and she did, and then she let him do things to her that, when added up together, amounted to sex. Most of what he did either hurt her slightly or felt annoying, but it was all over quickly. She didn't really like the guy, Cesare was his name, but she just wanted to check "lose virginity" off her to-do list, and he just wanted sex, too, so there was a low-stress businesslike feeling to the whole encounter. Plus, her parents would lose it if they knew, which was an added bonus.

"Beautiful, beautiful," Mr. Boy was crooning, leaning over her and snapping away.

Yes, she was beautiful. "Too bad you aren't Elvis," she said to Mr. Boy.

"But I am Elvis," he said without missing a beat. He curled up his wormy lip, and it didn't look so bad. "I'm the King, baby."

Mr. Boy was cool. Ava loosened up even more. She felt her vagina getting slickery and the hot lights felt good and she knew she was enjoying herself, maybe more than she was supposed to.

"Turn toward your friend," said Mr. Boy.

So she did, and she caught sight of Nance scribbling something in a little notebook. What was she writing? Ava felt herself getting tense again.

"That's a wrap," said Mr. Boy.

On the way home, Ava felt calmer than she had in a long time. She sat back in her seat, not feeling compelled, for the time being, to check herself in the mirror, because she was beautiful, Mr. Boy had seen her naked and confirmed it.

"That thing we just did cost a lot of money," Nance said, her eyes darting over at Ava.

"Thank you very much," Ava said.

"It'll be worth it. This is just the beginning for you, my dear. You're going to get on that show and get rich and famous and show everybody!"

"Show them what?"

"You'll be a star!" Nance leaned forward like she was pushing the car with her upper body. "Nobody will mistreat you ever again."

"Really?" Ava didn't believe this for a minute. People were always mistreating people.

"We'll show them," Nance muttered, pounding her little fist on the steering wheel.

Ava didn't really want to show people anything. "If my mom finds out about this," she said, "I'll tell her it was your idea. It *was* your idea."

Nance tightened her grip on the leatherette wheel, her mouth in a tight line. She looked like Miss Clavel's evil twin.

"But thanks *so much,*" Ava said, "for taking me and paying for the pictures. It was *so* nice of you and I *really* appreciate it."

"Does your grandfather ever go for walks by himself?" Nance said, not seeming to hear the thanks. "Is there any place he goes on a regular basis?"

"He likes the Cracker Barrel," Ava said, because she couldn't think of what to say to Nance's nosy questions, and she herself liked the Cracker Barrel. "He doesn't get to go there much," she added, and Nance smiled.

He'd drawn their locations on a grid for maximum efficiency, and since a lot of the shops were on South Monroe, he decided, on his first Saturday off from McDonald's in three weeks, to work his way south on Monroe. Actually, he didn't *get* the day off—he was taking it off. It was Memorial Day weekend so they'd be swamped at McDonald's, but he'd called in anyway and left a message for his boss, Oinker, saying he was sick, which might mean he'd get fired the next time he went in. He'd worry about that later.

All the antique stores in town had wimpish names: Remembered Treasures, Grandma's Attic, the Ding a Ling, Miss Sandy's, Old Glory, Sisters, Something Nice, Southern Chicks. Antique stores were for old ladies. If you didn't already know that, the names of the places would be a big hint. He felt conspicuous and clumsy going in, but his Geiger counter helped. As soon as he opened the trunk of the Pontiac and took out his Geiger counter—a blue metal machine about the size of his forearm that looked like a cross between a car window scraper and huge dildo—he always felt better. He had a purpose. He was a man with a machine, a man on a mission. The women in the stores watched him curiously as he waved his machine over the merchandise, but they watched him with respect. Or, maybe they were just scared of him, which was okay, too.

He ticked the stores on South Monroe off his list, one by one. At the next to last store, Grandma's Attic, his was the only car parked in front of the shop. With his trusty Geiger counter in hand he opened the door, setting off the usual electronic bell sound, and stepped inside the tepid air-conditioning. The room smelled both dusty and moldy, like all the shops he'd been in. This one, though, had a stinky cinnamon-scented candle burning somewhere.

He took in his surroundings. Long room with no windows except the dirty plate glass ones in the front. No other customers—no visible people, period. Typical stuff. Lots of old dishes, toys, random furniture, shelves of paperbacks, cases of costume jewelry. He didn't see any clocks, but there had to be some, maybe hidden, even buried. He would cast a wide net.

He switched on his Geiger counter, turning it to signal with a blinking light rather than sound, and started up the aisle, swinging his machine slowly over the shelves of junk. On the little Geiger counter screen the dial occasionally jumped around and the light flashed on and off, picking up random bits of radioactivity here and there, but nothing substantial.

"Hey, hon." A woman's voice. She was planted on a chair behind a counter, reading a magazine. She sat there so motionless that his eyes had swept right over her, detecting no life in that vicinity. "What'cha got there?" she asked him. Dark helmet hair and fat. Jabba the Hutt, wearing red plastic jewelry. Sucking on a lollipop.

Otis told her that he was trying to find radioactive things for a school science project. He could have just asked her if she had any old clocks, but he didn't want her help, because that would mean more conversation and interference on her part.

"Nothing radioactive in here, hon," she said. She pulled the red lollipop from her mouth and shook it at him. "Better not be."

"Mind if I look?"

"Just be careful with that thing. Don't go breaking any of my valuable merchandise." The lollipop went back into her mouth.

"I won't break anything," he said. She might've been kidding about the valuable merchandise, but he had a hard time telling if people were kidding. He just hoped she wasn't going to keep asking him questions, because if she did, he'd have to move on to his final location—Sister Sandy's. Or was it Miss Sandy's?

He swept his Geiger counter over a box of dolls with china heads, then over a shelf of Happy Meal toys—might be a clock or watch hidden anywhere—moving steadily toward the back of the room and away from Jabba the Hutt.

"There's an article about the Red Hills Horse Trials in here," Jabba announced. "You go to that?"

Otis told her that he didn't go, not volunteering that Ava went every year. He didn't want to give Jabba any information she might use as a net to trap him into talking to her.

"Who'd want to gallop a horse over these gigantic fences?" she asked. "Sheesh. Even after Christopher Reeve they do it. You could break your fool neck."

Otis hated it when people made pronouncements like this, because he never knew if they expected a reply or not. He opted for not speaking. The light on his Geiger counter was just flipping on occasionally. So far no clocks at all. He kept moving, like a shark. Sharks probably had radioactive stuff in their stomachs, because they'd eat anything. Funny how he was terrified of sharks but not of radioactivity.

By this time he was at the back of the room and he noticed another room to his left, a whole room next to this one, a room where there wouldn't be any Jabbas watching over him.

He moved into the other room, waving his

wand over dressers, coffee tables, souvenir ashtrays, raggedy couch pillows, and stacked flowered tablecloths. He bent down and stuck the wand back into a corner where there were some iron piggy banks.

"Well, if it ain't the spaceman."

Otis, startled, backed into a brass floor lamp and steadied it before it fell.

Rusty, the goth girl who lived in his neighborhood, the minister's daughter, was sitting in an old yellow lounge chair with a stack of comic books in her lap, a can of Coke resting on the arm of the chair.

Otis hoped she wouldn't spill the Coke. He worried about things like drinks spilling. "What are *you* doing here?" Otis said. Rusty was the last person in the world he'd thought would hang out at Grandma's Attic.

Rusty took a big swallow of her Coke and belched. "This is my grandma's shop."

"Your grandma is *the* Grandma?"

"So they say." She took another sip of Coke and then flung the empty can into the room behind her. It hit something and rolled a ways.

"Pick up whatever that was!" Jabba yelled from the next room, but Rusty didn't budge.

"I'm perusing these comic books while I wait for Royce," Rusty told Otis. "You know Royce, right?"

Otis did know Royce. Royce and Rusty were a

scary couple, pale, skinny, dyed black hair, permanent smirks on their faces. They walked the streets of Canterbury Hills and the halls of Sunny Side High School like two ghouls risen from the graveyard. Why did Rusty have to be sitting here in Grandma's Attic? Weekends were when he was supposed to have a rest from people like Rusty.

Otis felt anxiety bubble up in his stomach, the way it did every morning when he went into Sunny Side High School, a horrible feeling he was used to and had learned to hide. He gravitated toward the teachers because most of them were patient with him and didn't openly laugh at him or whisper about him or ignore him. Except his English teacher, Mr. Lennon, who seemed to find everything Otis said sidesplittingly funny. The teachers were getting paid to put up with him, it was true, but for Otis the knowledge of this fact was only a small humiliation compared to the myriad other humiliations visited upon him, either on purpose or not, by his fellow classmates. Fresh in his memory was yesterday's history class, when, toward the end of the hour, he'd opened his mouth and began to speak—offering up tidbits about World War II bombers—information he'd read somewhere—and as he was talking about P-51 Mustangs, and P-47 Thunderbolts and B-29 Flying Fortresses he saw the teacher, Mr. Fusek, shaking his head at someone, so Otis looked around. Half of the class was rolling their eyes or covering their ears, and the other half was snickering. This was bad enough, but even worse was the realization he'd had later, on the bus going home, that they'd probably been doing this all year long and he just hadn't noticed.

There was just one more week of his junior year to endure until they got out for the summer. And this would be a great summer. This summer would be his summer! The summer of his triumph! Surely he could handle Rusty for a few minutes, since she wasn't attached to Royce and they were in a totally different place than usual.

He switched off his Geiger counter and glanced around the big room—a huge walnut bed, a red dinette set, a glassed-in bookcase, racks of what looked like old prom dresses, but no clocks. "What kind of comic books are you reading?" he asked Rusty, just to stall.

"*Radioactive Man*. From *The Simpsons*. Ever seen him?" Rusty held up a comic book with a Bart Simpsonish–looking character on it, dressed in a superhero suit.

Otis had never heard of Radioactive Man. Was this just a coincidence? Or was Rusty mocking him? Was this a planned prank? But Rusty hadn't known he'd be coming in here. Like usual, Otis was taking too long to reply to someone, which made him seem even more gooney. He needed to say something quick, something safe. "There was a big earthquake in Indonesia. Six thousand people were killed."

Rusty tossed her dyed black hair. Even from here, Otis could smell cigarettes. She mimicked Otis. "I heard about the earthquake in Indonesia." Then back to her own voice. "Is that an alien detector you got there? The only alien in here is my grandma. Did she give you a hard time? She doesn't like men, only horses. Hey, isn't *unguent* a great word? It's my new favorite."

"I'm looking for clocks. The old kind, with glow-in-the-dark dials. The bigger the better."

Rusty did her smirk. "You're so twisted. Hey. Want to come to a party with us tonight? Me and Royce. FSU party. Free beer and other stuff, if you get my drift." Instead of lowering her voice, she'd raised it. Her grandma would hear!

"Can't, I got plans," Otis said. He'd learned that most invitations he received weren't sincere, so it was best to say no straightaway just to be safe. And he really did have plans. When he was done building his model breeder reactor—the youngest person ever to build one, the only civilian to ever build one—*then* he could take time out to go to parties. People would be having parties in his honor!

"What plans? Jerking off to Internet sites about aliens?"

"I don't believe in aliens," Otis told Rusty.

"There's no definitive proof, from any reliable source, that any so-called alien beings or their crafts have ever visited Earth."

"Whatever." Rusty slouched back in the chair. "You look normal, but you're like totally abnormal. Are you going to pull a Columbine one of these days? Just let me know when so I can sleep in that day." Rusty smiled at him again, a nice smile this time, and Otis saw that she was still as pretty as she used to be in elementary school, even under all that black eyeliner and dark lipstick. Rusty had been a born-again Christian in elementary school. Back then, she went around telling everyone that her father was a minister, and she was always inviting other kids to her church. What had happened to her? She used to be a cheerleader in middle school, but now she skulked around the edges of everything, making fun.

Desire came over Otis with surprising force. He really, really, really wanted to tell Rusty what he was doing in the shed, exactly what he was making, how much work it had been, how difficult it was to do it, and how much acclaim he was going to get for making it. The closer he got to being finished, the harder it was, he'd discovered, to keep his mouth shut. And the fact that she was reading *Radioactive Man*—that had to be a sign! "I'm building a model breeder reactor in my shed," he blurted out.

Rusty looked at him and waited.

"It's a source of nuclear power," Otis said, and then he explained it to her using a metaphor he'd read somewhere: a breeder reactor is a power source that never needs new fuel once successfully up and running. Imagine you have a car and begin a long drive. When you start, you have half a tank of gas. When you return home, instead of being nearly empty, your gas tank is full. A breeder reactor is like this magic car. A breeder reactor not only generates electricity but also produces new fuel. There was no way he could possibly assemble the thirty pounds of uranium needed to make a true breeder reactor, he explained to Rusty, but he figured he could make a smaller one, a model, the size of a shoebox, that would perform like the real one.

"But why?" Rusty asked him, and she seemed genuinely interested, but he'd been fooled before. "Why do *you* want to make one?"

Otis told her how his granddad, after he'd moved in with them, gave him a book called *Atoms to Electricity* that was about nuclear power. In the book was a detailed diagram of a breeder reactor. Once he saw that drawing, almost a blueprint, he was hooked. Otis had never doubted that he had the persistence and focus and intelligence to make a reactor. Asperger's was good for something. And the fact that nobody had successfully made a *safe* one yet spurred him on. "Teams of scientists had been experimenting with breeder reactors under top-secret circumstances in well-equipped labs," he told Rusty, "but the government—well, Jimmy Carter—outlawed them in 1977 because one of the by-products is plutonium, which is used in nuclear bombs. So no one is officially making them anymore. But I'm going to show everyone that I can make one at home, using everyday stuff I put together on my own. I've already made the neutron gun. Radium is the most effective fuel for the gun. The best source of radium is old clocks, clocks made in the twenties and thirties. Last week I found three in an antique mall out on I-10. I got five total, but that's not nearly enough."

Rusty was playing with something hanging from a cord around her neck, a multicolored drawstring bag like the medicine bags worn by Native Americans. "In other words," she said, "you're going to blow us all to kingdom come."

"No," Otis began, but Jabba interrupted him, calling from the next room in her piercing voice.

"Rustifer! What you doing in there?"

"Going wee wee on the furniture, Granny!"

"Come help me sort these clothes!" Jabba yelled.

"Hold on a minute," Rusty yelled back. She unfolded herself from the old yellow chair—it did look like she'd gone wee wee on it—and stood up, a graceful fairy creature from the dark side, and beckoned to Otis. "There's a big ugly clock over here somewhere," she said, leading the way to the back of the room, winding between tables and chairs. In a dim corner, on a little kid's dresser shellacked with frolicking lambs, there sat a couple of sparkling pink ceramic lamps with no shades and—a clock.

Otis switched his Geiger counter on and held it up to the face of the clock like a match to a flame. The needle on the dial shot up and the little red light started blinking like crazy. "Shazam," he said.

"Indeed," Rusty said. "That's one hot clock."

"How much is it?" he asked Rusty.

Rusty bent over and fished around for a tag. "Seventy-five bucks. A steal, right?"

Otis stared at the clock, a big fat plastic thing with a black face and green hands. The hands had been painted with radium, but there wasn't enough radium on the hands to make the Geiger counter go nuts like this. What was the source? There must be more inside the clock. He felt his heart tripping along as fast as the light on his Geiger counter was blinking. "I only have thirty bucks," he told Rusty.

"We offer layaway," she said.

"I need it now."

"Well, she won't go down that much." Rusty shook her head. Then she said in a low growly voice, "Just take it. I'll show you where the back door is."

"Steal it?" Otis had never stolen anything in his life.

"Beatrice!" Jabba's voice sounded far off. "Royce just pulled up! You aren't leaving until you help me sort these clothes!"

Rusty bent toward Otis, her medicine bag brushing his arm, and breathed her cigarette breath on him. "You'll be doing us a favor, right, getting this nasty thing out of here. And you need it to save mankind, right?" Rusty picked up the clock and thrust it into Otis's arms, grinning at him.

Suddenly Otis had a mental picture of Rusty from third grade, long before she went goth, standing at the front of their classroom, grinning in just this way, wearing an Atlanta Braves shirt, her hair in two ponytails sprouting out above her ears, holding up a baseball she'd caught at their spring training camp in Lake Buena Vista. Otis had been so jealous.

"He who hesitates is lost," the older, scary Rusty hissed at him.

There was no question that this clock should be his. It had a nice weight in his arms, the same weight as his mini poodle, Parson Brown, his boon companion. "You won't tell anyone, right?" he asked Rusty. "About anything. What I'm making. You know."

Rusty scrunched her eyebrows, thin black lines that looked like they'd been plucked and darkened. "Never!"

It was too dark back here for Otis to read Rusty's expression, but he knew he wouldn't have been able to read it even in the bright sunlight. "Do you still have that baseball? From spring training?" Otis asked her, but Rusty was already shoving him toward the back door.

It was the next afternoon, Sunday afternoon, before Otis could get free of the rest of them—free of chores and homework and anything else his mother could find for him to do—and escape to his shed. Once inside he locked the door, propped open the windows, switched on the fan, and sat down on his stool with his stolen clock in front of him on the table. He would have to work as fast as he could, now that he'd broken the law and could be arrested at any minute. If she missed the clock, Jabba could find out who he was and where he lived easily enough. It was exciting, being a lawbreaker, handling stolen property. He might have to break a few more laws before it was all over, but he was sure that he'd be pardoned once it came to light what he'd accomplished.

Otis loved his shed. It was hot in the summer and cold in the winter, always stank of burned something and was full of insects; but it was his very own uncomfortable, stinky, buggy place. And even though it was full of dangerous, unstable chemicals, it was the only place he felt truly safe and at home. His mother said that people with Asperger's often did not get irony, but in this case, the irony was not lost, even on him.

Back when he'd first decided to embark on his quest to make a model breeder reactor, he'd spruced up the shed in preparation, giving it a coat of white paint inside and out, hanging a poster of the periodic table on the wall, arranging an old green carpet he'd found in somebody's trash on the floor. He'd taken the old dehumidifier from the basement and plugged it and a desk lamp and fan in with extension cords. Along the wall were two sets of metal shelves lined with jars and vials of ingredients he'd collected or created to make his breeder reactor. Books his grandfather had given him were propped on one shelf: *Atoms to Electricity* and *Nuclear Power, Friend or Foe?* alongside a framed black-and-white photograph of his much younger grandfather, in a white lab coat, at the University of Iowa. Another shelf held Otis's logbook and a notebook and drawings he'd made, plans. He loved that word. *Plans*. It made him want to rub his hands together and cackle.

And he loved all his tools and equipment, no matter how humble others might find them to be.

From a nail in the corner hung a paper mask and rubber gloves and a cracked lead-lined suit, one he'd pilfered a while back from the chemistry lab at school—he wouldn't really call that stealing, since they'd been about to throw it away. On the table, beside the stolen clock, sat a blowtorch and a frying pan and a Bunsen burner. Also on the table lay his most prized possession—his neutron gun. He'd fashioned it from a block of lead with a hollowed-out center in which he would place a chunk of fuel.

Stored in the corner were boxes of defective smoke detectors he'd bought at a discount from First Alert, so that he could remove the americium chips and weld them, with a blowtorch, into a big ball. Originally he'd planned to use americium as fuel, because it was easier to find. Granddad had been the one to suggest smoke detectors as a source for americium. He always answered Otis's questions and gave him practical suggestions to what he thought were hypothetical questions about how to obtain ingredients for a breeder reactor, without having any idea that Otis was actually following his advice. Of course, the fact that the old man had dementia helped along these lines, but it seemed that dementia was also making his grandfather act flakey.

What was the deal with his grandfather getting locked in his shed? Had the old woman really pushed him in, or had something else happened? Had Granddad and the old woman been snooping around together? How had they found the key where he'd hidden it in the crook of a tulip tree? Otis never allowed anyone into his shed. Had his grandfather forgotten that the shed was off limits? This was another reason that he needed to hurry and finish his reactor. Before too long his grandfather would be completely gone, either mentally or physically or both. Otis wanted to surprise him with the completed reactor—surprise and impress him and make him proud. He wanted to be just like his grandfather when he grew up, only smarter and richer and more famous.

Atomic energy was Otis's passion, had been ever since Granddad had sent him some old nuclear energy textbooks that spoke in glowing terms about the future of nuclear science, about massive power and thrilling discoveries. His grandfather was the only other person Otis knew who shared this passion. Everyone else was afraid of it and refused to recognize its possibilities. So the two of them had exchanged letters about the textbooks—the old man refused to try e-mail—and spoke on the phone at least once a week.

But after Grandma died, when he was still living in Iowa, Granddad started losing his memory. He'd be driving to the grocery store and get lost. He forgot to take his medications and missed doctor appointments, wore dirty clothes to church, and didn't pay his bills. People from Iowa City called his mother all the time to report on his worrisome behavior. Mom cried about it, and Dad tried to comfort her, and eventually the two of them drove up to Iowa and moved him down to Florida. They gave him the guest bedroom down in the walk-out basement, where Otis had his room. Now that he lived right in the same house, his grandfather was even more available to discuss nuclear energy and answer Otis's questions about how to get materials for his reactor.

And he was making great progress. He'd already spent an afternoon last week taking apart the three clocks he'd found at the antique mall on I-10 and scraping the radioactive paint off the dials, but afterward he had less than a quarter of a pill vial full of flakes to show for his work. He would have to find many more radioactive clocks, but this big stolen one from Grandma's Attic was a good start.

With a screwdriver he pried the face off his stolen clock. There, inside, glued to the back of the clock, was a tube of liquid and a little folded piece of paper. The paper read, in faded black ink, "Here is some more radium paint to touch up your clock! Enjoy!" This was too good to be true. This was better than finding a hundred old clocks. Enjoy!

He picked up his Geiger counter and switched

it on, holding it up to the vial of paint. The flashing light went wild. He switched it off and sat back down, and feeling that the occasion called for a celebration, began cackling and rubbing his hands.

Then he heard something else, someone else, close by, laughing, a throaty chuckle, imitating him. Nobody was at either window. He jumped up, unlocked the padlock on the inside of the door, and threw it open. There, at the top of the driveway, with her back to him, walking briskly away, was the old lady who'd been hanging out at his house, the one who'd found the key to his shed and locked Granddad inside.

"Hey," he yelled at her. "Old lady! What do you want?"

She turned around and waved but kept walking.

He stood there in the doorway, gazing out at the lush backyard without seeing anything, holding his breath. She must've been spying on him. Surely she wouldn't be able to figure out what he was doing, a ditzy old lady like her who belonged in Grandma's Attic. But maybe she wasn't ditzy at all. Maybe that was an act. Maybe she was some sort of government agent, reporting on his activities. Who would suspect an old lady of being a spy? The government wouldn't want a kid like him accomplishing what none of their scientists were able to do.

Otis stepped back and slammed his shed door closed. Another reason to hurry and complete his project. For some reason, he thought of Rusty, imagined telling her about this development. He wanted to tell her. He would tell her. Beatrice. Rustifer.

But first, there was the radioactive paint to open.

Part Three JUNE 2006

CHAPTER 6 *Suzi*

Turned out it happened at a nothing game, an early morning scrimmage with the Trojans, a fairly kick-ass team, which was, like Suzi's team, made up of girls from a few different middle schools. It was on a Saturday, and Soccer Dad was there, pacing and yelling from the sidelines—fortunately Suzi couldn't hear what he was saying. Nance had come to watch, too. She'd driven out to the field by herself and had brought her own lawn chair and was sitting at midfield holding a goofy-looking umbrella over her head. Poor woman must really have no life. Why couldn't it be Mom sitting there, watching her? Mom, as usual, had better things to do. She had to take Ava to support group and then out to lunch so Ava would feel good about herself even though she had to go to a support group. You had to be autistic—and whine about it—to get her mother's attention.

The fourth quarter started and Suzi's team, the Sharks, were behind by four. Their coach, Annika, eight months pregnant, was sitting on the bench, legs spread, chin in hand, like she'd already given up. Her goalie coach, Jorge, was pacing around, yakking on his cell phone, probably telling his son to clean up his room. Important stuff.

All the action right now was down at the Trojans' goal, where the ground, being in the shade, was still damp. For the whole game the Sharks kept driving it down but couldn't get it in. The Trojans' goalie was Suzi's friend Mykaila, who sprang around the goal box like some demented kid's toy: Mykaila in a Box.

Suzi, from her post, called out directions. "Maddy, mark up!" It was so hot the ground was doing the wavy thing.

She was hoping, praying, that the Trojans wouldn't bring the ball down to her goal box again. Her knee was hurting. In the past she'd had other injuries, mostly minor—a concussion; a sprained ankle when she fell in a hole in back of a goal in Monticello (crappy field); sprained fingers; and, when extension diving, had bruised her elbow.

But her lingering injury was her left knee, which she kept twisting when she landed on it just so. The bursa sack in that knee, according to the PA, had gotten inflamed. She really needed to rest it, so she'd be ready for soccer camp in July, but how could she do that? It was wrapped up tightly today, making her feel like Lurch on the *Addams Family*. Things could be worse, she kept reminding herself. Another goalie she knew, in a game just a month earlier, clutched the ball close to her face after she'd captured it—a big no-no—and had gotten kicked in the jaw. Now this girl's jaw was broken and her mouth wired shut.

Stay down there and get a goal. Please. Her teammates in their ghostie gray jerseys reminded her of soldiers on a battlefield, some with current injuries and some haunted by past injuries: Janie with her shin splints and Haley with her torn ligament and Amanda's turf toe and Maddy's broken nose.

Whoa. The Trojans' center defense, a hulking s/he, delivered a slot ball down the field toward Suzi. Their right midfielder pounced and kept it moving. Suzi tensed up into the attack position. Take it away, she urged her teammates. Take it. Because of her knee, part of her dreaded having to defend their goal, but at the same time this was when she liked the game best—when it was up close and tense and she couldn't think about anything else. The Sharks' midfielders weren't doing their jobs. Mia tried. Ali tried. A Trojan forward, little blond devil girl slipped in there, swiped the ball, and dribbled it toward Suzi.

Suzi stepped out into the penalty box. Once she came out she was committed. She had a personal goal for each game: to come out of her box at least twice. She'd already come out twice, and those two had gotten by her. Not this time.

She clapped her hands, spit on her gloves, watching the ball, and here it came, zinging toward her from left field and she lunged forward, her weight on the bad knee, and her kneecap popped.

At least she'd stopped them from scoring.

She lay there on the ground, trying to breathe. She lay there, feeling like she was underwater, the pain in her knee like a weight pulling her down. Her father was bending over her, Annika, Mykaila, her team members, saying things, but they were above the water and their words were muffled. None of this was surprising. What *was* surprising was the fact that she felt so relieved. *That's that*. She marveled at her lack of emotion. But then Nance was kneeling beside her, getting down into the water with her, stroking her hair, holding her hand, and that's when Suzi started crying.

Suzi didn't listen to her iPod or to Star 98. When her friends and Davis called, she had nothing to say. She didn't feel like reading or MySpacing. She didn't want to be out on the couch in the den, watching TV. She wanted to lie in her room under her purple and orange sixties mod-daisy-patterned comforter and do nothing.

Unlike Ava's room, which underwent a radical change every few months—Ava threw out all her dolphin posters and everything dolphin-related when she plunged into Elvis—or Otis's room, which never had anything but science crap in it, Suzi's room—the smallest of the three kids' bedrooms—was layered with things from every stage of her life and every interest she'd ever had. Her white iron bed, which her mom had rescued from a junk store and painted pink for her second birthday. The black wool carpet with colored butterflies that Suzi herself picked out at T.J. Maxx when she was four. Her old posters of animals and newer ones of rock groups—My Chemical Romance, Panic at the Disco. The clutter on her desk and dresser and in the corners of the room and under the bed—plastic Pooh figures, lip gloss, shells, bird feathers, ticket stubs, crayons, soccer trophies, Brownie badges, dusty photos of her friends, stuffed animals, American Girl dolls. Her bookcase full of board books and picture books and complete collections of Nancy Drew, Little House, Ramona, Narnia, Harry Potter, and more recent additions, books about Our Changing Bodies and Crushes and sexy vampires and Cool Girls Kicking Butt.

On Suzi's left knee was a brace thing that went up to the middle of her thigh. She was going to have to wear the brace and keep her knee immobile for three to four weeks, and then she'd have to do physical therapy for the rest of the summer. She'd have to use crutches for at least six weeks. She could cheer her team on from the sidelines, but she couldn't participate in any drills or weight training sessions, and, of course, no practices or games. No Olympic Development soccer camp. She was done with soccer for the summer, maybe longer, depending on how she healed.

In the evenings, her father tiptoed into her room like she was on her deathbed. He'd come in and talk and talk, update her on the latest tropical storm development, describe his day at the office assembling training packets—whatever the hell those were—and usually he'd ask her if she wanted to watch a movie with him, but she always told him she didn't feel like it. Although he never said so, she could tell that her father was sick, sick, sick with disappointment about the Olympic Development soccer camp. He wore a pitiful hangdog expression that drove Suzi nuts and after a while made her angry. Like she could help what happened! Play soccer yourself, she wanted to yell at him. But she felt sorrier for him than she did for herself, because he was old and had nothing but his job and she was young and had her whole life ahead of her. A *great* future ahead of her, Nance had said.

Her mother, brisk and unsentimental as always, brought her snacks and meals and pain meds on a tray, but didn't have time to sit with her.

Ava kept looking in at Suzi like she was an animal in a zoo, and once she brought her a crayon-drawn get-well card, which was sweet, but when she came in to deliver it she spent the whole time watching herself in Suzi's full-length mirror.

"Why do you keep doing that?" she asked Ava, even though she knew what Ava's reaction would be.

"I'm not doing anything."

"You look fine. Stop worrying."

"I'm *not* worrying. Just leave me alone." And off she went, storming out of the room, leaving Suzi alone and realizing how much she missed Ava, not Ava as she was now, but the old Ava.

The old Ava used to read Nancy Drew books aloud in a pleasing, dramatic voice. She and Suzi played with their American Girl dolls or their stuffed animals or played dress-up—Ava the servant girl and Suzi the benevolent princess—or go fish or Dogopoly or school—Suzi the teacher and Ava the pupil. They would play together for entire days. Now all they did was fight, which was sometimes fun, but mostly tedious, and sometimes, like now, totally inadequate.

Otis never came to see Suzi, but he did encourage Parson to come in and keep her company, which Parson did for a while, until she heard the back door open and someone more interesting come into the house.

Her granddad wandered in and sat on the end of her bed and looked at the floor, and then at her. Occasionally he patted her brace. "Now what did you do to your knee, kiddo?" he kept asking her.

Only Nance had time to sit with her, bring her brownies and magazines, the kind of teen magazines her mother would never buy for her. Sometimes she brought her knitting, a brown woolly thing, and said she was knitting Suzi a sweater. A sweater? Obviously the woman hadn't lived in Florida very long.

Nance hadn't mentioned the Italy trip again. Suzi was disappointed that Nance had given up on it so easily. It would've been something to look forward to. Although, with her bad knee, they probably couldn't have gone this August anyway.

"We're having Grandparents' Day at my church," Nance told Suzi one evening after she'd given her a mango smoothie from Tropical Smoothie. She rocked in a rocking chair at the end of the bed, tapping her sneakered foot on the floor. "You're supposed to bring your grandchildren to church. Would you like to be my granddaughter for the day? It's Genesis Church, where my neighbor, Buff Coffey, is youth minister."

"When is it?" Stalling.

"This Sunday," Nance told her. "Aren't you about ready for a change of scenery? I can help you get in and out." She gave Suzi a wink. "Bet there'll be some cute guys there."

What would an old lady know about cute guys? But Suzi was bored out of her mind and her friends were already making excuses about why they couldn't stop by, and Davis was losing interest in her because she couldn't roller-skate—hell, couldn't even walk—so it was probably no time at all until he moved on to a girl who could put one foot in front of the other and who actually liked him back. There was plenty of time to lie here and think about how miserable she was.

"I don't know." Her mother was slumped over the sink, washing dishes. "Isn't that a church of wackos? Like a cult?"

Suzi had to admit that she knew nothing about the church. She'd had to hobble into the kitchen on her crutches to talk to her mother, since her mother rarely came to her.

"Do you really want to go?"

Suzi shrugged. "It's for Grandparents' Day."

"What?" Her mother turned away from the sink. "Is she calling you her granddaughter?"

"No," Suzi said, wondering why her mother would care. "I'm just a stand-in."

"She said that? Stand-in? You're sure? She didn't say that you *were* her granddaughter? She never said that? Or hinted at that?"

Suzi was confused. What exactly, had Nance said? Why did it matter? "Uh. No, she didn't. She's not deluded or anything. I don't think."

"Oh my God." Her mother turned back to

washing the dishes, scrubbing at a muffin tin like she was performing the most important job on earth.

"Why not put that in the dishwasher?" Suzi suggested.

Her mother only scrubbed harder, working on every muffin indentation. "The dishwasher doesn't get this clean," she said, and then sighed loudly. "We need to go back to church."

That would never happen. They went to church only a couple of times a year, because her mother said she didn't want to have to get up early on the weekend and hurry around making everyone get dressed and have to look presentable herself and then—horrors!—be forced to chitchat with well-meaning strangers!

"Dad would really like it if we went to church," her mother went on. "Maybe Granddad could go with you and Nance."

Suzi didn't want her granddad dragging along after them. "I don't think he'd like that kind of church," she told her mother, even though she really had no idea what kind of church it was.

"Probably not." Her mother turned off the water in the kitchen sink and snatched up the dish towel. She frowned at Suzi. "I just don't know."

"It's a church, not a satanic temple."

What was Mom worrying so much about this for?

• • •

Mom needn't have worried, because by the time she sat down in the church, Suzi was too tired to even *consider* joining a cult. Most of her energy and focus was used up getting into the backseat of Nance's car and then out again in front of the church, which was in a strip mall; then across the sidewalk and through the front door; through the lobby, which was like one you'd fine in a fancy hotel with marble floors and a guest services desk and couches and armchairs and even shops selling coffee and T-shirts and CDs; and then into the sanctuary, which was like an auditorium with padded seats and thick carpeting. She and Nance sat at the back, at the end of an aisle.

The room was huge. Red and purple spotlights shone on the stage, where, in front of a metallic backdrop a rock band played. In front of the rock band, six singers, three white and three black, exhorted the congregation to stand and feel the spirit. Suzi, thank God, couldn't stand, and neither did Nance; but they watched the semicool-looking singers on the screen lead the congregation in a bouncy song about Jesus that went on and on. Big cameras were stationed on platforms here and there, and images of the band and musicians were projected onto two big screens on either side of the stage, along with the words to the songs.

The congregation was roughly 70 percent

African American and the rest white, with a few Asians sprinkled here and there. Some people wore jeans, even old people. Quite a few tattoos. An African American woman in a silver suit and hat sat in front waving two flags in front of her, like a starter at a car race. There was a lot of hollering and swaying.

During the offering, "Late Breaking Genesis News" played on the screens—announcements about upcoming church events. Neither Nance nor Suzi put any money into the white offering bucket passed down their row.

Nance leaned over and said to Suzi, "This is an unusual church."

"I'll say."

A chuckling African American man took the stage, made a few jokes about his short stature, and then introduced the youth minister Buffington Coffey, who was delivering the sermon, the regular pastor being out doing the Lord's work somewhere else. Reverend Coffey wore jeans and a plaid button-down shirt untucked. He had a handsome face and long sideburns, like somebody from an Abercrombie ad. Then he started talking about taking his little girl swimming in the Gulf, and Suzi quit listening.

Nance, who'd slipped a beige cardigan sweater over her pink church dress, kept glancing over at Suzi and smiling, patting her hand.

Suzi was slumped so she could stick her leg out in the aisle, and she felt self-conscious. Her bare feet, in the ugly sport sandals her mother made her wear, were freezing, and, not being an old lady, she hadn't thought to bring a cardigan. Maybe the cold was what made people here so lively. A middle-aged white woman with a long flowing skirt and bare feet was swooping and genuflecting in the aisle near Suzi, like she was hearing music on an invisible iPod.

Okay, this church was bizarre, but more bizarre than any other church? Just not as civilized as Faith Presbyterian, where people wore better clothes and sat quietly like they were half asleep.

Nothing was mentioned at all in the service about it being Grandparents' Day. Maybe Nance had got that wrong.

Now the Reverend Coffey was talking about a vision he'd had that morning, and Suzi perked up. Who didn't like a vision? He paced back and forth on the stage so they could get the full benefit of him, but Suzi watched his screen image rather than the actual him, because that way she could see his face more clearly.

"I saw a field," he said, "a huge field, that stretched as far as I could see. I was standing in this field and I was a child, and God was there, too. He was my father, and he was standing a little ways away with open arms, asking me to come to him. 'I will catch you,' he said. 'I will hold you up. I am always here for you! I'll be here for you when your job evaporates, when your earthly relationships fail. I am all knowing, and all loving, and all protecting. That's what a father's love is.' Now I know." Here the Reverend Coffey stopped and stared out into the congregation. He had long eyelashes and dark eyes. "Now I know that many of you have never experienced that kind of love from a parent. And you want it. You need it."

True, Suzi thought. She did need it. It was like he was talking directly to her. Cool!

"But you *can* experience that love with God," the reverend went on. "With him, you can feel that safety, that protection, that unconditional love you've always yearned for. Just step forward. Move toward him. He's waiting for you."

Okay, Suzi didn't mind God waiting for her, but she really wanted her mother. Why couldn't it be her mother, waiting there for her in that huge field? She pictured her mother standing in a field, a soccer field, and then she started thinking about soccer and pretty soon the sermon was over.

After the service came to a close, Nance introduced Suzi to people around them. "This is my granddaughter." The first time she did it, Suzi wondered if she'd just slipped up. But then she did it three, four, five times. Some people shook

Suzi's hand—clasped it—and others hugged her. They asked after her knee and said that Suzi should pray on it and ask God to heal it. "We just love your grandmama," said a cute old African American woman wearing blue jeans. "She's a precious jewel."

After most people had cleared out of the auditorium, Suzi and Nance made their way through the lobby.

"Hope you don't mind that I told people you're my granddaughter. I'm sure that Helen would've been just like you." Nance's eyes had gotten watery.

Don't cry, lady; that's all I ask. "It's fine," Suzi said, pausing to rest.

They approached the reverend, who was shaking hands with people leaving the church. "This is my *adopted* granddaughter," Nance told him, after he'd greeted her profusely, clasping both her hands in his. "Suzi, this is Reverend Coffey, our neighbor in Canterbury Hills."

Reverend Coffey was even taller than he'd looked onstage and built like a football player. "Just call me Buff," he said. He had longish, wavy brown hair and looked like Orlando Bloom, with the same jutting chin and thinnish lips. And those eyes! He turned to Nance. "This girl is a true gift from God," he said, about Suzi. Then he said to Suzi, "Hope you'll be back next week. And come to youth group. I'm the leader."

He looked intently into her eyes, as if there was more going on at youth group than just your standard Bible-related activities.

Nance offered to take Suzi to Dunkin' Donuts after church, somewhere Suzi hadn't been since she was eight.

"Let's bring your grandfather with us next week!" Nance said in the car.

Suzi, sprawled out in the backseat, was surprised that Nance was just assuming she'd be going back to Genesis Church, and she was even more surprised to discover that she was actually considering it.

"Your granddad doesn't get out much," Nance said. "I think he'd enjoy it. Don't you?"

"Maybe." Suzi had never thought about her granddad being lonely, but she supposed he must be. "I thought you said today was Grandparents' Day."

"I just made that up," Nance said. Her eyes met Suzi's in the rearview mirror and then slid quickly away. "I wanted you to come with me. I shouldn't have lied, though. I'm sorry."

That was strange. A church lady telling a lie like it was no big deal.

"I would've gone anyway," Suzi said, but that might have been a lie also.

As soon as Nance got Suzi settled at a table in Dunkin' Donuts with a few cream-filled delicacies, surrounded by glum-looking people getting their sugar fixes, Nance announced that while Suzi was eating her first donut, she'd drive down the road and fill the car up with gas and be back in two shakes of a jiffy jack's tail. "Save me the biggest one," she told Suzi, pointing at the donuts.

Suzi watched her drive off, pulling into the traffic on Monroe in her oddly aggressive manner. Why couldn't she have waited to get gas? Why the urgency? She drove right on by the Shell station on the corner. But maybe she had a particular brand of gas in mind. The thing was, after Suzi had eaten all the donuts but one, she sat there and sat there. She looked at her watch. Nance had been gone for half an hour. Suzi's braced knee, propped up on a red vinyl chair, was throbbing. It was time for more pain meds. They were a few miles from Canterbury Hills or she might've set off walking—if she hadn't been injured.

Should she call someone? Nance herself didn't have a cell phone. She'd have to call home and ask one of her parents or Otis to come and get her. Otis would be mean about it. And she didn't want to get Nance in trouble, make her look like a flake. But where the hell was she? Suzi called Mykaila and chatted awhile, told her about the church service, about the fetching Reverend Coffey, told her she was stranded at Dunkin' Donuts. Not a bad place, Mykaila observed. If you have to be stranded. Maybe Nance was in an accident! Mykaila suggested hopefully.

Suzi ate the last donut, then waited another half an hour, then another fifteen minutes, then, finally, called her mother. She'd thought her mother might be angry at having to come get her, but she wasn't. No, instead of being angry or feeling bad about Suzi getting stranded, her mother was worried about what had happened to Nance.

In the van, Suzi told her mother that it really hadn't been Grandparents' Day at church after all, but that Nance had pretended to some people at church that she was Suzi's grandmother. "I think she's confused," Suzi said. "Maybe she's getting Alzheimer's."

"Oh God," her mother muttered, like it was the end of the world or something.

When they drove by Nance's house, her bottle green car was in the carport.

"Should we stop?" her mother asked Suzi. "Should we go in and make sure she's all right?"

"Let's go home," Suzi suggested. "My knee's really hurting." Crazy old bat. It was a shame, really, because she'd gotten rather fond of the old thing. But what if she'd pulled this sort of stunt in Italy somewhere?

When they got home, her mother spent twenty minutes talking to Nance on the phone, or, rather listening to Nance talk, and murmuring consoling phrases, like "I'm sure it was" and "She'll understand."

The hell I will, thought Suzi. What would possess somebody to behave like that, after she'd introduced Suzi around as her granddaughter? Was this the way Nance would treat her actual granddaughter? Good thing she didn't have one.

When her mother finally got off the phone, her face looked thoughtful. She told Suzi that Nance was very apologetic and said that it would never happen again.

"Why'd she do it?"

"She got upset, thinking about her daughter," her mother said. "Her daughter died. Did she tell you?"

Suzi was pleased to report that she knew all about Helen, who'd died of cancer.

"I guess her Helen loved donuts, and Nance got overcome with memories being in Dunkin' Donuts," her mother said. "That's no excuse. But she said she'll make it up to you and hopes you'll forgive her. I'm just telling you what she said."

"She just left me there."

"I know, I know. But people do crazy things when they're sad."

"I'm sad, and I don't do crap like that."

Her mother sat down in a kitchen chair like the wind got knocked out of her. "*You're* sad?" she said. "What's wrong, honey?" Like, you're not allowed to be sad.

Duh, she wanted to tell her mother. Why do you think? You only care about Ava. It was too awful to say aloud, and her mother would just deny it anyway. "My knee, duh," Suzi said, glad she had a go-to pain source that her mother had to acknowledge.

"Oh, yes, that," her mother said, sounding relieved. She glanced out the window into the sunlit branches of Granddad's beautiful live oak tree as if she wished she were outside instead of in here. "Nance has been so nice to all of us, so helpful. She's adopted our family. I hate to just cut her off."

"I'm not going to just cut her off," Suzi snapped. Her mother would look for an excuse to cut anyone off. "She wants to take Granddad to church with us next week."

"Oh, really?" her mother said. "I'm sure he'd enjoy that."

Anything to take the old man off her hands. Suzi had said the right thing once again.

"I guess we could give her another chance," her mother said.

Marylou CHAPTER 7

Before Nance/Marylou actually met Wilson, she hadn't realized how complicated, and potentially unsatisfying it could be, trying to enact her revenge. She hadn't even considered the possibility that Wilson might be losing his marbles, might not remember what she *required* him to remember.

On the third morning she read the *New York Times* to him, or pretended to read it, the two of them were sitting alone in his little den, drinking cups of coffee that Caroline had brought in; and he asked her if she was the one who'd sent him the package, which gave her hope that he did, finally, grasp the situation.

She said that, yes, it had been she who sent him the package full of photocopies of documents and letters from the government study, linking her and Wilson and Helen.

He asked her why she'd sent it to him.

She said to remind him of what he'd done.

He gave her that blank face. At least he was wearing his hearing aid today and had put on trousers with a short-sleeved button-up shirt tucked into them, instead of his usual bathrobe and pj's.

"You're as bad as a Nazi," Marylou explained to him. "You're a monster. Experimenting on human beings without their knowledge or consent. I should call you Heinrich. Or Adolf."

He actually smiled. "Or Godzilla," he said.

The smile was insufferable. "Do you know who I am?" she asked him.

"I believe I do."

"Who? Who am I?"

The annoying little white poodle was out in the front yard, barking fiercely at Paula Coffey, in her white visor, jogging by. Wilson said, "You're Mrs. Archer. Mrs. Archer with the lovely blue eyes."

"I told you. My real name is Marylou Ahearn."

His eyes behind their trifocals swept her up and down. "You look nice today."

"Go straight to hell."

He nodded. "Not yet," he said, and crossed his legs so that his white calf showed. He glanced out the window, and she did, too. The dog was silent, but the city recycling truck was nearby, slamming glass bottles around. Moss hung in ghostly swaths from the huge live oak tree in the front yard. The sunlight coming into the room made her feel drowsy. The smell of warming dust made her feel drowsy. She didn't want to feel drowsy. It was happening again. His bobbing and weaving was wearing her down. The previous two times she'd "read the newspaper" to him she'd given up badgering him after a while and just sat there, making small talk about Memphis and gardening and the weather, hoping that her mere presence was making him miserable, occasionally imagining flying across the room and strangling him. Breaking the table lamp over his head.

Then, because such images were so preposterous, she'd start wondering if maybe he was really the ogre she thought he was. Maybe he hadn't really known what he was doing with that experiment and so on, until she actually found herself making excuses for him, trying to make sense of the fact that she and this nice, polite, rather handsome gentleman were sitting together, talking about daylilies, when what she really wanted to do was to kill him.

One day, after spying a key in the fork of a tree, she'd taken the opportunity to lock Wilson in the toxic garden shed, hoping that he'd suffocate in there or inhale enough deadly fumes to have a lasting effect. She knew that even if *he* hadn't figured out who pushed him into the shed, *they'd* have to have figured out that she'd done it; and she planned to vehemently deny it when they confronted her. But nobody in the family even mentioned it to her the next time she showed up at their house to "read the paper" to Granddad, who seemed just as unflappable as ever.

Today, she decided, she wouldn't give up. She took a sip of the strong coffee and set down her mug. She wasn't going to fall back on small talk. She was done messing around. She informed him that she'd moved to Tallahassee with the singular goal of killing him.

"Is this another one of your jokes?"

"I am going to kill you. How much clearer can I be?"

He folded his arms on his chest. "Don't talk like that. I could report you to the police."

"You could," she said, leaning forward, struggling to keep her voice low so that Caroline, nearby in the kitchen, wouldn't hear her. "But if you told the police, it would all come out, what you've done. It would get in the papers. Your family—your daughter and grandkids—and all of greater Tallahassee will hear the details about how *you* are responsible for poisoning eight hundred women. And their unborn children."

"Oh. Well. There's already been a hearing in Washington," he said. "When that fellow from Arkansas was president. Hillary's husband. I gave a deposition for the hearing. And afterward the subjects were compensated. OJ was involved, too, somehow. The rental car guy."

"*I* am a subject," Marylou said. "Here I am. I got some money, but I do not consider myself to be compensated. I am an uncompensated individual. I've had many medical problems. And my daughter, Helen, died of cancer. At age eight. Can you imagine watching your child suffer and die, Adolf?"

He stared fixedly at his hands, which were now in his lap. "I'm sorry your daughter died."

"Are you sorry that *you* killed her? *That's* what you need to be sorry for."

Would he say it? She watched his face closely. A shadow passed over it. "I'm not feeling well," he said.

"You don't feel bad enough, in my opinion."

He seemed to sink even farther into the ugly chintz chair. "I need to lie down."

"You'll have plenty of time to lie down after I kill you."

His voice sounded faint. "That's funny."

"Do you think I'm a stand-up comedian? Why did I say I came here?"

He picked up his coffee mug, a thick brown and white thing that looked like a passable murder weapon. "To read the paper to me," he said. "And it's very good of you." He took a sip of the coffee.

"I'm *supposed* to read the paper to you. But notice I'm not. What am I doing?"

"You're pestering me about something."

"*Pestering* you?"

He looked over at the *Tallahassee Democrat* on the couch, tucked up close to Marylou where she could snatch it up and pretend to read if Caroline should come in. "Have we read Arts and Leisure yet?" he said. "Let's see what movies are playing."

"Listen. I'm going to keep telling you, as many times as it takes. I was one of the pregnant women you gave a radioactive drink to. In 1953. And here I am today, in 2006."

He smiled at her, turning on the charm. "You look fine to me."

"I'm not fine. My daughter died of bone cancer."

He shook his head and sighed. "My wife died of cancer. She played her piano right up until the end. She played hymns, songs from *West Side Story*, everything."

Marylou couldn't help herself. "*West Side Story*? Yuk."

"They have a piano here, but nobody plays it."

"Cry me a river. It's not the same thing. Helen died of cancer because *you* gave it to her. You gave me the radioactive cocktail and told me it was good for me. It was vitamins, you said. So *you* killed Helen. Can I be any more clear?"

"*I* gave you a cocktail?"

"No, you idiot. You were in charge of the study. At Memphis University. One of your minions gave me the drink. Nurse Bordner. But you were the doctor in charge. It was your study. You came by to say cheerio right after I'd drunk it. 'We appreciate your cooperation,' you said."

"You've got the wrong person," Wilson said.

"No, I don't, but we'll move on. I also saw you on the day Helen died. Do you remember that?"

He shook his head, so she refreshed both her memory and his.

It was on a February day in 1963. Helen lay on a bed at Memphis University Hospital—white sheet, white gown, white walls, gray girl—hours away from death. Marylou and Teddy were crouched on either side of her with their winter coats on. Teddy's coat was red with a plaid hood.

Why hadn't they taken their coats off? By then Helen's face had lost much of its Helenness, her lovely curving mouth now a hole drawing in ragged, irregular breaths, her formerly plump freckled cheeks hollow. Marylou and Teddy said soothing things to the part of Helen who was there with them, kissed her forehead, alternately clinging to her and squeezing her hands and stroking her hair, hoping to get some last response, some acknowledgment that she knew them and knew she was loved—they would've been overjoyed to see her eyelids flickering—but there was nothing. How long had they done this? Were they crying? Or were they subdued and numb? Marylou had no idea.

What she did remember was hearing, at some point, behind her in the doorway, a rustling sound, and she'd automatically turned around, expecting to see one of the nurses or Helen's doctor, but by that point, even if it had been President Kennedy himself she wouldn't have cared. But it wasn't President Kennedy; it was the same doctor she'd seen the day she'd been given the "vitamin cocktail" at the same hospital almost ten years earlier. Dr. Wilson Spriggs.

Once again he was standing in a doorway, even though it was a different doorway in an entirely different wing of the hospital. But she remembered him, even though his dark hair was graying and longer, curling around his ears, and his glasses were smaller and wire framed and he wore a fat paisley tie instead of a bow tie. He still looked foppish and pretentious. She had no idea in 1963 that the "vitamin drink" had given Helen the cancer that was killing her, and that Marylou and Helen had been guinea pigs in Dr. Spriggs's secret government study, one of many such studies going on in the country back then. She didn't know any of those things, but she hated Dr. Spriggs just the same, hated him for standing there useless and vain, for not saying anything to her or Teddy, even though he must've known what was happening in that room, whether he knew exactly who they were or not, and she hated him for his ability to walk away, as she imagined, untouched and unharmed.

"An angel of death," Marylou told the old Wilson now. "You were the angel of death."

"I'm sorry you think so." There was a pause while Wilson took another sip of his coffee and set the mug back down with a shaky hand. "Are you feeling all right?" he asked her.

"I'm tired," Marylou said.

"Have you been getting enough sleep?"

Actually, she hadn't been. There was some funny business going on around her house at night that kept her awake. Just the night before she'd heard someone, around midnight, prancing around on her roof like a reindeer. The next morning a big hunk of roof shingles lay on the ground beside the garbage can, which convinced her that it had been a person on the roof, not an animal. As much as she longed to tell somebody about this—someone like her former husband Teddy—she would not allow herself to tell Wilson. So she said, in a mincing voice, "'Have you been getting enough sleep? Have you been drinking your radiation like a good girl?' Don't be pulling that doctor crap with me."

"I am a doctor," Wilson said. "Tell me who you are."

"I'm one of your guinea pigs. I'm leaving now, but I'll be back. You are going to pay for what you did."

"What is it you think I did?"

"You know what you did."

Wilson frowned, looking bewildered. "Why are you so angry at me?"

"I'm not only angry at you, I'm going to kill you. I just haven't figured out how."

"You'd better go," he said, looking alarmed for the first time. "Right now."

Marylou stood up. "When I come back tomorrow you won't remember anything we've talked about, and you won't remember that I said I'm going to kill you."

"You don't know that."

"Okay. What did I just say?"

He squirmed around in his chair, blinking like a spotlight was in his eyes. "It's been real nice talking to you, but I'm not in a position to buy anything right now."

It was so hot, walking home. Canterbury Hills was deserted in the middle of the day. She was glad that Buster was at home in the air-conditioning. The houses and trees receded, and it was all about the asphalt, pushing the heat up into her face. The heat here had a different quality than the heat in Memphis. In Memphis it was like a withering blast furnace, but at least there was movement in the blast. Here, she felt like a fish struggling in a hot shallow pond. It was unnatural to move in such heat. She tried not to cry, but tears leaked out of her eyes. She didn't want to look conspicuous. She felt faint, but she kept going. Telling him about the day Helen died, that had taken it out of her. She hadn't talked about that day in years. Her right hip was aching again. One foot, then the other. She would force Wilson, somehow, to acknowledge the depravity, the horror of what he'd done, and when it was clear that he understood and after he sincerely apologized to her, then she'd kill him, and she no longer cared how she did it. But right now the son of a bitch was too jolly. He refused to be miserable while she was turning the screws. Before she snuffed him out, she wanted him miserable. But how in the world could she change the outlook of a happy fool?

Desperation was the mother of invention. By

the time she got back to Reeve's Court, Marylou had devised a brand-new attack plan. She would continue with her efforts to make Wilson remember and apologize, but she would also take steps to destroy his family, the way he'd destroyed hers. It would surely make him miserable to watch his family suffer, the way she'd had to watch Helen and Teddy suffer.

Rather than killing all of them, which she didn't think she had the guts to do—and, even if she did manage to do it, there was no way she wouldn't get caught—she would get to know them better, each one of them, and then set about disrupting their lives. She would make sure that Wilson knew what she was doing, that it was *she* who was causing them trouble and that she was doing it because of what he'd done to her, and to Helen, and to those eight hundred other women and their children and husbands.

It was easy enough figuring out the best way to mess with each member of that family. She hadn't spent twenty-five years as a high school English teacher for nothing. She was good at sizing people up, at displaying a kind of false cheeriness that made them feel comfortable with her, and she had an instinct about what people really needed—which usually wasn't what they thought they needed. The only hitch was that she didn't purely hate them, the way she did Wilson. These mixed feelings made it a little more difficult to plan and carry out a single-minded campaign to destroy them. But she would do her very best for Helen's sake.

Suzi was a shining light, and for this reason she was a bit of a tough case, because although Marylou resented Suzi for being the sort of girl Helen would have been, for living the kind of life that Helen would've lived—Helen, who was bright and beautiful and wise and kind—she also liked Suzi for those very reasons. Right away, Marylou saw that Suzi was tired of striving to be perfect. There was no religious training in that household, and Suzi could use some. Marylou saw great religious potential in Suzi, and Suzi's becoming a rabid Christian would have the added bonus of upsetting her liberal parents. Suzi already considered herself a Christian, but she'd been attending a Presbyterian Church, which was almost as bad as Unitarian. However, for Suzi to simply become a Southern Baptist, like Marylou, while that would be horrible for her parents, would not go far enough. Suzi needed exposure to one of those giant churches that met in buildings that resembled a Walmart. She needed to become the kind of Christian who quoted Bible verses irresponsibly and judged other people and scared them away. It seemed like a true gift from God that Marylou just happened to move across from a minister at the Genesis Church, a church that she'd hoped would fit the bill in every way. When she actually went to Genesis Church, though, she discovered that most of the people there weren't scary or judgmental, but were just like the people at First Baptist in Memphis. Surprise! She actually liked Genesis Church, even if the minister did sling too many metaphors around in one sermon. It felt good just to be going to church again. She'd missed First Baptist more than she'd thought she would.

Six months ago when she first came up with the idea to kill Wilson, back when she was living in Memphis, she'd started going to church again. Since she was spending so much time thinking about sinister things, the least she could do, she reasoned, was to think about God and his love twice a week at church so that she wouldn't become a total sociopath. And rather than kill other people who were stand-ins for the person she really wanted to kill, like serial killers did, she'd be kind and generous to others and hone in on the one who deserved to die. And her plan had worked extremely well. Since she'd started planning to kill Wilson, and then decided to destroy his family instead, she felt no animosity toward anyone but him. Almost none at all!

The first Sunday she'd lured Suzi into Genesis Church she'd gotten drunk with power. Thank God she'd gotten scared out of her wits and left her at Dunkin' Donuts, unable to proceed with her impulsive plan to take Suzi out to Lake Jackson, propose a canoe ride, and then brain her with an oar. That didn't pan out. Now she was back on track with her goal: creating Jesus freak Suzi.

At the same time she was seeing to Suzi, she was mounting her campaign on all fronts. Otis and Ava. There was something anxious and vulnerable and permanently innocent about both of them. Their mother tried to explain to Marylou that they had some sort of disability, and Marylou could see that there was definitely something different about them. She'd had quite a few students like them over the years, and although many of them had been troublesome and frustrating to deal with, she also found such students engaging because of their peculiar interests. They were always social outcasts, usually ignored and sometimes persecuted, and that broke her heart.

But she steeled herself and proceeded with her plans to derail Otis and Ava, telling herself it was for a good cause. She steered Ava away from her studies and toward the trashy world of modeling and shallow self-absorption. Otis she would merely expose by writing a letter to the EPA. There was all kinds of illegal stuff in that shed. She didn't have to be a Nobel Prize–winning scientist to tell that.

Vic she felt little to no sympathy for. He was

detached from his family, and nothing that went on in his house seemed to affect him. Vic was a cretin not to realize what he had. Work would be the best place to get him, so she signed on to be a scorer at FTA. She would cause as much trouble there as best she could.

Caroline was a neurotic, insecure woman, obsessed with Ava and merely tolerating everyone else. She was in desperate need of someone to help her and support her, the way her husband should've been doing, but Marylou did not intend to be that person. The best thing to do to Caroline, Marylou decided, was to pretend to be helpful and supportive but all the while work behind the scenes to poison everything Caroline took for granted.

Vic and Caroline needed to shit or get off the pot, as Teddy would've said. Their marriage stank to high heaven, but she wasn't going to be the one to point this out to them. Let them wallow in their own filth while she dirtied the rest of their nest.

Of course she would have to make sure that, while she was doing her dirty deeds, the family would tolerate her, even want her around. In the long run, it probably would work in her favor that she'd left Suzi alone at Dunkin' Donuts—it had established, in the minds of the Witherspoon family, that she was scatterbrained, which could come in handy later on. The truth was, she was the furthest thing from scatterbrained. Well, maybe not the furthest thing. But none of the Spriggs family members—except Wilson whom she'd told outright that she planned to kill him but it didn't seem to faze him a bit—suspected that she was guilty of anything but being a pathetic and annoying busybody. They did probably suspect her of locking Wilson in the shed, but they'd never said anything to her about that. And Wilson, she knew, would never tell on her. He seemed not to care how badly she treated him or how much she threatened him.

In addition to her crushing-his-family agenda, she kept up her efforts to make him remember. Even though she reminded him every so often that she planned to kill him, he willingly climbed into her car. She took him to Barnes & Noble, "for a treat," she told Caroline; and the two of them sat in the coffee shop for an hour and a half while she showed him books about the horrors of radiation. He sipped his café mocha and nodded, not even bothering to defend radiation, glancing around at the other café customers, especially the young pretty college women bent over their fashion magazines. Finally he announced that it had been a real pleasure talking to her, but didn't they have any lighter reading material available at this bookstore?

Another day she took him to a nearby park, and they sat on a bench in the shade and watched the kids and their parents play on the thick plastic slides and jungle gyms, all connected to big plastic fortlike contraptions, so unlike the thin metal playground equipment Helen had enjoyed. And no more concrete under the equipment—now it was poky, splintery fresh-smelling cedar chips. Marylou spotted a little girl with long blond hair and fair skin like Helen's and pointed her out to Wilson and reminded him again that he'd killed Helen. "Who is Helen?" he asked her. She'd told him a million times, but she'd try again. How could she begin to describe Helen?

She told him about how Helen used to love playgrounds and that there was one near their house in Overton Park with an old shell of a fire truck in it that Helen loved beyond reason when she was four, loved sitting in it and turning the wheel and making the siren noise, and she'd really wanted to be a fireman, and Teddy bought her a fire hat and toy fire trucks and books about fire trucks even though Marylou didn't approve of encouraging something that a girl could never do, and had actually told Helen one night at dinner that girls could never be firemen, and Helen had physically attacked her mother, calling her a liar. The next day Helen threw away all her fire-related items, and now Marylou regretted saying such a thing to Helen, for all kinds of reasons, because of course today she could've been a firefighter if she'd wanted to be, but beyond that, why had she felt compelled to throw water on Helen's dream? This wasn't the kind of memory Marylou wanted to relive about Helen, and had never told anyone about this before, and in fact she never spoke about Helen anymore to anybody.

She realized she was trembling and then realized, that, sweet Jesus, Adolf was actually holding her hand, and she was letting him. She screeched and flung his hand aside.

Kids stopped their play and turned toward Marylou and Wilson.

"Are you all right?" said the nearest mother, wearing the playground mother's uniform of baggy shorts and baggy T-shirt. Cedar chips hung from the front of her shirt.

"Ants," Marylou said, brushing off her hand. "I got rid of them."

After the playground got busy again, Wilson spoke up. "I remember that fire engine," he said. "I used to take Caroline to Overton Park every Saturday, when she was in elementary school. She howled when she had to get off the swings. Remember that big monkey they had there in the late sixties, in the zoo, the one that used to get mouthfuls of water and spit on people? After he started doing that he disappeared. Wonder what they did with him. Poor bastard."

Marylou did remember that monkey. He was as big as she was. "He probably got used in a radiation experiment," she said. She grabbed Wilson's upper arm and squeezed it hard. "No, wait. You only used humans for those."

"The zoo was never the same after he left," was all Wilson said.

"I could spit on you, if it would make you feel better."

"No thanks. Don't think it would."

One Sunday she took Wilson to Genesis Church along with Suzi, hoping he'd feel the need to repent, but afterward he claimed that the sound system had screwed up his hearing aid and he couldn't make heads or tails of what they were singing and saying. "All sounded like caterwauling to me," he said.

Another time, in the evening, she took him for a walk around the neighborhood and as they were plodding down Nun's Drive, him walking twice as slow as she was, she got an idea and stopped. "Just wait here," she told him.

"What? Why?" It was nearly dark, and the crickets were striking up their chorus.

She pointed at a nearby house, no lights on, no cars in the drive. "Got to run ask my friend something. Be right back."

She marched up the driveway as quickly as she could with her stiff ankle and gimpy hip. Fortunately her "friend" didn't seem to have a dog. The back of the house was dark, too. How could she possibly explain herself if someone caught her? She was sneaking around just like the person who climbed up on her roof at night. She would hide back here until Wilson wandered away.

Suddenly, motion lights came on over the patio like a play was about to start, and she ducked into the shadows. That metal patio furniture. Bright colored chairs with backs like oyster shells. And a brick fireplace with a spit. She hadn't seen chairs like that, or a fireplace like that, in years. Not since the fifties, not since that horrible patio party at Teddy's boss's house.

She hadn't wanted to go to the damn party in the first place, mostly because she didn't know anyone there. When they arrived, there were three couples sitting in the same kind of metal chairs on the flagstone patio—much like this one—drinking orange-colored drinks with cherries and colored umbrellas floating in them. Two of the men were dark, hairy, and bespeckled, just like she expected engineers to look, but the third man was blond and tanned like a country clubber. He was Teddy's boss. The women were a bit harder to categorize. One wife was young, dark, and overmade-up. She was smoking a cigarette and scowling. Another wife was fat, fair, and pleased with herself. The third wife was old and wrinkly with white hair—she looked as old as a grandmother, though probably she was only fifty. It was impossible to figure out who went with whom.

The bossman stood up to shake their hands. His wife, it turned out, was the overmade-up smoking woman. She stubbed out her cigarette in a huge pink ceramic ashtray and asked them if they wanted mimosas, gesturing at a big glass pitcher on a white metal table.

Teddy asked for Coke, Marylou for lemonade. They were Baptists, after all.

"Oh, come on, drink a real drink!" cried Mrs. Boss. It appeared that Mrs. Boss had had a few mimosas already.

Teddy glanced at Marylou, then shrugged. "Guess it wouldn't hurt none. Never had one of those things."

Marylou felt annoyed by how quickly he gave in. "I don't drink," she said. "But thank you."

Mrs. Boss poured Teddy's drink in a tall fluted glass, dropped an umbrella and a cherry into it and handed it to him. Then she went into the house for a few minutes and returned with a clear, fizzy drink in a plastic tumbler for Marylou. No cherry or umbrella for her! "Tonic water," Mrs. Boss said out of the side of her mouth.

Teddy sipped his mimosa and exclaimed about how good it was.

"Invented at the Ritz in Paris," Mrs. Boss said. "Over there, we drank mimosas in the morning, but what the hell. I say they're good anytime."

"Buck's fizz," said Bossman. "That's what the British call them."

"A manmosa has beer instead of champagne," added one of the hairy men. "Ever tried it that way?" he asked his boss, who shook his head.

"Uggh," said Mrs. Boss, swinging her bare, tanned leg. "Sounds disgusting."

Marylou, feeling swollen and pale and unsophisticated, sat in a springy metal chair, sipping her bitter, bubbly tonic water. She was plainly pregnant, wearing a ruffly flowered maternity dress, but nobody asked her about her baby. Nobody seemed interested. Instead they discussed some of the people they worked with, one of whom had just been arrested for indecent exposure at the Memphis Zoo, a scandal everyone but her seemed to know all about. So the next time around she accepted one of the mimosas. Mrs. Boss—Vivian?—poured more drinks for everyone, announcing that there was another pitcher waiting in the fridge.

Charcoal was smoking in the fireplace grill in the corner of the patio, but nobody was paying any attention to it, and there wasn't any meat in evidence. There weren't any finger foods or snacks available either. What kind of cookout was this? Marylou slurped down her drink, and had another and another, and by the end of the evening she and Vivian were lying in the yard sticking their stockinged legs up in the air, talking about how they were hanging off the side of the world! Wheee! Teddy had had to carry her home.

Nowadays pregnant women knew better. What kind of damage had she done to Helen that night? Maybe all those mimosas had contributed to Helen's cancer as well.

The motion lights went dark. Play over. The end. Marylou was back in Tallahassee, trespassing in some stranger's backyard. She crept around the side of the house, a two story with aluminum siding, and peeked around the corner. Wilson, damn him, was standing there, under the streetlight, where she'd left him. She stepped behind a prickly waist-high holly hedge and watched him, not minding the mosquitoes whining around her face. As long as she wasn't standing on a fire ant nest, she could stand there forever.

He glanced left, then right. Somebody down the street slammed a car door. A bat swooped in a figure eight under the streetlight, but he didn't appear to notice. He probably had no idea where he was or what he was doing there. Finally, he backed up and lowered himself down onto the edge of the lawn that sloped right up to where she was hiding.

She could sneak away now, walk back home, and it might be a while before anyone found him.

But someone would find him, eventually, and eventually he'd be returned to his proper owner. His family would be very angry at her, but she might worm herself out of being blamed, since they seemed to be willing to believe anything that made their lives easier. But *he* wouldn't care. Either he'd remember and forgive her, or he'd forget. Exasperating creature. She watched him a while longer, his white shirt and white hair glowing under the streetlight. The sharp smell of gasoline wafted up from the nearby garage. Her ankle went from stiff to achy. A car with rock music blasting came rushing past him, too close, but he didn't budge. She didn't feel sorry for him, she didn't. But this wasn't any fun.

Without deciding to, she broke through the hedge and strolled boldly down the strange lawn toward him, the ground soft from armadillo tunnels, praying she wouldn't slip and fall. Hello, Canterbury Hills, I am making myself right at home here! "Yoo-hoo," she called to Wilson. "Avon calling!"

He didn't turn around. He didn't even glance at her.

"Ready?" she said in a chipper voice. "My friend, Vivian, Viv, was making mimosas and wouldn't give me one." His legs stuck straight out in front of him, like a kid's legs. Her white tennis shoes were half the size of his. "You got big feet. But then so does Viv."

His cheeks were well shaven and smooth for an old man, but he smelled like fresh sweat. "Help me up," he said. "Take me home."

Glad that she wasn't yet as old and stiff as he was, she pulled him to his feet and he walked off by himself, a little way down the street, and then turned around, facing her.

"Am I going the right way?" he asked.

"What is this, some existential drama?" she said. "Keep walking and find out."

He exhaled loudly. "Just go ahead and kill me," he said, "if that's what you want to do. I'm right here. Get it over with."

She almost burst out laughing. It was just like her fantasy, the one she'd had the first time she'd seen him in his yard overwatering his azalea bushes, when she wished he'd just pop up and ask to be killed and hurry up about it. "Should I hurry up about it?" she couldn't resist saying.

"Please."

"No. I won't. You can't make me." She went forward, took his arm, and they started down the block in the direction home should've been in. Immediately she felt uneasy. Nun's Drive looked different in the dark. Houses seemed to have rearranged themselves, driveways looked like streets, streets like driveways. Lights in the houses made them seem even more remote. One house had a huge TV, glowing blue and green like an aquarium, that took up most of a wall.

Two large-sounding dogs in someone's backyard barked ferociously. He was leaning on her, making it hard to walk. "I've changed my mind about killing you," she said. "But I'm not done with you. You are not off the hook, Adolf."

"Verna Tommy will have left the light on," he said. "She never forgets."

That night Tropical Storm Alberto crept over the Florida Panhandle. The next morning the weather channel reported that near Homosassa two people who did not evacuate required water rescue. And at Egmont Key State Park a woman fell off a boat when a band of showers and surging currents made navigation difficult; her husband and a friend drowned after jumping in to save her without life jackets, though the woman returned safely to the boat.

Marylou went outside into her twig-littered carport to get the newspaper, and she discovered that her blue rug had mysteriously reappeared. A couple of mornings ago it had *disappeared* from the bottom of the steps, and she'd looked all around the yard but couldn't find it. Who, she'd wondered, would want an ugly little Walmart rug? And now it was back in the same place, looking exactly the same. Somebody had come out in a tropical storm to replace the rug, just to make her think she was losing her mind.

It was similar to the mysterious tennis-shoe

thing. One morning Marylou'd found a brand-new pair of men's black Converse sneakers, size 10, on her front porch. She threw them away, but the next morning there was another pair, exactly the same kind and size, in the same place. It might've been the same pair.

Was there some message intended? What did a disappearing and reappearing rug and black tennis shoes mean? She couldn't tell anyone about this stuff, because it sounded crazy. She had no idea who would do such things, but, in her moments of paranoia, Marylou suspected that it must be someone who saw beneath her nice old lady exterior and was trying, in the creepiest sort of way, to let her know that she wasn't fooling everyone.

CHAPTER 8 *Vic*

Alberto. What a wimp. And Vic had had such high hopes for him.

On June 8 he'd watched baby Alberto hatch in the western Caribbean, held his breath as the baby burst out of his red egg, causing a colorful disturbance on Vic's computer screen as he crawled slowly northwest, fed by sweet winds. By June 10, toddling around Cuba, Alberto had blossomed into a tropical depression, and his predicted path was smack-dab into Florida's

Gulf Coast. When he read this forecast, Vic, down in his basement closet, silently raised his fist in celebration.

Vic's boy wobbled in the Yucatán Channel—increased wind shear—but he hung tough. On June 11, a red-letter day, he intensified into Tropical Storm Alberto, and Floridians started paying him the attention he deserved. It was hard for Vic to discuss the lad with family and friends and not sound gleeful. And then, praise be, on June 12, the NHC predicted that Alberto would attain hurricane status before he made landfall—in the Big Bend, the armpit of Florida, near Tallahassee! Vic celebrated by having three beers after dinner. But, alas, on June 13, Alberto, weakened due to an infusion of dry air, came straggling ashore fifty miles southeast of Tallahassee, near St. Marks. He remained just a run-of-the mill storm—undernourished and undistinguished.

Yeah, sure, there was flooding, storm surge, downed trees, power outages, and Alberto fathered a few impotent tornadoes; but all in all, he turned out to be a disappointment, an underachiever, a failure. Utterly forgettable.

Meanwhile, there was the rest of his life, which at that time was the portfolio project. Vic's other baby.

The portfolios included samples of each student's work in the subjects they took—lab write-ups, essays, the solutions to story problems, the whole shebang. Scoring them was a bitch, and it was Vic's job to try to figure out how to train people to do that scoring as fast and accurately as possible. Otherwise, students (and ultimately their teachers and their schools) would be assessed on the basis of nothing other than standardized tests.

Portfolios from ten pilot high schools were pouring into FTA offices. Vic and his staff had to read through some of the writing samples and, for each subject area, assemble the packets that they could use as examples to train their scorers with. Vic had persuaded his supervisor that Gigi, with her Ph.D. in English, would be an excellent person to train the language arts scorers. He finagled her a temporary raise. Since Vic was a language arts person himself, he would help Gigi.

Vic and Gigi spent hours alone in a conference room piled high with cardboard boxes labeled Language Arts with the name of the high school written underneath, reading through hundreds of writing samples to find examples of different ways a student could get a score of one, two, three, and so on, so that they could photocopy the samples for training packets. Sometimes they read the papers aloud to each other or asked the other one's opinion on what score a certain paper should get, and in between reading and discussing student work they talked about themselves and their families and graduate school and their lives since graduate school.

In the hallway, outside the open door of the conference room, there periodically came the deep buzzing sound of somebody pressing a button on the soda machine and the clunk, clunk, clunk of a can of soda falling down the chute and then the trickling clink, clink, clink of coins in the change slot. It was pathetic how much Vic loved hearing those sounds when that machine was buzzing and clunking and clicking for him and now, for Gigi, too.

Gigi sipped her fresh Diet Coke and Vic cracked open his Mountain Dew, and the dreary green walls of the windowless conference room and the fake wood tables and the chemical smell of industrial carpet and the frigid recycled air—everything was transformed into something magical by the presence of Gigi, with her wild mane of hair and dark blue eyes and lively personality. Vic's life had gone from shades of gray to Technicolor. He felt like he was back in graduate school, when he and his fellow strivers used to go out for beer and gossip and to flirt and argue and dance. He hadn't realized how much he'd missed it.

Sitting across from each other at the end of a long table, surrounded by the manila folders that Vic saw in his sleep, they talked about the

American Lit. professor they'd had who thought every short story had a hidden key planted by the author that unlocked all the meaning, and the Modern American Poetry professor who only wanted to discuss the boring dreams she'd had the previous night, and the grad student who wrote stories about a young man (much like himself) who hitchhiked around America, sleeping with women and causing their long-awaited menstruation cycles to magically resume.

Gigi updated Vic on her love life. She'd been married and divorced—her second marriage—since graduate school. She wasn't seeing anyone at present, because she'd gotten very choosy. She was over forty and she didn't want to waste any more time on losers. Both her husbands had been alcoholics, and she wasn't going to make that mistake again.

"Travis has problems," Gigi said. "He gave me so much grief in high school. Talking ugly, punching holes in walls. Refusing to get out of bed. The doctors didn't know what was wrong with him. Oh, they *said* they knew. Slapped disorders on him left and right. ADD, ODD, OCD, bipolar. You ever wonder if we're doing the right thing, getting our children saddled with all these labels? Seems like every other person has Asperger's these days. Hell, Travis might even have it. I sent him to one of those support groups just to see if he felt comfortable with those people."

Vic suggested she call Caroline for advice. He didn't really feel competent giving advice about Asperger's, and he didn't want to waste precious time with Gigi, talking about Asperger's. He was sick to death of Asperger's. Sometimes he wished old Hans Asperger had never been born. Vic didn't even like to speak the A-word aloud to people not in the know. It usually elicited either chuckles ("Did you say *ass* something?") or blank stares. And the word *autistic* was even worse, as it conjured up head-banging devil children. But Caroline never hesitated to throw those A-words out like firecrackers. Although she wouldn't admit it, she enjoyed the disturbance those words caused. If asked why she brought it up with people, she would say that she was only making people aware so that they'd be more sympathetic to Ava and Otis, cut them some slack, realize that they weren't just weird but weird for a reason.

But Vic would argue with her. We're all on the spectrum somewhere. Why label people? We're all weird. And aren't people with obsessions more interesting than those who have no idea what they like? Some people turn their obsessions into great careers. About the social problems. Who doesn't just not "get it" sometimes? Some of us are more "typical" than others, that's all.

So Vic, sitting in the suddenly cozy conference room with Gigi, finding himself unwilling to waste time deconstructing Asperger's with Gigi, segued into Ava's obsession with Elvis, thinking Gigi would find it as bizarre as he did.

The thing about Gigi was, he could never predict how she'd respond to a question or what take she'd have on a situation or a subject. Of course, if he'd been married to her for twenty years, she might have been as predictable as he found his wife to be. But he realized that he didn't really know Gigi well at all, and he wanted to remedy this situation. He looked forward to hearing what she had to say, even if she disagreed with him.

"I suppose you like Bob Dylan better," was Gigi's response to his complaining about having to listen to Elvis music nonstop.

"Well, yeah. He wrote his own songs, for one thing."

"Dylan was a poseur! Rich Jewish kid pretending to be an Oakie. He did write some great songs. It's apples and oranges, anyhow. Elvis was an interpreter. He drew from all sorts of music and put his own stamp on it."

"He didn't have such hot taste. 'In the Ghetto'? Come on." Vic was surprised to find himself feeling energized, and it wasn't just the Mountain Dew. Unlike the spats with his family, he was actually enjoying this little tiff with Gigi.

Gigi tossed her loosely curled blond hair over her shoulders. High-maintenance hair, Caroline called it. Caroline had recently cut her hair short and stopped coloring it. It was her hair—she could do what she wanted to with it—but looking at Caroline's gray streaks made him feel old.

"Here's the thing," Gigi told him. "Elvis didn't get access to some really good songs because the Colonel insisted that Elvis get all the royalties. You have to understand Elvis's background to understand why he didn't fight the Colonel. You're just like everyone else who doesn't like Elvis because he was white and Southern." She poked Vic in the chest with her well-manicured index finger. "Face it, Vic Witherspoon. You are a snob."

Vic swatted her finger away. "Didn't know you were such an Elvis fan."

"I'm not," she said. "It's just my duty to fight Yankee misconceptions. I'm a Johnny Cash fan, myself. Now. Listen up. Is this a good example of a three?" She held up an essay and read a pitiful little movie review of *The Incredibles* that was four sentences long. The first sentence said, "Listen up, dudes and dudettes," and the last sentence said, "You just gotta see the movie your own self!"

"Any misspellings? How's the punctuation?" Vic asked her. "It might be more of a two."

"I can't bear to give this poor kid a two," she said. "He's got some flair."

"How do you know it's a he?"

"This is a three or I'm walking right out of here."

Vic swept his hand toward the door. "Feel free. Dudette."

She checked her big red watch. "How long till happy hour? Can you go out after work for one drink?"

"Maybe. Just one."

Gigi, who must've picked up on his reluctance, smoothly shifted gears and asked about Suzi's knee injury. "Must be hard on *all* of you," she said.

Vic felt she'd seen through him, knew that he cared too much about Suzi's soccer career. He had yet to inform the director of the Olympic Development soccer camp that Suzi wasn't going to be there. He read their thrice weekly e-mails, enthusing about the upcoming camp, the outstanding coaches, the successes of former campers. He just wasn't ready to give it all up yet. "Actually, Suzi's doing really well," he lied. "She's been going to church with Nancy Archer. That church where your brother is a minister."

"Suzi has too much common sense to fall for that nonsense. How's Oats?" Gigi used Suzi's baby nickname for Otis.

"Oats is Oats." Vic told her about the smoke

detectors, and about how he'd just seen Otis taking a box of old alarm clocks into the shed.

"What's he doing with old clocks?"

"It's a big secret." Vic was ashamed to let people know how little he really communicated with his son. His only son. He *wanted* to communicate with him. He *tried*. Just last week he'd taken Otis to see *X-Men*, but during the previews Otis exploded when Vic gently pressed him about exactly what he was doing with the smoke detectors and clocks. Otis got up and stormed out of the theater before the movie'd even started.

The only thing Otis really cared about was science, and it had always been Wilson, not Vic, who'd encouraged Otis in his scientific endeavors. Vic was a liberal arts person, so he'd readily allowed Wilson to step in. When Otis was little, Wilson sent him an endless supply of mechanical things: robots, model kits, radios, tape recorders. Otis spent hours taking things apart and reassembling them to see how they worked. He strung together batteries to use as a power source for an electric blanket on Boy Scout camping trips. He fashioned a battery-powered skateboard that Caroline had to confiscate after he fell and split his head open. At one point Wilson sent Otis an old book called *The Golden Book of Chemistry Experiments*. Otis started experimenting with all sorts of chemicals and even made some chloroform that he administered to Suzi, which knocked her out cold. *The Golden Book* was sent back to his grandfather. Now, apparently, it was something to do with smoke detectors and alarm clocks.

Gigi kept talking. “Maybe Oats plans to hide those clocks around your house and set them for different times. Wake up, people! It’s happy hour!”

“Not yet,” Vic warned her, and opened another student essay, this one entitled “The Terrible Trip.”

“Hey,” she said in a quieter voice, leaning toward Vic. “Bring Avie out for a riding lesson this weekend. I miss her.”

Vic said that he would. Gigi asking about his children reminded him of where his true priorities lay—that they weren’t here, and they weren’t with Gigi—and after a while he realized that the conference room had lost its magical sheen and had been restored to its drab state; and as usual, he couldn’t wait to get the hell out of there. He told Gigi he’d be skipping happy hour, explaining that Suzi would need him at home.

In late afternoon, sunlight hung in columns through the canopy trees on Live Oak Plantation Road, which, because they spread out so graciously, never made Vic feel claustrophobic, even though he’d grown up on the prairies of the Midwest. And, turning into Canterbury Hills, he was struck once again by how much he loved his neighborhood, the sheer ordinariness of it. It was the sort of neighborhood he'd always dreamed of living in.

Vic grew up in a house in West Branch, Iowa, that looked, from the outside, as if it had been abandoned. Until he got old enough to mow the grass, it grew so high that the neighbors called a lawn service and took up collections to pay for it. His father, who was always reading and writing and teaching, never seemed to notice the grass at all. And then there was his mother's rock collection. These weren't little rocks, or even hunks of interesting and unusual minerals, but big ugly gray-brown boulders she carted home from rivers and creeks in their aged station wagon. She dropped these monstrosities randomly around their overgrown yard, which made mowing even harder for anyone who dared to try it. The Fortress, people called their house.

Vic bided his time until he could get out. He enjoyed his afternoon paper route because he loved studying other people's neat little homes; smelling the dryer lint from their laundry rooms; imagining the quiet, mundane lives that were lived within. He bet nobody in those houses accidentally fried eggs in a frying pan lined with motor oil as his mother once did after his father had used the pan to catch oil draining from the station wagon.

For years Vic had congratulated himself on the splendid, impulsive idea he'd had of applying to graduate school at FSU. He'd been working in marketing and publicity at the University of Iowa Press, and one snowy day, eating his tasteless sandwich in the lunchroom, he'd happened upon a spread in an old *National Geographic* about Maclay Gardens in Tallahassee and Iowa was all over for him. And he'd never been sorry about leaving the Midwest behind. Tallahassee was great! Florida was great! Why would anyone not want to live here? Of course, some sourpusses might take issue with not only the hurricanes and rising insurance rates and rampant, heedless development and lack of state money for education and Governor Jeb Bush and fire ants and palmetto bugs and alligators and vicious exotic pets turned loose and humidity and heat and March, which, although breathtakingly lovely, was when spring breakers and serial killers and long-lost friends and relatives descended upon the Sunshine State. But most of the time Vic didn't care about any of that, because every place had its drawbacks, and he loved living in Florida.

And there was his very own yellow brick house with the white picket fence, the smooth carpet of St. Augustine grass that, for some reason, this summer, didn't sport even a patch of brown fungus. If a big hurricane came and washed his house away, he would miss it. He truly would. As he pulled in behind the house and parked the car at the bottom of the driveway he felt a bittersweet tang, as if his house were already gone.

For Vic, being around Suzi had always been relaxing, like sitting in front of a fire, basking in the warm glow of her competency. Not that she was always easy to be around, by any means. But up until she hurt her knee, she'd been on a steady course—good grades, excelling at sports, and friendships—whereas Ava and Otis were much loopier and uncertain in their passage through the days. They got A's in some subjects and F's in others, could flawlessly recite their lines in *Guys and Dolls* but had trouble cutting up their meat. In a conversation with Ava and Otis, you never knew, from one minute to the next, whether they'd approach you eagerly or flail and curse at you. And being around them out in public, watching them interact with other kids, Vic always felt on edge, expecting a misstep and hating himself for it, overwhelmed one moment with pity, the next with pride, his hopes rising and plummeting. There was always distance between himself and his older two children, even though he loved them with all his heart. With them he always had to think before he said or did anything; and because being with them often felt like work, he'd gradually started spending more time with Suzi. He wasn't proud of this fact, but there it was.

That's why he depended so much on Suzi to be the calm center of his life. Watching her decline was extremely disturbing.

That evening after work, when he went into her messy room and sat on the bed beside her, she merely glanced at him and went back to staring up at the swiveling ceiling fan. She wore her shorty pj's with fairies on them and had an old polyester afghan she'd dug out of the back of the closet covering her injured knee.

Vic worried about leaving her at home all day, because her mother was too busy with Wilson and Ava to pay much attention to her. Oh, Suzi could take care of herself. It wasn't that. On one occasion, years ago, when Suzi and Ava and Otis had, for one time only, an incompetent babysitter who did nothing but sit on her butt and watch TV all evening, occasionally going outside to call her boyfriend and smoke a cigarette, eight-year-old Suzi made dinner for herself and Ava and Otis—sandwiches and cheese grits and a fruit salad—then put the leftovers away and washed the dishes, took a bath, and put herself to bed. "I figured I was second in command," she told us later. It didn't occur to Ava or Otis to step in and take over, or even help.

Vic reached over and stroked Suzi's unkempt, curly hair.

She flinched, the way Ava always did when he tried to touch her.

"What've you been doing today?"

"Praying about my knee. It's not working."

Vic decided to leave that one alone. "Help me make something for supper."

"Where's Mom?" Suzi said accusingly, like he was keeping her mother away.

"They won't be home from therapy till seven."

"Figures."

"Want to bake some cookies?"

"You don't get it," she said loudly. "My knee hurts!"

Vic knew he should stop pushing her, but he couldn't seem to shut up. "You'll feel better if you get up and move around some. And your knee will heal faster."

In response, she rolled over and faced the wall. "I. Don't. Want. To. Do. *Anything*."

Vic found himself wanting to yell at her, shake her. Stop this at once! You're my only normal child and you'd better stay that way! Then another voice, a wiser voice, came over the loudspeaker in his head: Get away from your child. Now.

He ducked out of her room and into his own, changed into shorts and a T-shirt, grabbed a can of sparkling water from the fridge—no beer left! Should've gone to happy hour—then went out back to sit on the screened porch, under the ceiling fan, which was uselessly paddling the turgid air. It was the golden time of day, mellow spotlights of sun gleaming between the branches of the live oak trees. Quiet except for the squirrels chittering in the limbs and the whine of a distant leaf blower. It was so hot out there in the summer that he always had this second story porch to himself. His own little tree house. Down below, Otis's white shed looked like the hut of a fairy-tale creature.

Their backyard was so totally enclosed by trees and shrubbery, they could cavort around naked if they were so inclined. Caroline had done that very thing one morning, peeling off her sweaty clothes after her run. She'd never do anything like that now, not since her body had decided to betray her by aging, but he wished she would. He would take off his own clothes and join her. He pictured the two of them, frolicking in the backyard, a gleeful, world-weary middle-aged Adam and Eve who'd returned for a second honeymoon in a much smaller, homelier Garden of Eden. If he told Caroline about this fantasy, she'd either bring up dirty laundry or laugh her head off.

The longer Vic sat there, sipping the unsatisfying sparkling water, the more he became aware of the work that needed to be done all around him. The porch smelled musty and the screens looked green. He needed to pressure wash again, needed to replace some mushy boards on the deck, and repaint the whole thing. But before he did any of that he would check the NHC Web site.

"Daddy." Suzi stood in the doorway, flushed and disheveled but determined, leaning on her crutches. "I'm sorry. I want to make cookies."

"I'm sorry, too," Vic said, rising out of the wicker chair.

"For what? You didn't do anything."

How could he even begin to explain what all he was sorry about? He was sorry she'd hurt her knee, sorry that he depended on her to prop him up, sorry that she'd been stuck in the role of the "only normal kid in the family." He was sorry that poor Wilson had had to come live with them and that poor Ava and Otis had Asperger's and sorry that his marriage had gone south and that he missed the days when it was just him and Caroline and sorry because Caroline felt so besieged and that he felt so inadequate that he was counting on a hurricane to blow their problems away. He was sorry that his life was slipping away while he sat on the porch feeling sorry. He was sorry that he was such a sorry son of a bitch.

"Forget it," he told Suzi. "How about peanut butter with chocolate chips?"

Gigi and Vic were finishing up the training packets—six example packets and six testing packets. The readers had been hired by Human Resources and would show up at FTA the following day, ready to be trained.

Vic was not only helping Gigi make up her packets but also supervising the other test specialists in math, science, and social studies, and he needed to go over their training packets with them later that day. He and Gigi were taking too long to make hers up, because, basically, she couldn't keep her mind on the task.

"If I have to read one more review of *The Incredibles* I'm going to kill myself," Gigi said. There were entire classes at one high school that had written reviews of *The Incredibles.* "I've never seen that movie and I never will. Just the thought of it makes me sick."

Vic smiled at her and picked up another essay to read.

Gigi pulled up the hood of her green sweater. "It's like a refrigerator in here," she said. "Aren't you cold?"

Because Vic wasn't seeing any bigwigs that day, he was wearing shorts and a polo shirt. He was cold, but it did no good to complain, because that's the way management liked it. "Get some coffee," he told her.

She shrugged. "Almost lunchtime."

The bank of fluorescent lights above them emitted a high-pitched buzz. Vic's left big toe throbbed. He wriggled it against the bumpy rubber sole of his sandal. Gigi's horse Cisco Kid had stepped on it. He'd been holding Cisco while Ava tightened his girth, and the dumb horse moved sideways, planting his hoof on Vic's sneakered foot. He hoped the nail wouldn't turn black and fall off.

"How can you stand doing this day after day?" Gigi blurted out.

"I do it with half my brain tied behind me."

"Is that any way to go through life?"

Why had he asked Gigi to work with him again? She hated work. She didn't know how to work. She didn't need to work. Her family had money. "We're not all independently wealthy," Vic told her.

Gigi spread her hands to check out her pink fingernails. She had beautiful hands, but they looked pale and cold. Vic could take hold of her hands, warm them for her. "Actually, I'm broke," she said. "I need this job."

"Your idea of broke is different from mine," Vic said.

She shrugged. "I'm going to teach more riding lessons, too. That ought to help."

She'd insisted he not pay her for Ava's lesson on Cisco Kid, so he'd offered to take her out to dinner sometime instead. It had been wonderful to watch Ava's total absorption while she rode and her straight posture as she posted around the ring. And he'd enjoyed seeing another side of

Gigi—the competent horsewoman, passing on her knowledge, neither one of them paying the least bit of attention to Vic. Despite the heat, it would have been a perfect afternoon except for three things: 1. Caroline had not wanted Ava to go because she was worried about her having another fall, so Vic and Ava had had to spend way too much time talking Caroline down; 2. During the lesson Travis, Gigi's son, had plopped down in the lawn chair beside his and had talked unceasingly about horse manure while staring at Ava; and 3. A horse had smashed his toe.

Vic's next paper was about the philosophy behind *The Little Engine That Could* and how it had helped the writer achieve her goal to become class president.

"Here's a perfect three," Gigi crowed, waving her paper at him. "A narrative that's all dialogue. It's a tree talking to a bird."

"Funny."

"Want to read it?"

"No." He wanted to put his head down on the desk and sleep.

Gigi smacked her lips and picked up another essay. "Yeah. Okay. This one's about *1984*. When are they going to put that book to rest? All it is, is an anticommunist manifesto." She spoke in a Valley girl voice. "Like, it's so cold war!"

Vic wasn't looking at her. He was trying to

make sense of the lines on the page in front of him. “Dear Sir,” the letter began. “I have some suggestions for alternative power sources that you may be interested in hearing about.” No, actually, I’m not, he silently answered the student, then told Gigi, “Let’s just read the fucking essays or we’ll be here all night.”

There was a few minutes of strained but blessed silence.

Gigi couldn’t keep quiet. “Vic,” she said, and waited until he finally glanced up at her. Her face was framed by the hood of her sweater, tendrils of blond hair wisping around her face. Little Green Riding Hood. “Is your toe bothering you?” She smiled at him, and he felt bad for being so cranky.

His toe, actually, was killing him. “Little Italy for lunch?” he asked her.

“You’re on. I’m gonna take me a bath in a hot bowl of pasta.”

The image of Gigi, naked, in a bowl of pasta, like a kind of old-timey black-and-white photo, filled his head and warmed him right up.

The following day they began training the newly hired temps who would score the sample portfolios. Gigi trained the Language Arts people, Ed did Science, Carol did Math, Sandra did Social Studies. Vic went from one conference room to the next, observing, answering questions when he needed to, making sure everything went well. The scorers were overeducated and underemployed, some of them mentally unstable (those people usually left after a few days), some of them happy to be out of the house and eager to stay out (these people tried to impress him at every turn, thinking that they might get a real job at FTA), some of them angry about being smarter than the trainers but having to score portfolios in an assembly line at two dollars over minimum wage. These people often challenged the trainers and had to be dealt with.

When Vic walked into the conference room as Gigi was getting ready to start the training, he did a quick inventory of the scorers and noticed many familiar faces, old hands who helped out on every project, and there in the back row, Nancy Archer, her accoutrements spread out around her—coffee mug, pens, pencils, notepad. She looked like a regal but mischievous queen. She waved at Vic, claiming their special relationship in front of God and everyone. He nodded at Nance, thinking, Oh shit. He remembered telling her about the project, suggesting that she might want to score, but never thought she'd actually follow through.

He sat down in the back of the room to watch Gigi—wearing a low-cut, sleeveless dress, high heels, and big hoop earrings—explain the training packets to the scorers. As soon as she'd finished, three of the scorers—an African American ex-military fellow, a young greasy-haired Harley type, and Nancy Archer—banded together to challenge her.

"Why's 'My Big Fat Halloween Party' a three and 'Lost in Kentucky' only a two?" Harley asked Gigi. " 'Lost in Kentucky' at least has a voice."

"I used to be an English teacher," Nancy said, "for twenty-five years. And I *never* would've given 'My Big Fat Halloween Party' a C, which is what a three is—am I right?"

Military Man read Gigi's rubric back to her in a sarcastic voice, and then waited for her to defend her scores.

Gigi kept glancing at Vic, her eyes panicky like a horse's. He nodded encouragingly at her, but even though they'd discussed the reasons they'd given the papers their scores, she didn't seem to remember their rationale. She stammered and blushed and giggled. "Well, let me think. I *know* I had a good reason. Can anybody help me out here?"

The rebels saw they were getting to her and stepped up their attack. How had this woman ever taught when she was a graduate student? Was she falling apart because Vic was there, watching her? He finally stood up and sent everyone on break.

Vic planned to spend half an hour with the

upstarts in his office, the three unhappy know-it-alls, letting them know, in the nicest way possible, that they were completely replaceable.

He spoke first to Military Man and then Harley, who both left his office in a huff and quit the project, and saved Nance for last. He was particularly angry at Nance, whom he felt was trying to take advantage of the fact that they had a personal connection.

"I'm sorry I upset Gigi," Nance said, sitting across from him. She was wearing a pinstriped jacket with a white bow blouse underneath. "I truly didn't mean to."

Vic flipped the overhead lights on in his office so as to create an official atmosphere. As in, This is a corporation you're dealing with, lady.

"Gigi's a real nice girl," Nance went on. "She's Buff Coffey's sister. I believe I saw you talking to Gigi at the roller rink. Is she a good friend of yours? Is that why she has this job?"

Vic said that Gigi was qualified to be doing what she was doing, having a Ph.D. in English.

"She might be smart," Nance said, "and she's real cute, but I could do a much better job training than she's doing."

Did she think Vic was going to let her take over Gigi's job? The arrogance! And after he'd been so nice to her that evening she came over, defending her against Caroline's sullen attacks.

"Gigi's doing a fine job. You need to give her a

break and not argue with everything she says. We made up those training packets together. I stand by all those scores."

Nance grimaced and raised a hand to her cheek. "I'm *so* sorry. Didn't mean to step on your toes. I didn't realize that you two were a *team*. I thought you were her supervisor."

"I am her supervisor. And we're working together. My toe's already been stepped on." He told her about Gigi's horse stepping on his foot, realizing as he did so that he was only making things worse.

"Oh, I see. I had no idea you two were *together*."

What the hell was wrong with this woman? "We're not *together*. We *work* together."

She swiveled around and gazed at some framed photos on the shelf behind her. "And," she said cheerily, "you're *good friends!*"

"We're friends."

"What a lovely picture of Caroline," Nance said, pointing at one Vic had taken of Caroline, tan legs and big smile, in front of the Grand Canyon, right after they'd graduated from college. With virtually no money, they'd taken the whole summer off to drive out West to places neither of them had ever been before.

Nance persisted. "Is Caroline a friend of Gigi's, too?"

"Mrs. Archer."

"Nance."

"Maybe working on this project isn't the best thing for you. You seem to be very unhappy with it."

"Oh no! I love it so far. I'm so sorry I've offended you. I won't say another word. I'll just score my papers and leave you and Gigi alone."

Vic reluctantly agreed to let her stay on, and Nance returned to the training room with her tail between her legs. She was just desperate for attention, Vic decided. For people to acknowledge that she was smart and knew her stuff. That put her into a category of people that Vic and Gigi could deal with.

That evening, after checking on Suzi and explaining to Caroline that he was dining with "some FTA people" he took Gigi out for dinner.

At one point, at the cozy corner table in Cyprus, surrounded by the elegance, candlelight, and fine wine they felt they deserved after such a hard day; when they were toasting each other with their wineglasses and imitating Nancy Archer and Gigi was looking at him eagerly, as in, Now what? he finally realized where he was headed. He kept hearing Nancy Archer's insinuating voice saying, "You're a team. You're *good* friends."

Vic, like any man his age, had done a few rounds with this problem. He knew full well that you couldn't help who you were attracted to. Forget about willing it away! He'd thought about this problem over the years and had come up with some theories and options and a solution that he thought would keep him on the straight and narrow. He called it Vic Witherspoon's Guide to Doing It and Not Doing It at the Same Time: The All-and-Nothing Approach to Marital Fidelity.

To begin with, attraction just springs up, that dizzying electrical field, and there it is. Attractions are often inappropriate. Usually inappropriate. If you're married, always inappropriate. In said inappropriate situations, he'd come to see, one had a number of choices. The smartest choice, and the one that was often the hardest to make and carry out, was to remove yourself from the company of the attractive person as quickly as you could and never go near her ever again. This was often not possible because of the circumstances that placed you in the path of this person to begin with, for instance, an attraction between coworkers like him and Gigi.

If you *can't* flee the attractive person, you can choose to hang close but not too close to this person, indulging in the glimmering edges of the force field, convinced that nothing's going to happen and that it's perfectly okay because: 1. Nobody else notices, including the person you're attracted to. (Everyone notices.); 2. The feeling is probably only coming from you and so, since it isn't reciprocated, you aren't in any danger of actually acting on it. (If the other person allows you to hang around her, she is attracted to you, too.)

So scratch that option. Here's the best solution he'd come up with, the one that seemed to make the most sense, the one he decided would work with Gigi: You hang around the attractive person *as much* as possible, bathing in the glow, waiting it out, telling yourself that even if the desire between the two of you is mutual and acknowledged, you'll have the power to resist.

This, he thought, was the best solution for two reasons: 1. The more you're around the object of such attraction, the more you're forced to face the fact that she does have a few flaws, a few unappealing qualities, and before long she becomes as ordinary as an old shoe, or your spouse, and you're breathing a sigh of relief that you didn't say what the hell and give in. 2. He'd used this method once, successfully, with another coworker, Wendy, a few years back—ten years, to be exact. Actually, he didn't breathe a sigh of relief until she moved away, but by the time she left most of the sparkle had worn off and she'd transitioned into being just a friend rather than a *friend*. Her pregnancy and the birth of her first child was undoubtedly a factor in the transition, but still.

Full disclosure—he knew the other methods didn't work because of a few slipups, a very few, none of which Caroline knew about. When he turned thirty-five, he'd determined that all that was behind him. The older he got, the more he had to lose, the less compelling became the prospect of upheaval and drama; and even if Caroline never found out, the pining, scheming, euphoria, and the wallowing in guilt would've taken too much out of him. Add to that his intense desire to avoid dueling lawyers; acres of counseling appointments; and most of all, heartbroken children. He'd prefer to just stay home, eat popcorn, and watch all of the above on TV.

So Vic was counting on the all-and-nothing approach with Gigi, because he had no desire to disturb his marriage any more than it was already disturbed—he didn't want to add to the damage that had already been done by the everyday wear and tear of life with three kids, two of them with "disabilities," and an old man with dementia. Also, he was already aware of some of Gigi's flaws: She overdid it with the eyeliner and revealing outfits. Her laugh was too loud and her Southern accent exaggerated. She didn't take the job seriously. She wasn't very good at it. She drank too much.

He told himself that nothing had happened between himself and Gigi at the Cyprus—they ate dinner and drank a lot of wine, hugged good-bye a little too long in the parking lot and went their separate ways. But he never mentioned to Caroline that Gigi was the only other person at the dinner, which broke the cardinal rule of All-and-Nothing—if he couldn't tell his wife about it, it was not nothing.

Later that night, his head heavy with pinot noir, instead of getting into bed where he belonged, he found himself in front of his laptop, checking the NHC Web site to see if there were any new developments, any new storms that might have potential.

There was nothing on his computer screen. Nothing.

Part Four JULY 2006

CHAPTER 9 *Caroline*

On the Fourth of July, at the Canterbury Hills neighborhood pond, Caroline sat on top of a picnic table, her father parked on the seat below her, watching fireworks shooting up from across the muddy water. Vic, looking young and trim in shorts and T-shirt, stood a few feet away, arms folded on his chest. Otis had wanted to stay home and watch the Space Shuttle *Discovery* launching toward the International Space Station, but Caroline had insisted he come out and get some fresh air. He'd walked down to the pond with them but disappeared into the crowd as soon as they got there. Ava and Suzi had better reasons for missing the festivities. Ava's nervous system couldn't tolerate fireworks, and Suzi's knee was giving her trouble.

Kids danced around with sparklers, and the smoke from stink bombs hung like a ceiling overhead. The smoke didn't rise in this humidity. Caroline wore jeans and tennis shoes, because of the mosquitoes and fire ants, but wished she'd worn a sundress and put up with the bites. She despised July Fourth and all the forced gaiety around it, gaiety that required one to endure the heat, eat bad food, and subject oneself to fiery things that banged and popped and had been known to "take out an eye" or "blow off a finger." She felt guilty about hating Independence Day, so she usually went overboard in the opposite direction—baking cupcakes with red, white, and blue icing; organizing a cookout; buying tons of sparklers and snakes; forcing gaiety on everyone else. This year she hadn't bothered with any of it.

Vic had come along only because she'd asked him to, but Caroline was glad he was here. She hadn't had a minute alone with him, and there was something she had to tell him. The other night at her Asperger's RDI group—Relationship Development Intervention—which always met at Caroline's friend Billie's house, a new mom had shown up, a woman who had the kind of straight blond-highlighted pageboy that three quarters of the women in northeastern Tallahassee sported, even though maintaining such a hairstyle in the raging humidity took buckets of time and money and products. This woman quickly let it be known that she didn't want to waste time discussing RDI, or what she called piddle-ass therapy. She wanted to talk about how the mercury in vaccination shots had *ruined* their children. "I'm involved in a lawsuit right now against drug companies," she'd said. "That's where we ought to be directing our energies! We need to be exposing these people. They've ruined thousands of kids with those vaccines. My daughter's life is ruined! My beautiful daughter is ruined!"

What a thing to say about your daughter, Caroline thought, but then realized she'd thought similar things but had never said them aloud. Sometimes, in her darker moments, she wondered if the reason she spent so much time trying to fix Ava was because she couldn't fully love Ava the way she was.

The women in the RDI group had tried to comfort the angry woman and counter her arguments, saying they doubted that the shots were the only cause, if they were a cause at all, and that they'd chosen to put their energy toward doing something to help their children now; but the woman didn't want to hear any of it. There was something about the way the woman went on and on, about her entirely understandable and justifiable but out-of-place anger, that stayed with Caroline and eventually drove her to do some detective work. And she'd unearthed something amazing, which was what she needed to tell Vic about.

Above the Canterbury Hills pond, a huge orange and blue blossom burst in the sky amid cheers and hoots of appreciation. Caroline gave up waiting for Vic to sit down with her, slid off the metal picnic table, and went over to stand beside him. "Listen to this," she began.

She told him how she'd gone snooping through

her father's bedroom and had found a folder in an envelope in one of her father's dresser drawers. The folder was labeled Prenatal Study—Memphis University Medical School. When she opened it, she discovered medical records and typed narratives with her father's name signed at the bottom.

On the papers were names of hundreds of pregnant women who'd been given, in the early fifties, prenatal cocktails containing radioisotopes at the Memphis University Medical School. It was part of a government nutrition study.

She'd known that her dad was involved in some experiments in the fifties, experiments he didn't like to discuss, but she'd had no idea what they were really about. In the folder was correspondence between Wilson Spriggs and someone at the Atomic Energy Commission regarding their radioisotope distribution program, which Dr. Spriggs was taking advantage of. The cocktails given to the pregnant women were made with radioactive iron that came from the Oak Ridge, Tennessee, uranium pile.

From what Caroline could figure out, a random sample of pregnant women visiting the prenatal clinic would have a blood sample drawn on their first visit, radioactive iron administered on the second visit, and finally another blood sample taken on the third visit to determine how much of the iron had been absorbed. The women were told only that they were getting vitamins that would be healthy for them and the baby. No consent forms were signed.

As she finished talking, a spidery, spangly star with tails whiz-banged overhead. "My favorite color!" yelled a nearby kid.

"Sweet Jesus," Vic said. "Your father poisoned all those people."

They both turned toward Wilson, who was holding a lit sparkler someone had given him, holding it like he didn't know what to do with it.

"You don't have to say it that way," she said, knowing how ridiculous it was to defend her father at this point, but she kept on. "They didn't think they were poisoning people. They thought they were helping their country. There was a cold war on! Anyway, I doubt *he* actually gave the women cocktails."

"It was his study," Vic said.

"Yeah. I know."

"I'm sorry," Vic said, finally putting his arm around her and pulling her close. He smelled like beer, but it felt good to be close to him again. When had they stopped hugging, and why, when it was such a comfort? Then he added, "Try to forget about it."

Caroline broke free of his arm.

Her father now sat with his head tilted up, gazing at the latest gold and silver explosion.

"Those people got a settlement," Vic said. "It's over now."

"But it's not over," Caroline said. "It's never over." She forced herself to breathe. "I think Nance was one of those women."

"Really?" She finally had his full attention, although she couldn't see his expression in the dark. "Is her name on the list?"

Caroline had to admit that it wasn't.

"Well then," Vic said. "Have you been talking to Billie again? You two and your conspiracy theories."

"I think she's using a made-up name," Caroline suggested. "I just figured it out after support group the other night. Why Nance showed up here in Tallahassee. I knew there was something too coincidental about her coming here from Memphis and her having gone to the same clinic where Dad worked. For a while I thought she was my real mom!" Caroline made this sound like a joke and hurried through it. "But now I know why she's here. My father killed her daughter. There was a Memphis postmark on the envelope that the papers were in. And her daughter died of bone cancer. She told Suzi."

"Sounds pretty far-fetched," Vic said, and before Caroline could reply, added, "Hey, isn't that Otis?" He pointed at a family sitting on a blanket a couple of yards away.

Actually, there seemed to be a family blanket

and an annex blanket. On the family blanket were Buff and Paula Coffey and their little girl, Angel, all cuddled up close. The older, black-haired, black-outfitted daughter, Rusty, sat cross-legged on the annex blanket with . . . Otis?

"What the hell?" Caroline said. "What's he doing with her?"

"I didn't know they were friends."

"He never tells us anything," Caroline said. "He knows we wouldn't want him hanging out with Rusty."

"Should I go over and talk to him?"

Caroline thought about it. She imagined Otis seeing his father, his embarrassment, his defensiveness. And herself having to talk to Paula Coffey. Being invited to join them. "I'll talk to him later," she said.

Nance lived in a white brick house at the dead end of Reeve's Court. Her front porch was festooned with hanging flower baskets, and there were pots of flowers all over the small front yard. There were rows of flowers along the edge of the house with no weeds in between them. It wasn't until Caroline was standing in front of the door, waiting for Nance to answer the doorbell, that she noticed that the red salvia in the basket nearest her were made of silk. She swiveled around. All the flowers in all the baskets were silk. She peered over the porch railing and studied the flowers down below. She'd stuck plastic flowers in the ground! Then why'd she have that garden hose snaking across the yard? And the full watering can? And she'd eagerly offered to work in their yard, saying she loved yard work! As Caroline was trying to process this, Nance, who was expecting her, answered the door with Buster at her heels, and, smiling, ushered Caroline inside.

The house smelled of ham and cookies baking. Nance, wearing a patio dress and purple tennis shoes, indicated that Caroline should sit on what looked to be a brand-new beige vinyl couch. She disappeared into the kitchen and brought out a plate of homemade peanut butter cookies and glasses of tea with sprigs of fresh mint in them.

She settled in the rocking chair across from Caroline, holding her glass of tea, which she'd wrapped in a yellow cloth napkin, and explained that since she'd been scoring portfolios part-time at FTA and helping out Caroline's family and going to Buff's church every whipstitch, she'd been neglecting her own housekeeping.

Caroline reiterated that they all appreciated everything she was doing to help them, and that she hoped Nance wasn't wearing herself out. And, besides, the house looked clean to Caroline. In fact, the room they were in was not only free of dirt and dust and clutter, but it was also free of personality. Every bit of furniture looked new, large, and beige, even the coffee table and the lamps. Framed photographs were lined up on a low table against the beige wall, but Caroline couldn't get a good look at them. She told Nance that her house looked neat as a pin.

"Don't look too close," Nance said. She had a rather large pecan-shaped head, and she sat up straight as if she had to balance her head on her shoulders, which gave her a dignified air. "I'm trying to get things done round here today," she told Caroline. "If I get distracted, it's all over for me. The TV has to stay off."

"I don't want to take up your time," Caroline said, like a salesperson. "I just wanted to pay you a visit, since you're helping out at our house so much."

Nance didn't respond to this illogical statement. "Well," she said, "there's somebody out there who *doesn't* appreciate me. Has it in for me, seems like. Keeps calling here and hanging up. Lets it ring twice, and then hangs up before caller ID clicks on. They know exactly what they're doing."

"Why would someone do that?"

Nance snorted. "Heck if I know." She told Caroline she'd been hearing strange sounds on the roof at night, like somebody was walking around up there. It drove Buster wild, she said. "Here's the scariest thing," she said, lowering her voice. "The other evening, round eight, I saw someone wearing a Richard Nixon mask peering in the kitchen window at me. I ran outside, but the person had run off. It was a grown person! Couldn't tell whether it was male or female."

"You should call the police," Caroline said. Maybe Nance was closer to totally losing her marbles than she'd thought. "You want me to call them for you?"

"Oh, no, no," Nance said. "They'll just think I'm a crazy old lady. Maybe Vic could come down here and spend the night sometime. He could catch them, I bet."

"Maybe." Vic would never agree to that.

Nance dabbed at her lips with her napkin and set down her glass and uneaten cookie on the doily-covered table beside her. Buster, lying beside her, stared intently at the cookie, as if waiting for it to leap up and dance.

Caroline resumed eating her crumbly cookie and sipping tea and asked Nance about working at FTA.

"It's a hoot," Nance said. "Just a hoot. I'm loving every minute of it. Except for that loud woman who helps Vic. Buff Coffey's sister."

"Gigi?" Caroline said.

"Flirty little filly," Nance said. " 'Tween you and me, she's terrible at her job. But Vic covers for her." Nance gave her a creepy little smile, cut her eyes toward her and then away.

"Sounds like Gigi," Caroline said, feigning

lightheartedness. At one point, back when Vic was in graduate school, she'd suspected Vic and Gigi of being attracted to each other—they always ended up side by side at parties—but Vic had always denied it. Gigi had always gotten plastered at those parties, but that was back when lots of people drank too much, she and Vic included.

"Now." Nance's voice changed and became confiding and caring, "Suzi told me that Otis and Ava have—Is it ass burger? What's that?"

Caroline went into her Asperger's spiel and after a while, as Nance's expression grew more quizzical and then doubtful, Caroline's mind started wandering back to the fake flowers in the yard. Did she actually pretend to water them and think she was fooling the neighbors?

Nance said, "Well, I can't tell there's a thing wrong with Otis and Ava. They're just as smart as can be. And cute. They seem perfectly normal."

Caroline took a deep breath. In the old days she would argue with people who said things like this, but it felt awful, really, to be put in the position of trying to convince someone that there was, really, something wrong with her children and that she and the doctors and therapists weren't just making shit up. So she didn't put herself in this position anymore. She looked at her watch and said she had to get to the grocery store.

"I'll be by to get Suzi for church in the morning," Nance said. "And there's a dinner at church tomorrow night and a special program on mission trips. One's to Mexico! At the end of the summer. Would you mind if Suzi went on a mission trip with the church?"

After the Dunkin' Donuts incident—even though Nance had proved to be reliable since then—there was no way Caroline would let Suzi go on any kind of trip with Nance. "Her knee won't be healed enough," Caroline said.

Nance sighed and raised her hand to her neck in a dramatic gesture. "She's such a precious girl, your Suzi. You're so lucky to have her. You have no idea how lucky you are."

"I'm fully aware of that."

"You know, dear," Nance said. "If you don't mind my saying so. You spend too much time fussing over Ava, and she's going to be fine."

"What I need is for people to stop telling me I'm a bad mother."

"Oh, dear, I'm sorry," Nance said. "I didn't mean that! I meant to compliment you. I know it must be hard, taking care of that bunch. If you and Vic ever want to get away together for a long weekend, just let me know. I'd be glad to step in and help out."

Although Caroline would never let Nance look after her home and kids, she did, for a few seconds, entertain the idea of herself and Vic going off on their own somewhere. He used to be such a good traveling companion. But she'd never talk him into taking a trip with her now. He was always working. Besides, it would be like going away with an old boyfriend she hadn't seen in twenty years. Too much awkward catching up. Together, they wouldn't be able to forget about their life at home the way she could if she were by herself. She thanked Nance for the offer, and then found herself telling Nance about getting Ava into Rhodes and moving up with her to Memphis.

"If that's what you want, you could stay in my house," she said. "I'll get rid of that little couple who're housesitting for me. The boy, Trevor, is so ugly his mother must've had to borrow a baby to take to church."

"I might take you up on that," Caroline said, but knew she wouldn't. She wanted a perfectly anonymous place to live in, like an apartment above a store downtown, a place with huge windows looking out over Main Street, a place completely free of clutter where she could just sit and contemplate the strangers walking past. She might even get a job in a clothing store, like Barbara's, the one she used to manage in Iowa City, when she actually had time to care about clothes and the people who wanted her advice about what to buy. It was all a fantasy, she knew that, but if Ava got into Rhodes, she'd do her best to make it happen.

"I know you must've missed your mama something awful, growing up without her."

Strange shift in subject, but Caroline nodded, deciding to go with it. "Wish I had a memory of her. Even one." She thought about mentioning the fact that she'd suspected Nance of being her long-lost mother but decided against it. It would make her seem too pathetic. This conversation was supposed to be about Nance, not her. "I'm so sorry that your daughter died," Caroline blurted out. She had to say what she'd come to say. "If you ever want to talk about it."

Nance flipped her hand in a dismissive wave, as if they were discussing who'd burned the breakfast toast.

"She died of bone cancer?"

"She died of medical negligence. I'd prefer not to go into it right now."

Bingo.

As Caroline was leaving, she walked over to the table with the photographs. She asked Nance which ones were of Helen.

"All of them," said Nance.

There was Helen at various ages: the wide-eyed downy-headed infant wrapped in a blanket; the six-month-old wispy-haired charmer clutching a cloth block; the solid toddler in diapers and a fluffy dress; the gap-toothed, freckled, blond girl wearing a plaid dress in a school picture; the serious Brownie scout sporting a sash full of badges, hair held back with plastic barrettes sticking out from under her beanie; then, finally, the sickly looking and pale patient under an afghan on a couch. Caroline studied all the pictures, looking for signs, markers, that might have foretold her fate. But Helen looked healthy and happy and like every other little girl until, suddenly, she wasn't. When had she started growing that tumor? When had it started hurting her? When did she realize that she was dying? There were no other people in the pictures with Helen—not her mother or her father. Just Helen. "She's beautiful," Caroline said, and turned to ask Nance more about her, but Nance had already stepped out onto the front porch and was holding the door open for Caroline to leave.

As Caroline stood on Nance's front porch in the stifling humidity, she gestured toward the yard. "Pretty flowers," she said.

Nance smiled. "Why thank you," she said. "They're hardly any work at all!"

Was she being ironic? Caroline had no idea. "Is Archer your real name?" Caroline asked her. "I mean, was it your name when you were married and had Helen?"

"No," Nance said. "Why?"

Caroline hadn't planned on asking this question, not so abruptly, so she didn't have a reason already in mind. She just spread her hands and shrugged.

"It was Quackenbush," Nance said. "That was my first husband's name. Bernie Quackenbush. Now, I don't want to be rude, hon," Nance said, stepping back into her house, "but I've got work to do round here. I'll see you in the morning!"

Back home, in the den, Caroline showed her father the folder full of documents about the radiation study. He leafed through it as if it were all news to him.

"Is this all true? You were head of this study?"

He nodded slowly, frowning. "Well, it appears I was," he said. "But I don't recall a thing about it."

"That's convenient."

Her father didn't respond. He shut the folder and gazed out his window into the backyard. What was he thinking about?

"Where'd this come from? Did Nance give it to you?"

"I believe she did. Yes, I believe she did."

"Why?"

"I've got to get out there and do some weeding. I haven't been out there in weeks."

"You were just out there yesterday."

"Was I? Didn't do a very good job."

"Was Nance one of the women in this study?"

"She keeps sniping at me. She's angry at me about something."

"I guess so."

There wasn't any Quackenbush listed among

the eight hundred victims. So she still hadn't given Caroline her real name. She was intent upon hiding her real purpose in being here, and Caroline didn't feel she should expose her. Had she moved to Tallahassee just to confront Wilson? If so, she must have been mightily disappointed, because he was refusing to own up to anything. But now that she was here, what did they owe her? That was the real question. What the government had done to Nance, what her *father* had done, was a travesty. Caroline and her family were obligated to help Nance Quackenbush, or whatever the hell her name was, however they could.

"Is this why my mother left?" Caroline said. "Mary Conner! My mother! Did she find out about this . . . study?"

"Well, now, that could be," he said, tapping his upper lip, as if the thought had just occurred to him.

CHAPTER 10 *Ava*

Suzi was acting strange, like her personality had changed when she hurt her knee. She actually started being nice to Ava.

"Come to church with me and Nance," she told Ava. "Please, Sissy? The minister wants to meet you."

Sissy? This was one of Suzi's tricks, but what part about it was the trick? "Why?" Ava asked her.

"I told him so much about you, that's why." Suzi was acting all hyper and shifty, swinging around on her crutches. She kept bugging Ava, following her around, pleading with her, until finally Ava said okay.

And that's how Ava came to be sitting in Genesis Church, which was next to the dollar movie theater, where Ava would rather be, watching *Akeelah and the Bee*. At least at the movies there was only one screen to watch.

Suzi sat on one side of her and Nance on the other. Most everyone else was standing up, swaying with their eyes closed, singing a song about the wind bending a tree in a hurricane. What did that have to do with God?

"There he is," Suzi said, elbowing her, pointing at one of the screens.

"Ouch," Ava yelled, pushing Suzi away. Ever since Suzi was little, she'd poked Ava, prodded her, yelled in her ear, tried to hug and kiss her, anything she knew that Ava didn't want her to do; and then when Ava pushed her away she acted hurt, even went running to their mother, crying about how she was only trying to be nice to Ava and how mean Ava was and so on.

Now, though, Suzi didn't react to the push. She even leaned closer to Ava. "There he is," she said again, pointing to the people singing up on the stage. "That guy in the middle, the tall one, who looks like Orlando Bloom. That's Buff. The minister who wants to meet you."

Ava said in her regular voice, refusing to whisper. "He doesn't look like Orlando Bloom. Why does he want to meet me?"

"He just does," Suzi said, making a "duh" face. She knew more, but she wasn't telling.

Nance scooted closer to Ava, too. Now Ava was in the middle of a human sandwich, being pressed into a pulp. "What are you talking about?" nosy old Nance asked her.

"Nothing," Ava said, and knew she'd sounded rude but didn't care. She didn't like Nance, even though everyone else in her family did. Ever since they'd gone to have those pictures taken and Nance had used reverse psychology on her to get her to pose naked, she didn't trust the woman. So, basically, she was in the middle of two untrustworthy pieces of bread. A pressed liar sandwich.

Nance leaned past Ava and repeated her question to Suzi. The two of them were BFFs. "I was just showing her Buff," Suzi explained to Nance.

The head minister—a roundish, baldish, friendly-looking man—jumped onto the stage, and the congregation finally sat down and collected itself, and he began talking, welcoming everyone on that fine summer morning.

It would've been okay if Suzi hadn't added, "Buff wants to meet Ava."

"Why?" Nance asked.

"Exactly," Ava said.

They shouldn't be talking now, because the minister was talking, but Suzi kept right on, explaining that Buff had wanted to meet Ava after Suzi had talked so much about her.

Nance frowned.

Ava lost interest in Buff, what little interest she'd had, because she'd just spotted Travis, the cuteish guy who'd visited her Asperger's group, sitting across the aisle. He'd spotted her first and was waving at her. He was wearing a felt hat with a feather through it, like Bartholomew Cubbins wore. People wore unusual clothing to this church. She waved back at him.

All through the endless church service, which both Suzi and Nance seemed to be really into, listening to the minister talk about stirring up the fire of God and walking out further into the water, she thought about *America's Next Top Model*. Nance had helped her fill out the application and everything was ready to be sent off, including the photos Mr. Boy had taken of her—not the naked ones, of course—and as soon as she sent them off, all there was to do was wait to see if they'd want to interview her in Jacksonville, and if they didn't, they were idiots, Nance declared. It was creepy that only Nance knew about what she was doing—except the guys in her Asperger's group, of course, which meant that Travis knew, but he'd probably have forgotten all about it by now. What would Elvis think of Ava becoming America's next top model? He would approve, because he liked models.

And what would Elvis think of this church? He'd probably like it, being kind of a Christian and a showy guy, but she didn't like it. It reminded her of a poor man's version of one of Elvis's Vegas shows. There was too much going on at once with the screens and music and live entertainment and headline news, everything way too loud. It was like they were trying to duplicate what it was like in her own house. Why would she want to go to church for more competing noise? What happened to church being quiet? Did everything have to be like a video arcade?

After the service was finally over, Ava wiggled out of the pew and into the aisle, catching her breath. Escape. She must escape.

"Hey, Ava." It was Travis, blocking her path. Along with the Bartholomew Cubbins hat, he was dressed in a blousy white shirt and olive-colored knickers with brown socks and flappy leather elf shoes. "What are *you* doing here?" Travis asked her.

"My sister goes to church here," Ava told him.

People were jostling into her and Travis and giving them curious glances and then big smiles. "What are you dressed like that for? Are you in a play?"

"I'm a volunteer at Mission San Luis. You should come up there sometime." Travis was taller than Ava, and not bad looking, his baby face balanced out by his sturdy build. He had a dimple in one cheek.

Before she could say anything in reply, like "sure" or "maybe I will," Suzi came up from behind, plowing into Ava and propelling her forward with her body and her crutches, causing her to bump into people who were making their way down the aisles and out of the church.

Ava protested, but Suzi kept pushing her in her aggressive way, like Ava was a soccer ball she was moving toward the goal. "Let's go say hi to Buff," she said.

Up near the stage, Buff was talking to an older couple, patting the woman's rounded back, his face furrowed with concern. He had nice thick, light brown hair, parted on the side. And a suntan. Didn't he worry about getting skin cancer?

"Buff," Suzi interrupted, shaking his elbow. "Here's my sister, Ava."

Buff dropped his hand from the older woman's humped back and turned his attention immediately to Ava. Wow. He glowed like a movie star. He clasped her hand in both of his. "So good to finally meet you."

"Okay," Ava said, glancing off sideways. Buff was sending her messages with his eyes that were too intense, and she couldn't interpret them.

"You are just as beautiful as Miss Suzi said you were!"

"Okay," Ava said, meeting his eyes briefly and then looking at Suzi.

"I never said that," Suzi protested, her face crinkled with disgust.

Buff wrapped his football player arm around Suzi's shoulders and gave her a squeeze, causing her to stumble with her crutches. Suzi's face changed from disgust to pleasure. Suzi's goal, Ava'd figured out over the years, was to get all the attention, in any situation, focused on herself, and she was so good at getting it that Ava didn't bother to compete.

"Nice to meet you," Ava mumbled, and began backing away.

"Wait, wait," said Buff, dropping his arm from Suzi's shoulder. There were other people, teenage girls and one eager "cool guy" type lined up beside Buff, waiting to speak to him. "Suzi and I would love to get you involved in our youth group—wouldn't we, Suze?"

Suzi nodded and did another fake, eager smile.

"Okay," said Ava. Thank God the word *okay*

had been invented. There was some debate about the origins of the word, she remembered reading somewhere. Some people thought that it came from the Choctaw Indians, and others that it came from the African slaves in America. . . .

Buff was talking to her again. "So, we're taking a youth group trip to Wakulla Springs next Saturday. Have a cookout, grill some burgers and brats, swim with the gators. What do you say? We'd love to have you." He was like a force, the combination of his personality and his manly good looks. Either you let yourself be drawn into his force field or repelled. That's how Otis would've described it, though he would probably be even more scientific, mentioning atoms, neutrons. . . .

"Can you come? Next Saturday?"

"Well . . ."

"I'll drop by to pick you both up myself."

"Cool!" said Suzi. "I can't swim, though, with my knee like this."

"You can sit on the beach, looking cute," Buff told her. "So I'll pick you both up next Saturday at eleven."

The boy standing at Buff's elbow couldn't contain himself for another minute. He elbowed Buff in the ribs. "You gonna pick me up, too?"

"With your foot odor?" Buff said to the kid, and elbowed him in the stomach.

Ava took this opportunity to turn and start

down the aisle, glancing around for Travis in the thinning crowd, but didn't see him.

There was Nance, though, sitting in the chair watching her, looking small and forlorn and pasty pale. Why was she staring at Ava?

Ava walked right past her and out through the bustling lobby into the blinding sunlight and the blistering concrete and all the cars, looking for Travis. He was gone.

"Who was that guy you were talking to earlier?" Suzi asked her when they were in Nance's car, racing home like they were going to a fire. "The one in the costume. I've seen him before. He's bizarre."

Ava didn't want to give greedy little Suzi any more information, or ammunition, than she already had. "I've never seen him before in my life," Ava said, remembering too late that Travis might be on the Wakulla trip and she'd have to keep lying. She was just as bad as Nance and Suzi. She was the liar filling in the pressed liar sandwich.

There was something else she'd been lying about. She had barely passed algebra last spring, and her mother had sent in her application to Rhodes College. But even though she'd told her mother she wanted to go there, she didn't, and she wouldn't. Ava had wanted to be so many things along the way as she was growing up; and maybe because of her mom's encouragement, she'd been certain she could do any of them, although she'd never admit this to her mother. Her father didn't care what she did, didn't expect her to accomplish anything, the way her mother did. She had no idea what she really wanted to accomplish, beyond being an Elvis fan and America's next top model. But being a fan wasn't a career and the model thing, if she did get it, wouldn't last long. All she knew is that she wanted to eventually be a grown-up—finish college, just a state school, nothing fancy, and live on her own for a while, then get married and have a family. But this wasn't anything she could ever say aloud to anyone. It was too ordinary, not flashy enough. More like a log cabin instead of Genesis Church.

Buff came for Suzi and Ava the following Saturday morning. He pulled up into their driveway in a big black SUV, the kind of car her parents always spoke scornfully of. He had called the day before and talked to her mother about the outing, and her mother later told Ava that he wanted to take his own car to Wakulla Springs because riding on the bus made him motion sick, and, well, since they were in the same neighborhood, he thought he'd just swing by to pick up Suzi and Ava. Her mom seemed to think it was okay, so it must be.

Buff came inside, in his polo shirt, knee-length madras shorts, and sports sandals, like something out of the Lands' End catalog, and talked to her mother for a few minutes in a soothing, reassuring voice, promising that he'd have her "lovely daughters" back by five p.m.

Even though Suzi sat in the backseat on the way down to the park, she managed to insert herself into the conversation constantly. Buff asked Ava questions about her interests, her plans, her goals. She told him she got As in everything except math, which was mostly true. She told him she planned to go to Rhodes College in Memphis, if she could get in, but beyond that she didn't know.

"I'm going to get a soccer scholarship," Suzi announced, "to one of those Ivy League schools, like Harvard, and be an archaeologist."

Ava let out a big sigh, and to her surprise, Buff winked at her.

"Must be nice to have it all figured out, Suzi Q," he said. "But the Lord might have other plans for you!"

"Huh," Suzi said, clearly doubting that anyone, including the Lord God almighty, could interfere in her plans.

Every time Ava glanced over at Buff, he was looking at her with that intense gaze that she didn't know the meaning of. After a while she forced herself not to look at him.

At Wakulla Springs State Park, which was about half an hour south of Tallahassee, they met up with the other youths, who were disembarking from a big white bus with *Genesis Church* written on the side. After the cool car ride, standing outside in the heat under the live oak trees felt comforting.

Three of the girls, who looked to be around Suzi's age, came rushing over to hug her and help her carry her swim bag and towel since she was on crutches.

Ava was pleased to see Travis climbing off the bus, wearing regular clothes and carrying a balled-up towel. He didn't see Ava and headed straight for the river.

Ava tried to follow him, just because he was someone familiar to hang out with, but Buff was gathering up the remaining youth group members with his arms. "Buff hug!" everyone said, and Buff prayed aloud right there in the gravel parking lot for God's guidance and protection and for everyone to have a safe and fun day. "Amen," all the teenagers chanted, and then they let out a whoop that startled Ava out of her skin.

Somehow, Ava ended up sitting beside Buff on the river ride in one of the white metal boats with open sides and a canopy roof—and she was aware that many of the other kids, who all seemed to want Buff's attention, were staring at her with unfriendly expressions, which she supposed meant they were jealous. Jealous! Of her! This included Suzi, who, red-faced and sweaty, struggled up the aisle of the boat on her crutches and still managed to shoot Ava a nasty look.

Travis merely smiled at Ava as he passed, not making any effort to sit beside her. He plopped himself down on a bench in the front of the boat, beside another boy, and the two of them passed a pair of binoculars back and forth.

Ava had taken this forty-minute-long ride down the Wakulla River countless times—with her family and visitors from out of state, and on outings in elementary school. The pale green water was always super-clear. You always saw the same things as you floated along—alligators half submerged in the lily pads looking like chunks of radial tires, turtles lined up on logs, egrets, herons, anhingas, and ducks—black snakes dangling from trees. And you heard the same stories about all the movics filmed there—the most famous being *Creature from the Black Lagoon*. But it never got old, somehow.

Buff took pictures of alligators with his cell phone, he said, to send them to his three-year-old daughter, Angel. He was very considerate of Ava and kept asking her if she could see the animal the guide had just called out.

"Buff. Hey, Buff." A young woman with a

cleavage-revealing tank top tapped Buff on his shoulder. “Why didn’t Rusty and Paula and Angel come?”

Buff turned around with his whole upper torso and flashed his smile at the girl, who had long brown braids. “Hey, Amber. They had a birthday party to go to.”

“Who’s Paula?” Ava asked Buff.

Amber, the cleavage girl, answered the question. “That’s his wife. She used to be a Playboy bunny!”

For some reason, hearing this made Ava feel sick. Playboy bunny! Was that the kind of woman Buff liked? Did all men, even ministers, want to marry women who looked like that? Huge boobs, like Amber’s?

Buff was shaking his head at Amber disapprovingly. “That was before she got saved,” Buff told Ava. “That life’s behind her now. She’s been cleansed in the blood.”

Yuck, Ava thought. And without even thinking about it, she stood and walked up the aisle and slid onto the bench seat beside Travis.

Travis said nothing but companionably handed her his binoculars.

“Anhinga on your left,” intoned the guide, an African American man with a trim gray beard who gunned the boat’s motor to underscore every announcement he made. “Also known as the snakebird. Water turkey.”

• • •

Later, they all ate hamburgers and brats and chips and potato salad and brownies in a picnic shelter behind the Wakulla Springs Lodge—a white, two-story, Spanish-style building housing a restaurant, hotel, snack bar, and lobby where Big Joe, a huge alligator killed by poachers, had been stuffed and was now displayed in a glass case.

Ava sat alone at the end of a picnic table, eating a large, well-done hamburger, delivered to her by Buff himself, watching Suzi and her posse at another table. Even though she'd just started attending this church, Suzi already had a posse, as their dad would say. Suzi, whose only complaint about her social life was that everyone wanted to sit next to her and thought they were her best friend, ate her lunch and talked with her posse, pointedly ignored Ava, pretending Ava didn't exist, not even caring that Ava was alone, even though she'd invited her.

Buff, too, was surrounded by chattering, laughing kids at all times, and after he finished cooking and eating he started throwing a football with some of the guys. The guys seemed to love him as much as the girls did. He was like the popular kid, only he wasn't a kid.

The smoke from the grill gradually died down. Travis sat under a huge live oak tree, reading a book that appeared to be a fantasy book, from the lurid cover. Why did guys like to read that kind of crap? What was wrong with the real world? Facts. True stories. Biographies. Ava had never liked made-up nonsense. She'd read the first volume of the Guralnick biography of Elvis five times.

Finally the group tidied their shelter and moved in a herd down to the changing rooms beside the lodge. Then they descended the tile walkway onto the narrow strip of sugar sand beach beside the river. Most of the kids threw down their towels and got in line to jump off the tall wooden diving tower.

Suzi's posse had positioned themselves close to the water, surrounded by cypress trees like a little fort. Knowing she wouldn't be welcome in Suzi's group, Ava positioned her towel in some sparse grass under a cypress tree and sat down feeling hideously self-conscious in her pink and black zebra-striped bikini. People were always telling her how thin she was, how gorgeous, but she never felt like she was either, at least not for long. She was always, it seemed, preoccupied to distraction by some flaw she'd detected in herself, on her body, something she couldn't stop worrying about no matter how much her mother told her she needn't worry, that she was making another big deal out of nothing. Today it was the fact that her pubic hair was sticking out of her bathing suit on the right side. She usually remembered to shave down there but had forgotten this morning. But why was it sticking out only on the right side? Then she noticed a slight pooch in her stomach. She shouldn't have eaten all those chips! She sucked her stomach in and it popped back out.

A shadowy figure loomed over her. Travis, wearing only swimming trunks and a baseball cap pulled down low over his face, clutching his towel and book. Ava couldn't take her eyes off his chest—hairless except for a silky dark nest in the middle. He asked if he could sit by her, and she said sure.

He laid out his striped towel in the sand, smoothing down the edges and sweeping off errant grains of sand. He arranged the towel so that it was precisely six inches away from her towel. Then he sat down like he was lowering himself slowly into a hot bath. He smelled like he'd used two bottles of sunscreen, but even so his skin was toasty brown, his arms dotted with enticing-looking freckles, and Ava had to restrain herself from connecting them with her finger. As soon as he was settled, he started in talking about the time when an alligator ate an FSU student at Wakulla Springs, a story Ava had already heard a hundred times. While Travis talked on, Ava took in the scenery. The diving tower was over to the far left of the beach, near the underwater spring where the river started, bubbling up from the deep caverns at exactly 70 degrees. Ava had always wanted to jump off the high platform, but had never had the nerve.

The lifeguard, a little rooster of a guy, sat in his squat lifeguard chair, talking to some teenagers who sat near him on an overturned rowboat. People swam in the designated swimming area and sunned themselves on two platforms anchored out by the far edge of the swimming area, near the ropes. Supposedly, the alligators, waiting on the other side of the river, wouldn't come into the swimming area because they didn't like crowds. (The FSU student who'd been eaten had swum over into the alligators' territory—he must've been drunk or on drugs, people said.) You could either believe the unlikely notion that the alligators respected the boundaries and take your chances, or stay safe, hot, and miserable on the beach. Ava always made sure there was somebody between her and the ropes when she went swimming.

There was a loud squeal and some wild splashing right in front of Ava and Travis. A group of white people, some of them wearing T-shirts over their bathing suits, were yelling and dunking each other, and the men were slinging their long wet hair about.

"Rednecks," Travis observed. "Did you ever notice how many overweight people there are in Wakulla County? Just take a look."

There were a number of fat people with red necks and, in fact, entire red bodies, out frolicking in the pristine water, people with many tattoos who had no business wearing bathing suits in public. Some of them sat nearby in their beach chairs, swilling beer and eating fried chicken.

"Don't make fun of fat people," Ava said, slapping her stomach, harder than she meant to. She shifted so as to hide her pubic hair.

"You're not fat," Travis said, his eyes evaluating her body like he'd just been evaluating the rednecks in the water. "All the guys were talking earlier about how hot you are. I told them you're going to be America's next top model."

Ava felt herself relax and well up with happiness. "Let's go swimming," she said, standing up. "Let's jump off the tower."

Travis adjusted his cap. "That tower isn't safe. There've been thirty-two accidents on that tower since it was built in 1933."

Ava took his hand and gave it a yank, pulled his hat off his head, and he came stumbling after her. He followed her up the steps of the tower, passing people who'd chickened out and were coming down. At the top the two of them waited in line with other mostly wet, shivering teenagers, and then, when the lifeguard gave them the signal to proceed, not allowing herself or Travis time to stare down and chicken out, she grabbed his hand again and the two of them leaped into the air and plunged down and burst through the surface of the frigid water, and she didn't even care that her bikini bottoms came down to her knees, she was having so much fun. They were both laughing and whooping when they came up for air, and without even discussing it they swam back to the tower. They jumped off again and then dog-paddled around awhile until Travis suddenly got scared of alligators and beat it back to the beach and Ava floated on her back with her eyes closed, which made her feel better than anything else in the world.

After a while she drifted back to shore and stumbled up onto the beach, feeling like a frozen fish, and collapsed onto her towel. Travis had taken his towel and moved on. The cute boys and Suzi's posse had also disappeared, but their towels remained. Ava stretched out on her stomach, thinking briefly about applying more sunscreen, and fell asleep. She woke up, feeling someone spraying something on her back. Travis?

"Hey, there! Sorry to bother you, but you're burning up, girl!" Buff. He held up a spray bottle of sunscreen.

Ava sat up, groggy, blinking, trying to arrange herself into an unhideous position.

"Thanks," she mumbled, smoothing down her damp, no doubt crazy-looking hair.

"Having fun?" Buff sat cross-legged in the sand beside her, dry headed, wearing a pair of dry navy blue bathing trunks and his polo shirt and Ray-Ban sunglasses.

"I am," Ava said, remembering jumping off the tower with Travis, holding hands, and how scared he'd looked the first time, how gung ho he'd looked the second time.

"Me, too," Buff said. "I'm glad you came." He dug into the sand with his heel. "Haven't had a chance to talk to you much."

Ava made a sound of agreement. What did he want? Was he going to start in about Jesus and being saved? She'd heard all that before—most recently from Suzi—and wasn't interested in hearing it again.

"I'd like to spend some more time getting to know you," he said. He gave her a smile, but his eyes were hidden behind his sunglasses.

"Why?" Ava blurted out. She wished to God she'd remembered to bring her own sunglasses.

"I just think you're an interesting person," Buff said. "I think we might have some things in common."

"Like what?"

Suzi and her friends rose up out of the water, Suzi's friends helping her hop up the beach, and they all plopped down on their towels again, laughing. Suzi, Ava remembered, had been told by their parents not to go into the water, because it might strain her knee. Suzi herself had told Buff she couldn't swim, but she must've decided to give it a try—good way to get more attention. Ava waved at Suzi, who appeared to be turning to look at her; but if Suzi saw her, she gave no sign.

"Here, look," Buff said. He opened up his cell phone and clicked around on it. Was he going to show her a picture of his wife, the Playboy bunny? Finally he found what he wanted and held the phone up so she could see.

There was so much glare that Ava couldn't make out the image at first.

"This is amazing," Buff said. "Very cool!" His deep voice got squeakier. "I'm totally down with this."

Ava took the phone and tilted it and saw a picture of herself, one of the ones taken by Mr. Boy. One of the naked ones, where she was lounging in a chair with a big dumb smile on her face. "Oh God."

"I know the guy who took it," Buff said. "He forwards me stuff now and then. Don't worry, I won't tell." He nudged her. "And don't get mad at him. He didn't tell me your name or anything."

Ava handed him the phone and glanced up at the river, but the entire scene before her, Suzi, the gallivanting rednecks, swimming tower, the river, the palm trees and pickerelweed on the other side, disappeared in the painful glare. "Then how'd you know it was me?"

"I recognized you from the neighborhood, and then I found out Suzi was your sister. Maybe you could pose for me sometime? I'd really like that."

"Hey, Buff," one of Suzi's friends was calling. "Come here. It's Suzi's knee. It's really hurting her."

Buff stood up and Ava hid her burning face between her knees. She'd never been so grateful for Suzi's need to suck up all the attention.

CHAPTER 11 *Otis*

The summer was more than half over. When school started in the fall, Otis would be a senior at Sunny Side High. His guidance counselor, Mr. Wilkins, had been after him all the previous year to start working on college applications, but his parents hadn't mentioned college to him in a long time—his mom obsessed with Ava getting into Rhodes, and his father fussed after Suzi—so Otis had let the whole thing slide. He had his own plans for the future, and they didn't involve college.

He, Otis Witherspoon, would be the first person ever, in the history of the world, to single-handedly create a successful (model) breeder reactor, and then . . . fame and fortune would follow. He could skip the college and graduate school part altogether. He'd be given a job as a prestigious respected young scientist with enough money and staff to build whatever he wanted to. Women would fall all over him.

This day, the day he'd be testing the neutron gun, would be a huge step forward for Project Breeder Reactor. The fuel he was using had been hard to obtain and had taken him weeks to procure and harvest.

First was radium. He'd scraped the radium paint off the old clocks, stirred in the contents of the tube of paint he'd found in the stolen clock, and added that to some radium he'd strained from a chunk of uranium he'd ordered online at amazon.com. Radium, check. Next, beryllium.

He'd called on a science geek friend, Bucky, a recent Sunny Side High School graduate who now worked at the chemistry lab at Tallahassee Community College, to ask for his help. Without asking questions, Bucky smuggled four strips of beryllium from the lab and sold them to Otis for twenty-five dollars each.

At last Otis had the proper fuel for his gun. Eventually he would fire it at some thorium in order to create the reaction, but first he had to test it. Because the neutrons released by the radium and beryllium through the gun would make no noise and have no charge, it would be hard to tell if it was working. Then he remembered a method he'd read about—one used by the Joliot-Curies in 1932. Paraffin, when hit by neutrons, throws off protons, which do emit a charge and could be detected by his Geiger counter.

One afternoon after he left his new job at Arby's he swung by Walgreens and bought a block of paraffin that was meant to be used in a foot spa. The following morning, he was up by eight o'clock, and soon after his dad left for work, Otis started down to his shed to don his lead apron and test his gun.

It had been nearly a month since he'd stolen the clock from Grandma's Attic, and he'd stopped worrying about the police showing up to arrest him. He'd decided that the whole shoplifting thing was just an aberration. He'd never stolen before and promised himself he never would again.

He'd also just assumed that he'd continue toiling alone in his wonderfully odiferous, sweltering shed, but his new friendship with Rusty had squashed this assumption. She'd started hanging out in his shed, watching him, asking questions, refusing to be deterred by his rudeness. She usually showed up around one p.m.—she slept until noon—and she'd bang on the shed door saying things like "Little pig, little pig, let me come in" and "Mr. Sharkey, white courtesy telephone, please" and "What da password today? Unguent? Lima bean? Toblerone?" until finally Otis gave up and let her in.

He was totally mystified. Why was this snarky girl paying so much attention to him? He'd made overtures toward pretty girls over the years—kind, shy girls who professed to love all animals and therefore should love him—usually by writing notes or contacting them on MySpace, but these girls always claimed they could only like him as a friend. Rusty—loud, mean, and self-confident—was the sort of girl he'd never even considered. But he found himself remembering things she'd said and wanting to tell her things, too. He supposed that meant that he liked her. But did he really want to keep explaining to her what he was doing? Let her in on his secret project?

The morning after he'd purchased the block of paraffin, she came knocking early in the morning, as if she'd known he'd be up to something special that day. When he opened the shed door, he stopped her from barging in like she usually did. "There's gonna be high levels of radiation in here." He gestured at the lead-lined apron hanging from around his neck. "I'm testing my gun."

"Cool," she said, pushing past him. She sat down on the stool that Otis usually sat on. Her stiff black hair looked like she'd brushed it the wrong way on purpose. "I stayed out all night," she said. "Want to hear what I did?"

"No," Otis said.

"I was messing with someone. That old lady. Mrs. Archer, right? I'm going to smoke her out of her den."

"You're going to set her house on fire?" He was relieved that she didn't want to talk again about sex or drugs, two things Rusty liked to talk about, two things that the very mention of made him feel inadequate.

"You're so literal minded!" Rusty said. "No, I'm going to force her to come clean. I mean, like, reveal her true identity."

"Good luck with that," Otis said.

Rusty flared her nostrils at him. She wore a black tank top with rips in it, which showed her black bra, and a short black-and-blue-plaid kiltish skirt and black high-top Converse sneakers.

"Don't you want to know why she needs to be smoked out?"

"She's a spy," Otis said. "I caught her snooping around my shed."

"Nope. She's a serial killer." Rusty sat there, waiting for him to ask how she knew that, but he didn't want to hear it.

"Is there a reason you wear black all the time?" Otis asked her. "If some day you wore something green, or pink, what do you think would happen?"

"Can't risk it, Biscuit." She rubbed her thin little hands together. "So, Igor, what are we doing today?"

Otis sighed and slipped on his rubber gloves. "Like I said. I'm testing my neutron gun," he said. "I told you it's not safe in here. I don't have any more aprons."

"Like that apron is any protection." She waved away his apron with a flick of her wrist.

Otis started to explain to her about the lead in the apron, but she interrupted him.

"Who gives a shit anyway," she said. "We're all gonna die." She smiled at him with her cracked pink lips, her pale face free of makeup. She had some dark stuff in the tear duct of one eye.

He said, "I love you."

She snorted. "Yeah, well, you don't know me, right? Just ask my dad how unlovable I am."

Otis didn't want to get into a conversation about moms and dads, so he extracted a paper face mask from the carton and slipped it on. He offered one to Rusty, but she shook her head.

"I've got my protection here," she added, shaking the tan leather medicine bag hanging around her neck.

"Do you ever take that thing off?"

"Never. Only when I'm in the shower."

Otis asked her what was in the bag, and she said it was a secret.

"Whatever."

"Okay. I'll tell you. There's some clippings from Royce's toenails and one of Angel's barrettes. They're the only two people I love in the world, right? And a little magnet with Buckwheat on it I stole from Grandma's Attic. I love my grandma, too. There's one of her chewed up sucker sticks."

She kept talking, sitting there on Otis's stool, so he tried to tune her out and focus on his task. He slipped on his face mask, then transferred the radium powder to a piece of aluminum foil and balled it up—hard to do with rubber gloves on—then did the same thing to the beryllium powder. It was hard to keep his mind on his task, because he kept picturing Rusty, not wearing her medicine bag or anything else, in the shower. He often thought about her when he was in the shower, which had lately made the whole shower business seem totally worthwhile. Why had he told her he loved her? She hadn't said it back, but she hadn't seemed surprised. He poked the balls of aluminum foil into the cavity of his gun and quickly wrapped the gun up with duct tape.

All the while, Rusty kept yakking. "That stuff reeks. Royce ran away." Royce the zombie boyfriend, last seen wearing an FBI sweatshirt.

"Where did he go?" His voice was muffled by the paper mask.

Rusty shrugged. "That's what they keep asking

me. His mom, his stepdad, the cops. Have you heard from him? Did he ever talk about wanting to go anywhere? They don't get it. We never talked about anything, right? We just smoked weed and laughed. Do you get high?"

Otis told her he didn't and then explained that marijuana was illegal, killed brain cells, caused auto accidents, and was a gateway drug. He had tried pot once, one day behind the gym at middle school. Some cool guys offered him some. It made him feel like he was losing his mind. Why would people seek out that feeling?

"There's other ways to get high," Rusty pointed out. "I bet some of the stuff you got here would work." She reached over and grabbed a vial of radium flakes.

"Put that down!"

"Just kidding. God! Hey. Did you know that your little sister's been going to our church? Your older sister went, too. How come you don't?"

"I'm busy." Otis positioned his duct-taped gun on the table and set the large block of paraffin in front of it. "Scoot back. There's a radioactive neutron stream going out of this baby." He couldn't see it, of course, but he imagined it until he almost saw it, a ray of sparkling, dancing particles shooting out.

Rusty scooted the stool back a few inches. "I hate going to church," she said, "but I have to go. Mom makes me. Mrs. Archer, the serial killer, was the one who brought your sister to church and introduced her to my dad. It was like she fixed them up. Really creepy, right? Your sister's a preppy bitch, but I feel sorry for her getting mixed up with my dad. It's all that witchwoman's doing. I hate her guts. One day I saw her digging up her yard on one side of her house, and then the next thing I know there's a bunch of plastic flowers stuck in there. Who would do that? She probably buried something underneath them. Probably body parts. I bet she's killing people, right? She tried to give me a donut once. I suspected poison so I dropped it. Why'd she move here, anyway? And why across from us? We need to figure out what she's really up to. Maybe if we devil her enough, she'll go away, right? Last night I snuck around her house and made scratching sounds on all her windows. Her dog barked and barked. I hid whenever she turned on the outdoor lights."

"Stop talking now," Otis said. He turned and picked up his Geiger counter from the shelf behind him.

Finally Rusty was quiet, watching him intently.

He switched on his machine and held it over the block of wax. The clicking started up immediately. Clickclickclickclick. .2 mrems! "It works!" Otis said, a wave of deep satisfaction rushing through him. He was going to do it. He was! He'd show everyone!

“Wow,” Rusty said, like maybe she finally believed he knew what he was up to.

Although he hated to do it, he switched off the Geiger counter, laid it down, and began ripping the tape off his gun. “I need to get some thorium to shoot the gun at. I don’t know where to get it.”

“I’ll help you,” she said. “This is so cool. I’ll help you.”

“Why?” Otis looked into her eyes, which were pale blue.

She was the first to blink and look away. “I’ll help you,” she repeated, “if you help me. Help me smoke out Mrs. Archer. Is it a deal?”

Otis was stuffing the aluminum balls back into the medicine vials—old Lexapro bottles that had Ava’s name on them. Ava who got everything, including happy medicine. He pulled off his gloves and the paper mask. “It’s a deal,” he told Rusty, who jumped up and kissed him on the lips.

Her lips were dry and rough but softer and sweeter than anything he’d ever felt in his life, and the combination of the successful firing of his neutron gun and his first kiss made that day his best ever.

Otis approached his granddad when he was sitting in his little den upstairs, after supper, watching *Antiques Roadshow*, the sound on the TV up so loud that the windows rattled. As soon as he saw Otis, Granddad picked up the remote and snapped off the TV.

Otis sat down on the couch.

"Good evening there, son," Granddad said, and Otis smiled. He loved it when Granddad called him *son*. "What do you know?"

"There should be a game show called that," Otis said, then repeated in a deep showy voice, "What do you know?"

"Good to see you, son," Granddad said. "How's Burger King?"

"That was three jobs ago. I'm at Arby's now."

"Oh, right." Wilson paused and gazed out the big square window into the front yard. "I've got to get out there and mulch those flower beds. I'll do it tomorrow."

This was something his grandfather had taken to saying every time Otis came into the den to see him. Granddad hadn't been going out to work in the yard, like he used to. Otis was dying to ask him about obtaining thorium for his gun, but it was really bugging him that Granddad kept repeating the thing about working in the yard over and over again. He asked Granddad why he didn't go out and work in the yard right then.

"That horrible woman will show up and harass me. I've told your mother I don't want her in here reading to me anymore. Every time I go out in the yard, there she is. I know her from somewhere, I just can't remember where."

"You know her 'cause she shows up here all the time," Otis said. It was scary how much his grandfather's memory was slipping. Otis didn't know what to do. Should he correct his grandfather, the way his mother was always doing? He felt bad for his grandfather when his mother got angry at him for something he couldn't help. She'd say, "You've already asked me that one hundred times, Dad!" The same way she got angry at Otis when he forgot to put gas in his Pontiac or got fired from another job.

"Why do you keep getting fired?" she'd ask Otis. "Don't you do what they tell you to do? Don't you follow the rules? How hard can that be?"

How could he explain it to his mother? Yes, there were rules at his jobs, or, what they called procedures, and he tried to follow them, but other people kept screwing things up. As soon as his shift started, the other employees began yelling at him, each one telling him to do a different thing now and to hurry up, and there was so much noise and so many hot things and loud people that it was hard to focus and he made mistakes, and pretty soon he would make too many of those mistakes. Also, he was too honest. At McDonald's, when one of the managers, Mitchell, a skinny African American man who wore big square glasses, was reprimanding Otis for causing a big grease spill and asked him, in a nice voice, “Do you think you can give me one hundred percent effort from now on?” Otis, instead of saying yes right away, as he later realized he was expected to do, thought about it. He thought about the job and how boring and demeaning it was, especially compared to what he’d be doing when he was a famous scientist. “No,” he told Mitchell. “I can give you sixty percent.”

Mitchell shook his head and sighed, but then to Otis’s surprise, Mitchell began to giggle, helplessly, and Otis laughed, too. When he left Mitchell’s office he assumed everything was okay, but as soon as he came into work the next day he was fired by an unsmiling Mitchell.

Wilson was staring out the window at the front yard, the way Parson Brown did when she wanted to go out but wasn’t yet making a fuss about it.

“My friend Rusty says that Mrs. Archer is evil,” Otis offered, pleased to drop the phrase “my friend” into the conversation.

Wilson gave the hollow-sounding guffaw he’d taken to emitting so often that even Otis noticed it. “Well, she sure is angry about something,” Wilson said. “She thinks I’m responsible for all the unhappiness in the world. She never lets up. ‘Do you know what you did, Dr. Spriggs?’ Over and over. I don’t know what the hell she’s talking about.”

"That lady's bonkers," Otis said. "She murders people and buries their body parts. We're going to do something about Mrs. Archer, Granddad. Don't worry. We'll stop her from bugging you. Okay?"

Wilson turned and looked at Otis as if surprised to see him sitting there. "Stop who?" he said.

"Mrs. Archer."

"Oh, yeah." He nodded, but it seemed like he'd already forgotten who Mrs. Archer was. Pretty soon he'd forget who Otis was! "I've got to get out there and mulch those beds," Granddad said again.

"Granddad. I need some thorium for my breeder reactor. Any ideas?" Otis had, a few months ago, given up the pretense that the breeder reactor was hypothetical, after he'd figured out that his grandfather didn't remember what they'd talked about from one conversation to the next.

"I believe," said his grandfather, "that propane lanterns, the kind you get at camping stores, would be a good place to start. Course, you'd have to get a whole lot of them."

Propane lanterns. Check.

"Let's play checkers," Otis suggested to his granddad, who agreed, seeming glad for the diversion. Granddad was always up for a rousing game of checkers.

• • •

Otis and Rusty went looking for propane lanterns in Otis's Pontiac—the car Rusty referred to as his serial killer car. At Walmart, Sears, and Target, the propane lanterns were pretty much the same price, and all expensive—from thirty to eighty dollars. And they didn't really need the whole lantern. At Sears they bought two, but all they wanted were the mantles that came with the lantern. Most lanterns came with two, and Otis wasn't sure how many he'd need. At Target they discovered boxes of replacement mantles, two to a box, but they were fifteen bucks a box.

After a whispered discussion, they decided to steal them.

Rusty went a few aisles away, where the fancy granola and gourmet food was, and he could hear her pretend to collapse, knocking some jars off the shelf. When he heard that Rusty was being fussed over by a couple of old lady customers and the lurking pimple-faced store clerk, Otis slipped six boxes of mantles into a battered canvas messenger bag adorned with a hammer and sickle, which used to belong to Royce.

In order to pay Rusty back, Otis had to agree to make some night raids on Mrs. Archer. Rusty instructed him to dress all in black and paint his face and hands with some black kiddie face paint she gave him.

At midnight one night he met Rusty in front of

the old lady's house. Then they ran around and around her house, swinging their propane lanterns and chanting "Odobee dumba lawee" over and over again. All this, including the chant, was Rusty's idea.

"Why are we doing this?" Otis asked Rusty at one point.

"We're driving her mad."

Inside Mrs. Archer's house, lights went on and Buster began barking.

"I bet she's mad, all right."

"Not that kind of mad. *This* kind of mad!" Rusty held the lantern up to her face and swung it in time to her chant, a hideous, leering grimace on her black-painted face, and Otis laughed so hard he nearly peed his pants. Which was okay, because it meant they had to extinguish their lanterns and call it a night.

The next step, Rusty decided, was to sneak into Mrs. Archer's house while she was at church with Rusty's family. Rusty was certain that Mrs. Archer had given her mother a key to her house but had no way of knowing which key it was, so she swiped her mother's entire key chain early Sunday morning and even pretended to look for the keys with her father, acting just as puzzled as her parents about what could've happened to them. She told Otis all about this grand act of deception while they were fumbling at Mrs. Archer's front door, trying key after key in her lock, the dumb dog Buster barking his fool head off.

Finally they found it and let themselves in.

It was a disappointingly bland house. Buster followed them around, wagging his tail. They opened her cupboards and helped themselves to some Lay's sour cream and onion potato chips and Entenmann's powdered donuts, leaving crumbs on the counter. They leafed through her *Time* magazines and *Tallahassee Democrat*s stacked up beside the coffee table.

In her bedroom they rifled through her old lady underwear and jewelry. Rusty helped herself to a pair of rhinestone clip earrings. There was a big bed with a pink bedspread and it looked soft and inviting. Otis lay down and folded his arms behind his head. The bedspread felt slippery beneath his calves. The pillow under his head was down filled and the pillow slip had pink roses on it. It smelled like old lady perfume. How kinky. He was lying on an old lady's bed.

"Look!" Rusty said, pointing.

On the bedside table sat an old-fashioned framed photograph of a little girl in a winter coat and fur hat, her hands stuffed into a fur muff, and she was laughing. Snow was falling all around the girl, but she was laughing. What was so funny? "Is that her?" Otis said. "Mrs. Archer, you think? When she was little?"

"It's evidence," Rusty said, and snatched up

the photograph. "Probably some little girl she killed. One of her victims, right? The police will want to see this."

For some reason, her saying this ridiculous thing made him want to kiss her. "Come here," he told her, and opened his arms.

Clutching the picture, she dropped down hard on the bed beside him and rolled over next to him. Rusty. Rustifer. Beatrice. She smelled like herbal something, like she'd just taken a shower. He wrapped his arm around her neck and brought her down close and they lay side by side and kissed, and kissed, and kept kissing, her showing him how to do it. It was pretty nice, very nice, but not nice enough. After a few more kisses he rolled over and pulled her underneath him. Oh, yeah. This was nicer. Much nicer.

"What the hell? What are you doing?" She struggled underneath him. He couldn't tell if she was joking or not.

"What do you think I'm doing?" He tried to kiss her again, but she struggled again and he let her go.

She slipped out from underneath him and sat on the edge of the bed, her back to him. Her shoulder blades, under her thin T-shirt, looked like a child's. "I need to collect more evidence," she said.

"You're taking this game a little too far," Otis said. "This is a game, right?"

"I'm serious, jerk!" Suddenly, with a grunt, Rusty hurled the picture across the room and it smashed against the wall. "This is not a game!" She whirled and lunged at him, pinning him to the bed, pulling his hair, scratching at his face, slapping and punching at him in the same random way Suzi used to attack him when she was little. Rusty didn't feel much bigger than Suzi had then.

Otis shoved her off him and scooted off the bed. She rose to attack him again, but he pushed her back on Mrs. Archer's bed, maybe a little too hard. His cheek stung where she'd scratched it. "You need to see a psychiatrist."

"I'm not seeing any more shrinks! You have no idea what my life is like. How dare you!"

What was she talking about?

He ran out of the house, leaving Rusty screaming after him, calling him names. He walked home in the suffocating heat, wondering how he'd gotten mixed up with such a maladjusted individual. He touched his cheek where she'd scratched it and his finger came away bloody. To think he'd told her he loved her!

He did love her.

But science was calling him. Science was reliable. Science was his true love.

Part Five AUGUST 2006

CHAPTER 12 *Suzi*

Buff's house was so different from Suzi's house. In Buff's house the furniture all looked and smelled new, and in the living room everything was blue and white, in the kitchen red and white, in little Angel's room pink and white. Everything matched! Buff's house had soft wall-to-wall carpet in all the rooms, even the bathroom; and the bathroom sinks didn't have dried toothpaste globs and lone hairs in them and old eye shadow and blush containers spilling over on the counters. At Buff's house there were dried flower arrangements in every room and a bowl of fresh fruit on the dining room table. There were family photos everywhere—of his family, not their dead relatives. Huge framed photos, taken outdoors, the kind where everyone in the family wears a white shirt. In all the pictures Buff looked so handsome, an older brother of Orlando Bloom. Paula's blond hair hung down in perfectly straight curtains. Rusty's wavy reddish brown hair was pulled back in a ponytail. Baby Angel had no hair. Except for Angel, they looked like an orthodontist's advertisement.

The whole setup—the family and the house—made Suzi angry because she knew that the reason they looked so perfect and that their house looked so perfect was because they didn't have two teenagers with Asperger's throwing fits and hoarding things and a stinky old granddad (she loved him, though!) and a dad who never came home and a mom who slopped around looking hideous and making nasty remarks and claiming to be too tired to do anything but hide in her room and read. If she lived in a house that looked like Buff's house, she'd bring friends home with her all the time. As it was now, she was always embarrassed when Mykaila and Sierra and Sienna came over, and she ended up apologizing over and over until they told her to shut the hell up.

Of course, Suzi knew that everything wasn't as dandy at Buff's house as it seemed. For one thing, Rusty had become a total reject misfit who wouldn't even babysit her own little sister, or maybe couldn't be trusted to babysit her. And there was something way wrong with a married man, a minister for God's sake, who was obsessed with Ava.

Suzi might have found Buff's obsession with Ava to be hilarious and *only* hilarious if not for two things: 1. Why Ava? What was so great about her? And 2. the fact that Ava wouldn't have any part of Buff. Ava hadn't been back to church since that one time, and after the Wakulla Springs trip she'd refused to go to youth group. She didn't have an appreciative bone in her body.

She was waiting for Elvis to rise up from his tomb and marry her. Did she not realize how *cool* Buff was? A hot minister! How cool was that? Maybe Buff would divorce his wife and marry Ava! Although nobody in their right mind, once they realized how annoying Ava was, would want anything to do with her. Of course, Ava was gorgeous to look at, prettier than Suzi, even, if you just *looked* at her.

Suzi could probably get Buff in big trouble if she told people about his obsession with Ava, and maybe she would, but she'd tell when she was good and ready. Her mother would *spaz* and she'd never let Suzi go back to that church again if she knew. Suzi couldn't bear the thought of that. She liked going to Genesis, she'd accepted Christ as her personal savior and planned to start reading the Bible, very soon. Her knee was healing, mostly because of her physical therapy, but surely all the church members—and Buff!—praying for her had helped.

When she closed her eyes at night she imagined Buff, like in his sermon, standing in that big green field, holding out his arms, and her running toward him. He would envelop her in a hug, but it wasn't the loving fatherly kind, it was the other kind; and when he kissed her it was like Orlando Bloom kissing Keira Knightley in *Pirates of the Caribbean*, not like Davis slobbering on her at the skating rink. She'd broken up with Davis by texting him, which she knew was tacky, but she didn't care. She'd moved on, in her mind anyway, to bigger and better things. Buff just needed more exposure to her and he'd catch on to what he was missing. Her. Not Ava.

But Paula had called their house last night and asked *Ava* to babysit. What a joke! Ava, babysit? She couldn't even take care of herself. It was disappointing that Buff had told Paula to call the Witherspoon house and ask for Ava, not Suzi. Her mom had answered the phone and tried to get Ava to talk to Paula, but Ava said no, she wouldn't, and left the room. So her mother, flustered yet again by Ava's rude behavior, just stood there holding the phone like a mutant.

"Give me the phone," Suzi told her mother. Then she got on the phone and told Paula that *Ava* couldn't babysit but that *she* could, even though she'd never technically babysat before, and that's how it happened that on Friday night, instead of hobbling through the mall with her buds, she was at Buff's house, playing Nancy Drew. Buff wasn't there, which was a bummer, but she could at least nose around and collect information about him. Just how far would he go in his ability to surprise her? He was a married minister obsessed with Ava. What other quirks lay below his shiny surface?

And she was entertaining Angel, whom it was

so easy to love. As requested, Suzi fed Angel some gluten-free noodles and meatless, sugar-free tomato sauce. And steamed carrots and broccoli all cut up. Naturally, Angel turned up her nose at the entire dinner. Suzi tasted it and pretended to love it, just to get Angel to eat more of it, but it tasted like crap. Cardboard crap. Angel ate enough, with a lot of coaxing, to earn a yogurt pop for dessert. Since she wasn't playing soccer right now, Suzi really had to watch what she ate. But tonight was special, so Suzi had one, too.

While they sat at the kitchen table and chewed and sucked on their yogurt pops, Suzi listened for sounds coming from Rusty's room, but heard nothing.

Paula had rolled her eyes when she mentioned that Rusty was holed up in her room, grounded all weekend. Suzi wanted to ask what for, but you couldn't ask that sort of thing. You need to ground her until she's twenty-one, she wanted to say, but she couldn't say that either.

Paula and Buff had gone for a Parents' Date Night with some other church couples, all smiles and seeming eager to be off on their own. Buff was as friendly to Suzi as usual, giving her a hug, smelling like richling cologne. They'd be back by ten thirty, Paula promised. She wore a low-cut shirt, revealing the top of her round balloon breasts. Implants! A minister's wife! Suzi was pleased to notice that Paula had a rather large behind, even though she exercised nonstop and seemed to eat only cardboard.

After dinner she and Angel played store (Angel's idea) and then school (Suzi's idea) and then Angel said she wanted to watch *VeggieTales*. Suzi got her into bed around seven thirty, read her a couple of wholesome children's books, the best one called *When Jesus Comes to My House* about Jesus dropping in on a little boy for a play date and the two of them building with blocks and having a snack together. Finally Suzi turned out Angel's light, feeling competent as all get-out.

All this time, Rusty had not made a peep in her room and hadn't come out once to see what was going on. There was a light on in her room—Suzi could see it under the door—but no sound at all. Maybe she'd snuck out and was causing trouble with her friends. Or, scratch that, she didn't have any friends. Suzi stood outside her door, listening as hard as she could, hearing nothing. If Rusty wasn't in there, Suzi would go in and nose around, see what she could dig up. She knocked.

"Yeah." She was in there.

"Hi, it's me, Suzi, the babysitter." She liked calling herself this.

"Otis's sister?"

"Right." Suzi had never been referred to as

Otis's sister before in her life. How would Rusty know Otis?

"Need something?"

"I'm just bored."

"Sorry, the booze is locked up," Rusty said. There was a rustling, then a creaking sound, and the door popped open a few inches. Rusty, with her hair pulled back in a ponytail and no makeup on, looked almost normal, except for the nose ring. She wore pink pj's with elephants on them. "Why, if it isn't the preppy, popular Miss Witherspoon."

Suzi made vague noises of protest, her face flushing. On the surface, being called popular was great. But the way Rusty said it, *popular* sounded like something worse than shallow and foolish, which it was, but how was it Suzi's fault that other people liked her? "Just wanted to see if you were really in here," Suzi said.

"Ta-da!" Rusty said.

Suzi looked over Rusty's shoulder but didn't see anything interesting in Rusty's room—no cigarettes, booze, illegal drugs, nasty books. The room was neat and clean, without even any pictures on the walls. No computer, no electronics visible.

"Come in, I guess, if you want," Rusty said. She stood back from the door.

Suzi hobbled into the room and Rusty quickly shut the door behind her.

"Sporting injury?" Rusty asked her.

Suzi told her how it happened, and surprisingly enough, Rusty actually listened as if she were interested.

She motioned for Suzi to sit down on one of the twin beds, which she did. Rusty plopped down on the other, lying on her side in her baggy pink pj's, head propped up, staring at Suzi with her big blue eyes. It was a mysterious room, not what she'd been expecting. All white, no other color to balance it out. No personality. It was like an institutional room, like a room in a crazy ward. *Girl Interrupted*. The white bedspreads had nary a wrinkle in them.

Rusty must've noticed her looking around. "I used to have all kinds of shit in here, but I took it to the Goodwill."

"Why?"

Rusty shrugged. "I want as little of my actual self in here as possible. It's my way of protesting."

"Dang," Suzi said. "That's harsh. On yourself, I mean."

"They can make me live here, but they can't make me enjoy it."

Suzi admired Rusty's zealous self-denial and wondered if she could strip her room bare this way. Nope. No way. She needed her comforting things. Her room was the polar opposite of Rusty's room. She and Rusty were opposite in every way, when you thought about it, but here they were talking. It was like a social miracle. Never would've happened outside this room. Rusty was two grades ahead of her but seemed way older. And she was easier to talk to than a lot of people. She didn't bother with meaningless chitchat, so Suzi decided to forgo it as well. "Why aren't *you* watching Angel?" she asked Rusty.

"I've been deemed irresponsible."

"How come you hate it here so much? Your dad's so cool!"

"You go right on thinking that. I know him, and he ain't cool."

"You should see my dad."

"I've seen him."

They both shared a nasty little laugh.

Suzi asked what was wrong with Buff.

"Let's just say, his fixation on your sister—it's not the first, and it won't be the last."

"How did you know he liked Ava?" For some reason, hearing this, rather than making Suzi angry or repulsed or frightened, gave her hope. "Did he tell you?"

"It's obvious."

"Doesn't your mom care? Does she know?"

Rusty sighed and rolled over onto her back. "She's the Great Wall of China."

"Huh?"

"She knows, but she pretends she doesn't. She blocks it out. Even though he's been in treatment."

"Wow," Suzi said, but she didn't know exactly what this meant. In treatment for what? Did she want to find out? Not really.

"For sexual addiction," Rusty added, staring at her ceiling. She sighed again.

"Wow," Suzi said again, thinking how peculiar it was for a daughter to be talking about her father this way. A minister with sex-u-al addiction. What did this mean? That he couldn't help himself? Again, in a way that Suzi knew was sick and twisted, this gave her hope. But she didn't want to know more.

"What were you doing in here?" she asked Rusty.

Rusty rolled over and pulled a book from under the bed. "I bring in one book at a time, and when I'm done, take it out and bring in another. Usually I get them from the library. Otis gave me this one. It's scintillating." She held up an old white paperback book called *Atoms to Electricity*.

"How do you know Otis?" Suzi asked, but she was wondering, Would she be able to hear Angel if she woke up?

"Night, night, Suze," Rusty said, flopping back on the bed. "Enough questions for now."

The following Wednesday Suzi stayed late after youth group and watched as Buff cleaned up. All the other kids had left. Buff was supposed to give her and Ava a ride home, but Ava, of course, wouldn't lower herself to attend youth group. Buff was rearranging beanbag chairs in the chat room, scooping them up and slinging them into a corner, while Suzi, because of her knee, sat on a folding chair and watched. The muscles in his back and arms rippled under his white T-shirt as he bent over and picked up the multicolored beanbags.

He was scowling. He'd been acting annoyed all evening. When one of the smaller boys, Nick, banged his elbow against a cabinet and doubled over in pain, Buff had told him to get over it. When one of the girls, Jackie, went on and on during check-in about a fight with her friend, he'd said, "That's lame."

"Where's Ava tonight?" he finally asked Suzi, kicking the beanbags into a mound. "Did we do something to scare her away?"

"You did," Suzi said boldly. "She doesn't like you."

Buff hesitated, glancing up at Suzi as if he were going to say something, then changed his mind. He snatched up the last beanbag chair, the one with a hole in it, and heaved it at the wall, and when it hit beans rattled out.

"But I do," Suzi said, her heart popping away like a string of firecrackers. "I mean, *I* like you." She hoped Buff understood what she was trying to tell him.

"I like you, too," Buff said, not meeting her eyes. He put his hands on his hips and surveyed the room.

Suzi knew what kind of like he was referring to. Pals. Buddies. "No, not that kind of like," she blurted out. "I *like* like you."

He finally turned, looking her up and down. "What exactly are you saying, honey?"

Why was he making this so hard? "You know."

He shook his head. "Okay, I know. But *you* don't know. You're younger than my daughter."

"Your daughter hates you." Because of all her sparring with Ava, Suzi had a knack for saying just the right thing at the right time, or maybe it was the wrong thing, depending on how you looked at it. But either way, her words usually had the effect she desired.

Buff walked over to the food table, where bowls of tortilla chip crumbs and plates of cookie crumbs waited to be taken to the kitchen. Buff slammed the table into the wall. "Wait for me in my office," he told Suzi.

Suzi stepped out of the chat room and stood a moment in the great hall, and she felt like cartwheeling across the cavernous room, dancing and whirling. She would have done it except for her lame knee. Ha-ha-ha, she was thinking, for some reason. Na, na, na. So there. She had no idea to whom these thoughts were addressed.

CHAPTER 13 *Marylou*

It seemed too good to be true, the morning that Suzi came knocking at her door. Marylou was wary about answering, because nobody ever rang the bell except Jehovah's Witnesses and the person who was harassing her, the coward who'd always run away by the time Marylou could step outside to look around.

Suzi had an eerie look on her face. She'd hobbled all the way over to Marylou's house on her bad knee, but the look on her face didn't seem to Marylou to indicate that she was in pain. On the contrary, it seemed like suppressed pleasure, the way Helen used to look when she came home from school, bursting with a story to tell her mother about some kid's bad behavior.

Marylou flung open the door, gave Suzi a hug, and invited her in, noticing that Suzi looked sloppy for Suzi, in an old T-shirt and sweatpants cut off into shorts and old flip-flops, her hair jammed down under a SeaWorld baseball cap.

"You should've just phoned me, honey," Marylou told her. "I would've come and got you."

"Could you take me to the library?" Suzi asked Marylou. "The big one downtown? It has some books I need."

Marylou told her sure, wondering why she hadn't asked her mother to take her, but pleased that she hadn't. She explained to Suzi that they'd need to wait until her pineapple upside-down cake finished baking. While Suzi flopped down on the sofa in the living room with Buster to wait, Marylou busied herself in the kitchen, loading the dishwasher and wiping counters.

She wanted to run over her options in her head once again, but she'd recently had trouble thinking clearly. Maybe it was the torpid subtropical heat here. It was hard to focus.

Okay. She'd tabled her initial plan to murder Wilson, because there wouldn't be any satisfaction in murdering him if he didn't know, or understand, why he was being murdered, but it wasn't that she felt any sympathy for the wretched old coot. Even after that nighttime walk on Nun's Drive when he asked her to go ahead and kill him. Oh no. She did not feel a bit sorry for him. In fact, after meeting with him and talking with him and observing him, she hated him even more than she had when he'd simply been an abstract bogeyman. It was easier to despise him now that she had particulars to focus on—his spotty, shaking hand waving in her direction like an underwater plant when he was trying to tell her something but couldn't form the words; his habit of farting like a pack mule when he walked; the way he sat three inches away from the TV screen and stared at the idiotic commercials for Depends diapers as if they were words of wisdom from on high. And him—some smart research doctor who thought he was better than everyone else! A Nazi doctor who treated pregnant women like his own personal guinea pigs! She'd stopped dropping in to see him because his decrepit condition depressed her. She'd decided to leave him be and take care of the rest of his family.

Marylou'd decided that Suzi, the first family member she'd met, was the person she wanted to focus on the most. She would continue to disrupt the lives of the others, but she'd devote most of her troublemaking time to Suzi. But trying to decide how to best use Suzi was just as difficult as pinpointing the best method of ridding the earth of the scum named Wilson Spriggs, the American Nazi. The problem was that she felt no desire at all to harm a hair on Suzi's head. She liked Suzi. Plain and simple. In fact, she liked her so much that she wished she could adopt her. Who knew why you liked one person more than others? She and Suzi were nothing alike, so it wasn't that. Marylou was reserved and calculating and expected people to intuit her stellar qualities without her having to do a thing—meanwhile ignoring all her weaknesses—while Suzi was earnest, open and self-confident, and enthusiastic about life. Marylou felt good just being around Suzi. And Suzi needed her, too, since her own mother had checked out long ago. The two of them, she and Suzi, needed each other.

And now, in her cake-smelling kitchen, stacking hot clean melamine plates in her cupboard, Marylou had another hand-slap-to-the-forehead moment. Instead of trying to create trouble for Suzi, maybe she should pour her energy into creating a *positive* relationship with Suzi. Make Suzi want to come live with her! Suzi needed to spend time with Marylou, lots of time; and gradually she'd become more and more estranged from her own parents; and soon she would turn, by her own choice, into the granddaughter Marylou had never had. The daughter she'd never had. The daughter Helen would've been if she'd been allowed by the American Nazi to grow up like her friends had. Healthy. Smart. Kind. Loving. Responsible. Sweet. Funny. The truth was, Marylou loved Suzi. How could this be? But there it was. The feelings she had for Suzi both delighted and terrified her, but she couldn't ignore them.

It had already been harder than she'd expected to drive any real wedge between Suzi and those hapless goats she called parents. The church thing, she'd thought, would do it, but she'd underestimated the mother's ability to avoid looking a gift horse in the mouth. What a strange expression that was. Was she, Marylou, the gift horse? She imagined herself with a horse head and Caroline peering into her mouth. One chomp would do it.

And she'd also underestimated the father's determination to focus on anything but his job and that nasty, slatternly coworker of his. Gee-gee.

She'd hoped that Suzi would embrace fundamentalist Christianity and become a zealot, but she was wrong there, too. She'd underestimated Suzi's ability to fold religion smoothly into her already well-rounded life like eggs into a batter.

It had also been hard to derail Suzi because she, Marylou, had so much to do! She was living in a new city; and living, period, took work. When she'd first moved to Tallahassee—ah, those halcyon days!—she had only her hatred of Wilson Spriggs to focus on. She knew nobody, had no place to go except the grocery store; and, on her first few visits to Publix, she'd looked around and decided that every old man she saw pushing a cart must be Wilson Spriggs. She was in the town where he lived, and it seemed like everyone she saw must be connected to him in some way, like they were all in some unfolding drama starring the Radioactive Lady and the American Nazi.

But now the people and places she saw in

Tallahassee had taken up their proper roles again. They were simply themselves, and she was forced to acknowledge them. She had to chat with the checkout girls at Publix and the woman at the hair salon (recommended by Paula Coffey) who cut her hair, and her coworkers at Florida Testing and Assessment who liked to discuss *American Idol* and *CSI* while eating their bag lunches. She had to find new doctors. Keep up with her prescriptions. Locate a reliable lawn service and discuss the state of her yard with the workers. (She actually hated yard work, and she'd put all the fake flowers around as a joke—she'd found them on sale one day at Walmart—but it was like the emperor's new clothes. Everybody acted like they were real, so Marylou didn't bother to explain.)

But mostly what took up her time was church. Even though it wasn't a Baptist Church, and it was the kind of church she'd always turned her nose up at, she found she actually enjoyed going. It was her own fault, allowing Buff and Paula to pull her into their lair, but not having many other obligations she could use as excuses, it was hard to say no. So she was now going not just Sundays and Wednesday nights, but she'd joined a women's Bible study group, which met for breakfast on Thursday mornings, and a prayer group, which met for lunch on Fridays. And her Sunday school class, the Wouldbegoods, was always doing community projects. They'd talked her into helping with the food pantry and the clothing drive, and it all took time! Marylou was busier now than she'd been in Memphis. "Busier than a one-legged man in an ass-kicking contest," Teddy used to say.

Six months after Helen died, Teddy'd left Memphis and gone away, up to Wisconsin, where his sister lived, just for a visit, he'd said, but then he kept extending his stay. Finally he told her he'd gotten a job with the City of Madison Parks and Recreation Department and eventually asked her for a divorce. A few years later he remarried and had three boys who were now grown. She knew this because for years they'd exchanged cards at Christmas and the occasional letter, until one letter from Teddy, coming right after what would've been Helen's twenty-first birthday, informed her that he just couldn't write to her anymore, and asked her not to write to him. It was too depressing, he said, to be reminded of her and Helen, because the two of them went together in his mind, and always would, and Marylou understood. She and Helen did go together, but in her mind, Teddy went with them, and she was incapable of putting it all behind her, even if she'd wanted to, which she didn't.

She was happy for Teddy that he'd been able to escape the weight of what had happened and create another life for himself, even if she hadn't been able to. She'd married Martin, of course, a few years after Teddy left, but, although he was a perfectly nice man, he was no Teddy, and she never could talk to him the way she'd been able to talk to Teddy.

For years she'd kept a notebook full of things she wanted to tell Teddy, things only she and Teddy would appreciate. Small things, mostly. *The oak tree in the side yard got struck by lightning and it split the trunk right in half, but I wouldn't let them cut it down. I took swimming lessons at the Y, and it turns out I'm a natural! Remember Marcia Jenkins, that sweet but homely girl from down the street who was in my junior honors English class? She married a Canadian Inuit! In their newspaper picture the two of them are rubbing noses. Remember how I used to hate prunes? Well, I've gotten right fond of them in my old age.* And so on.

After she got caught up with planning to murder Wilson, she shut that notebook, Notes to Teddy, for good. Teddy would never understand, or condone, her desire to get even. Living well is the best revenge, he always reminded her. That's what he'd said when she expressed to him her anger at her own parents, telling him how they'd abandoned her at her grandmother's house in Little Rock so they could go off gallivanting in Hollywood. Teddy, while not making light of her anger, had encouraged her to forgive them, and after a time she had. But forgive Helen's death? Never.

Suzi Witherspoon was the first young person she'd met, in all her years of teaching Sunday school and high school, whom she thought she could love the way she'd loved Helen. She had to go carefully with Suzi. Not make any mistakes. It was even possible that if she was able to have a grandparent-grandchild relationship with Suzi, her anger about Helen would dissipate and she could get on with enjoying the rest of her life. Live and let live, as Teddy would've said. It could happen, couldn't it? Maybe it wasn't too late.

The timer dinged and she removed her pineapple upside-down cake from the oven. She was supposed to take it to a potluck supper her Sunday school class was having that evening. Perhaps she could talk Suzi into coming with her.

The Leon County Public Library, where Marylou hadn't been before, was a two-story affair with large plate glass windows, built in the seventies. It was full, on this summer afternoon, of mothers with small children and office workers and scantily clad teenagers and people who appeared to be homeless napping in the air-conditioning.

Marylou had loved going to the Georgian-style, three-story library in downtown Little Rock when she was a child. Her grandmother would drop her off there a couple of afternoons a week, and in her memories of that library it was always summer. She relished the time by herself, the drowsy heat and whirring fans and smell of old book covers, sitting in the same plaid chair in the children's room and deciding which five books, in the stack of mysteries she'd selected, she really wanted to check out, the same lady librarians working behind the counter, probably they were only in their forties but they looked, to Marylou, to be 140.

In the Leon County Library it was all DVDs and CDs and banks of computers. Suzi rode the elevator upstairs to get her books, and Marylou wandered to the back of the room downstairs where there was a children's section. She leaned against a long bookshelf and glanced through children's books—some of the same ones she'd read to Helen—*Three Little Horses* by Piet Worm, that strange book with the gorgeous illustrations of Blackie, Brownie, and Whitey dressed up like princesses—but she was also secretly watching the children sitting around her, industriously coloring the free coloring sheets handed out by the librarian and fighting with their siblings while their mothers searched the library catalog on the computer.

After a bit Suzi reappeared, limping—she'd left her crutches at home—with three books she was clutching to her chest. "Ready to go?" That excited look again.

"What you got there?" Marylou asked her casually.

Suzi blushed a deep scarlet under her SeaWorld cap. "Just some random books."

"Oh. Okay."

But Suzi really wanted to show her. She crowded closer to Marylou, who was already jammed up against the shelf. Suzi displayed her books one by one: *A Teenagers Guide to Sex*, *What Your Parents Won't Tell You About Boys*, and *What Boys Are Really Thinking (and Should You Care?).*

"Huh," Marylou said, nodding, and sighed. Typical teenage stuff, she supposed. But did they have to get interested so young?

"Can I spend the night at your house tonight?" Suzi asked her. "So I can read them? All my friends are busy or out of town."

Marylou decided to ignore that last part and said sure, but would Suzi like to attend the Sunday school potluck with her?

"No way," Suzi said vehemently.

So maybe Marylou was wrong about the folding in of the religion. Maybe Suzi'd already gone off it.

"That's where the guy is. At church."

"What guy?"

"Him." Suzi held up the books again, glancing around as if she was afraid of someone listening in, although nobody was close enough to hear them.

"The young man you're interested in?"

Suzi snorted. "He's not that young."

Remain calm, Marylou told herself. "How old is he?"

"Old. Really old."

Marylou felt faint and gripped the bookcase behind her. "It's just a crush, honey. Those come and go."

To her horror, Suzi's eyes filled with tears. "We did something we shouldn't have done."

Marylou led Suzi over to a miniature table and chairs and they perched, squatted really, on tiny kid chairs. Help, Marylou thought. What should she say? She'd never been a parent to a teenager. And the ones today were nothing like the ones she'd taught years ago. Or maybe they were, but the ones she'd taught in the 1950s knew to hide things better.

"So you let him . . ." Marylou trailed off, wanting, and not wanting, to know the details.

"We had sex!" Suzi said, not even bothering to whisper.

Marylou glanced around the kids' section, wild-eyed. Every person she looked at, mother and child, was staring back at her.

Suzi went on, talking too loudly. "I thought I wanted to, because I love him, I really do, but I wish I'd waited. I wanted to wait till I got married. Or at least engaged."

Marylou whispered, "Honey. You're not . . ."

"No!"

This time Marylou didn't even bother to look around. She felt that righteous anger welling up in her again. She'd missed it. "Did he force you?"

"I'm such a slut."

"You are not a slut."

Suzi went on like Marylou hadn't spoken. "*I* asked *him*. I thought I wanted to. I love him. And he wants to meet me again. Tonight! I told Sierra and she thought I should go tonight, but she probably thinks I'm a slut and is telling everyone."

Marylou scooted her little chair toward Suzi and hugged her, comforting her as best she could. Why would sensible, sweet little Suzi do such a self-destructive thing? The poor kid!

Finally Suzi lifted her head from Marylou's shoulder and whispered, "Don't you want to know who it is?"

No, she thought. But she said, "If you want to tell me."

The lip quivering again. The repressed smile. This next revelation, Marylou realized, was really the shocking part about what Suzi wanted Marylou to know. The other stuff was just warm-up.

"It's against the law, having sex with a young girl," Marylou heard herself say. "Whoever did this to you could be arrested. Should be."

“I know, I know. I don’t want him to get into trouble. His wife can’t find out. Ever.”

Marylou gripped the seat of her chair. “He has a wife?” She’d been picturing some nasty, sly-faced older teenager, not someone with a wife.

“I can’t tell you.”

“You’ve got to tell me. This can’t go on.”

“That’s why I’m telling you. I guess I don’t want it to go on. I do and I don’t. It all started because of Ava. It’s her fault. I just offered myself as a replacement for her. Since she wouldn’t. His daughter told me that’s what he wanted, since he likes to look at pictures of young girls on the Internet. I felt sorry for him ’cause Ava was being such a jerk to him. She could’ve said no nicely.”

“Who is it, Suzi?”

Suzi was sobbing now, and it look a long time before she could speak his name.

That night Suzi went to sleep in Marylou’s bed, with Buster. Marylou skipped the potluck and sat on her screen porch in the dark. She had to figure out what to do, who to talk to, which of the emotions swirling inside her to express, and to whom.

Mostly she felt terrible for Suzi, because she knew, from her own experience with a nasty uncle, that this event would affect her the rest of her life. This sort of thing happened to a lot of girls, but that fact didn't lessen the pain of it, not one iota. She also felt terrible for Paula and Rusty and Angel, but not as bad as she felt for Suzi. It was awful, not being able to take away what had happened to Suzi.

Suzi had begged Marylou not to tell, not yet, and Marylou had promised; but of course she had no intention of keeping this promise. If Suzi wouldn't tell, she would. But who should she tell first, and how should she tell them? For some reason she found herself wanting to tell Wilson, the only person around who would listen and remain calm(ish) and help her come up with a plan. But, no, that was ridiculous. She couldn't tell Adolf. Should she tell Caroline? The police? Buff's wife? Buff himself? She'd always thought there was something slick and shifty about Buff—a proper nickname for a grown man? So why was she so surprised? But a thirteen-year-old girl? That was different from fornicating with lusty choir women. Reverend Coffey was depraved. She wanted to run over and pound on Buff's door, and she just might do it.

All those people must be told. She hated to be the one to tell, the one to start a chain reaction of events that would hurt lots of people and would draw attention to her in a way she wanted to avoid, seeing as most people she knew here didn't know her real name or why she'd come to Tallahassee in the first place. But she could deal with all that. What was worse was the paralyzing guilt, worse than she'd ever experienced before; and she couldn't argue herself out of it, the way she'd learned to do when she started berating herself about the radioactive cocktails.

Because this whole thing was her fault. It was *her* fault. She had taken Suzi to that church for her own devious purposes and delivered her into the clutches of that creep. Could she ever stop ruining the lives of innocent people? First her own daughter and now Suzi. The Radioactive Lady, it seemed, was just as destructive as the nasty shit she'd swallowed.

She could be sitting anywhere, on any screened porch in August, the heat cradling her, the cicadas in the live oak trees doing their metallic buzzing that sounded like *hot, hot, hot,* she could be in Memphis or Tallahassee or Little Rock and it didn't matter because only her internal landscape counted at the moment, and it was a familiar landscape, a place she'd found herself many times, a safe, cool numbing place she might call Freeze. Freeze wasn't like the Stop in Go-Stop, Go-Stop, behavior that Teddy had always teased her about. Freeze was more like: I'm checking into the Econo Lodge and I'll see you later. She'd spent time in Freeze after her parents had hopped into their Studebaker and driven away from her grandmother's house, and for a time after Uncle Pat molested her.

She'd lived in Freeze for years after Helen died.

She sat there in her teak patio chair for she didn't know how long, deep in the land of Freeze, not able to move, or think, or feel. Then she heard a rustle outside. Sometimes when she was sitting out here at night she imagined a giant cockroach creeping through her backyard or an armadillo as big as a collie. There was something prehistoric about this landscape. But the rustling she was hearing now sounded like a person. A person creeping through the tangle of shrubbery and vines along the back of her house. It was nearly midnight, so her tormenter had just assumed that, as usual, she'd be in bed. She remained motionless on the dark porch, barely breathing. When the shadowy figure came into view at the sliding screen door, *it* froze in surprise.

"Graahhhh," Marylou bellowed, hauling herself out of Freeze with her own angry voice, not even sounding like a human being, lurching to her feet and snatching up an empty candlestick—the old lady did it on the screened porch with the candlestick!—yanking open the screen door, letting the candlestick fly at the fleeing figure. It missed by a mile.

But she'd seen who it was. Now, at least she knew.

Vic CHAPTER 14

There'd been five tropical storms and only one named hurricane so far this summer—Ernesto—and Ernesto hadn't amounted to squat. With a name like that, what would you expect? All predictions had been for Ernesto to swing into the Gulf, but by the time he rumbled over eastern Florida, he was only a mild tropical storm. Now Vic had a new friend: Grayson. Another wimpy name, but who knew? Grayson was passing over the Dominican Republic this very day, and all forecasts had him headed toward the Gulf.

The portfolio scoring was going swimmingly. Training sessions for portfolio scoring were over, and so for the scorers, the relative excitement of training and qualifying had given way to the drudgery of scoring, of just showing up and getting through the portfolios. Each had to be scored by two readers. Readers scored each essay on a bubble sheet and slipped the sheet into an envelope so that it wouldn't influence the other reader's assessment. Gigi had to be on call to answer the scorers' questions and resolve nonadjacent scores, and Vic was back to overseeing all the trainers. This batch of scorers, surprisingly sane and reliable, were working quickly, and it looked like they'd be finished ahead of schedule. Ron, Vic's supervisor, was as pleased as he'd ever been, and Vic expected a raise and a promotion when the project was over.

Nance was one of the stalwarts. She hadn't missed a day. She was there every morning at eight thirty, carrying her lunch in a red oilcloth bag—turkey sandwich on whole grain bread, a ziplock bag of pretzels and another of baby carrot sticks. She either ate with some fellow senior scorers or ate alone and perused *People* magazine. She never gave Gigi or him any more trouble about scoring; in fact, she never said much to Vic at all, but sometimes when he was chatting in a corner of the room with Gigi, laughing with her, making plans for after work, he'd glance over and catch Nance staring at him. It was unnerving.

He and Gigi had taken to eating their own lunches at a picnic table outside, telling themselves it was because they were the only two people at FTA who wanted to deal with the heat. Inside it was so cold that at first the heat felt wonderful, and being alone with Gigi felt wonderful, too. The picnic table, an old wooden one, was back under some giant pine trees, always covered with pine needles and sap, but that didn't deter them. It felt like time travel, like junior high, eating lunch with his girlfriend.

On this particular Friday, a week before the end of the project, they swept the needles off the table, plopped right down in the sap, and gobbled their brought-from-home sandwiches—his peanut butter and honey and hers chicken salad wrap—chewing and smiling but not talking. They both wore sunglasses. His wire framed, hers white-framed cat's eyes.

Vic shared his strawberries and blueberries and vanilla yogurt, and Gigi shared her sesame sticks and Milano cookies, and then they drained their sodas, wadded up their trash, and, leaving their lunch boxes—his Scooby-Doo, hers Lily Pulitzer—went for a walk around the parklike grounds of FTA. By then the heat had thawed him and was cooking him, but he didn't want to go back inside, even though their lunch hour was nearly over.

It was strange how, when Gigi first started working with him, they'd done nothing but talk, and now they didn't talk much at all. As they strolled on a paved path through a weird little glen dotted with stone benches that nobody ever sat on, Vic felt pulled toward Gigi, the same way he'd once been drawn to his former FTA coworker Wendy, the pregnant one, the one on whom he'd practiced successfully his all-and-nothing technique of avoiding adultery. He and Wendy used to saunter along these paths on their lunch break, and he had wanted nothing more than to wrap her in his arms, big belly and all, but he never did. They'd never even kissed, not once.

He and Gigi had already kissed, many times. They'd been having drinks and sometimes dinner every night after work. Hugging good-bye in the restaurant parking lots had escalated to kissing good-bye and finally to making out in her car like a couple of adolescents at a drive-in movie. It was ridiculous, shameful, and exhilarating.

Now he wanted more, or told himself he wanted more. He wasn't sure which. As they moved together down the path, he was aware of the curve of her breast, the dimple in her left cheek, her hair bouncing on her bare shoulder. They walked down a little hill, Gigi's sandals clacking on the pavement, and followed the path into a grove of pines, Gigi a few steps ahead of him. The hem of her wildly colored dress hit her a couple of inches above her knees, her freckled calves tightening each time she took a step. He imagined lifting her dress over her head, revealing nothing but her underneath. What was she thinking? Why didn't she say anything? But he didn't say anything either. He wasn't ready yet. He was committing petty crimes, getting used to the idea of himself as a criminal, working up to the felony. It wasn't too late to go straight, he reminded himself. He savored the excitement of teetering on the edge, feeling young and reckless. Nowhere near dead.

Gigi had stopped and turned toward him, one hand on her hip, like a model posing—Hipster in

Hicksville. The two of them were at the edge of the FTA property line, marked by a barbed-wire fence. Across the fence was a pasture; and way off, under an oak tree, a group of Cracker cattle, brown with white spots, stood patiently waiting for the sun to go down. Little egrets hopped among them, eating bugs.

He pulled Gigi into his arms and kissed her neck, her ear, her lips. "You feel so good," he managed to say.

She struggled away from him. "How long are we going to play this little game?" she asked him, sounding more hurt than angry.

Drunk with lust, no blood in his brain, he took the question literally. How long? Huh. Let's see. Out in the field, fire ant mounds were scattered around like huge brown sand castles. "Would you look at the size of those ant hills?" he said.

Gigi harrumphed and gave him a shove. "Such a boy," she said, and began clomping back up the path toward the low, flat-roofed brick building, sixties faux-prairie architecture gone amok. A landscaping guy on a golf cart crossed behind Gigi and waved at Vic. Had he seen anything? Why was he waving?

Gigi, a siren in her mod dress, kept walking toward the building and another afternoon of game playing, and before he knew it he was jogging after her.

• • •

Later that afternoon, after the scorers had gone home, Vic wandered into the language arts scoring room to ask Gigi if she was ready to go to Andrew's. She had her back to him, so he snuck up on her as she sat at a long table under those god-awful lights, bent over a portfolio, her hair now drawn back in a messy ponytail with a plastic grip, moss green sweater wrapped tightly around her. As Vic tiptoed toward her, holding his breath, he wanted to wrap his arms around her and nuzzle her neck again. His all-and-nothing plan of action hadn't worked worth a damn. And to answer her earlier question, he wanted to end the game right now. He was ready, even eager, to do something incredibly stupid and cruel and destructive. There was an almost painful relief in this realization. Let's just go to a hotel, he would say. Forget the drinking and the dinner and the extended foreplay. In his mind, he was already there. They were already there, the full length of their naked bodies locked together on a bed, her legs parting.

Just as he was about to lean down and embrace her, he saw what she was doing with her yellow number-two pencil on the bubble sheet. She was erasing one scorer's score and changing it so that it matched the other. He watched her do this to another score sheet without even looking at the portfolio, let alone reading the essays to determine which was the right score. For a few seconds he actually considered pretending he hadn't noticed, but as he watched her change score after score, his desire shriveled up and anger replaced it. Finally he said in a low voice, "*What* are you doing?"

She shrieked and threw her pencil. "Fuck!" She turned to Vic, her face flushed, from either embarrassment or surprise or both. She didn't answer his question but stood up and backed away from him, trying to recover her equilibrium.

"How long have you been doing that?"

She shrugged, like one of his teenagers. "I don't know. Couple of days."

There was noise in the hall, a clanking sound, which could have been the janitor emptying the trash can. There could be straggling scorers lurking about or other FTA employees. He tried to keep his voice down. "You're compromising the whole project! How can you know which is the right score unless you read them?"

She took a few more steps away from him, arms folded on her chest. "What difference does it make? I mean, come on!"

"One's right and one's wrong. That's the difference." Ironic, him saying that, after what he'd just been thinking about sex and hotels.

"Oh, really?" she said, trying for coy. "Didn't you say yourself that all holistic scoring just pretends to be unbiased?"

"I said it *tries* to be unbiased."

Gigi smiled a tight little smile and displayed her palms, like, *same difference*.

Vic dropped down onto a nearby table. It was happening again, and he'd so hoped that it wouldn't, not with Gigi. He was weary, so weary, of being saddled with the task of trying to make unreasonable people see reason, which he'd been doing, it seemed, all his life. The most unreasonable people of all had been his own parents.

Caroline swore that the Asperger's gene, if there was such a thing, must've come from Vic's side of the family, and he really couldn't argue with that. Vic's father always wore his trousers, as he called them, belted up above his waist and too short besides. You could always see his black socks, even in the summer when he wore sandals. Vic drew his father's attention to these fashion errors, but his father couldn't have cared less. For a while Vic's father played drums, badly, in a small circus that toured Iowa, and before Vic knew enough to be embarrassed, he went to hear his father's band accompany Tonja, the henna-haired trapeze artist, as she swung by her knees over their heads. The absurdity of it was stunning. But Vic's father was a college professor, and, among his university colleagues, eccentric behavior was tolerated, even expected. The man taught in the English Department, after all. He taught the Bible as literature, and he was an atheist! What sense did that make?

His mother collected unbeautiful, unnecessary things—magazines, dolls, Kleenex boxes—and stacked them around their house, forcing the occupants to walk ever narrowing pathways between the rooms. Forget about sitting on the furniture. His mother never once answered the phone or the door, not wanting, she explained, to be put on the spot.

By the time his parents went into assisted living they decided, after never exchanging a cross word in their entire marriage—or not one Vic remembered—that they hated each other so much they had to have separate apartments. But even that wasn't enough, because they ran into each other around Melrose Meadows and became offended by the other's cruel or show-offy or childish behavior. They called Vic to complain about each other, but nothing he said made a bit of difference, and they died, three years apart, bewildered about why they'd ended up alone.

And the unreasonableness went on. There was his wife, who was convinced that Nance was one of Wilson's radiation victims, even though she had no evidence whatsoever for her theory. There was Ava, to whom he'd explained over and over again that if she didn't learn to deal with her anger and quit physically attacking her sister she'd attack somebody else someday and end up in jail. Suzi, who wouldn't do her physical therapy exercises, even though she claimed she wanted her knee to get better. Otis, who hid out in that infernal shed all the time. Wilson, who wouldn't go out of the house by himself anymore because he was convinced that a bogeywoman was waiting to get him.

Vic had assumed that he wouldn't have to take up the mantle of village explainer, or village scold, with Gigi, not because of her behavior, which had never been especially reasonable, but because of how he felt when he was with her. He'd thought, he'd hoped, that *he* could be unreasonable, too, at least for a while, when he was with her, but it seemed that it was not to be. Sigh.

"We've got to try to make scoring as accurate as possible," he told Gigi. "That's what we're here for. There's a lot of money riding on this project." He sat down on the edge of the table, hating himself for saying these things and her for making him.

She shrugged and looked down at the floor. "It's so boring, reading all those essays."

"Lots of kids are going to get the wrong scores. Doesn't that bother you? What if it happened to Travis?"

She wrinkled up her nose and grimaced. "I haven't been doing it the whole time. I was just trying to hurry, so we could get out of here." She stepped forward and started to hug him, pressing her breasts against his chest. How easy it would be to give up, give in, say to hell with his job the same way he'd been planning to—let's admit it—say the hell with his marriage. But he kept his arms at his sides.

She finally gave up and dropped her arms, cocking her head and making Bambi eyes at him. "Let's talk about this at Andrew's," she said.

"I'm not going to Andrew's," he said. "I'm going home. I need to figure out what to do about this."

"I'm really sorry," she said, stepping back, her face now pale. "I really didn't think this was that big a deal. You didn't act like it was."

He hadn't? Maybe he hadn't known how important the project was to him. How important his job was. "I've got to think," he told her. But so far, thinking too much, about the wrong things—in other words, rationalizing—was what had gotten him into this mess.

"Fine." She started gathering up her stuff—her glasses, her pens and pencils, her pack of gum, not looking up at him.

When he turned around to leave, he saw Nance in the doorway, her small neat figure, standing there, watching them, purse slung over her shoulder, that red lunch bag clutched in her hand.

"Why are you still here?" He had no idea how much she'd overheard.

"I want to talk to you."

He turned back to Gigi, but she'd gone.

In his office, seated behind his desk, he felt better. "About Gigi," he began.

Nance picked up a picture on his desk—Soccer Suzi, from two seasons ago. "You and Gigi have a thing going."

"Of course we don't." So maybe she hadn't overheard his argument with Gigi. He felt relieved. "Is *that* what you wanted to talk to me about?" he asked her. "Not that it's any of your business."

She set the picture of Suzi down on his desk, facing her, and gazed at him, her face troubled rather than judgmental. But her words were harsh. "You need to be paying more attention to your family."

He thought about protesting, making excuses, but didn't have the energy. "Yeah. I know."

"Talk to them. Talk to Suzi. Ask her how she is. Ask her what's been going on."

"Why don't *you* tell me, if you know something."

Nance shook her head. "You ask her."

"Okay, I will. Now. About Gigi." Vic suddenly found he wanted to confide in Nance about Gigi cheating with the portfolios, ask her advice.

"Forget about Gigi!" Nance slammed her fist on his desk, causing his desk light to blink. "I can't stay here anymore and watch you flirt with the Dixie chick. I was going to tell your wife about you and Gigi. I *want* to tell her, but I'll leave that to you. This is my last day here."

"You're quitting?"

"Got that right, sailor." She flung her red lunch bag into his trash can. "Now go home and be a husband and a daddy." She stood up and marched out.

Vic sat behind his desk, stunned. Should he find this funny? Should he be offended? Outraged? The woman had threatened him, for God's sake. What had happened to the sweet little old lady who'd sat in his living room two months ago, eating cake and complimenting? Who was this nasty busybody? Whoever she was, she had some nerve.

When Vic pulled into the driveway he saw Otis standing in the lower part of the backyard holding a blue metal wand about as long as his forearm. He was shirtless and barefoot, which was unusually careless for him—worried as he usually was about sunburn and fire ants.

He had his back turned, and so Vic tried to sneak up on him. This seemed to be his day for that. Catching people in the act. Except that he knew what Gigi was doing as soon as he saw her.

With Otis, not so much. Vic was struck, again, by how strange it was that his son was a man with hair on his chest, six feet three inches tall, an inch taller then Vic was.

Otis was looking at a little screen on the object, which had a gauge with a red flashing light on it.

"Is that a Geiger counter?"

Unlike Gigi, Otis didn't jump or yell or even seem startled, because he wasn't. Of course, he'd heard his father's car and seen him coming. He was just ignoring his father, watching the needle jump on his machine.

"Oats. I asked you a question."

"Just a minute," he said, not looking at Vic, wanting only for his father to go away.

Vic stood there, trying to be patient, when God knows he wasn't in a patient mood. He felt guilty that he'd allowed himself to be shut out of Otis's life, and he was angry about having to feel guilty. He knew he should fire Gigi and never have a thing to do with her again and come clean with his boss and risk losing his job; tell Caroline about his dalliance (not an affair, not yet); go in and ask Suzi what was new in her life, as Nancy Archer had commanded him to do, but he didn't feel ready to do any of that.

Finally Otis turned around and looked at him, eyes unfocused. "Huh?"

Vic asked him the question again.

"Er, well, yeah. Geiger counter. Used."

"Why do you need it? There's no radiation in our yard, is there?" Vic knew he should stop talking, but he kept on, running his trap, giving Otis an out. "So, why are you doing this? Just for fun?"

"Yeah," Otis said, smiling that angelic, surfer-boy grin. "Just for fun!"

"So, what's it say? Is there anything radioactive?"

Otis looked at Vic like he was the stupidest person to walk the planet. "Do you hear any clicking? That's what it does if something's radioactive. Anyway, there's small amounts of radiation everywhere."

"Why's the red light blinking and the needle jumping around?"

"That just shows you it's working. Okay? God!" Otis went from 0 to 150 in a split second. "Can't I do anything around here without people asking me a hundred frigging questions?"

Vic took a step back. "Come with me to get some ice cream. I won't ask you any more questions. We'll just talk about whatever. The weather. There's another tropical storm out there. Grayson."

"I'm already doing something, in case you can't tell."

"I love you, Otis."

No reply.

"Just wanted you to know." Vic turned, deciding not to go into the house and face any kind of music at all, and trudged back to his car. There probably wouldn't be any music inside his house to face anyhow. Caroline wouldn't want to stop whatever she was doing to listen to his tale of woe about Gigi cheating. She'd barely even noticed that he'd been going out after work almost every night. Suzi, whom he'd been instructed to talk to, had been staying at a friend's house for the past couple of nights and probably wouldn't even be there.

Driving all the way home just to leave again was unreasonable, but this thought pleased him. He could be unreasonable all by himself. He didn't need Gigi for that. Most people would say that rooting for a hurricane to hit Tallahassee was unreasonable as well. Why did they all expect him to be the reasonable one? Screw all of them. Fuck all of them.

"I love you, too, Dad," Otis tossed over his shoulder.

Not having any idea where he was going, Vic cranked up the Volvo and backed out of the driveway like hellhounds were after him, a very unreasonable way to drive.

Caroline CHAPTER 15

Caroline had not been able to have a decent conversation with Suzi. Suzi was avoiding her, staying over at Nance's house, and she'd come back home this evening, only, she informed her mother, to get some clean clothes. In the past Suzi had been something of a home girl—didn't really like being away from home. So what was up? Suzi clammed up whenever Caroline asked her what was going on. Was she angry at Caroline for something? But Caroline knew better than to get aggressive about asking what was wrong. That would just drive Suzi farther away. She resolved to be patient.

That evening Vic must've been working late although he hadn't called, her father was watching *Antiques Roadshow* in his lair, and Otis was working at . . . Wendy's? Caroline was carrying a basket of clean clothing into Suzi's room and noticed that the door to Ava's room was closed and there were voices inside. Suzi was in there, talking to Ava! That in itself was something of a miracle. The two of them used to hang out together in Ava's room all the time. When they were little they played games with their dolls and stuffed animals, and when they were older they read aloud or made up clubs or businesses or TV shows in which they'd star as two sisters who rescued animals. But lately, when they weren't fighting, they steered clear of each other. Caroline was so glad they were talking that she nearly swooned. She stepped closer to the door so she could hear what they were saying. She'd never been above snooping, spying, rifling through drawers. Whatever went on in her home was her business.

She heard Suzi say, "He posed me."

"Naked?" Ava said.

Caroline's body stiffened. She strained to listen with everything in her being.

"He posed me like this." Some rustling and thumping noises. "And like this."

More rustling and thumping. Then the two of them snickered.

"That's nasty," Ava said. "Then what?"

Caroline's hand went to the doorknob and she fought the urge to burst through the door and demand details. She knew she'd find out more if she could make herself stand there and listen as long as she could stand it.

"Then," Suzi said, "he put his, you know, his thing in my mouth."

"I've never even done that."

Oh. My. God.

"He wants to see me again," Suzi said. "He needs me to do this stuff with him because his wife won't. Don't you think he's cute?"

Holy shit. Wife?

"He's okay," Ava said.

Silence. Keep talking, Caroline thought. Keep talking, or I'll beat it out of you.

"He's so old," Ava added.

There was some rustling and low talking Caroline couldn't hear.

Ava said something that sounded like, "Are you going to?"

Suzi spoke a little more loudly. "Nance won't let me. She said that if I don't tell she'll call the police and Paula and make me tell Mom and Dad."

Paula? Nance? Police? Caroline took a deep breath and tried to calm down. Don't yell, she told herself. Don't scare the poor child. But she was shaking so badly she felt like she was going to fly apart.

She opened the door slowly and went in. She must've set the laundry basket down, because she wasn't carrying it anymore. Both girls looked startled but quickly composed themselves. They were both sitting on Ava's bed.

Caroline opened her mouth and words came out. "I heard what you were saying. I need to know what's going on."

"Nothing!" Suzi said, and actually smiled. She scooted backward on the bed and snatched a purple Elvis-head pillow and clutched it to her chest. What poses had she just been doing a minute ago? Caroline was glad she hadn't seen Suzi do them.

Ava, on the other hand, was sitting up straight and bug-eyed, watching her mother.

Caroline heard how calm her voice sounded and marveled at it. "I heard you say you gave some man . . ." should she say *blow job?* "You're way way too young for that kind of thing. I want to know who it was."

Now Suzi looked scared. She dug her chin into the pillow she was clutching.

"Honey, tell me who it was," Caroline said, and then couldn't help adding. "I can't believe that you told Mrs. Archer and she didn't tell me."

"She *wanted* to tell you," Suzi said. "I begged her not to. He'll get into so much trouble."

"It's Buff," Ava said. "That minister dude."

"That *jerk,*" Caroline said, the shock like ice water filling her body.

"Yeah," Ava said. "Jerk."

Suzi reached over and gave Ava a shove. "Thanks a lot. That's the last time I tell you anything."

"He's wolfish," Ava said. "He tried to get me to do it, but I wouldn't. I told him no. Did I do the right thing, Mom?" Ava wanted to be praised for her good decision, highlighting the contrast between herself and her sister. Every occasion was one for sibling rivalry. How could Caroline even be noticing these things right now?

She walked over and sat down on the foot of

Ava's bed. "You did the right thing," she told Ava. "But I wished you'd told me. Both of you."

"It's too embarrassing," Ava said.

Suzi's face looked scary blank. Caroline scooted over and tried to hug Suzi, but she shied away. "I only did it," Suzi said in a robotic voice, "so he'd leave Ava alone. I did it so she wouldn't have to."

"I was never going to," Ava said. "I'd never do that."

Shut up, Ava. "I'm so sorry you felt you had to do it," Caroline said. Understatement of the year. Of the century.

"That's what I do," Suzi said. "Do things to make other people feel better." She sighed and stared up at the poster on Ava's wall—a black-and-white photo of Elvis on his Harley, taken by Alfred Wertheimer. The quintessential good boy trying to act bad. Was that what Suzi had been doing?

"He probably does that kind of stuff all the time," Ava said.

"That doesn't help!" Suzi shrieked and slapped the side of Ava's head.

"Owwww," Ava howled.

Caroline, moving quickly, caught Suzi up and held her and kept murmuring that it would be okay, that Suzi wasn't in trouble, that it wasn't her fault. But her mind was spinning into the future, toward what she had to do next.

She left the girls in Ava's room; and on the way out she tripped over the laundry basket, stumbled, and nearly fell, and then wished she'd fallen so she'd have a legitimate excuse to cry. She already had a reason, which wasn't the same as an excuse. She wanted to cry, to scream, to rant and rave, but she couldn't make Suzi feel worse than she already did. This was about Suzi, Caroline told herself. Keep the focus on helping Suzi get through this.

In her bedroom she dialed Vic's cell phone number, but he didn't pick up. He'd been staying late at work every night. Or at least he always said he was at work, and when he did come home he'd sneak straight down to his computer to check that damn hurricane Web site. Lately all he could talk about was Hurricane Grayson, a category 1 that had come ashore in the Keys that afternoon. She felt a burst of anger toward Vic for not being available. She could follow that train of thought a long way. He was never really available. When it came to her and the kids. Except for Suzi's soccer. But since he didn't have soccer anymore, he'd simply disappeared into hurricanes and work.

Gigi! She was probably working with Vic. Ava must have Gigi's cell phone number, because of the riding lessons. Oh shit. Gigi was Buff's sister. She dialed Nance's number.

When Nance answered, Caroline just started talking. "Suzi told me about Buff."

“I’m sick about it.”

“I bet you are,” Caroline said, allowing a bit of her anger to spill over, even though she knew that Nance wasn’t the right target. She railed at Nance and Nance just listened.

“Call Child Protective Services,” Nance finally suggested.

For some reason this suggestion made Caroline even angrier. “First I’m coming over there to talk to Buff. Are they home?”

“It’s Wednesday night. They’re at church.”

Caroline forced herself to take a breath. “Then I’m going to church. Now. To tell him I know.”

“Can I come with you? I’d like to help any way I can.”

Caroline punched the off button on the phone and wished she had one of those old-fashioned phones that you could hang up by slamming the receiver down, making a point. Fuck you, was the point she wanted to make.

By the time she got to the Genesis Church, the service was more than half over. She stood in the foyer, with the gleaming terra-cotta tile floors, and peered through a round window in the door that opened into the sanctuary. *Sanctuary* didn’t feel like the right word for that room. *Arena*. There was a band set up on the stage, but the spotlight wasn’t on them—it was on some man, evidently the minister, who was up there on the stage preaching, and people in the audience were shouting out "Praise Jesus" and "Amen" and waving their hands in the air. The minister's voice rose and dipped, rose and dipped. It was mesmerizing. She couldn't see Buff anywhere. What was his real name? She refused to think of him by that harmless, cuddly nickname. Honey, don't you trust old Buff?

"Hey there," said a quiet voice at her elbow. A dark-haired woman, very slight, wearing a long skirt and no shoes, stood beside her. "You're welcome to go in," she said. "Lay your troubles on the Lord."

"Don't have any troubles."

The woman smiled and held up her bare foot, bony and supple. "God doesn't care how you're dressed."

Caroline had no idea what she was wearing, so she checked. A tank shirt and an old pair of holey shorts with green deck paint on them. So what. She imagined herself bursting into the sanctuary and making a big scene, but that would be too melodramatic. They'd throw her out and she wouldn't get to say all she had to say.

"Is Buff in there?" she asked.

"First row on the right." She pointed. There he was, sitting in a row of men, staring up at the minister but probably planning his next sexual encounter with a minor. Smug bastard.

"What's his real name?" Caroline asked the woman.

The woman frowned. "Why, Buff is his real name, far as I know." She flapped her hand, bye-bye, and slipped into the arena.

Caroline stepped back and paced around the foyer, glancing into the Sunday school rooms that opened up off to the side. All these rooms had stages in them as well, miniature versions of the big stage in the big room. In the KidZone she spotted Paula Coffey, Buff's wife, up front with a guitar, leading a bunch of preschoolers in a song.

Caroline took her phone out and called Vic again and got no answer. This time she left a message, explaining, in a flat, terse voice, what had happened and where she was and why.

Church finally ended with a wild burst of singing and clapping, and then people started filing out. Caroline sat down in a big plush armchair in the corner of the lobby. She'd wait for Buff to come out and she'd surprise him. She imagined the look on his face and squeezed her knees together to keep from flying apart. The smell of popcorn and coffee was making her feel queasy. She wished she had a weapon. Anything sharp would do. Or hard. She imagined smashing a hymnal into his face. She suddenly remembered the face of the teenage boy who lived next door to her family in Iowa City. Artie

Finnegan. She'd been only five or six. Had he done something to her? She'd gone into his house with him once but couldn't remember a thing about it.

She couldn't sit there any longer. The surge of people leaving had slowed to a trickle and she got up. She walked over and looked through the door and saw Buff standing with his wife, Paula, up front near the stage. How'd Paula get in there? Paula was holding a squirming blond toddler. Angel. Another young couple stood there, talking to them, laughing. Behind them, the band was packing up their instruments. Caroline felt paralyzed for a minute, imagining how Paula was going to feel, but the self-satisfied look on Buff's face sent her forward, propelled her up the aisle. She stood behind him, her teeth chattering.

She finally had to say, "Excuse me."

All four adults and the toddler turned to look at her. Everything was happening in slow motion, like the time her car spun off the icy road in Iowa and landed in a ditch. She couldn't stop that and she couldn't stop this.

Buff smiled quizzically. Paula just smiled. The toddler stared.

"I'm Suzi Witherspoon's mother," she said. "Remember me? Remember Suzi?"

Buff's mouth opened.

"Soo-see. Soo-see Widderpoon!" Angel said.

"Suzi's such a great girl," Paula gushed.

"Yes, she is!" Caroline said heartily, idiotically. Her ears were ringing. She'd never been this angry in her life. "What's your name?" she asked Buff. "I don't mean Buff. I mean your real name. Not your nickname."

"Ah, it's Buffington. Buffington Coffey."

"Buffington Coffey! Buffington Coffey!" said Angel.

"Well, Buffington Coffey," Caroline repeated and then let loose with a string of foul language and accusations and threats that scared the hell out of her.

Paula cowered and she and Angel backed away, and the other couple stepped back, too. Only Buff stood his ground, listening, as if she were reciting Bible verses.

"There's been some mistake," he said when she stopped. "Would you like to come back with me to my office? We can talk in private." Then he addressed his wife. "There's nothing to this. Suzi's got some problems."

"She does now!" Caroline yelled. "After what you did to her." She went on and on, saying that there was no way in hell she'd go back to his office and did he want to take nasty photos of her and get her to suck his dick, too?

There was quiet after this last outburst, and then she heard a rumbling behind her. It was Vic, growling like a bear, running up the aisle. He tackled Buff, like the football player he'd been in high school, and then started whaling on him, beating the tar out of him, and Caroline was glad, very glad.

Buff didn't fight back but lay there like he deserved it.

CHAPTER 16 *Ava*

She hadn't been to Mission San Luis since elementary school, and what she mostly remembered was the long climb uphill to get there. Otis had dropped her off at the bottom of the hill and zoomed off to God knows where, refusing to wait, even when Ava promised she'd just be a few minutes. He was off on some Otis errand of mysterious importance. But actually she was glad that he'd gone, glad to be left alone and entirely free of her family.

It was late afternoon. On top of the hill the live oaks shaded the paths and buildings. She followed the path to the right, past the friary and the huge thatched-roof church, seeing no one until she noticed a few people gathered in front of a cottage across the field. She had no idea what sort of craft or trade Travis demonstrated—had no idea whether or not Travis was even working today. But she needed to talk to him. Talking to someone she didn't know well on the phone made her nervous, and he wasn't on MySpace, so she'd taken a chance and come here. She'd taken a chance! She didn't usually take chances.

A gaggle of little boys in baseball caps raced past her, going the opposite way, red-faced and shouting. She approached the cottage. There were gardens around it and a small bonfire in a clearing. The smell of meat cooking wafted up from an iron kettle in the fire. A costumed woman was holding forth near the fire, while an earnest middle-aged couple in matching T-shirts and shorts, with big smiles plastered on their faces, looked on.

The talking lady, who wore an ivory linen mantilla and silver earrings and an ivory linen bustled dress, turned to include Ava as part of her audience, and Ava felt obliged to stand and listen.

"That's my cook," the talking lady said, pointing to a darker, younger woman sitting on a log nearby, sewing. "She's fixing our stew for dinner. I have to keep an eye on her so she doesn't burn it."

The young woman, also in costume—a much simpler one—didn't even look up.

"I've just been at the church, saying my rosary," the talking lady went on, as if they'd asked. "My older brother is the friar here, and another brother is the merchant trader. He has three ships anchored down at St. Marks. He takes the things we make here in the village and trades them in Havana for things from Europe, like playing cards and tools and olive oil. There's his stand." She gestured at a little thatched-roof stand across the path, where animal skins hung on a line.

"Is there anyone working there now?" Ava jumped in.

"My brother has just set off down the Wakulla River with some Indians in canoes, headed for St. Marks, carrying more of our products to trade. I've been praying for their safe return."

Ava guessed that this meant that Travis wasn't acting as the merchant trader today. She stood there, swatting gnats away from her eyes, wishing she could swish her ponytail like a horse's tail.

The talking lady gazed quizzically up at the sky. "Oh dear. Looks like rain."

Actually, it didn't. But it was cooler today than it usually was in August, or so everyone was saying. Only in the mid-eighties, with low humidity. It could be because Hurricane Grayson had gone back out into the Gulf. And then, who knew what it would do?

"Heavens, I need to bring in my children's beds before it rains!" said the lady. "I set them out to air this morning. My husband and I and our ten children live in that cottage."

A black rooster and some speckled hens darted past, weaving this way and that.

The man listening asked the talking lady if the hens were hers.

She couldn't give a straight answer, it seemed. "I lost three hens to hawks last week." She went on and on, in her phony antiquated English, when Spanish would've been more accurate. Ava listened as long as she could stand it. Finally she interrupted and asked her if Travis was working there today.

"He's a soldier, down at the fort," she told Ava. "Would you like to see inside my cottage?" she asked her group. The nice couple followed her and Ava turned and hurried off toward the fort.

She wanted to talk to Travis about everything that had been going on at home. Things had been bad, very bad. Travis might not be glad to see her at all, since Rev. Buff was his mother's brother, and his uncle, but this was another chance she had to take. The red dust on the paved path got between her flip-flops and her feet, and she wished she'd worn sneakers. She didn't have much tolerance for the physical irritations that most people could just ignore, but if she banged her head hard on something it didn't seem to hurt her as much as it would most people. Most people. She got tired of most people. Travis wasn't like most people, either.

A log stockade enclosed the white stucco fort.

Inside, Travis was talking to the group of sweaty little boys. He wore the same white collarless shirt and breeches with the braided belt and felt hat that he'd been wearing at church, the same brown knee sock thingies and leather shoe boots. "Ava!" he said, and she could tell he was really glad to see her. He held up his finger, meaning, wait a minute. So she did.

A set of military spears with wooden handles and wicked-looking blades hung on the wall behind him, and he explained the differences among them to the boys. They were different kinds of pole arms, he said. One was for fighting on horseback, another type had different-shaped blades to demonstrate rank. The boys made sounds of approval.

Then he showed them the matchlock and flintlock muskets hanging on another wall and some swords lying on a shelf right at the boys' eye level.

The boys crowded close to the swords, itching to pick them up. They weren't even listening to Travis, she could tell. Each one wanted to snatch up a sword and stab something.

Finally Ava couldn't stand it anymore. "You boys need to get out of here," she said. "Time's up. Move along."

There were four of them, and they all looked at her with varying degrees of surprise and annoyance on their faces. Then one of the boys said, "Vamoose," and they all took off together out of the fort like a school of little fishes.

"Is there anyone else in here?" Ava asked him, and Travis said no.

"When are you going to be on *America's Next Top Model*?" He leaned back against the clay shelf that was built into the wall. "I've been watching it every week."

Was that all he cared about? She leaned against the shelf next to him. She told him she wasn't interested in being on that show anymore.

"Good," he said. "It's really lame."

That made her feel better. "You didn't come to support group yesterday."

He shrugged, lifting his tricorne back off his forehead. There was a slight indentation in his forehead and Ava longed to touch it the way the boys had longed to touch the swords.

"I don't need to go to that group," he said. "I don't have Asperger's."

"What *do* you have, then?"

"You mean like what disorder? I don't know and I don't care. I'm just going to live my life. Screw all that disorder and syndrome shit."

"Tough talk," Ava said. She knew she would think of herself as someone with Asperger's syndrome for the rest of her life, and it felt like a huge, unfair burden. If she ever voiced this sentiment, someone would point out that everyone had burdens of one kind or another.

That was the Christian way to look at it, but she wasn't a Christian, so did she have to look at it that way? It sucked. Period. But at least she could read about Asperger's and make sense of herself, and how many people could say that?

"Did you just come here to yell at me for not coming to group?" Travis said. "I didn't think you'd care."

"I'm not yelling. I care."

"That's good," Travis said, and they both leaned in awkward silence. Ava kicked the toe of her flip-flop in the red clay floor. Outside there was the sound of birds, a rooster crowing, and the boys somewhere yelling and whooping.

"I wish I could just stay in the seventeenth century," Travis said.

"Why?"

"My mom. She's always in a bad mood. Either drunk or trying not to drink or has a hangover. Do you drink?"

Ava shook her head. "I mean, I have a couple of times." That was a lie. She'd tasted wine once and hated it. In high school she'd never been invited to the parties where kids drank. Her few friends in high school had been the uncool supersmart girls, now gone off to good colleges across the country, who'd had slumber parties where they watched *Gilmore Girls*.

Travis straightened up, turned around, reached up and removed one of the rifles from the wall.

What was he going to do with a gun? "Is that real?" Ava asked him.

"Of course," he said. "We're not supposed to let visitors hold them, but do you want to?"

Ava shook her head.

He took aim at something outside the front door. "We keep our gunpowder kegs in a room back there, if you want to see."

"No, thank you," Ava said, and then asked him if he knew about Buff and Suzi, and when he said no, she told him what had happened, and she told him how her mother had confronted Buff at church and that he'd denied doing anything, and how her father had beaten Buff to a pulp and how Buff had threatened to press charges, and how that didn't sound good, even if she wasn't sure exactly what it meant, and how her parents had reported Buff's abuse of Suzi to the police and he'd denied everything to them, too, and how Suzi had just been crying in her room and going to counseling appointments, and her mother had been crying, too, and her dad had either been angry and yelling or not speaking to anyone.

Travis had lowered the rifle and was frowning at her. "Why are you telling me all this?"

"Since he's your uncle, I thought you'd want to know. Bob's your uncle!" she couldn't help adding.

"*Buff's* my uncle. He'd never do anything like that. He's a minister!"

Ava couldn't believe that he was standing up for Buff. She'd thought he'd be on her side, on Suzi's side. "You don't believe Suzi? You think she's lying? She's not a liar."

Travis lifted the long gun to his shoulder again, sighting an imaginary target across the room, and Ava felt like slugging him. It seemed very important, suddenly, to prove Suzi right and Buff wrong. But how to do it when she wasn't there with them? Actually, she knew how to do it. She could reveal her secret to Travis, about Mr. Boy taking the naked pictures of her and Buff showing her that he'd seen them. But if she told Travis, she'd have no control over the information anymore. If Travis told anyone, more people would get in trouble, including her. But she really, really wanted Travis on her side, and Suzi's side, and telling on herself was the one way she could think of to get him there.

"Hey," Travis said, hanging the musket back up on the wall. "Would you like a tour of the mission? We close in forty-five minutes so they won't care if I leave my post. I'm in training to give tours. What I want to do eventually is work on the archaeological dig. They've found some cool stuff—pottery, bowls, tools. I'm going to FSU next year and majoring in archaeology. I'm going to get my own apartment. Have you been watching the news about Hurricane Grayson? There's a storm warning for the entire coastline of Florida. Atlantic and Gulf coasts. First time that's ever happened." He started walking out of the fort, and Ava had to catch up.

Okay, so he didn't want to talk about the Buff thing, and Ava realized she was sick of hearing about it and talking about it and thinking about it, and glad not to have to tell Travis what she didn't want to tell anyone.

He and Ava went into the friary and then into the gorgeous church with the high thatched roof, which let in tiny beams of light, wisps of straw floating down, and the dirt floors and glowing religious paintings, then they walked over to the Indian council house. She could see why Travis liked it here so much. Up on this hill there was a touch of a breeze every now and then. And the traffic on Pensacola Street was just a faint murmur.

As she was walking around with Travis, she had three realizations, none of them directly related to what she was looking at. The first realization was that looking at the pictures and the places and imagining what went on in Mission San Luis felt like a key into a new kingdom. Re-creations of the past. *She* wanted to re-create the past. She wanted to immerse herself in history. The history of something. She would major in history. History, she realized, was what she cared about most. She'd been skirting around this knowledge for some time. She'd been most interested in the *story* of Elvis, in his history, even more than his music. She'd loved reading books about how horse breeds came to be, about the origins of foxhunting and what sort of people had gone in for it. The subjects weren't as important to her as the stories. What sort of history she might want to study, the time period, at what college, she didn't know yet. But she knew. History! That's where she wanted to be. She felt something in her settle and lift at the same time.

The second realization was that she really liked Travis. She felt happy around him. Relaxed. Even today, with all the stress at home. He was cute and smart and interesting, and she wanted to go out with him. Not out-out, like going steady, but she wanted to go on a date with him and see what happened. She hadn't had any fun dates ever. But she felt ready to try again.

The third realization wasn't so good. It struck her that she'd been remiss in keeping her secret from her family, especially now that Suzi was in such a bad way. It wasn't Travis she needed to tell. She needed to tell her parents. Suzi, surprisingly, hadn't ratted on her about the naked photos, but she needed to rat on herself.

If she told her parents about her experiences with Mr. Boy and Buff, her story would add more weight to Suzi's case. It would also get Ava into trouble, but was that such a big deal now? No,

Suzi was her little sister, and she needed her help. Ava rarely got to feel like the big sister with Super Suzi as a sibling, but this would give her the chance. It would upset her parents even more, though. She hated to be the cause of more pain and conflict, but she had to do it.

She and Travis were standing at a display of knee-high pottery jars in the Indian council house, a large circular structure that could accommodate three thousand people, and Travis had gone quiet and was watching her. “What are you thinking about?” he asked her. “Are you bored? I’m sorry, I talk too much.”

“I was wondering how I was going to get home,” Ava said. She wasn’t, but she should have been, since Otis had roared off before she could make arrangements with him to pick her up.

“I can take you,” Travis said. “We could get ice cream first, if you want.”

“I want,” Ava said, knowing she’d remember this afternoon for the rest of her life, walking around Mission San Luis with Travis, realizing that she liked him, realizing what she wanted to study in school, realizing that she had to help her sister, come what may. Two great things and one awful thing in one afternoon. And there was Hurricane Grayson, which might or might not cause a lot of trouble.

Why did the good and the bad have to come together? It seemed, often, that they did.

CHAPTER 17 *Otis*

Finally, the day had come. He got up early, dressed, ate a hearty breakfast of twelve toaster waffles before anyone else got up, enjoying the solemn ceremonial feel of this occasion, this day, August 12, 2006. A day that would appear in future science books, in news stories, in TV specials, maybe even movies. All this wonderful fallout would take a while, but right away, at least, he'd be in the local news. His story would wipe Hurricane Grayson off the front page of the *Tallahassee Democrat* and would do the same to the stories about Reverend Buffington Coffey, and give Rusty some peace and quiet.

He missed Rusty. She hadn't been around since all the fuss started with Suzi and Rusty's father. He'd texted Rusty and asked her to call him, but she didn't, so he called her and left voice messages, saying that he missed her and that his reactor was nearly finished and he wanted her to be there when he put it together. When she didn't call him back, he called again and added that he was sorry for everything that had happened with her father, and that he didn't blame her and that he really, really liked her—he didn't mention the word love again—but she wouldn't text or call him back. There was so much he needed to tell her, so many things he'd had to do without her.

She'd missed out on the blowtorch. He loved his blowtorch. He loved the roaring noise, the metal mask he wore, the bright flame, and she would've loved these things, too. She could've helped him take apart the replacement mantles that the two of them had stolen from Target, extracting the thorium strips. She could've helped him dump the strips into his cast-iron frying pan, and he would've let her fire up his blowtorch and reduce those suckers to ash. Watching Rusty do it would've made it even more fun.

Next he'd had to isolate and purify the thorium from the ash, and he'd had a little chat with Granddad about how to do that. Granddad had suggested using lithium fragments to absorb the unwanted ash. Lithium batteries, his grandfather said, would be the best source.

He wanted to tell her how Granddad had become a virtual prisoner in his den, with himself as his own jailor. He was so scared of being accosted by Mrs. Archer that he never went outside anymore. He gazed longingly at the front yard, commenting on the yard work that needed to be done, but he wouldn't venture out. He wouldn't even go on walks with Otis and Parson, which had been one of his favorite things to do.

And his mother, who usually fussed over

Granddad almost as much as she fussed over Ava, had stopped reading to Granddad and asking after him and bringing him snacks. It was all about Suzi now, taking Suzi to counseling, talking to Dad, in loud enough voices that even somebody who wasn't trying to eavesdrop could overhear, about the four other girls from the youth group who were also pressing charges against Buff.

When he heard all this talk about Buff, Otis thought of Rusty, whom he realized now must've known something was screwy with her father. She'd called him a phony and a perv, and he felt really bad for her. She must feel so embarrassed and ashamed to have everyone know. And the worst thought he had was that maybe her father had tried to do some of the same things to her. Maybe he *had* done them. Otis had read about men doing those things to their daughters, but he'd never tried to imagine how a daughter with that kind of father might feel. In fact, until he started wondering about Rusty and missing her and feeling bad for her, he'd never thought much about anybody other than himself—maybe because he'd never really spent a lot of time with another person, outside his own family, that is. Gotten to know her. Shared experiences with her, like stealing and vandalism and creating dangerous nuclear devices. So this is what it feels like, he realized, to let another person into your world. It felt much more dangerous than any nuclear device he could create, because he had no idea what the possible chain reaction would be. But when he thought about all the bad things he and Rusty had done, it made him happy, and he was glad of all of it. He thought about her at night, in bed, until he ached, and there was only one thing to do for that, but a different sort of ache came back right after. He missed her.

So, in order to keep the memory of Rusty alive, he went out and shoplifted lithium batteries from CVS and Walgreens and Target and Walmart, even though he could've paid for them. Once he got them home, he cut them in half with wire cutters and removed the shiny lithium strips and dropped them in a beaker of Crisco oil to prevent oxidation. Then, donning his gas mask, lead suit, and latex gloves, he put the thorium and lithium into a sealed aluminum foil ball and dropped it into a pan of oil, cooking it on his propane stove for half an hour. When he tested the ball, after it cooled, with the Geiger counter, all indications were go.

Then he had the thorium all ready to shoot the gun at. He had the beryllium strips for part of the fuel, but his final step was to transmute the radium—obtained from the clocks and the hidden tube of paint and the chunk ordered online—into a workable form. He ordered some barium sulfate online and mixed it with radium and strained the brew into a beaker. In the beaker it emitted a glow that told Otis it was ready.

A few days earlier he'd loaded up his gun with his uranium and beryllium and tried shooting it at the thorium. Nothing happened, nothing that could be measured with his Geiger counter. He tried this for three successive days with no results, and he began to get agitated.

That night he drove by Rusty's house, looking for her, but it was shut up tight. No cars there, no lights on. Another night he walked over to her house, dressed in black, wanting to propose some Mrs. Archer harassing if she was up for it. The black SUV was in the driveway, but no lights were on. He knocked on Rusty's window, but there was no response, so he snuck across the street and did some halfhearted Mrs. Archer tormenting by himself—tossed some gravel at her windows, picked up a flowerpot with fake daisies in it and placed it on the roof of her car—not very original tricks, but it was something to honor Rusty, and he slunk back home, missing her.

He discussed the problem of his gun not firing with Granddad, who suggested that in this situation one might slow the neutrons down using a filter of water and tritium, which could be obtained from night-vision gunsights. Otis looked them up online and discovered that night-vision gunsights cost more than a thousand dollars apiece. For two days after this discovery he wandered about in a daze, and one evening, when everyone else was all worked up about some new revelation in the Buff case—a fifth girl, one from Buff's old church, had just come forward—Otis just walked into his parents' room and took his father's credit card from his wallet and ordered three gunsights to be sent to him FedEx overnight.

When the box arrived he took it with shaking hands to his shed. He carefully pried the sights open, and when he realized that he could extract the tritium, a waxy substance, and reassemble the gunsights with no evidence that they'd been pried open, he decided to scrape the tritium off all three of them, using coffee stirrers he'd lifted from Wendy's, and then return the gunsights to the company, claiming they were defective. That way, as long as his father didn't check his credit card balance until after the sights had been returned, he'd get away with it. A brilliant plan, if he did say so himself.

August 12, 2006. He stepped outside onto the back deck. Another coolish, airy day, sunny but not hot, scuddy white clouds blowing across the sky. A great day to complete his project. Wanting to give Rusty one more chance to be there when he made history, he stopped outside his shed and called her cell phone again. This time she answered. She didn't sound happy to hear from him. She sounded sullen and snippy, like the old Rusty used to before he got to know her. Remembering that she usually slept late, he apologized for calling at eight thirty in the morning, but she said she was already up, had been up, and what did he want already?

Otis ignored her bratty tone and asked where she'd been, why she hadn't called him back; and she acted annoyed, as if he were merely pestering her. "Why do you think?" she said. "Duh. Anyway, I don't live in your neighborhood anymore. I don't live in Tallytown anymore." She told him that she and her mother and Angel were staying down in Lloyd, twenty miles away, with her mother's parents. Then she added that her mother was divorcing her father, whom she would henceforth refer to as the demon seed.

Otis told her he was sorry, but he didn't know if that was the right response to her parents' getting a divorce.

"Seriously, don't be," she said. "It's a big relief, right? Now I don't have to lock my door."

Otis felt a chill, even though it was plenty hot in his backyard.

"I meant I'm sorry about all of it," he said. "I'm sorry it happened."

There was a sniffling sound. Was she crying? He hadn't meant to make her cry, so he started talking, quickly relating the trial-and-error process he'd been through in the past few days, the gunsight scam, shoplifting the batteries, and how today was the day he was assembling the entire thing and how he knew, just knew, it was going to work.

He heard the sniffling again, which puzzled him, but then he realized she was laughing. "What's so funny?"

"Oh, nothing. You. You're so . . . I don't know. Earnest."

"Okay." Otis didn't know why that was funny, but he realized he was smiling, too. "I wish you were here," he said.

"Me, too. Good luck with your whatsit. I'll be there in spirit, cheering you on."

"When are you coming back?"

She sighed. "Nothing's been decided. I won't be living in Canterbury Hills again, that's for sure."

"You'll visit, though. You'll come see me. I could drive down to Lloyd."

"Uhmm. Don't think my mom would be too glad to see anyone from your family right now."

Otis protested that he hadn't had anything to do with the "scandal" and that it wasn't fair to blame him, and Rusty agreed and said it wasn't fair but that nothing was and that she had to go now and please don't call for a while. "I took one of your radium paint chips," she told him. "For my medicine bag."

"Don't!" Otis said. "Don't put it in your bag. Throw it away." Why was he getting so upset?

"Sheesh," said Rusty. "Okay, spaceman." She hung up.

So, on the big day, Otis went into his shed alone and, feeling something of a letdown, after he'd put on his lead apron and mask and plastic gloves, he wrapped the uranium powder and beryllium in little foil cubes and arranged them around a block of carbon inside the lead gun, then wrapped the thorium ash in foil packets and distributed them around the outside layer of the gun, next to the packets of uranium and beryllium. Then he wrapped the whole thing up with duct tape and weighed it. It weighed two pounds. He set it down and left the shed, locking the door behind him. The deed was done.

Although everything had changed for Otis, he didn't feel it was the right time to break the news about his invention. Not until he knew for sure it was working, he told himself. For the next couple of days, three times a day, he checked the level of radiation in his shed with his Geiger counter, recording his findings in his logbook. Every time the reading was higher, until finally the needle went to the top of the dial, which meant at least 50 mrems. He hadn't decided how and when to reveal to the world what he'd made, and he wished he could talk to Rusty about it. He didn't want to announce his accomplishment until he'd made good and sure it was working.

One day he decided to measure the levels outside his shed, and he picked up radiation all over the backyard. How much was too much? He'd never cared enough to find this out. But when he saw Parson sniffing around in the yard, right where he'd been picking up radiation, he grew uneasy. He scooped her up and brought her inside.

That night he visited his grandfather in his den and posed that question. How much was too much?

For once his grandfather looked at him straight on. "Why are you asking, son?"

Otis, settling himself into the chair, was startled. His grandfather had never directly questioned him like this.

When Otis didn't respond, his grandfather, who was staring at him, said, "You aren't actually thinking of making one of those things, are you? Because that would be very foolish."

Otis felt himself flushing.

"You don't want to endanger people's lives. Make them sick."

Otis nodded, but he thought of Rusty and Parson Brown, and he himself felt sick inside. Did this mean his grandfather would not be proud of his accomplishment? If his grandfather wasn't proud, would anybody be proud? He didn't intend to endanger lives. He wanted to prove that it could be done, and done safely.

"You worked with radioactive materials and it didn't hurt you," Otis said. "You said it was a lot safer than people realized."

His grandfather turned back to the TV set, to the news hour that he watched every evening. "Bad business about your sisters," Granddad said. "Terrible. Your mother just told me. I knew something was wrong around here. Why did she feel she had to protect me? I'm their grandfather!"

"I don't know," Otis said. Had the news about his sisters jarred something loose in Granddad? He seemed more with-it than he had in a long while. He pictured Granddad's head full of marbles, shaking and clacking.

The man on the news hour—the old guy with the bags under his eyes—was going on about Hurricane Grayson, which had made landfall again over Naples and was moving northeast across south Florida, flooding everything and drowning people. There was nothing about the war in Iraq, but lots of interesting facts about the hurricane.

"Areas in Florida have already received up to twenty-five inches of rain, causing serious flooding. Alligators were seen in flooded neighborhoods after high water forced them from their habitat. Hundreds of homes were flooded in

Brevard and St. Lucie counties; some locations were inundated with up to five feet of standing water. Early estimates from Brevard County show ten to twelve million dollars in damages to homes and infrastructure. Hurricane Grayson had caused the drowning of one person swimming off Neptune Beach and another swimmer in Duval County. Three people were killed in traffic accidents. A twenty-eight-year-old kite surfer was critically injured in Fort Lauderdale when winds associated with Hurricane Grayson slammed him face-first into the ground and then dragged him through streets until he hit a building."

Otis got caught up listening to the report and when his grandfather said something to him again, he'd almost forgotten what they were talking about.

"I was involved in a research study, a long time ago," his grandfather said. "We thought we were doing the right thing, but we weren't. We hurt lots of innocent people. Caused deaths. I don't want you to ever take those chances."

"I won't," Otis said in a matter-of-fact voice, but his ears were humming and he couldn't concentrate on either his granddad or the news show.

"How 'bout a game of checkers?" Granddad asked him.

Otis told him maybe later. He got up and

walked out of the room and through the empty house—everyone was gone these days—out the back door and down to his shed. There was a full moon, and the sky was unusually clear, smattered with stars. He got his Geiger counter from the shed, turned it on, and began sweeping it around the backyard. The dial on the Geiger counter glowed in the dark, and Otis saw that the radiation levels in the yard were now up to the top of the dial, just like in the shed. But all this meant was that if he stood there beside the reactor for fifteen minutes he'd be absorbing 50 milligrams of radiation. A dental X-ray was equal to 150 milligrams, and that was way safe! The only thing was that this particular Geiger counter didn't measure levels higher than 50. It was a piece of crap. So he actually had no idea of the true level being emitted.

His insufficient instrument registered top of the dial radioactivity three houses away.

There was always the Marines. A good option, if it weren't for the Iraq war.

CHAPTER 18 *Suzi*

Anne Frank was her go-to girl. Suzi stayed in her room as much as they'd let her, rereading Anne Frank's diary for the millionth time so that she wouldn't feel sorry for herself. After all, all that had happened to Suzi was that 1. She'd hurt her knee playing soccer and had missed Olympic soccer camp; and 2. She'd given a grown man a blow job. Big deal. It wasn't like he'd raped her or she'd been forced to hide in an attic for years. And she hadn't done it to protect Ava, as she'd told her mother. That idea had occurred to her only after the fact—that she'd been protecting Ava.

She *was* glad that it had happened to her and not to Ava, because Ava had already had enough counseling and attention and hand-wringing focused on her. Now it was Suzi's turn. She'd always thought of Ava as the weaker one of the two of them, but she was thinking differently now. Now she admired the way Ava had told Buff to buzz off. Ava had had no problem telling Buff to forget it. That boded well for Ava in the future, she'd heard her mother saying to her father one night in the kitchen. (This was another good side effect of the "crisis"—her father was no longer working late every night.) But what did *her* behavior say about *her* future?

The fact that her parents thought that Buff had forced her to do it, or talked her into doing it, made Suzi feel bad, because, actually, as she'd told Nance and Ava, it wasn't that way at all. She'd seen an opportunity, and she'd taken it.

Suzi'd decided not to try and correct her parents' version of the events, because she had the feeling that they would see Suzi as the innocent party no matter what. And she didn't want them to think she was some kind of oversexed slut. She'd thought Buff was attractive, and the truth was that she was just curious to see how far he'd go, and what *it* would be like with an experienced guy. She was curious! Did that make her a slut? Were sluts just curious? *Slut* wasn't a word she'd ever imagined applying to herself, but then most sluts probably didn't think of themselves that way either. She hadn't wanted to do anything much with her ex-boyfriend Davis or any boys her own age. They were so goofy and clueless and easily embarrassed and self-centered and insensitive and would've blabbed all over school. Buff never would've told a soul. It was her fault it had all come out in the open. If only she hadn't told Ava. But she had to tell somebody besides Nance, who'd been horrified but had tried to hide it. And Ava was the only person she knew who wouldn't judge her, who would listen and ask for details, but in a nonjudgmental way. She hadn't told Ava the whole truth, though. She hadn't taken off her clothes and posed for Buff. The blow job was the only thing that actually happened.

And now four other girls from the church, girls she didn't know, had come forward and told on Buff. He did this all this time, apparently, which made Suzi feel as special as a booger. How'd he even have time to write sermons when he was so busy pushing his penis on people?

Now she wished, wished so much that she hadn't done it, because the more she thought about it, the more unnecessary the whole thing seemed. She could've happily gone her whole life without smelling that oniony rubbery thing which was like a persistent thin-skinned animal trying to slide down her throat. And she could've happily gone her whole life without enduring Buff's treatment of her. He hadn't hugged or kissed her or even looked her in the eyes. He hadn't removed any of her clothing or his. Didn't turn off his office light. Just unzipped his pants, pushed her down until she was sitting on his desk and then got down to business. He hadn't even acted like he enjoyed it. It was more like he was performing some grim duty, encouraging himself with nasty words, which made Suzi feel really icky. And then afterward, there was his refusal to even pretend it meant something to him. He'd driven her home without saying a word, and she was so stunned by his behavior, and hers, that she didn't speak either.

What had she expected? She'd expected hugging and kissing and professions of love, and maybe undressing and fondling, if they hadn't been in an office. But what had happened—she hadn't even known that men acted like that. She had to wonder: Did other men do such things? She found herself staring at the men walking past her house, in the car beside hers, her friends' fathers, her own father! Grown-up, painfully ordinary men. Surely not!

For years she'd been warned repeatedly, boringly, about perverts, and had never thought much about what a pervert might do once he got hold of you, but now she supposed she knew at least some of it. She was ashamed, and disappointed in herself for not following Officer Friendly's advice. She hadn't run away or yelled or kicked him in the balls. Which she'd just assumed she'd do. She'd assumed she was brave and bold. She was Suzi! But, no, she'd stood there like a wimp and did as he asked, even though it made her sick. And the worst thing was—she'd asked for it! But why? Why had she?

When she got brave enough to ask her mother these questions, her mother's response, after hugging Suzi, was to get on the phone. She called around, polling people about counselors; and many of them recommended Doris as the best person in town for "this sort of thing."

Doris was the calmest woman Suzi'd ever met—soft-spoken and kind but no-nonsense and unflappable. On the old side. On the nondescript side. But Suzi kept watching Doris and marveling—Doris was a real counselor! Like the kind Ava went to!

Doris had told Suzi in no uncertain terms that it was a very *good* thing that her mother had overheard, because this kind of thing needed to come out in the open and not be a secret. That was the worst thing about it. The secret part. And Nance should've told her mother right away, Doris said. She said that Suzi really needed her parents' protection against men like Buff.

When Suzi explained that she'd started it, that she'd told Buff she was available, Doris explained that Suzi was too young to understand the ramifications of what she was doing. She'd gone along with Buff because she didn't know what would happen, and once she got into his office she was too intimidated, too frightened to act. Buff obviously had a lot of problems and was so immature he felt it was okay to act out the way he did.

When Suzi thought of Buff's behavior, his heavy breathing and dirty talking—had he really compared her mouth to a pussy?—and his violent pumping away as "acting out," Suzi wanted to giggle, but she stifled it because Doris was so serious. The thing was, Doris said, Buff was the adult, and he'd abused his position of authority that the church had given him, not just with Suzi and Ava but with all those other girls. It was a good thing, for everybody's sake, that his behavior was discovered and stopped. Suzi was *not* responsible for any of the pain this was causing anyone. No, the blame lay squarely on Buff's shoulders.

Tears sprang to Suzi's eyes—again—and she felt so many conflicting things, it made her dizzy. She felt so grateful to be sitting there, talking to Doris, able to unburden herself to somebody who knew how to respond. And she knew that Doris was right. It was Buff's fault. But was she entirely innocent?

Doris kept talking, asking her things, and Suzi answered as best she could, but one thing she could never tell was that she was relieved to be there with Doris not just because she could unburden herself but because, at last, *she* was the one who needed help and support, *she* was the one in need of attention, *she* was the one with the problem, and most important, now *she* had her mother's undivided attention. She felt guilty about this, and a little angry. Did you have to get yourself sexually abused (as Doris called it) to get some attention in her house?

The shit hit the fan again with Ava's revelation. After Ava told their mother about Mr. Boy and the nude photographs their mother blew another gasket. She went down in the basement and told their father, who was monitoring Hurricane Grayson on his computer. He came up and called the police and reported Mr. Boy, whose real name was Mr. Boyle. Both her parents were furious at Nance and blamed the nude photo thing on her. They invited the poor woman over without telling her why.

It was early evening when her parents, Suzi and Ava, Nance, and her grandfather sat down in the living room. Nance, for some reason, had insisted that Granddad be there. The two of them sat next to each other on the couch, Suzi next to Nance, with her bum leg propped up on the coffee table, and her parents sat in armchairs. Ava sat on the ottoman in her baggy pajama shorts and huge sleep T-shirt, even though it was only seven o'clock. Her face was dotted with three big blobs of white acne medicine, even though she had no acne now and had never had any. You could point this out to Ava until you were blue in the face and it never sunk in.

Otis was wandering around the neighborhood with his Geiger counter, thank God. This whole thing would embarrass him; and he wouldn't understand it, having never had a girlfriend, or even had a crush on a girl, in his entire life.

Nance, looking sporty in a navy-and-white-striped dress, admitted that she'd taken Ava to the photographer's, and said she'd only done it to help Ava, because Ava really wanted to go on *America's Next Top Model*.

"As if!" Suzi barked out.

"I never really cared about the *Next Top*

Model." Ava, ignoring Suzi, addressed Nance. "It was mostly your idea. You paid for it."

Nance looked down at her white veiny hands, and they all waited to hear what she was going to say. She didn't say anything.

"Regardless," said her father. He had stubble on his cheeks and the hair on his crown stuck up in wisps. How long had it been since he'd taken a shower? He was obsessed with the hurricane—staying up all night to check on it like it was some bad kid he was keeping tabs on. He had to know exactly where it was, where it was going, how big a troublemaker it was. All day yesterday Grayson had churned across the Florida peninsula, he told his family, moving very slowly, *gaining strength over land*—very unusual—causing massive flooding. The flooding was so bad that President Bush had declared the entire state of Florida a Federal Disaster Area.

This morning he'd informed them that Grayson had swept through Melbourne, breaking a record for the amount of rainfall accumulated, and back out into the Atlantic again. Where would it go now? Who cared, as long as it didn't come here. But it might come here. It might! It was a screwy storm, zigging and zagging all over the place as if it were toying with the entire state.

Right now it was sunny and clear here in oblivious Tallahassee. The air-conditioning in the house had shut off for a while, and the birds in the hedge by the living room windows could be heard twittering idiotically through the closed windows; and there were morons out walking their dogs and jogging as though there weren't a huge storm nearby. Hide! Hide! It might be coming! Suzi wanted to yell. Parson was sleeping under the covers on Suzi's bed. She was no fool. Okay, Suzi was officially losing her mind. She wished she could hold Parson now, smelling her comforting doggy smell, kissing her pointed snout.

"You should never have done that without our permission." Her father was lecturing Nance in an angry voice about the photo session.

"I realize that," Nance said. "I'm so sorry."

"I'm over eighteen!" Ava said. "I don't need your permission. God!"

Her mother wouldn't let Ava take any blame. She addressed Nance. "You shouldn't have let that creep take nude photos of her," said her mother, who was sitting in her favorite red chair by the window. "Now they're all over the Internet. What were you thinking?" Her mother looked spooky because of her short hair.

Nance kept worrying her hands in her lap. When was she going to start defending herself? What could she say? There really was no excuse for what Nance had done, Suzi thought. None. And she'd thought Nance was so sensible.

Vic sat back, folding his arms on his chest. "I'd like to strangle both of those fuckers with my bare hands." He pinched his mouth together. She'd never heard her father talk this way, use this kind of language. "Should have killed that asshole while I had the chance," he muttered. Buff had gotten a restraining order against her father.

"Just let the police handle it," Suzi suggested. "Those creeps aren't worth it." This was a line she'd heard on a *CSI*, she realized as soon as she'd said it.

"Please don't kill them, Daddy," Ava said, her face screwing up like she was ready to cry. She thought he was really going to do it! Ava was so naive.

"When I think of what those men did, it's all I can do to sit here." The short haircut made her mother's eyes look larger and angrier. She was rocking slowly back and forth. "I'd like to cut their balls off. They both deserve it."

Suzi couldn't believe that her parents were talking about wanting to kill people and mutilate their privates. Her parents!

Granddad appeared to be listening to all this and understanding it. "Come on now, you two," he said. "You're scaring the kids here. It's not right, this ugly talk."

Nance finally looked up and started talking, and what she said was so astounding that Suzi could barely believe it. She told them all that she'd been one of the women in Granddad's radiation experiments in Memphis in the 1950s, and that she'd suffered health problems ever since and lost her eight-year-old daughter, Helen, to cancer, because she'd been tricked into drinking radiation for Granddad's study.

What?

"I knew it," Caroline crowed. "I told you, Vic!"

Nance went on talking, saying she'd testified in a government investigation during the Clinton era and had been financially compensated, but years later she'd found out that Granddad was living here in Tallahassee and had decided to come here and kill him. The way he'd killed Helen.

He'd killed Helen. Granddad killed Helen? And Nance was going to kill Granddad?

Suzi looked at Ava. Ava was staring at her with a frozen face, but Suzi could tell she was just as shocked as she was.

"My God," Suzi's mother said to Nance. "Are you kidding? You were planning to kill him?"

"She's not kidding," Suzi's father said.

"I was never more serious about anything in my life," Nance said.

Kill Granddad? He was the sweetest thing in the world, or at least he'd been five minutes ago, before she found out he'd killed Helen in his experiment. That was beyond what even Suzi could imagine. What was wrong with all the adults in this room, all former or wannabe murderers?

"Did you kill her daughter?" Ava asked Granddad.

"Of course not!"

"You did, Dad, indirectly," her mother said. "You know you did."

"He won't admit it," Nance said.

Granddad just shook his head.

"I guess you blame the U.S. go'ment," her father said sarcastically.

So her mother and father already knew all about Granddad's experiment. What else had they been hiding around here?

Nance spoke up again and added that when she realized that Granddad's memory wasn't right and that he was just a harmless old man, she decided that it wouldn't be worthwhile to kill him, so she'd decided to get even with the whole family. She'd targeted Ava and tried to get her involved in modeling because her parents wouldn't like it and tried to turn Suzi into a religious freak because her parents wouldn't like that either, but none of it was satisfying because she really liked both girls and didn't want to hurt them.

Nance said all this really fast, and it was too much for Suzi to take in at once. But Suzi kept thinking, *She wanted me to be a religious freak?*

That's why she invited me to church? She scooted as far away from Nance as she could get, scooted until she was smashed up against the arm of the couch.

"But see what I ended up doing," Nance said. "By trying to get revenge, I hurt lots of people. People I care about." She turned and smiled a suck-up smile at Suzi, but Suzi just made a disgusted face, an expression Mykaila had perfected.

"What did I tell you?" her mother said to her father. "I told you she was one of Dad's subjects. Maybe you'll believe me next time." Her mother, once again, was focusing on the wrong thing.

Her father smoothed his hand down over his face as if he were trying to iron the frown off it, but it didn't work. "Shit," he said. "Shit, shit, shit."

Suzi stood up and limped over to the ottoman and lowered herself down next to Ava, the only person in the room, in the world, who had no pretense, who wasn't hiding anything, who was always exactly like she appeared to be. She laid her head on Ava's shoulder, smelling the medicinal acne stuff, the most wonderful smell in the world. *Please, please don't move away from me, Ava.* And instead of scooching away, Ava draped an arm awkwardly around Suzi's shoulder. There was an uneasy silence. Suzi tore her gaze away from Nance's profile and turned it, once again, on her granddad, the accused murderer, who sat there, with a slightly puzzled expression, on the other side of the woman who'd planned to murder him.

"Did you hear that, Granddad?" Suzi burst out. "Nance wants to kill you! Doesn't that bother you?"

"Wanted," Nance said. "I *wanted* to kill him."

Granddad said, "Why would you want to do that?"

"You know why," Nance snapped at him.

He shook his head. "Can't say as I do."

"I've told him, many times," Nance said, "but he always forgets."

"How were you going to kill him?" Ava asked. Leave it to her to focus on the method! How Aspergery. But now that she'd asked, Suzi really wanted to know, too.

Nance sighed. "Never could decide."

"So you're *not* going to kill him," said her mother, to the aspiring murderer. "We don't have to worry about that, do we? My God." She sounded ready to cry. "We've got enough to worry about."

"Oh, no, no," Nance said. "I gave that idea up long ago. I love all of you. I truly do. I just wanted to come clean 'cause I'm hoping to keep you from doing the same sort of stupid things I did. By hurting your kids I'd hoped to hurt you and Dr. Spriggs, but it all backfired. Please promise me you won't try to get revenge on Buff. Enough people have been hurt."

"I never would've guessed it," her mother said. "You seemed so nice."

"Nice!" her father spat out. "Not hardly. And I'm not promising anything about not getting even."

"Well," Nance said to her father. "Maybe there's some soul-searching you need to do." She fixed him with a stern look, and he flushed. Her father, the man with a restraining order against him, the one who wanted to strangle two men with his bare hands.

Suzi lifted her head from Ava's shoulder. "What about Otis?" Suzi asked, realizing that Otis had been left out of the equation. "What were you going to do to him?"

"He's doing enough on his own," Nance said, but stunned as they all were, nobody asked her to elaborate.

"Mom," Ava said. "Travis's birthday party is on Friday. At Alligator Point. He wants me to ride down early with him, on Thursday night. So we'll beat the storm."

"Go to the beach when a hurricane's coming," Mom said. "What kind of sense does that make?"

Ava went on a tirade about how important the party was to Travis and how his grandmother had lived at the beach for years and that this would also be a hurricane party and that she would be *just fine*.

• • •

People from Genesis Church started calling their house, talking to Suzi's mother, asking her to please come to church on Sunday night with Suzi for a "ceremony of healing." Her father said there was no way in hell he was setting foot in that church, and her mother agreed that she felt the same way. Suzi felt that way, too. After all, she was no religious freak.

"Ten or twelve people from the church have sent notes, saying they're sorry," her mother told her. "Which is nice, I guess. But what they need to do is put that disgusting pig behind bars."

"What's a ceremony of healing?" Suzi asked.

Her mother shook her head. "I imagine a lot of praying is involved. I think they need to do less praying and more castrating."

"Praying never hurt no one," Suzi told her mother. Suzi's grandmother Verna Tommy used to say that.

"Oh," Suzi's mother said, and swooped over and snatched up Suzi in a fierce hug that made her eyes water.

Marylou CHAPTER 19

Marylou tried to carry on her daily activities as if nothing had changed. But everything had changed. She was no longer working at FTA. After attending church on Wednesday night and finding Buff Coffey up at the pulpit, she decided that she'd no longer have anything to do with Genesis Church. She was no longer bent on destroying Wilson and his family. All the oomph had gone out of her. Her days lacked focus. She'd slipped into idle mode.

She took Buster for his five a.m. walk in the coolish air. The birds were unusually quiet. On the news it was all Hurricane Grayson, which had made landfall yet again—the fourth time for one storm, a record—sweeping back from the Atlantic into New Smyrna Beach; and now it was working its sodden, massive way west across the Panhandle. It was a slow-moving storm, they said, causing widespread flooding, spawning tornadoes. If her house got flooded, what would she do?

She wished she were back in Memphis. She missed her high-ceilinged house with its tall windows, her hollyhocks by the front door, the moldy-smelling metal glider on her front porch, the urban sounds of her neighborhood, and even her old friends—Virginia from church, Gladys from her high school teaching days—friends she'd lost touch with because she'd withdrawn into her protective shell after her second husband of only two years, Martin, died. Why had she done that? She kept hearing her own words echoing in her ears. *Revenge just hurts more people. It's not worth it. I've hurt people trying to get revenge. I've hurt you and your family.*

But had *she* really done the hurting? Had it really been her fault that the photographer who took those photos uploaded them on the Internet and Buff saw them? Well, yes, okay, because, as Caroline had said, she should've stood up to Mr. Boyle, told him he couldn't take those photos. If they hadn't been taken, none of this would've happened. She shouldn't have taken Ava there in the first place. If only she hadn't moved to Tallahassee. If only she hadn't read the article about Wilson on the Internet. If only Martin hadn't been killed in the accident. A semi ran into the back of Martin's Jeep on the interstate, claiming he didn't see the line of cars stopped ahead of him. Turned out later he'd been smoking pot. The truck driver, not Martin. If Teddy hadn't left her. If Helen hadn't died. If she hadn't gone to the clinic at Memphis University. If Wilson had only realized what the hell he was doing by conducting his so-called experiment. If there hadn't been a cold war on to instill wrongheaded thinking throughout the land. If radiation hadn't been discovered by that sick and twisted couple, the Curies. Okay, maybe that was going too far. But even if these things hadn't happened, let's face it, other awful things would have.

Marylou stood with Buster beside a wooded lot and let him sniff around in the dirt. She was so tired. She felt like a limp noodle. This kind of thinking wasn't helping. It just led back into the land of Freeze, where nothing she could do would ever matter. She missed having a sense of purpose, even if it was a malevolent one. Had she really decided that revenge was pointless, the way she'd preached to Wilson and his family? It was true: she had no desire to exact revenge on them anymore. They had suffered, but not the way she'd intended; and Wilson, the great scientist, was no closer to acknowledging the wrongness of his deeds than he had been when she'd first moved here. Suzi's suffering, and her family's suffering, had been pointless.

But maybe, argued her inner Radioactive Lady, the problem was that *certain* people hadn't suffered enough! A certain *person,* that is. She gave Buster's leash a sharp tug and he glanced up at her, puzzled, but then seemed to shrug—goofy old lady—and started ambling along again. Buster was so forgiving. Unlike her. That horrible Ceremony of Healing she'd accidentally attended at Genesis Church. She'd gone for regular Wednesday night church, but once there she'd gotten a nasty surprise.

That night there were no ministers, no singers, no band, and the cameras weren't even going. The giant screens were blank. There was nothing to look at except a woman playing an organ. "Sweet hour of prayer! Sweet hour of prayer! That calls me from a world of care and bids me at my Father's throne make all my wants and wishes known."

During the last verse of the hymn, Buff, wearing a dark suit, emerged from a door next to the stage, followed by Paula and Rusty and Angel. "This robe of flesh I'll drop and rise to seize the everlasting prize . . ." There was an intake of breath. The organ kept warbling, but most people had stopped singing.

"Damn," Marylou said aloud. She'd been missing Suzi's company in the seat beside her, even though she knew that Suzi would never be coming back to this church. Why had Marylou thought that *she* could come back like nothing had happened? She'd assumed that Buff would surely have resigned in disgrace, but she'd underestimated him once again.

Buff strode up onto the stage, and his family scuttled over toward the seats, Paula's and Rusty's eyes downcast, and Angel, in her mother's arms, looking around curiously. They sat down three rows ahead of Marylou.

Marylou scooted around on her seat cushion, the buttons in the fabric biting into her haunches. She wanted to bolt, but she had to see what happened next. She couldn't imagine what Buff was going to say. How could he stand up there, facing them, after what he'd done? But he did face them, and his face didn't look so hot. There were dark circles underneath his eyes. He looked gray and haggard, like he'd lost weight. His trousers hung on him. Where's your big dick now, buddy?

Buff opened his mouth and said that he'd decided not to lie anymore. He talked about how sorry he was, how he'd hurt so many people, how he'd let his family and his congregation down, and then he began to sniffle. "I've had a demon inside me for many years," he said. "I've tried to fight it, but it keeps coming back. Lord, I've tried to fight it. Sexual addiction. Addiction to pornography. Please help me, friends. Please help me fight this thing."

"We will, we will," said members of the audience.

"Friends, please forgive me. With your help I can beat this thing. With your help and the Lord's help, I can become a whole man again."

"Bullshit," Marylou said in a loud voice.

"Oh, Lord," said the elegantly dressed black

man sitting next to Marylou, his eyes trained on Buff. “Oh, lordy, lordy, please, lord.”

Three rows in front of her Paula was sobbing, too, and so was Angel, but Rusty sat there stiff-backed, and Marylou squirmed for all three of them.

But what happened next was even worse. Buff looked around and started picking out people to plead forgiveness of. “Forgive me, Danielle.”

“I forgive you!” Danielle, whoever she was, burst out.

There was a big upswelling of approval from the congregation.

After that, when he spoke to one of his victims, she answered back that she forgave him. So there were more than four victims. Seven, at least.

Finally, when he’d run through the list, plucky Paula dashed up on the stage with him, hugged him, and said she forgave him. At least he didn’t ask poor little Angel to forgive him. Rusty walked up to the stage, too, but she didn’t cry and she didn’t hug him and Marylou could tell she wasn’t anywhere close to forgiving him. Her mouth was all clenched like she was holding lots in.

Then people in the congregation went up and began hugging Buff and his family and praying with them and laying hands on them, and that’s when Marylou got up and walked out, wishing to God she’d done so earlier.

Buff. The Reverend Buffington Coffey.

Now, walking Buster, she kept replaying that ceremony in her mind, that maudlin, self-pitying display, making it all about him, not his victims, forcing people to "forgive" him just so he'd feel even less regret about what he'd done. He had stopped lying and confessed, and that, she guessed, was a good thing; but no doubt he'd hire some shyster lawyer who would get him off and he wouldn't even lose his job and his family would come back to him and pretty soon he'd start doing it again, probably to Angel and Rusty along with other people's daughters, because that kind of person never stopped, that was a proven fact, much as people wanted to believe otherwise. You can forgive them until the cows come home.

She and Buster were back on her street, and she found herself staring at Buff's two-story house that, in the early morning light, looked like something from a magazine cover: *Show Off Your Stunning Split-Level!* His wife's car wasn't there, but his SUV was. He was in there, right this minute. What was he doing? Probably having a good dream about all the people he'd fooled at that so-called ceremony.

Marylou, with a surge of energy, began walking more briskly toward home, Buster trotting to keep up. She'd been trying to get revenge on the wrong person, that was the problem. Wilson had done something awful, monstrous even, had caused deaths and disfigurements, but in a way, he himself had been brainwashed by the cold war mentality. And he hadn't kept on doing it. He hadn't tried to seek forgiveness in a showy, public way. As she walked along, Marylou realized she was full of energy again, a scary, humming kind of energy. Gas. Go. Return of the Radioactive Lady. And this time she would not be deterred.

She rang Buff's doorbell close to seven a.m.—a Friday morning, so if he wasn't up he should be up. She wouldn't have been surprised if he didn't answer right away—she wouldn't have wanted to talk to anyone if she were him. And she expected that, when he did, he'd be either under the influence of sleeping pills or unshaven and miserable looking, liquor on his breath, weak and pathetic, the way he'd looked at the ceremony of hoodoo.

She intended to lean on the doorbell until he answered, then give him the cake and leave. She had no desire to sit and watch him eat it. Didn't think she could.

But she should've known! He answered the door right away, smiling, freshly shaven, with swim trunks, a T-shirt, and flip-flops on. "Well, good morning to you!" he said. "To what do I owe this honor?"

She thrust out her cake. “It’s two nice big slices of my fresh pineapple upside-down cake,” she said, trying to do a passable imitation of a kind smile. “Excellent for breakfast!”

He thanked her and asked her to come in and share the cake. She demurred.

“Aw, please come in for just a minute,” he said, standing back from the door. He took the cake from her—plastic-wrapped on a paper plate. She hadn’t wanted to give him the whole cake in case he decided to give some to someone else. He took her arm and pulled her inside. Was he suspicious of her?

She stood there, in his spotless kitchen, her mouth dry and her heart thudding in her chest. “It’s cold in here,” she said.

“I keep the air-conditioning up too high,” he said, setting the cake down on the counter. “Paula’s always turning it down. She’s not here now.”

Marylou nodded.

“Come. Come sit down.” He gestured at the living room.

“I can’t. I really need to go.” She tried to swallow. “Are you going swimming?”

“It’s my nephew Travis’s birthday today. My sister, Gigi’s, having a party for him down at Alligator Point. They thought it would take my mind off things.”

“How nice,” Marylou said flatly. Would two

pieces of cake be enough to kill this man? She certainly hoped so. "What about the hurricane?"

"Eh." He shrugged her question away. "More waves for us!" He crouched down like a surfer, swaying on his board.

"I hope you like pineapple upside-down cake," Marylou said.

"I love it. It's my favorite kind of cake. How'd you know?"

Marylou shrugged. "Lucky guess."

"I'm going to gobble it right up! Won't you join me?"

Marylou protested and began moving toward the door.

"Mrs. Archer," Buff said, fixing his face in a sincere mask. "I just want to thank you for standing by me. With everyone's help, with my family's support, and the Lord's gracious love, I can beat this thing. Your help means so much. And your prayers. And this cake!" He took her hand in his warm paw and she let him hold it.

You're warm now, sinner, but not for long. That was the Radioactive Lady talking.

"Paula said she'd consider moving back in with me. I really miss her and the girls." His eyes teared up and she had the sudden urge to poke them, hard.

"Cake goes down better with milk!" Nance called out as she stepped out the door. "Milk and cake make everything better!"

• • •

Marylou hid in her house for a while, not allowing herself to think about what she'd done. She tried to watch a cooking show, but kept imagining the round girl chef pouring antifreeze into her polenta with porcini topping and her rotelle with broccoflower and albacore tuna. Finally, surging with restless energy, she clipped Buster's leash on and dragged him outside where it was balmy and fresh as if all the oppressive stagnant air had been sucked up into the gray sky, where dark clouds were now scooting across in a businesslike manner.

Buff's black SUV was parked in his driveway. He hadn't made it to the birthday party after all! What a shame. She refused to imagine what might've been happening to him inside. So this was what it was like, she thought, to just not think about the consequences of what you'd done. Not really so hard after all! Wilson had done it for years. Keep moving, that seemed to help.

Vic CHAPTER 20

Vic's secret wish had been granted. He'd wanted a hurricane and along came Grayson. He couldn't enjoy it, though, because here he was, driving right through Grayson to retrieve Ava from Travis's grandmother's beach house.

The night before, Travis had come by their Friar's Way house to pick Ava up and she'd gone off with him to Alligator Point, overnight bag in hand, over Caroline's wild protests.

"His mother and grandmother and their friends will be there, not that it matters. It's his birthday. He wants me there. I'm his girlfriend." Ava lifted her chin proudly.

"But the storm, the storm!" Caroline wailed. "There'll be way more flooding at the beach."

"I'm going," Ava said, and she went.

The next morning Nance woke them up at seven thirty, dropping by unannounced to take Wilson out to breakfast. She didn't say a word to Vic about the little talk they'd had in his office after he'd caught Gigi cheating. In fact, she spoke only to Caroline and Wilson, which was fine with him. As Nance and Wilson drove off to their impromptu Cracker Barrel breakfast, Vic's boss called to tell him that FTA was closed because of the hurricane. Vic started calling Ava not long after that to see if she was all right. Ava didn't answer her phone, so by nine thirty Vic was headed south along Highway 98, a two-lane road hemmed in on both sides by the Apalachicola National Forest. It was agonizing not being able to drive any faster than forty-five. For some perverse reason he pictured Ava floating away in the beach house or clinging to driftwood in the surging sea. Or her drowned body washing up on the beach. What kind of a man was he, thinking such thoughts, torturing himself by imagining the very thing he couldn't bear? If anything happened to her because of this storm, he'd blame himself for wanting the damn thing in the first place.

Nearby pine trees swayed back and forth so far that it was hard to believe they didn't snap. Pinecones and pine straw jounced off his windshield and then away. The sky before him was grayish green. Instead of driving into a storm, it was like he was bringing the hurricane across the Panhandle with him. Grayson had proved to be bizarrely unpredictable, with his four separate landings in Florida, his back-and-forthing, his swelling and shrinking—storm-hurricane, storm-hurricane. Now his path was depicted on TV as a yellow brick road lined with red propeller-shaped spinners zooming over the Panhandle toward Perry, fifty miles southeast of Tallahassee.

The Volvo's wipers slashed back and forth on high, rain spattering the windshield with a loud tearing sound. He'd tried to listen to NPR to take his mind off Ava, but the rain was so loud he had to turn it up full blast to hear it. Convenience stores had lights on inside, but their parking lots were empty. All the traffic was headed the opposite way, up toward Tallahassee. His was the only car headed down to the big wa-wa, as Suzi used to call it. Angelo's Seafood Restaurant was boarded up. On the Ochlockonee Bridge the wind slammed into the left side of the car like it wanted to push him into the water.

Alligator Point was a long skinny peninsula like a finger curving out into the water—the Gulf on one side and the Little Alligator Bay on the other. Vic felt even more vulnerable driving out onto the peninsula, palm tree leaves turned inside out, tree trash flying. The KOA Campground was deserted. He struggled to keep the car on the road.

Travis's grandmother's house was one of the few old bungalows left on Alligator Point, which was now, like its snootier cousin, St. George Island, full of new stilted houses on steroids. There were a few vehicles parked near her house but in the center of the peninsula, mostly battered SUVs, Jeeps, and pickup trucks. Vic figured they'd parked there to stay clear of the water. He planned to be in the house only a minute, so he parked right in front.

When he stepped inside, Gigi called his name and rushed up to hug him like he was her long-lost cousin. "What're *you* doing here?" she kept exclaiming.

Vic hugged her stiffly, aware of other people watching.

"I came for Ava," he told Gigi. Everyone had to speak loudly over the storm. "We need to get home before the roads flood."

"Oh, no, stay and have some lunch," Gigi said. "It's barely a cat. two!"

"It could get bigger."

Ava, in a gauzy coral-colored dress, ran up to greet him, followed by Travis in his Sponge Bob bathing trunks and a sweatshirt. "Can I stay and have cake? Travis hasn't opened his presents yet. I'm sorry I'm wearing Suzi's dress. Please don't tell her. Everyone here loves Elvis! There's a three-legged dog on the beach and he won't come in."

Ava was having a fantastic time, that much was clear.

Vic grabbed her and hugged her and she forced herself to accept it, and he agreed that they could leave after cake.

Caroline had been flabbergasted that Gigi's and Buff's mother was having a party, after Buff's name had been all over the papers for molesting children. How could she? But it made perfect sense, in a way. Old money. Stiff upper lip, and all that. She must be determined to pretend that nothing had happened, that her son would be somehow pardoned, and that life should go on, even in the midst of a hurricane. The lady was as nutty as the Mad Hatter.

Present at the Mad Hatter's birthday/hurricane party were a handful of people, some salty preppy types, some working class, all mostly older people who were probably, like Gigi's mom, permanent residents of Alligator Point. They were all drinking, mostly beer, happy to have an excuse to tie one on, the sort of diehards who routinely ignored hurricane warnings, money or age or machismo allowing them to romanticize the notion of going down with the ship, which was, actually, the same sort of romanticizing Vic had been doing, wanting to *be in* a hurricane.

A group of men sat around a TV, watching the weather channel with the sound off, swapping hurricane stories in raucous voices. A dark, wizened man told about growing up in Miami and being sent out to pick avocados off the trees in the yard prior to the storm so the wind couldn't hurl them through the windows. A man with a white beard relayed that, up in Georgia, Hurricane Floyd had ripped all the green pecans off his trees and flung them into his bathroom. Sixteen wheelbarrows worth.

One fellow, who was drinking a Bloody Mary and appeared to be pregnant, told about how a few years ago, here on Alligator Point, during Hurricane George he'd passed out on his sofa, dead to the world, after a hurricane party like this one, his arm dangling down off the side. In the middle of the night he'd woken up with his hand underwater. He'd managed to get out of the house and tried to drive away from Alligator Point but had ended up wrecking his brand-new

El Camino in front of the campground and abandoning it. “Time I got back there, couple days later, somebody’d stripped my car bare, made a skeeter out of it.” He cackled, and his listeners roared appreciatively.

Okay, maybe Vic had been too judgmental. Another way to view this situation was that these people were relaxed, and they’d been through more storms than Vic had, so what the hell? Why not join them? Ava and Travis had disappeared, so he went by himself into the kitchen, where two matrons in wrap skirts were unloading plastic bags of frozen food, stuff they’d removed from their own freezers and brought to the party so it could get eaten up before the power went out. He helped himself to one of the charred steaks that had been grilled in the garage, speared a baked potato, and scooped up some coleslaw, plopping it all on a plastic plate, and grabbed a beer. He sat down on the living room couch to eat.

Gigi nestled beside him, swigging a fresh beer. She wore a black-and-white striped tank top and white flouncy skirt, freckles dusting her nose, her mane of hair pulled back in an appealingly messy ponytail. Gigi herself was an appealing mess. Had he thought that his attraction to her would simply disappear? He found himself wanting to confide in her, to talk to her about the whole Buff thing, tell her how angry and disgusted and sick about it he was but also wanting to make clear that he wasn't mad at *her, only her brother;* and he wanted to tell her he'd decided not to tell his boss about her cheating, but people kept coming up and interrupting them, asking Gigi to introduce him.

The people also kept bringing him beers and he kept drinking them. At one point he escaped to use the bathroom, and on his way back out Gigi's mother caught him. "Vic, so good to meet you," said Maude Coffey, a tanned woman in a raspberry-colored sundress and a streaky helmet of hair. She could have been anywhere from sixty-five to eighty-five. "Gigi's told us so much about you."

Vic mumbled something and glanced around the room for Gigi, but he couldn't see her anywhere in the mix of tropically arrayed, blissfully oblivious guests.

The wind raged and rain pelted sideways against the house, now accompanied by a bass line of thunder, making it hard to hear Maude, who spoke in a quiet, hoarse voice. "He's got a court date coming up in two weeks. Matt Sandy's defending him, but I'm worried."

It took Vic a while to figure out that *he* was Buff, her son. Why was she telling this to Vic, of all people? "Matt Sandy," Vic said. "He gets all the drug dealers off."

"The therapists call it 'sexual addiction.' He's

been in treatment twice, but so far it just hasn't taken. Guess we haven't found the right program." Blinking back tears, she grabbed hold of Vic's arm. "He's not a bad person. He truly isn't."

Vic took a deep breath. "You might've warned the members of his congregation," he said in what he hoped was a reasonable tone. "How come he's not on some registered sex offender list? We like to keep track of those in our neighborhood."

Maude fixed him with her lavender eyes, now damp and slightly reddened. "He's never been in legal trouble before. Nobody's ever pressed charges." She must have read the expression on Vic's face. "I'm sorry for the girls, too, of course I am, but is taking him to court going to undo what happened? What about his own family? Buffy's making himself sick over this. He was too sick to come celebrate Travis's birthday."

"Sick is the least of what Buffy ought to be," Vic said. "Prison's too good for the son of a bitch."

Maude's mouth gaped open and Vic backed away from her.

Time to go.

He found Ava and Travis in the sunroom on the back of the house, sitting side by side in beach chairs, holding hands and watching the storm between strips of duct tape somebody had crisscrossed over the windows.

Vic crossed the sunroom, over to a large red cooler on the floor. He opened the cooler and dug out a bottle of Beck's, then he kicked aside the beach towels lined up against the space under the door. Here was his chance to really *be in a hurricane*.

"Where are you going?" Ava asked him.

"Sir, it's not safe out there. The wind is gusting at fifty knots."

Vic promised them he'd be careful and be right back and stepped out onto the patio, stung by wind-whipped sand and rain. His T-shirt and shorts instantly soaked through. He turned to his right, backing underneath the eaves, so that the wind and sand weren't coming right into his face, and gulped down the cold beer. This house stood level to the beach, a row of protective dunes in front of it, sea oats on the dunes blown flat. In between the dunes he could see the water, waves coming fast, right up to the dunes. Slap, slap, slap. Shingles on the roof above him flapped, and the mast of a nearby Hobie Cat, which nobody had seen fit to secure, clanged and whanged. Here he was, in a hurricane. Not as thrilling as he'd hoped it would be.

The patio door groaned open. "Mr. May-ture!" It was Gigi, stepping out onto the patio behind him. "I been looking for you!" She was carrying a bottle of Miller Lite. Her soaking-wet hair whipped wildly around her face. Eyes squinted against the wind, she tipped toward him, arms outstretched, beer breath and soft lips coming closer, but he quickly turned his head so she'd kiss his cheek. People were watching. Ava and Travis were watching.

Vic drained his beer and set the bottle down on the flagstones. It clunked over and rattled away.

She was leaning against him, staring out into the Gulf. "No birds out today! I love pelicans!" she said, yelling over the racket. "Aren't they cute?"

"You should've told me that your brother's a pervert."

Gigi just stood there, staring out at the Gulf, one hand shielding her eyes. "I swear to God there's a boat out there."

Vic peered out at the horizon but didn't see any boats.

Gigi took another slug from her bottle. "I hope they send the fucker up the river for good. Then Mama will realize she has a daughter and not just a fucked-up crazy-ass son."

"Go back inside," he said. "You're ruining my storm experience." He meant this as a joke, sort of.

"You're a dick," Gigi said. "You always tried to act so together, but I knew. I knew about you and old what's-her-name. After Larry's party."

"How'd you know?" He never wanted to remember old what's-her-name.

"Everybody knows, Duckie. We called her Radio Station, 'cause anybody could pick her up, 'specially at night." She reached over and pinched Vic's lips together. "Your mouth looks like a duck's. I always wanted to say that. Hey! Duckie! Let's go ride us some dolphins!" She spun around and began maneuvering her way, barefoot, across the slick patio and then up the wooden boardwalk toward the water, wind and rain blowing her sideways, her hair like an inside-out umbrella. She disappeared between the dunes.

What could he do but follow? On the boardwalk the wind was much worse, sand burning his bare legs and arms. He cupped his face to keep the sand out of his eyes. It was worse than being out in a blizzard. It was hard to walk straight. He felt like one of those show-off reporters on Weather Channel, who stood outside in hurricanes, dancing around like Rumpelstiltskin.

At the end of the boardwalk, where there was usually sixty or so yards of white beach, there was now only water and howling wind. And Gigi. Gigi stood facing away from him, in the water up to her knees. He yelled at her, but she didn't turn around.

A cooler lid cartwheeled past him into the water, an aluminum chair just behind it. The wind kept nudge, nudge, nudging and Vic allowed himself to be scooped up and deposited into the Gulf with Gigi, staggering and hopping along instead of dragging his feet like they told you to do to scare the stingrays away. He'd never liked the cloudy water at Alligator Point, didn't like not being able to see the stingrays and the sharks that might be lurking, but that uneasiness had never stopped him from going into the water. He'd always just figured that if it was his time to be stung or bitten, so be it. Beer helped. Would there even be any rays or sharks out in this weather? The warm water now was murkier than ever, and he couldn't even see his own sandaled feet.

When he reached Gigi, he grabbed her arm and they both lurched around in a silly dance. Then she plopped down and crouched there in water up to her chin. She took another swig from her bottle, like it was an ordinary beach day.

"We need to go in," he yelled at her.

"I love you, Vic," she yelled back. "So there. I love you." He couldn't see her eyes, hidden by strands of her dripping hair, but he knew that, even in her drunken state, she was watching his face carefully.

"Shit." He glanced behind him. He and Gigi were further from shore now, and at a different angle than they had been earlier.

"Shit! What the hell kind of response is that? I'm sorry I fucked up at FTA okay? You still mad at me for that? Is that your problem?"

"There's plenty of problems." They were both yelling the sorts of things that last week they couldn't have even imagined speaking aloud. "I'm married. You're a drunk. Your brother molested my daughter. Take your pick." He was angry at her, angry at himself, but in a way the anger felt just as trumped-up as their earlier lovey-dovey stuff. Loving her, hating her . . . had he trumped up all of it?

The water lapped at his hips. The wind was now behind them, shoving them, trying to bully them out into that vast expanse of brownish gray water studded with whitecaps. He and Gigi were moving, dancing around together. He couldn't blink the salty water out of his eyes. Again he begged her to come back with him.

She started giggling and pointed. "Your hair."

"What the hell is wrong with you?"

A bigger wave broke over them, knocking Gigi backward. She came up laughing, spitting water, holding her beer bottle safely aloft, but now she was treading water, and he was immersed up to his shoulders.

Vic held out his hand to Gigi. "Come on. We're getting washed out to sea."

Gigi ignored his hand, pouting. "Don't care."

Washed out to sea. Did he really say that? Sounded like an old pirate movie. Sounded too fucking metaphorical. There was something unreal about the whole scene. Now *he* was treading water. He turned. Travis and Ava were at the end of the boardwalk, two figures waving at them. A curtain of lightning dropped down over Little Alligator Bay.

"Lightning," Vic yelled, making a grab for Gigi.

Gigi swooshed sideways, away from him. "You're happy to play around till I tell you I love you. And you drink just as much as me."

"I never drink as much as you."

"Fucking liar!"

Why were they having this insane fight? Being drunk was like experiencing the world as drawn by crayons—all bright and dark outlines. Nuance and detail and complexity all gone!—I love you! Let's have fun! Pelicans are cute! You're a dick! I hate you! Liar!—Everything was clear and everything was stupid. No wonder drunkenness was such an appealing way for people to get through life.

Ava and Travis, at the end of the boardwalk, were jumping around and waving frantically. And there were now other people standing at the end of the boardwalk with Ava, waving. Maude, in her raspberry-colored dress. The pregnant man with the skeeter car. They were all soaked, staggering forward and backward in the wind, like people in a cartoon. It would've been, under other circumstances, comical. It wasn't funny. Not at all. None of this was funny.

Gigi dunked underwater and came back up,

spluttering and wiping her eyes. Was she crying? There was no sense blaming her, he realized. He'd led her on. He was proud of himself for having wise thoughts at a time like this, even though he was still treading water. He spoke to Gigi in what he hoped was a calm and calming, gentle voice. "Please come in with me."

She grimaced. "I'm not going anywhere. Especially with you, asshole." She raised the beer bottle, drained the water out, then cocked her arm back and tossed it at him, and before he could throw his hands up, it struck the side of his head and bounced off. She covered her mouth, laughing. "Oops," she said.

Vic clutched his stinging head. "You bitch." He was speaking B movie dialogue. This whole scene was out of a B movie. Pirate May-ture (aka Duckie) and the Drunk Vixen Get Swept Out to Sea. Never in his life had he imagined himself in such a melodramatic scene. But why not him? Why should he be immune? Life wants to be a B movie. Everyone's life. Even his. Get drunk, act on your impulses, shout out stupid shit you'll be ashamed of later—B movie!

Another curtain of lightning, behind the houses, this time a wraparound curtain instead of a café curtain, and then the deep chuckle of thunder.

"I'm just your midlife crisis," she said. "I'm your shiny red sports car, motherfucker."

He rubbed his temple. Why couldn't he just swim away and let her drown? A band of stronger rain washed over them, then another. A line of heavier thunderstorms coming in. "You're just like your brother," he bellowed. "A cheating, self-pitying sociopath." That had a real ring to it.

Gigi barked with laughter. "Who's the one cheating?" she yodeled. "What do you call what we were doing, Duckie? You're just pissed 'cause you're stuck in a crappy job and you're not even a member of your own famdammly."

It was the remark about his family that made him want to quit fighting. "My daughter's trying to save us," he said. "So's your son."

Ava and Travis were wading into the water, lumbering toward them, terrified expressions on their faces.

Gigi turned to look. "Hey! It's Avis and Trava!"

Vic dove under the water, scooped her up and, clutching her under his arm, hauled her ass and his out of the water.

On the way home with Ava from Alligator Point, Vic could drive only twenty miles an hour. Lightning flashed all around them and Ava screeched every time. Ditches were full up, more than full, and the overflow crept out across the road, forming rivers. In Carrabelle they drove through a lake of unknown depth where the road used to be. They were in it before he could stop, so he had to keep going. Tree branches flew in front of them. They swerved to avoid a plastic kiddie pool. Stoplights swayed manically over their heads.

He'd swallowed three quick cups of coffee in Maude's kitchen, so now he was a wide-awake drunk with a throbbing knot on his forehead who had to take a leak, driving with his precious, terrified towel-wrapped daughter shivering beside him in the car, but he still thought it was a better option than staying at the party. If he'd stayed, he would've done something even more asinine than he was doing now. God, just get them back safely. He felt he'd barely escaped some alternate life in which he and Gigi acted out scene after scene of their B movie. He knew he'd have to straighten things out with Gigi once and for all the next time he saw her. He'd have to come clean at FTA. But for now he felt lucky to have escaped.

What almost caused him to have a wreck, right before he tackled the Ochlockonee Bridge, was his cell phone ringing. The unexpectedness of it startled him. He veered into the other lane, overcorrected, and spun sideways, his tires spewing up water. Fortunately they were the only car on the highway. Their Volvo had stopped in the wrong lane and he eased it back into the right one. He flipped open his phone without bothering to read the caller ID. "What?" he said into the phone, his heart thudding. No response. "You scared me to death," he said to whoever had called him.

Ava was staring out the window at a little clearing in the woods. "That's where Mr. Ugly used to sell his peanuts, isn't it, Daddy?"

There was nobody on the line. He didn't recognize the number when he glanced at it. He snapped the phone shut and kept driving. After a minute he told Ava, "Mr. Ugly hasn't been there in a long time."

Caroline CHAPTER 21

Caroline rang the doorbell of the house on Evergreen Street. It was only seven in the evening, but the sky had already darkened. She and Otis and Suzi stood on the deep front porch, waiting. It was an old Craftsman-style house, beige stucco and green trim, with steps and a railing leading up from the sidewalk and a little apron of a yard in front, all in surprisingly good shape. There were lights on upstairs. Caroline rang the bell again. Distant thunder rumbled, and a great gray cloud shaped like a steep cliff was creeping across the sky toward them from the Mississippi River. Did Grayson stretch all the way up here? Surely not. But there was a storm brewing. Wind blew damp air and exhaust fumes over from Madison Avenue, which mingled with the smell of the gardenia bushes around the porch.

"Somebody's got to be in there," Caroline said, and leaned on the bell again, longer this time. Otis walked over and peered in a window, and Suzi sat down on a glider. They didn't have any luggage with them, because they'd left home in such a hurry.

On the sidewalk in front of the house, an anorexic-looking lady in baggy clothes walked up with three black Scottie dogs on three separate leashes. "Hurry up. Poop!" she ordered her dogs, who kept sniffing the grass but not pooping. The wind was picking up, blowing the woman's hair into her eyes, whipping around the empty plastic poop bag she carried.

"We're camping out right here till they answer the door," Caroline told her children.

"They can't hide forever," Otis said, peering in another window.

"We ride to victory!" Suzi yelled.

They'd just driven nine hours to Memphis from Tallahassee and they were all zonked but pleased with themselves for having found the place.

Finally the door was flung open by a bearded young man wearing shorts who looked disheveled and hassled, his wire-frame glasses askew. He held an empty cardboard box in his hands.

Caroline, Suzi, and Otis looked past him into the living room, into the house owned by Marylou Ahearn, alias Nance Archer.

"Help you?" asked the young man.

"We're looking for Marylou," Caroline said. She had trouble saying that name in connection with Nance. Nance and Marylou seemed like two different people.

"She was by here earlier this afternoon," the young man said. "Around four thirty."

"Was there an old man with her?" Suzi asked.

"And a dog?" Otis asked.

The young man wrinkled his brow and exhaled loudly. "Are you selling something? 'Cause I'm broke."

Caroline explained that they were friends of Marylou's from Tallahassee and that they were concerned about her and wanted to catch up with her to see if she was okay.

"Marylou has friends in Tallahassee?" he asked, stepping back to let them inside. "She sure didn't have many friends in Memphis." He shut the heavy oak door behind them and quickly locked it. They all stood there in the foyer beside an old player piano. "She did have a man with her," the young man said. "Wilson somebody. And her dog. Butter. He's in the living room."

"Buster," Otis said.

"Who is it, Trev?" A sturdy young woman with a long dark braid and fluffy bangs, wearing overalls, walked into the foyer carrying an armload of books.

Caroline explained that they were friends of Marylou's, and the young woman, who'd introduced herself as Katya, said, "You just missed Elvis Week. Did you come to see Elvis?"

"Not hardly," Otis said.

Katya invited them into the living room, where she turned on a floor lamp and then set her stack of books, which all looked old and serious, on the floor. Caroline and Suzi settled on a rose-colored sofa and Otis on a leather ottoman. Buster hopped up on the sofa beside Suzi, who bent over and kissed the top of his head.

Katya plopped down on an Oriental rug, crossing her legs underneath her. Her bare feet were dirty on the bottoms. The young man, Trevor, set down his empty cardboard box and perched on the arm of the leather chair.

It began to rain, and the raindrops blew against the tall windows in the living room.

"Marylou showed up here earlier today and told us we had to move out," Katya said. "We were just house-sitting, but, yeah, we expected a little more notice."

"I don't expect anything from anyone," Trev said. He had the entire alphabet tattooed around his hairy left calf.

"Um," Katya said, hugging her knees. "We're graduate students at Memphis University.

English and philosophy. Trev's getting ready to take his thingamajiggers. His exams."

"If I don't pass, I'll be driving a bus," Trev said.

Caroline looked around the living room. Old, comfortable furniture. Ceramic ashtray in the shape of Arkansas. Coffee table book about the Holy Land. Piano with a hymnal open on the music rack, old black-and-white pictures of dead people on top. This was a house that Marylou had lived in for a long time. "Did the man with her, Wilson, did he seem okay?" Caroline asked the couple.

Katya pulled her braid over her shoulder and swung the end back and forth. "He seemed fine to me."

"Nobody ever seems fine to me," said Trev.

"He wasn't, like, trying to get away?" Suzi said.

"Or signaling for help?" Otis said.

"Why would he be doing that?" Trev said, dropping down onto the chair. He was interested now.

Lightning flashed outside, too close, and when it thundered, the lamp wavered.

"Ooh, I hate storms," Katya said, hugging her knees.

How much should they tell Trevor and Katya? How well did Trevor and Katya know Marylou? Had Marylou told them anything about why she'd moved to Tallahassee?

Before Caroline could decide what to say, Suzi blurted out, “She kidnapped my grandfather!”

“No kidding,” Katya said, exchanging a glance with Trevor.

“Well, not kidnapped,” Caroline said. “They left town without telling us, and my dad’s having memory problems. I’m not sure how aware he is of what’s going on. We think that she took him against his will.”

“This is unbelievable!” Katya exclaimed, clapping her hands together. “Marylou, a kidnapper! Wow!”

“Nothing anybody does surprises me,” Trev said.

“Where’d they go?” Caroline asked the young couple. “After they left here?”

“Sightseeing, probably,” Katya said. “Maybe she took him to Graceland! Everyone ends up there.”

“Are they coming back?” Caroline asked them. “Where are they staying tonight?”

“Assumed they’d stay here,” Trev said. “Otherwise, why’d they tell us to get out?”

Lightning loomed right out front of the house. Katya screamed. Suzi squealed and plugged her ears. Thunder rattled the windows. Afterward they waited a minute, but nothing else happened. Suzi cautiously removed her hands from her ears.

“My grandfather was a scientist,” Otis said.

"He was a nuclear researcher. He wasn't always as out of it as he is now."

"He grew up here in Memphis," Caroline added, "but I doubt he remembers much about it. He needs his medications. Are you sure he seemed all right?"

"He was smiling," Katya said. "We thought they were a couple!"

"That's false!" Otis barked out. "She hates him. He hates her."

"Lots of couples hate each other," Trev added.

"So you don't approve of their relationship?" Katya said.

Suzi snorted. "They don't have a relationship," she said.

"Looked like it to me." Katya smiled mischievously.

"If you call Marylou planning to kill him a relationship!" Caroline said, thinking *What the hell?* She needed to talk to someone about Marylou's insane behavior. So she and Otis and Suzi related to Trevor and Katya how Marylou had been a subject in her father's experiments in the fifties, and that she'd always blamed her father for her daughter's death, and then how, just recently, thanks to Google, she'd located him in Tallahassee and plotted her revenge, and that she'd used a fake name and everything.

Trevor burst out laughing, a startling bray. "Marylou Ahearn? Kill someone? That figures."

"No way!" said Katya.

"Way," Otis said. "She told us herself, after she'd changed her mind and decided not to do it."

"At least, we hope she really changed her mind. That's why we're a little worried."

"So how did you know they came here?"

They told Trevor and Katya that Marylou had called them from the road and left a message, explaining that she'd taken Wilson to visit Memphis and not to worry, she'd bring him back soon, etc. Since it was just Suzi and Otis at home with Caroline—Vic and Ava being down at Alligator Point—the three of them decided to go ahead and follow Marylou to Memphis, just to make sure everything was okay.

They knew Marylou had a house in Memphis, so they stopped at Marylou's Tallahassee house—Suzi knew where there was a hidden key—and looked through some of her bills and letters and papers, hoping to find the address. They found the address, but they also discovered that Nancy Archer wasn't her real name.

"That's far out," Katya said. "Nancy Archer."

"*Attack of the Fifty Foot Woman*," Trevor said. "Worst movie ever made."

"Oh, Trev," Katya said. "You would know that."

There was a lull in the conversation. Caroline knew she should try to call Vic again. She'd left messages for him, telling him what had happened and that she and Suzi and Otis were leaving for Memphis, telling him Marylou's real name and her address, but as time went on and he didn't answer or return her calls, she got angry and turned her phone off. Otis never had his on, and Suzi's battery was dead. She decided she'd check her messages and if he'd called she'd call him back when she was good and ready.

"You're welcome to stay here and wait for them," Katya said, unfolding herself from the floor. "Back to work, Trev."

Caroline felt herself relax a little. Whenever she closed her eyes she saw green interstate signs. So far, it seemed, Wilson and Marylou were okay. And, although she hadn't let herself acknowledge it yet, she was happy to be back in Memphis. The rain seemed to have stopped. "How about if I go get everyone some barbecue?" Caroline suggested.

"I don't eat meat," said Trev, pushing his glasses up on his nose.

"Since when?" Katya asked him, and he shrugged.

"Maybe Suzi and Otis can help you pack your things up," Caroline suggested.

Trevor's mouth lifted into a sort-of smile.

Last December, when she and Ava visited Memphis, she'd gone with Ava to Graceland one afternoon. While Ava pored over the exhibits in the house, Caroline zipped through and settled outside on a concrete bench in the Meditation Gardens, where the tour ended, to wait for Ava.

It was warm for December and flies buzzed here and there. Beside the Presley family graves were garish but touching arrangements of silk flowers and trinkets and teddy bears and cards and pictures of Elvis on easels. The fountain, between Caroline and the gravestones, sparkled and spattered. All the benches in the garden were painted black. There was a black iron fence around the fountain and another one around the semicircle of grave markers. An airplane droned overhead.

Caroline found herself watching the other visitors filing through. A late fortyish woman with bangs and chin-length hair, carrying a purse with a picture of Elvis on it, kept sniffling and patting the grave markers like someone who'd just lost her entire family. A younger blond woman wearing jeans and a jean jacket sat in front of Elvis's grave and read a pamphlet which looked, from the illustrations, to be religious in nature. A British couple—a man with dyed hair and a toupee to match—were walking around talking, too loudly, about the thrill of finding their names, which they'd scrawled in pen, still visible on the wall in front of Graceland after all these years. A tall, thin, Asian man appeared, took pictures, and left. Two smiling short, stout,

German-sounding women in their sixties relit a vanilla scented candle on Elvis's grave. What was wrong with these people? They were acting like Elvis was some martyred saint. What did they hope to gain by coming here? It didn't make any sense to Caroline.

A man with a roaring leaf blower came along the path. A swirl of leaves eddied around her feet.

"Mama!" It was Ava, in her white T-shirt that said La La La I Can't Hear You. Ava looked like an angel, standing there in the sunlight, with the drops of the fountain in an arc around her. Ava never called her Mama anymore, and Caroline cherished the sound of it. Ava darted over and sat down on the bench beside her mother.

"Mama, you know what?"

Caroline took Ava's hand.

For a few seconds Ava allowed her hand to be held, but quickly, hating to be confined, she pulled her hand out of her mother's grasp.

In spite of herself, Caroline felt hurt.

"I've been thinking. Elvis had Asperger's. The way they described him as a child, always staying to himself, not having friends, not making eye contact. He was a total klutz. He dry washed his hands all the time, and walked sort of hunched over when he was a kid. And he was so good at music. Never had any lessons. A musical savant."

"Well," said Caroline. "That's a possibility."

"I just feel like . . ." Ava looked away. "I'm embarrassed to say." For Ava to be embarrassed to say something was highly unusual.

"I'm listening."

"Okay." Ava took a deep breath and let it out. "I feel like Elvis can help me, with my life, with my, you know. My Asperger's. Maybe he can heal me. Cure me."

Was this the reason all these people came to the Meditation Gardens? Did they all feel the need to be healed? Like going to Lourdes? "You don't need to be cured of anything," Caroline told Ava. "You're fine just the way you are."

"Then why do you keep trying to fix me?" Ava said.

"I'm just trying to make things easier for you. Help you."

"Huh," Ava said. "Well stop helping me all the time."

Caroline felt the familiar sting of being unappreciated, misunderstood, and hating herself for being so petty. Parents were never appreciated. She knew that. But knowing it and not caring about it were two different things. "All right, I'll stop helping you. Elvis can help you."

"Fine." Ava got up and wandered down the path toward a split rail fence that overlooked a rolling pasture and in the distance a barn.

Although she knew better, Caroline stood up and followed her. Groups of visitors, wearing their headsets, were strolling along the paths between the house and Vernon Presley's office, the racquetball court, and the Meditation Gardens.

She joined Ava at the fence, and both of them leaned against the rails and gazed at the horses grazing a few yards away—six horses, paired head to rump, swishing their tails in each other's faces, the way horses do. One of them was a palomino.

"I wonder if Elvis rode any of those horses," Ava said.

Caroline slipped her arm around Ava's waist. "Elvis's horses are long gone," she said.

Ava scrunched up her beautiful, angelic face and began to weep.

These sorts of public meltdowns rarely happened anymore, but they did happen, and you could never predict or control them. You just endured them.

"Those poor horses never knew what happened, when he died," Ava sobbed. "They waited and waited for him to come see them and feed them and ride them, but they never saw him again. They didn't understand."

"They had each other," Caroline said, stroking Ava's hair. "See? Look at them out there, taking care of each other." Tears ran out of Caroline's eyes, too. Whenever Ava cried, Caroline cried.

"Why'd he have to die? Why'd he take all those drugs? Why?"

Caroline was aware that other people were standing off a ways, staring at them, including the British man with the toupee. She had to think of something to say to calm her daughter down.

"Maybe he knew things would never get better for him," Caroline said. "Maybe he just gave up. But that's not going to happen to you. Or me."

"I know that!"

At last Ava allowed Caroline to hug her, and Caroline buried her face in Ava's sweet, sweaty hair. *Oh, when are you going to grow a shell like the rest of us?* is what she was thinking. And was also thinking, *Ava still needs me!* And, *I can't do this anymore!*

The next day she dropped Ava off at Graceland and decided to explore the city on her own. She'd visited there many times when she was growing up, but it was simply her birthplace, the place where her father had grown up, a backdrop for family reunions. As she drove through Midtown she felt like she'd been wearing smudgy glasses that had been removed. The past was visible everywhere: 1920s bungalows, Art Deco buildings from the thirties and forties, neon signs from the fifties and sixties. She drove past a sign in the shape of a smoking cigarette and one that had a white shirt with no body in it, waving an empty sleeve, advertising Happy Day Laundry. Every particular she saw was interesting and worthy of scrutiny, because it was in Memphis.

Memphis was where she'd lost her mother. The whole city seemed poised to reveal something important to her, something about her parents. Their past lives, their youth, their spirits even, seemed to be living on here in an alternate universe. In this part of town she could be back in the fifties, for all the buildings had changed. Was it possible to fall in love with a city?

Downtown she'd parked her car beside the Peabody Hotel and took a walk down Main Street. Trolleys, mostly empty, clacked past her. There was the Chisca Hotel, once the broadcasting home of WHBQ radio and the *Red Hot and Blue* show hosted by Dewey Phillips, who'd played Elvis Presley's first single, "That's All Right," for the first time on his show in 1954.

One street over, on Mulberry, was the Lorraine Motel, where Dr. Martin Luther King, Jr., was shot, now the National Civil Rights Museum. She passed a building which was once the Alonzo Lott School for Waiters. Sunlight slanted on the brick storefronts and coffee shops, the fire station. She could open up a clothing store in one of these buildings. Caroline's.

In the distance was the Arcade Restaurant, and across from the Arcade was Earnestine and

Hazel's, which had once been a church and then a pharmacy and a brothel. Now it housed a juke joint called Soul Burger.

The Arcade was a touristy spot because it had been used as a setting in several Hollywood movies. Locals sniffed at the food because the rolls weren't homemade, but Caroline loved the old brick building, the neon signs in the huge plate glass windows, the Memphis memorabilia on the walls, the soda fountain and the boomerang pattern in the Formica on the tabletops. It was the oldest restaurant in the city, and it was down at the end of South Main.

In the Arcade she'd sat in one of the turquoise and tan booths and ordered coffee and sweet potato pancakes and indulged her fantasy of living there, in one of those buildings on Main Street, working in a quiet and orderly store surrounded by beautiful clothing that she'd chosen herself, talking to people who actually wanted her advice and suggestions, feeling competent in her own life again.

And now, driving through Memphis, on her way back to Marylou's house with the tangy smelling white bags of barbecue and sides in the backseat, it felt unnatural being in Memphis without Ava, but it also felt fine. She was starting to understand that she and Ava would probably keep needing each other, coming apart and then back together, for the rest of their lives. It was up to her to make the first real move, to take a short step away. Neither Mom nor Elvis could make everything all right for Ava.

Caroline hadn't been able to step away, at all, ever, because part of her, deep down, was sure that she was somehow responsible for Ava's autism—that it was caused by something Caroline ate or drank or did while she was pregnant, or that her genes were bad, or the fact that her labor had gone on for a week and Ava had been yanked out by forceps with the umbilical cord wrapped around her neck. And those fucking mercury-laced shots.

Like Nance, she'd blamed herself all these years, but unlike Nance, she hadn't had a single evil doctor to share the blame. It was just her and the guilt and Ava, and somehow, she was going to have to practice, putting them aside, little by little.

Back at Marylou's house Caroline and her kids and the couple sat down in the kitchen, which smelled like old bread and old sponges. The round table took up too much space in the kitchen. The wooden chairs were tall and spindly, their seats hard and too short, the chair cushions thin and hard and lumpy from years of butts pressing into them. Despite the discomfort, it felt like they were having a party. Trevor decided to cast off his vegetarian scruples just for that evening and accepted a sandwich with a sigh. They all dived into the greasy barbecue sandwiches—pulled pork on white bread with a pickle, fries, beans, and slaw—that Caroline had dumped onto Marylou's thin china plates. Katya asked Suzi what she liked to do, and Suzi told her about soccer and how she couldn't wait to get started again in the fall, and Caroline felt relieved.

Then Otis started talking about how they should start selling Elvis relics on eBay, and Suzi chimed in with some suggestions about what they could pocket and sell—leaves from the trees on the grounds of Graceland, threads from the carpets inside the mansion. Katya and Trev got into the discussion, proposing that they all go into the Elvis relic business together.

"There are other Elvis sites to harvest from," Katya said. "Like Lauderdale Courts, where he grew up. Humes High School."

"We'd have to wear disguises, so they wouldn't be suspicious of us, coming back to Graceland, over and over again," Suzi said. She grinned at her mother while slurping up sweet tea through a straw, happier than Caroline had seen her in months.

"They're used to people hanging out at Graceland every day," Caroline said, and told them about the people she'd seen in the Meditation Garden.

"I'll sit by Elvis's grave and weep and fall out while you guys steal things," Katya said. "This could be way more lucrative than being a TA."

"I'll impersonate a German tourist," Trev said. "Wear a toupee. Pretend I can't read any signs."

"Otis could be an Elvis impersonator," Suzi suggested. "He's already got the pigging-out thing down."

Otis kept stuffing french fries into his mouth. "You could be a Donald Duck impersonator," he said.

"Or Michael Jackson," said Suzi.

"Michael Scott!" said Otis.

"I'll be Kelly Osbourne," said Caroline.

It was almost like a dinner at home but without the edge.

They had just finished dinner and were helping Trev and Katya pack up endless cartons of books, when Caroline decided to check her messages. There were six from Ava and four from Vic.

Wilson CHAPTER 22

She tricked him. She'd told him—and Caroline—that she was taking him out to the Cracker Barrel for breakfast, and he'd had no reason to doubt her and he was dying to get out of that house, but then, before he knew it, the three of them—she and Buster and Wilson—were on the interstate driving toward Panama City, and she told him where they were really going. It stunned him at first, that she could be so audacious, so bold, as to think she could get away with such a stunt.

"Why are we going there?" he asked her. Pine trees went whizzing past in the rain—he was way too old to jump out of her car, even if it were barely moving.

"I'm taking you back," she said. "Where we met. Where I got the radioactive cocktail. To jog your memory."

"I remember all I need to remember."

"Not in my opinion."

"And yours is the only one that counts, I guess."

"You got that right."

Why hadn't he allowed himself to be talked into getting a cell phone? Caroline and Vic and the kids wouldn't have any idea where he was. They'd be worried sick. He voiced this worry to Marylou.

"I'll call and let them know you're safe in an hour or two. Or three. After we've gotten a good head start."

"So you changed your mind again? You *are* going to kill me?"

"This is just a little outing. I need to know for sure that you remember who I am and what you did with that experiment, that you understand how terrible it was, and that you're truly sorry. Then I'll take you home."

"I know who you are and I understand what I did. It was terrible and I'm truly sorry. There's an exit. Turn around."

"You're just saying that."

He wasn't just saying that. It was true. He'd just waited too long to tell her, hoping he might not have to. "I have to use the bathroom. Right now. Pull over."

"There's a rest area three miles up the road. Don't try anything funny."

At the rest area he considered accosting a stranger and telling him what was happening, but knew that people would think he was a senile wacko. He thought about sneaking off into the woods, but then he'd be a senile wacko lost in the rainy woods. Buster would follow his scent and give him away. Maybe he could run across the interstate and hitchhike back. No, she'd be the only one who'd stop to pick him up.

He did manage to find a quarter in his pocket and the number for Vic's cell phone on the emergency card Caroline had put in his wallet, but as he tried to make the call Marylou and Buster came up behind him and Marylou hung up the phone. He gave up and got back into the car with her.

• • •

It stopped raining and the sun came out. They got off the interstate and onto a two-lane highway that plowed straight up through north Florida and Alabama, through tiny towns with gorgeous old houses, their yards dotted with scraggly palm trees, past pecan groves and fireworks shops and fruit stands, past the Bama Nut Shop, past one Mexican restaurant after another, and periodically Wilson forgot why he was riding along through the Deep South, and what year it was, and where exactly he was going, and he started enjoying the ride, because he hadn't taken a ride like this, through the country, in a long time, then he wondered why *he* wasn't driving, and then he turned and saw Marylou and thought, again, *Oh Christ*.

Marylou talked and talked, telling him about how she and Teddy had met at Little Rock Community College, where they were working toward associate's degrees, Teddy on the GI Bill. They'd both had small parts in a production of *Our Town*, Teddy as Simon Stimson, her as Rebecca Gibbs. She'd been terrible in the play, but Teddy'd lavished her with compliments at the cast party, and she did the same to him, even though he hadn't been so hot himself.

After they got married Teddy couldn't find work as an industrial designer in Little Rock—didn't really look that hard, truth be told—so thcy moved to Memphis where he eventually got a job at a tool and die shop designing custom parts for mechanical cotton pickers. Before that, though, when they were in public housing, she'd finally gotten pregnant with Helen.

She told Wilson how for years after she'd been slipped the radium she hadn't felt right, had felt tired and anemic, put on iron pills by her doctor, but that Helen had seemed fine until that Christmas morning when the little girl had come to her parents—she and Teddy lounging in bed, Helen up early checking her stocking—and showed them the lump in her right thigh, a hard lump like a peach pit lodged under her skin. "But it doesn't hurt," Helen kept insisting. It took a little over a year for her to die, Marylou told him. Imagine, watching for more than a year as your child died.

"I can't imagine it," Wilson said. "It sounds like the worst thing in the world. I am so sorry." How could he possibly convey how sorry he was? He could throw himself off a building or under a train, but what good would that do? He was going to die soon anyway, either by natural causes or by Marylou's hand. He'd once read that a writer called John Jay Chapman, a nutcase who'd lived around the turn of the century, had stuck his hand in an open flame in order to do penance for having beat up another man who was flirting with his fiancée. Mr. Chapman had burned his hand into a stump, but the fiancée had married him anyway. Wilson could do something like that, he supposed.

"So what's your story?" Marylou asked him, accelerating past a van so fast her dashboard rattled. Sitting beside him, she looked like a little white-haired pixie. She wore a white T-shirt that hung down like a dress over her white slacks. The interior of her car, a Ford Taurus, was neat as could be. When he commented on this, she informed him that it was a rental car. A pinecone air freshener swung from the rearview mirror. "Let's hear why you thought that radiation study was a good idea," she said. "I wait with bated breath."

Rather than demonstrating that there wasn't much problem with his memory, as far as the study went, which would put him in the position of admitting he'd only been pretending not to remember, he told her instead about the time in his life he remembered best, which was being in the Army Air Corps during the war, stationed in England and then Italy and occupied France. He'd flown the P-47 Thunderbolt, a single-engine plane that looked like a milk bottle. Jugs, people called them. He and his fellow fighter pilots went on bombing missions, blowing up aircraft, railroad tracks, bridges, truck depots. He'd once taken out a Messerschmitt 262, a Swallow, one of the world's first jet-powered fighter/bombers. Those things were bad, bad news for the Allies, he told Marylou. How come? she asked. Because, he said, the Swallow could've won air supremacy back for the Germans if they'd come on the scene earlier or if the war went on much longer. So you're saying that if it weren't for you, we'd be speaking German today, she said, and actually gave him a little smile.

He told her how once he'd had to make a crash landing in a barley field near the Rhine, his plane so full of dust he'd thought at first it was smoke. He had no idea whether or not he was behind enemy lines, so he hid in a ditch until he saw a Jeep coming down the road toward him, pulling a portable ack-ack, or antiaircraft outfit, two black men driving. When he saw the black men, he knew he was safe.

"Look. There's one of your black men now!" Marylou said, pointing out Wilson's window at a man sitting on the porch of a neat little house. "But now he's old, just like you!"

Marylou, it had to be said, had a good sense of humor. Not everyone did. Lila hadn't, but Verna Tommy had. Mary Conner he could barely remember. Wilson rolled down his electric window, and Buster popped up from the backseat and stuck his snout out into the wind. "Help, I'm being kidnapped!" Wilson yelled at the old man on the porch.

"Oh, quit," Marylou told him.

The man on the porch lifted his hand in the all-purpose rural salute—kidnapping, apparently, being no big deal—and Marylou and Wilson and Buster left him behind.

They were now driving behind an open truck piled high with watermelons, which Marylou was tailgating. Wilson asked her (once, twice, seven times?) to please keep her distance; and Marylou, finally fed up, veered over onto the shoulder, jerked to a stop, and asked him if he'd like to drive.

He hadn't been allowed to drive a car for a year, his license had expired and his family wouldn't let him renew it because of his memory problems, but he didn't tell Marylou any of that. He was pleased as could be to get behind the wheel of a car again, and thought briefly about hightailing it back to Tallahassee, now that he was in charge, but if he tried to do that, Marylou would raise a ruckus. So he took them the rest of the way through Alabama and then Mississippi and on up to Memphis, Marylou operating as navigator.

In Memphis, after stopping by Marylou's house on Evergreen Street to drop off Buster and give the young people notice—he didn't understand who the young people were and why they were living in her house if they weren't related to her—Marylou got behind the wheel again, even though they were both tuckered out, and drove him to the Memphis University Hospitals and Clinics, which had been remodeled, but was, behind the face-lift, recognizable.

"This is Dr. Wilson Spriggs," Marylou told the nurses behind a reception desk. "He's a very distinguished doctor who began his career here at this clinic. He wants to revisit his old haunts. It's very important to him. I brought him all the way up here from Florida."

One of the older nurses, with gray wings of hair framing her face, said, "I believe I have heard of Dr. Spriggs." The other three nurses looked over at her, waiting for her edict. She furrowed her forehead. "You should've called ahead." She glanced at her wristwatch. "It's five till five. What did you want to see?" she asked Wilson.

"He wants to see the OB clinic," Marylou said.

"I want to see the labs," Wilson said.

The nurse, after telling her underlings that she'd be back in a few, walked Wilson and Marylou to the elevators.

Wilson's back felt stiff after his long ride in the car, but he was exhilarated, too. "Sixth floor," Wilson said.

And the winged nurse, who was wearing a baggy yellow uniform, took hold of Wilson's elbow and said, "That's right, Dr. Spriggs!

They're still on the sixth floor!" and gave him a big smile. She might've been cute if her haunches had not been so large. "But this late on a Friday afternoon, I hope somebody's still up there."

Marylou, trailing behind them, looked like a forlorn white ghost. "Whatever happened to Nurse Bordner?" she asked, but nobody answered her.

The sixth floor, unlike the first floor and lobby of the hospital, was essentially unchanged—a coat of paint perhaps, new lighting. The locks on the doors looked sleeker and more efficient than the locks he remembered. There was the same smell, though, a smell that came rushing back to him, slightly sweet with a layer of bleach underneath. Off the long hallway were the labs with the Bunsen burners and beakers and centrifuge machines, the lab techs bent over test tubes, siphoning away with their pipettes. His friend Ebb Hahn had worked in that room there, processing blood samples from Wilson's radioactive iron study. What were they working on in there now? He had no idea.

They passed the biohazard labs, where the workers now wore goggles, caps, paper gowns, and latex gloves—fancier versions of the same old stuff—and the central supply room where two women loaded beakers into the steam machines. Martha Meharry used to work in there, perched on a stool between loads doing the jumble and crossword in the *Commercial Appeal*.

Their nurse stopped beside an office that said Nuclear Medicine on the door. "This here's Dr. Wilson Spriggs," she announced to the secretary inside, and then ducked off down the hall.

The secretary, a pinched-faced woman, sighed, then got up from her desk, disappeared into a warren of offices behind her. She emerged shortly with two doctors in tow, two doctors who looked remarkably, eerily, like Wally and Theodore Cleaver.

Wally and Beav, in their pressed plaid dress shirts and tasteful neckties, grinned at Wilson, who was wearing his yard clothes. They shook his hand—one of them shook it twice—and told him how much they admired him, how much they admired his work on the therapeutic use of radioactivity in the treatment of cancer. "This gentleman published the seminal articles on radioisotope therapy," Wally informed the secretary, who was feigning interest while playing solitaire on her computer. Seminal articles! The adjective, one Wilson had used himself once upon a time, sounded absurd and pompous to him now.

The two doctors also mentioned Wilson's work at the University of Iowa, his treatment of malignant effusions in lung and uterine cancer, what a pioneer he'd been, how he had changed the field, and so on and so on.

Wilson, bleary-eyed from the drive, felt like he'd stepped into another dimension. He was unable to believe that these two men had heard of him and that he was being treated like something other than a pariah. He glanced at Marylou, who glared at him. She hadn't come here to witness this. Wilson didn't know how to introduce her so he just stood there like an idiot.

Finally Marylou spoke up. "Howdy, fellas."

"This your wife?" Beaver asked Wilson, reaching for Marylou's hand.

"I'm his guinea pig," Marylou said, but she shook the Beav's hand and then Wally's. "Dr. Spriggs experimented on me in the fifties. Remember the radioactive cocktails?" She mimed drinking one. Thumb and pinky extended, head tilted slightly back, glug, glug, glug. "Yep, I drank the Kool-Aid!" When she made this gesture, when she mimed drinking the cocktail—the jauntiness of it, the self-mockery, and also the refusal to be denied—Wilson wanted to catch her up in his arms.

"Wow," Beaver said, shaking his head, gazing at Marylou like she was a specimen. "Look at you now!" he said. "So many years later. You're doing so well! Those experiments weren't nearly as bad as the press tried to make them seem."

"Everyone who knew anything knew they were

only administering trace amounts," Wally agreed. "The media just didn't get that. She's living proof. And the two of you are friends! Amazing."

"It is amazing," Wilson said, and he felt, for the first time, how amazing it was.

Marylou took a deep breath, and Wilson wondered if she was going to launch into her litany of woes, wondered if she was going to tell them the story of Helen's death. He wouldn't blame her if she did. Those two bozos deserved to have their bubble burst, at the very least. But, no, she surprised him again.

"What's really amazing," Marylou said, "is how boring the three of you are. You're boring the socks off me right now."

Wally and Beaver actually glanced down, whether out of embarrassment or to see if she really had lost her socks, he couldn't tell.

Wilson knew he had a choice. He could stay here and bask in the false but gratifying praise or leave with Marylou, who wasn't having any of it.

He took Marylou's hand. "Actually, gentlemen, my friend here is not doing well at all. She hasn't been doing well for a very long time. Thanks for your kind words. And good luck with whatever you're doing. I'm sure it's very important, but in my book you're like a couple of blisters who've shown up after the real work's been done."

Marylou allowed him to lead her out the door, down the hall, down to the first floor, and out of the hospital, where they stood under the awning. "I'm ready for a little drinkie poo," she said. "How about yourself?"

Wilson was momentarily confused. Where was he? He knew he should know. How could he have left the familiar labs and then stepped outside and not known where he was? Where was home now? Where was he supposed to go? How was he supposed to get there? Would Verna Tommy be there waiting for him? Would anyone be expecting him?

"Oh God," Marylou said, jerking on his hand. "Listen. I've got to tell somebody. I did something horrible."

"You?" Wilson said. "I can't believe it. You couldn't even bring yourself to kill me."

And she told him about Buff.

CHAPTER 23 *Marylou*

Rather than going back to her house on Evergreen Street to spend the night, she decided they should splurge and stay at the Peabody Hotel, since she'd never stayed there, and because, for some reason, this was turning into a pleasure trip rather than an abduction. Wilson told her that being kidnapped by her was the best time he'd had since Verna Tommy died—which she was thrilled to hear, even though odds were he couldn't remember good times even if he'd had them. She herself felt as if, even though she was achy and bleary-eyed from the car ride and disappointed by the hospital visit, the foreign phrase *having a good time* could be applied to her as well.

Instead of feeling weighed down by her past, as she'd often felt when she was home in Memphis, the fact that she was in the company of the wicked Wilson Spriggs, the last person on earth she'd ever imagined hanging out with, and that the two of them were fixing to shack up at the touristy Peabody Hotel, a place she'd never thought she'd stay, made her practically giddy.

Grinning like imbeciles, she and Wilson reserved room 624. After nine-dollar glasses of wine in the lobby while the Peabody's famous ducks waddled out of the fountain and over to the elevator to ride up to their penthouse coop, after listening to the player piano play Cole Porter songs and pretending that an invisible black man was at the keys (for a time they called him Topper and they became George and Marion), after dinner across the street at Automatic Slim's Tonga Club (coconut shrimp for Marion, sassafras smoked chicken for George), when they were both lying in their separate beds, with the orangey lights of downtown Memphis seeping through the gauzy curtains of room 624, Wilson told her again that two slices of cake laced with antifreeze would only have made Buff sick but wouldn't have killed him.

She already knew he'd been sick. As she and Wilson had driven away from her house back in Tallahassee, raindrops just beginning to fall, she'd glanced over and seen Buff staggering around in his side yard, wearing his bathing trunks, throwing up in some bushes.

Wilson promised to tell no one, ever, what she'd done.

In a way, his knowing about her evil deed created the tit-for-tat situation she'd been hoping to achieve when she moved to Tallahassee in April. It wasn't the same kind of tit-for-tat—his life for Helen's—but, in this new version, she knew all about his reprehensible experiment, tit, and he knew that she'd tried to kill someone, tat. She hadn't known how much antifreeze would kill Buff, but killing him had been her aim. If Buff was dead right now, she'd be a murderer. And only Wilson knew.

Before they fell asleep, wearing their clothes, Wilson said, from his double bed beside hers, "I went for months, years, without talking about that study. I'd think about it sometimes, feel sick about it. It made me even sicker when I realized how much I *didn't* think about it. Just tucked it away somewhere in my mind and went about my business. But I needed to talk about it. I feel better talking about it."

"Just call me Oprah," Marylou said. But then she told him that he was the only person left in the world she could talk to about Helen, the only other person she knew personally who'd been involved with the experiment, even if they'd been on opposite sides.

He admitted that his was the wrong side, but he said there had been a cold war going on and he was scrambling to get grant money. He was an ambitious young scientist trying to get data, a doctor trying to help determine how much radiation was safe. Back then, these sorts of studies were being conducted all across the country. They knew virtually nothing about radiation, but they'd all thought that small amounts had to be safe.

She listened, forcing herself to remain silent. Part of her understood. Part of her never would. But it made her feel calmer to hear his side.

Unlike Teddy, who'd had to detach from the past to go on living, she realized that she didn't feel alive, unfrozen, unless she held the past as close to her as possible, so she could take it out and examine it whenever she wanted to, with someone who'd been there, too. That was why she felt comforted by the presence of Wilson Spriggs. That, and she'd always, from the first time she saw him, found him to be attractive, that foppish dandy in his bow tie.

From the next bed Wilson began to sing, in a warbling, cracking tenor: "'I will tell all the world / Of my young Southern girl, . . . / I love you, Mary Lou Brown.'"

"Very interesting," Marylou said. "But stupid."

"Ain't it?"

"You can't remember my last name. But I like the young Southern girl part."

Then she paused and stretched, her old bones cracking and creaking, the elastic waist on her linen pants sliding up. Even though they'd spent nine hours in the car today and then toured the hospital, walked around downtown Memphis, her ankle and hip ached only a little. A four, on a pain scale of one to ten. "Have you ever seen the movie *Attack of the Fifty Foot Woman*?" Marylou asked Wilson.

"Don't think I have. But I am losing my memory."

"Well, shoot," she said. "Come over here and I'll tell you all about it."

When she and Wilson dropped by her house on Evergreen Street around noon, she saw Caroline's minivan in the driveway. And Vic's Volvo. The jig was up, whatever the hell that meant.

When she and Wilson went inside, she was expecting to be yelled at, castigated, attacked even. It was a stupid thing she'd done. No doubt about that. One of many stupid things. She hadn't thought they'd come after her, though, and it was jolting to see them—Caroline, Vic, Ava, Otis, and Suzi, sitting in her Memphis living room. Parson Brown herself was sprawled out in Marylou's favorite leather chair. Buster lay in front of the sooty cold fireplace, possibly dreaming of Christmases of yore and hoping for a yuletide blaze.

"Your hair looks darling now that I'm getting used to it," Marylou said to Caroline, which wasn't the right thing to say, she realized as soon as she'd said it.

Caroline ignored her. "Dad!" Caroline said, all goggle-eyed, and rushed forward to hug him. "Are you okay?"

"I'm perfectly fine. I'm having a good time, in fact."

"I've got your medications here."

It was only then that Caroline looked at Marylou, glared really. Anyone could see that Caroline longed to flail at Marylou, claw her eyes out, but before she could Suzi came over to Marylou and hugged her. Then, after some fumbling and awkwardness, they all sat down, Wilson and Marylou side by side on the couch, with Suzi next to Marylou.

"Things are bad at home," Vic told them, running his hand through his wild-looking hair.

He sat in the padded rocking chair wearing lime green swimming trunks and a wrinkled, too-tight cotton oxford shirt and looked like he'd been driving all night with the windows down. Nobody had gotten enough sleep, and they had all, Wilson and Marylou included, been in the same clothes for a while, since none of them had packed for this crazy trip to Memphis.

"What's the storm damage like?" Marylou asked him. "How's Canterbury Hills?"

"The pond's flooded," Vic said. "Lots of trees down. Power outages all over the city. We went through some bad stretches coming back from the beach, didn't we, Ava."

"Scary," Ava agreed. She sat in a straight-backed chair nearest the door.

"But when we finally got home," Vic said, "that's when we heard. The EPA came and got Otis's shed."

Vic told them how, even though the storm was in full swing, their neighbor John Kane saw their car pull up and came over and told them what had happened while he and Ava had been down at the beach and Caroline, Suzi, and Otis were on their way to Memphis. Earlier that afternoon, before the storm hit, a flatbed truck and a van had pulled in the Witherspoons' drive and a handful of people got out of the van and donned white astronaut suits like something straight out of a science fiction movie.

Mr. Kane watched with some other neighbors as two spacemen went into their side yard and removed refuse from the old shed, dust billowing up around them. A burned, chemical smell hung in the air, making the bystanders choke. Three other spacemen wrestled a huge industrial-size vacuum cleaner over the Witherspoons' front lawn. Mr. Kane finally got up his nerve and approached one, who he realized from looking through its plastic face mask was a woman wearing purple lipstick. She said, through an intercom device, that they were from the Environmental Protection Agency. No, there was nobody in the house. No, she couldn't tell him anything. Nothing. Sir. Please. Step away. Keep back. Sir. The two vacuumers stopped their vacuuming and stared at him menacingly until he retreated to the sidelines.

The astronauts, John Kane said, must've vacuumed up every speck of dust and debris on every blade of grass and shrubbery, trampling the flower beds and smashing all the azalea bushes. Then they dumped the shed remains and whatever they'd vacuumed up into black steel drums. They loaded the black drums onto the flatbed truck and roared off for parts unknown.

"What was in that shed?" John Kane had asked Vic, and Vic could tell that John was scared to death but trying to be nice.

Vic told them he didn't know. Technically, that was the truth.

But when Vic and Ava arrived in Memphis and told Otis what had happened, Otis had finally come clean and explained to his parents and siblings what he'd been up to.

"You were actually *building* a model reactor," Wilson said now. "You actually followed my directions? I never thought you'd . . ." he trailed off, and Marylou knew that he was going to say, I never thought you'd be so stupid, but he didn't, and she was glad he didn't say it.

"You told him how to do it?" Caroline asked her father. She and Otis shared the love seat, but at opposite ends.

Wilson admitted that, sure, he'd answered Otis's many questions about how to construct a breeder reactor—but he'd thought it was all theoretical!

"I did it, Granddad!" Otis said, clenching his fists on his thighs. "I got all the parts myself, and figured out how to put them together and it worked. It actually worked!"

"That's quite an accomplishment," Wilson said. "No doubt about that. You're a genius, son. You really are." There was pride in his voice as well as bafflement.

Otis rocked back and forth, a smile on his face, and it was similar to the way Ava paced when she was happy or excited. This was what he'd been wanting. His grandfather's praise.

"Otis didn't protect himself," Vic told Wilson.

"He only used a paper mask and gardening gloves. You failed to impress upon him how dangerous those elements are."

"But I did!" Wilson said. "I told him that real radioactive research is done in full protector gear, in sealed chambers with lead-lined gloves!" Then he paused and his tone changed. "At least I think I did. No, I know I did."

"You did," Otis said cheerfully, still not, Marylou thought, grasping the enormity of what he'd done.

"It's our fault, Vic," Caroline said, "for not paying attention. We should've been monitoring what he was doing." Even so, she couldn't help making excuses for Otis. Arguing his case. While she talked, Marylou watched Otis, wondering how he felt being dissected like a specimen in front of his family. His blank, handsome face revealed nothing.

Caroline said she'd been talking to him about the consequences of what he'd done, and she realized that being on the autism spectrum had prevented him from thinking things through, from evaluating the possible consequences. He'd gotten caught up in the scientific possibilities, in doing something nobody had ever done before. It wasn't because he lacked empathy. He just had a one-track mind. All he could focus on was the attention he'd get if he succeeded and the glory that would be heaped upon him, the thrill of being crowned a young scientific genius. Heck, she said, probably most of the scientists working on the atomic bomb had an autism spectrum disorder. What else would explain their lack of foresight?

"You're in good company, son," Wilson said.

"That's hardly relevant," Vic snapped.

"Well, at least the shed's gone," Marylou said. "Hopefully the EPA got it all."

"You put that deadly stuff in our yard," Vic said. "Next to our house."

"That's bad," Wilson agreed.

"Ohhhhh," Ava howled.

Suzi started crying. "We won't ever be able to live there again."

Marylou patted her hand.

"We haven't seen the EPA report yet," Otis said. "The levels might be in the safe range. The federal government says that people can get up to five thousand mrems of safe exposure per year. There was only fifty last I checked. I think there was only fifty."

"We won't go back unless we *know* it's safe," Vic put in.

"How will we *really* know?" Suzi said, wiping her eyes.

"We won't," Caroline said.

"I'm sorry," Marylou told Vic and Caroline. "I suspected for a while that he was messing with radiation, but by then it was too late. Course, it doesn't scare me, 'cause I'm already radioactive." She'd meant to lighten the mood, but it didn't work.

"There's more bad news," Caroline said. She stood up, scooped Parson up into her arms, and held her like a flopped-eared baby. And Marylou had thought Buster was spoiled.

"We just got a call," Ava added, round-eyed with all the drama. "Buff is dead."

"What?" Marylou grabbed Wilson's hand and squeezed. He squeezed back. "How?" was all she could manage to say.

"Somebody came into his house while he was asleep," Vic said. "Smashed his head with a baseball bat."

"Oh my God," Wilson muttered.

"That's horrible." Marylou sagged with relief. Not that he was dead, but that she hadn't been the one who killed him. She tried not to picture Buff's head being smashed with a baseball bat, and mostly succeeded in not picturing it.

"Who?" Wilson said.

"They don't know," Caroline said. "But there are plenty of people with a reason to kill him."

Marylou glanced over at Vic, who was gazing back at her. She couldn't read his expression.

"It wasn't me." Vic ran his fingers through his stiff, windblown hair. "Although I did think about it."

Parson struggled out of Caroline's arms,

righted herself on the floor, shook her ears, and sauntered over to curl up next to Buster, who merely opened an eye and closed it again.

"Well," Marylou said, squeezing Wilson's hand. "You can all stay here as long as you want. Take a little breather."

"I should get back to work," Vic said. "We'll have to find a place to stay. For who knows how long. Jesus." He ran his fingers through his hair again. "I can't even think about it."

"I'll stay here for a while," Caroline said. "Rest up before I wade back in. Just the thought of everything we'll have to do exhausts me." But she didn't sound exhausted. She sounded exhilarated by the prospect of staying in Memphis. Caroline had been miserable at home, and the whole family had known it, even though they might not have realized they'd known it.

Marylou decided it was time for good news, or at least what she considered to be good news. "Wilson and I have decided to get married," she announced.

Silence. Someone gasped.

Then, bless her heart, Suzi leaned over and hugged Marylou, planting a kiss on her forehead.

Caroline shrieked, "Dad! Are you crazy?"

"Yes, but that's beside the point." Wilson fixed Marylou with puppy dog eyes. The goofball.

"And we're ready now," Marylou added. "We

want to do it right away. We don't have time to diddle around."

"Get married at Graceland! At the chapel!" Ava said, jumping up and doing her pacing thing, the skirt of her coral dress swishing back and forth. "Please? That would be so marvelous."

"I'll vote for marvelous," Wilson said. "Long as there aren't any Elvis impersonators, except me singing 'Mary Lou Brown' to my bride."

"You want to get married at Graceland?" Caroline asked with irritated disbelief. "This is insane." She glared at Marylou. "My father has dementia. Are you prepared to take care of him? He doesn't have money, if that's what you're thinking."

Marylou decided not to rise to the bait. "I'm aware of all that," she said calmly. "We'll take care of each other." She sounded like a different person talking. Donna Reed, maybe. Where was the Radioactive Lady? Still there, shaking her head incredulously. Cue the birdies and the violins. Disgusting. Marylou was glad she hadn't disappeared altogether. Take a chill pill, Nance.

The Witherspoon family sat there staring at her and Wilson, waiting for them to say more. Wilson squeezed her hand but didn't speak, so Marylou plunged in. "I know it's not like a young couple getting married," she told them, "but it's something to celebrate, don't you think? We want you all there with us."

"I don't really feel like celebrating," Otis said. "I feel bad about our house. And I feel bad for Rusty."

"And for Angel," Suzi added.

They were silent for a minute, all of them thinking about Rusty and Angel, trying to imagine how they must be feeling but knowing they couldn't really know how bad it must be. The air conditioner cut off, and Marylou's old Bakelite clock on the side table, in the corner, ticktocked away. The room needed a good cleaning, which wasn't surprising. That graduate student couple, who couldn't even clean their own eyeglasses, wouldn't have noticed dust if it had reared up and bit 'em. But it was so good to be back in her old house.

Finally Vic broke the silence. He leaned forward, clasping his big hands on his knees. "We'll be at your wedding," he said. So Vic did have an earnest side. Who would've thunk it? "It's great you found each other," he went on. "It's a miracle, under the circumstances. We do need to celebrate. Congratulations, both of you." But he didn't sound happy. He sounded wistful and a little sad, and Marylou knew that he was sad about the state of his own marriage.

Caroline forced a smile. "Well, right after the wedding Suzi and Otis and Ava need to get back to Tallahassee. School starts next week."

"And soccer." Suzi lay her head on Marylou's

shoulder. Dear Suzi. Now she'd be her real granddaughter.

"Wilson and I will take you kids back to Tallahassee," Marylou offered. "You can stay at my house. Your mother and father should stay here and have a little vacation together."

Vic and Caroline glanced across the room at each other, their expressions tentative and hopeful. Marylou had never seen this kind of interaction between them. They usually faced off from their corners, entrenched in their positions, ready to defend themselves. Now they appeared vulnerable. It was hard to watch. What if one rebuffed the other one?

"I do have some vacation days coming," Vic said quietly, as if he didn't want to get too hopeful.

"I wish you'd take them," Caroline told him. Then she gave him a shy smile.

There was a sudden lightness in the air, the way it feels when a storm has finally passed over. A relief, renewed purpose. Mama and Papa were friends again! They *do* like each other! Life could go on! These thoughts, Marylou knew, were flitting around their circle, joining them together in joy like the Holy Spirit did at Genesis Church. Marylou expected someone to get up and dance, would've done it herself if she wasn't nearly eighty.

It didn't last. Of course, they couldn't let it last.

"*I'm* not going to stay with Marylou," Ava announced from her chair where she sat like a queen, swinging her crossed leg. "*I'm* going to get an apartment. With Travis."

Suzi guffawed and Ava shot her a black look.

"Buff's nephew Travis?" Caroline said. "Gigi's son?"

"He can't help who he's related to."

"That's not the point, and you know it," Vic bellowed.

And they were off—Caroline lecturing Ava about how she was too young to take such a step, and that, anyway, she shouldn't move in with a man, any man, before she'd really gotten to know him, Ava arguing that she was old enough to make her own decisions, and Vic chiming in occasionally, agreeing, for once, with his wife, then gradually settling back in his padded chair, his eyes fluttering like he was fixing to doze off.

After a while Suzi got up and limped off into the dining room with her cell phone, texting someone. She called over her shoulder, "I'm going to pour us some Sprite! We're going to celebrate Granddad and Nance's engagement! I mean Marylou and Granddad. Ava, change out of my dress!"

"Into what, fool?" Ava yelled back.

Otis drifted out onto the front porch and settled in the glider, which squeaked back and forth as he pushed it. Was he thinking about what he'd done, regretting it, or was he planning how to make his next nuclear device? Who knew? But Otis and Ava were now her grandchildren, too, and she liked feeling responsible for them.

So she just sat and listened to everything, to all the new noises in a house that had been silent for so many years, thinking, *This is my family now, certainly not a happy family, but my family, happy enough, and in time perhaps, happier.* Okay, they could be described as a pack of neurotics desperately in need of family therapy, and she, the Radioactive Lady, wasn't a paragon of stability herself, but so what? You get what you get and you don't care a bit. That was a little rhyme Helen used to say all the time. She'd learned it in kindergarten. Marylou had found it annoying . . . she did care what she got, dammit! Funny that she should remember it now, remember Helen saying it then, as if she were saying it now. You get what you get and you don't care a bit.

"That glider really needs to be oiled," said Wilson. He scooted closer to her.

"Yes, indeed," Marylou said, and rested her head on his shoulder. "But for now, let's just let it squeak."

ACKNOWLEDGMENTS

I was inspired to write this novel after reading Eileen Welsome's book *The Plutonium Files*, in which she used her Pulitzer Prize–winning investigative-reporting skills to uncover the truth about secret medical experiments conducted on vulnerable, unsuspecting American citizens during the cold war. It is a great American book. The medical experiment portrayed in this novel—radioactive cocktails given to pregnant women—actually took place at Vanderbilt University in Nashville, Tennessee, but I moved it to a fictitious hospital in Memphis, my favorite city.

Another amazing book that grabbed me by the collar is *The Radioactive Boy Scout* by Ken Silverstein, a superbly written true story that not even Hollywood could've concocted. Many of the details about Otis's breeder reactor come from this book, but as a fiction writer I also changed some things to fit my story. If I've gotten anything wrong about breeder reactors, the fault is entirely mine.

Hurricane Grayson, which appears in this novel, is a fictitious storm. For answering my hurricane questions, I thank Team Hurricane: Carissa Neff, Forrest Anderson, Christie Grimes,

Wendi Taylor Nations, Cadence Kidwell, and especially Beauvis McCaddon.

The Lillian Smith Center for the Arts provided me with space and time to write this novel. I'm forever grateful to Florida State University for keeping body and soul together. Thanks to my colleagues and students in our creative writing program for being the outstanding people they are. In particular I'd like to thank my assistant, Kristina Vogtner, for all her enthusiasm and smart ideas.

Many thanks also go to: Tricia Young, for being Tco. Mary Lou Sheridan, for being Mary Lou and not Marylou. Miranda Stuckey, soccer player extraordinaire, who answered all my soccer questions. My gal pals in the RDI Group—you've saved my life many times over. Mike Croley, who hosted and tour-guided me around Memphis a number of times. Tad Pierson of *American Dream Safari*, for taking me on tours of Memphis in his pink Cadillac. Janet Burroway and Patricia Henley, whom I can call day or night to discuss writing and anything else. Alison Destry Jester, for graciously spending way too much time hashing out the plot of this novel with me and for putting up with me for two weeks every summer. The Tarts—Joanna Harper, for offering me a lovely place to work out the final kinks in this book; Michele Messenger, for her graphic design genius; and Lauren Heath and Lisa Dowis, for keeping me laughing.

I couldn't have pulled it together without the encouragement of my wonderful agent, Gail Hochman. At Doubleday: Cory Hunter and Nora Reichard are true treasures. My brilliant editor, Alison Callahan, performed magic on the manuscript and understood better than I what I was trying to do.

Most important, I'm grateful to my family. My mother, June Stuckey, applauds me even when she must think I'm insane. My daughters, Flannery and Phoebe, took time out of their busy lives to help me choose character names, act out scenes, and give me sage advice about the behavior of teenagers. My husband, Ned, as always, was right there with me every step of the way. I appreciate him more each and every day.

Center Point Publishing
600 Brooks Road • PO Box 1
Thorndike ME 04986-0001 USA

(207) 568-3717

US & Canada:
1 800 929-9108
www.centerpointlargeprint.com